D0041947

Oct 20

Tree-
House
Comix
Proudly
Presents

DOG MAN

WRITTEN AND ILLUSTRATED BY **DAV PILKEY**

AS GEORGE BEARD AND HAROLD HUTCHINS

WITH COLOR BY JOSE GARIBALDI

graphix

AN IMPRINT OF

SCHOLASTIC

FOR DAN, LEAH, ALEK, AND KYLE SANTAT

Library of Congress Control Number 2016932063

978-0-545-58160-8 (POB)
978-1-338-61194-6 (Library)

25 24 23 22   20 21 22 23

Printed in China   62
First edition, September 2016

Edited by Anamika Bhatnagar
Book design by Dav Pilkey and Phil Falco
Color by Jose Garibaldi
Creative Director: David Saylor

DOG MAN

~~the~~ Behind the Scenes

One Time, George met Harold in Kindergarten.

nice to meet you.

me too.

They became best friends and started making Comics.

Their very first comic was a epic Novella called:

The ADVENCHERs of DOG Man

Akshin

LAFFS

FLEAS

by George and Harold

Over the years, they made **TONS** of DOG Man Comic Books.

DOG MAN FLIPPY

DOG MAN in SPACE

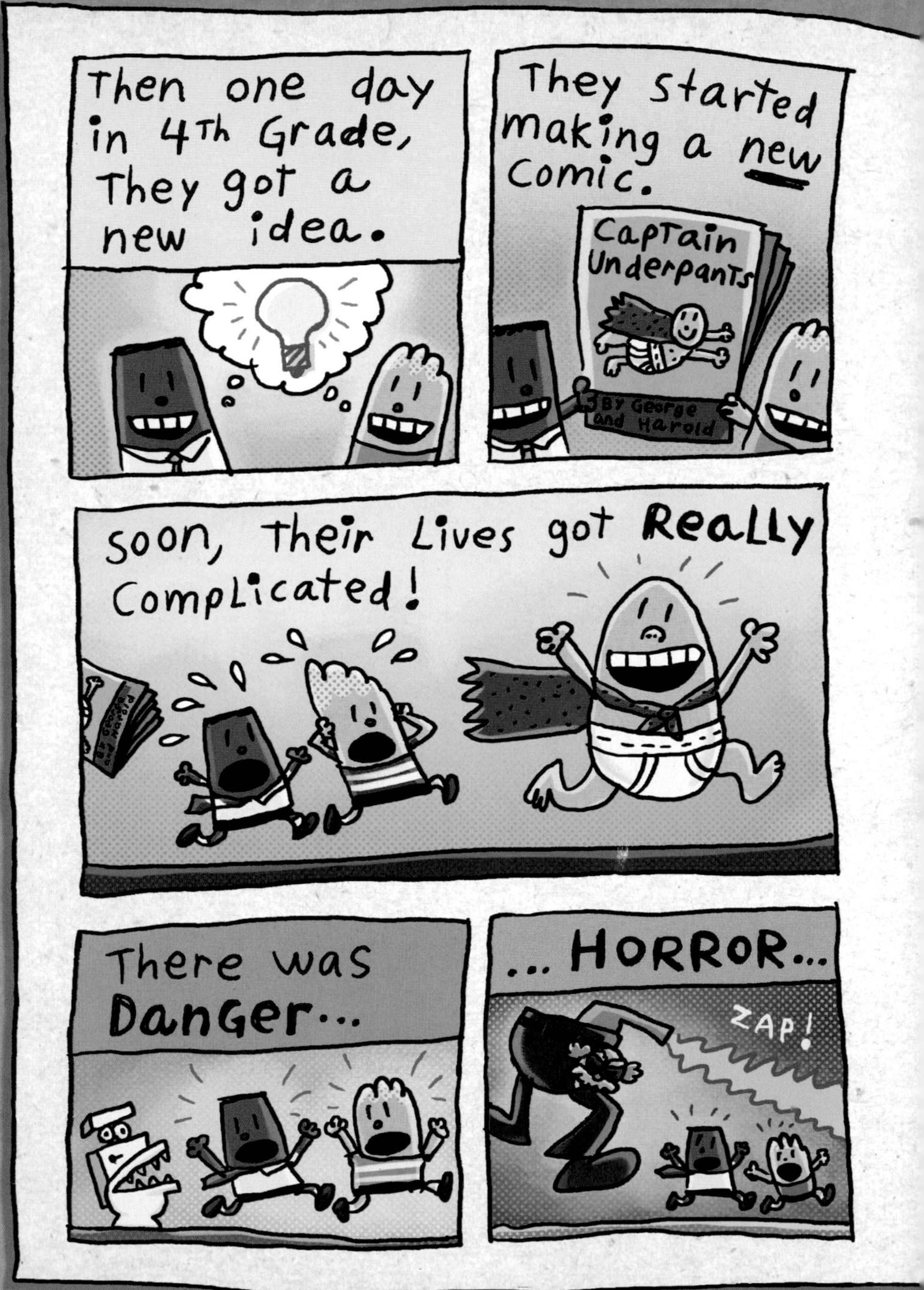

Then one day in 4th Grade, They got a new idea.
They started making a new comic.
Captain Underpants
By George and Harold
soon, their Lives got ReaLLy CompLicated!
There was Danger...
... HORROR...
ZAP!

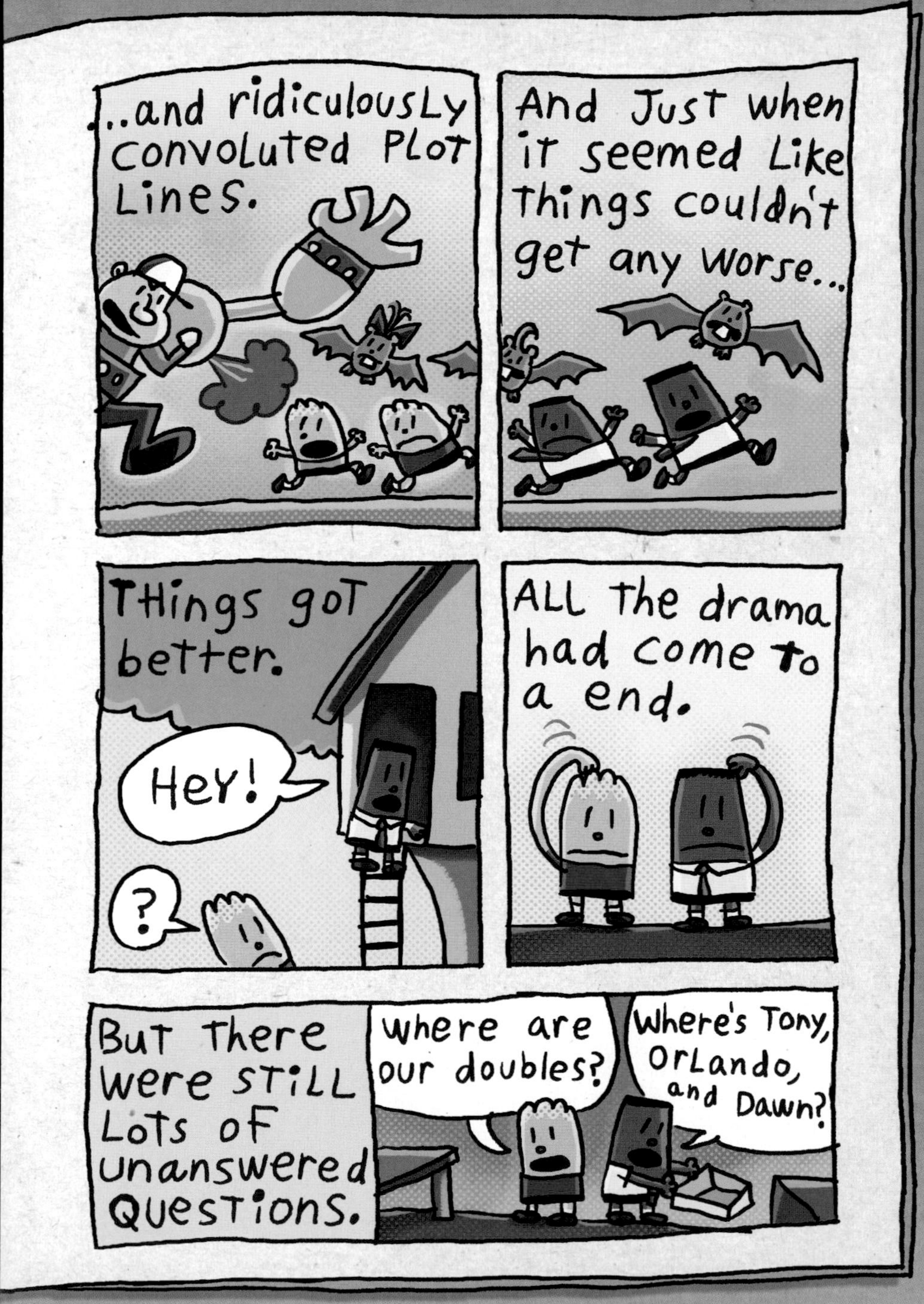
..and ridiculously convoluted plot lines.
And just when it seemed like things couldn't get any worse...
Things got better.
Hey!
?
All the drama had come to a end.
But there were still lots of unanswered questions.
Where are our doubles?
Where's Tony, Orlando, and Dawn?

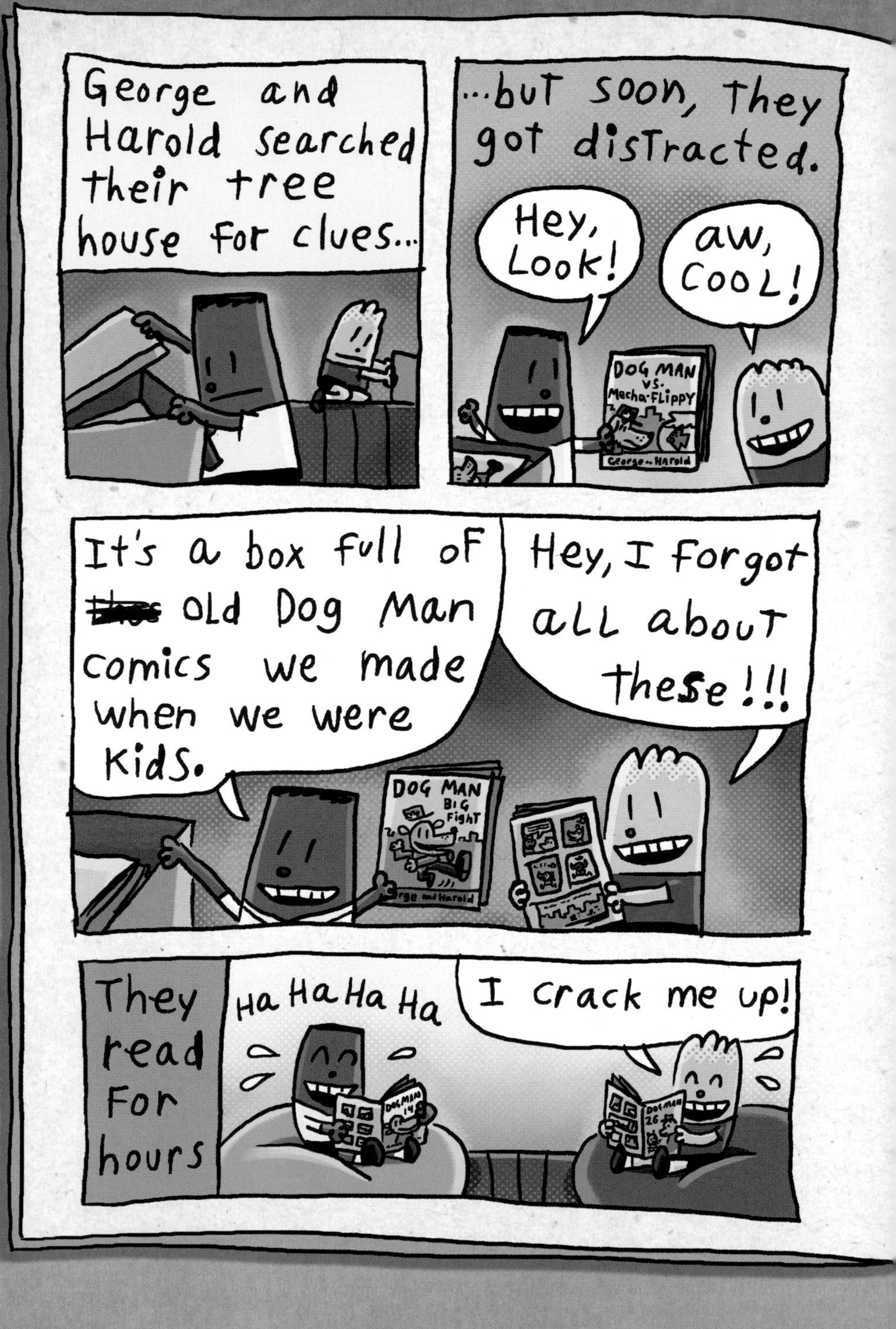
George and Harold searched their tree house for clues...
...but soon, they got distracted.
Hey, Look!
aw, COOL!
DOG MAN VS. Mecha-FLIPPY
George and Harold
It's a box full of old Dog Man comics we made when we were kids.
Hey, I forgot all about these!!!
DOG MAN BIG FIGHT
They read for hours
Ha Ha Ha Ha
I crack me up!

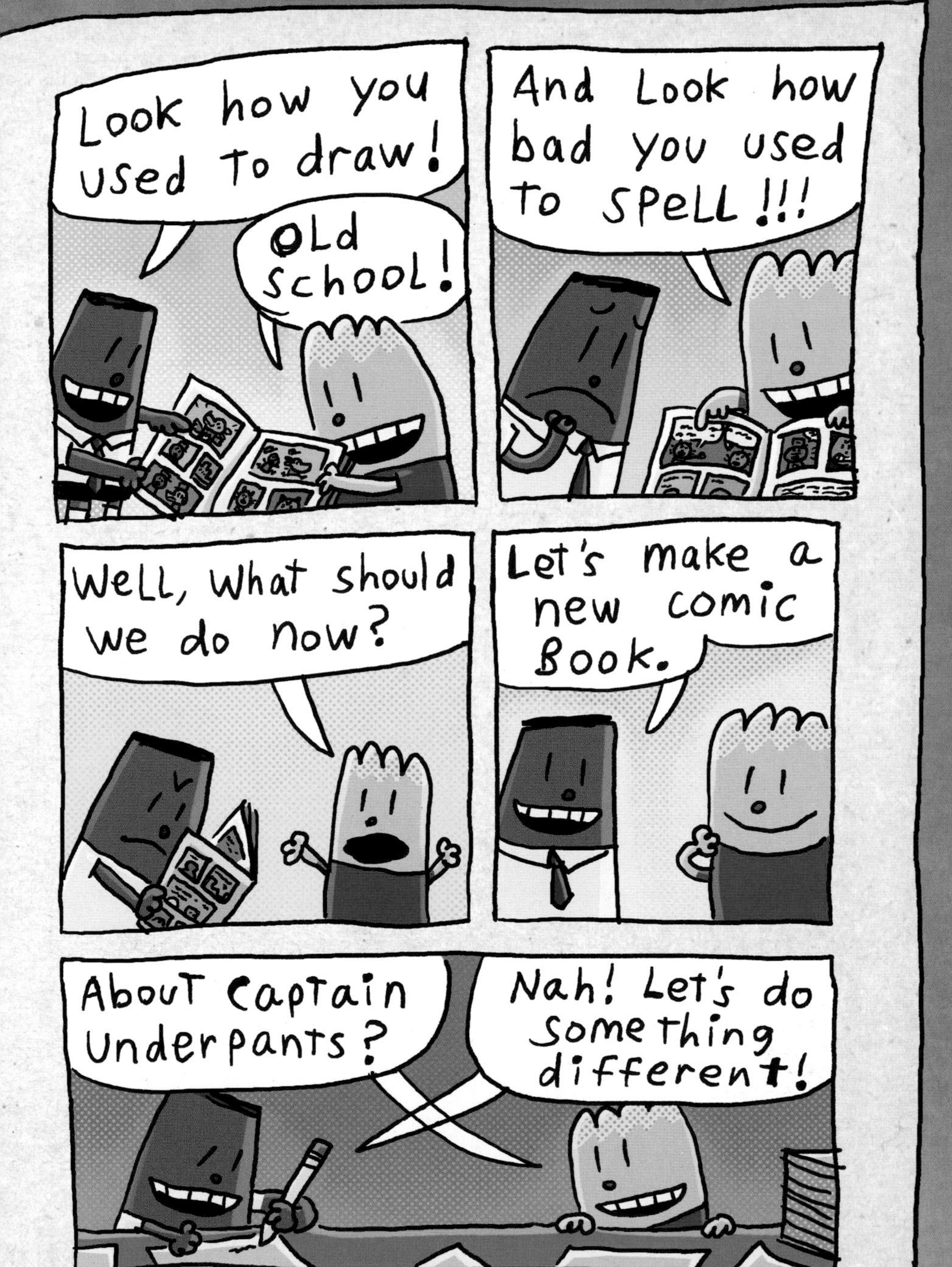
Look how you used To draw!
OLd School!
And Look how bad you used to SPeLL!!!
WeLL, What should we do now?
Let's make a new comic Book.
AbouT Captain Underpants?
Nah! Let's do Something different!

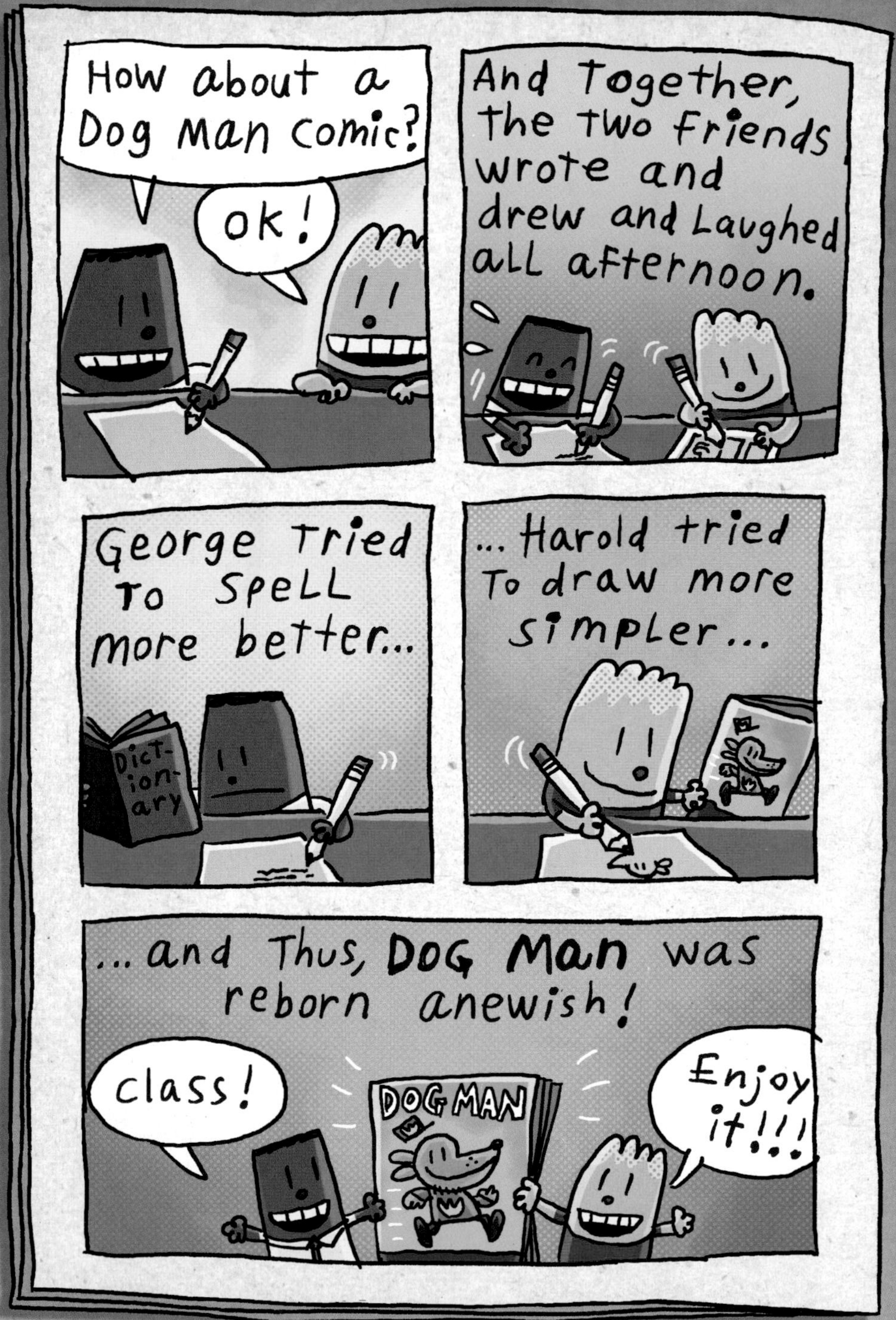
How about a Dog Man comic?
ok!
And Together, the two friends wrote and drew and Laughed all afternoon.
George Tried To SpeLL more better...
Dict-ion-ary
... Harold tried To draw more simpler...
... and Thus, DOG MAN was reborn anewish!
class!
DOG MAN
Enjoy it!!!

DOG MAN

CHAPTER 1
A Hero is unleashed

By George and Harold

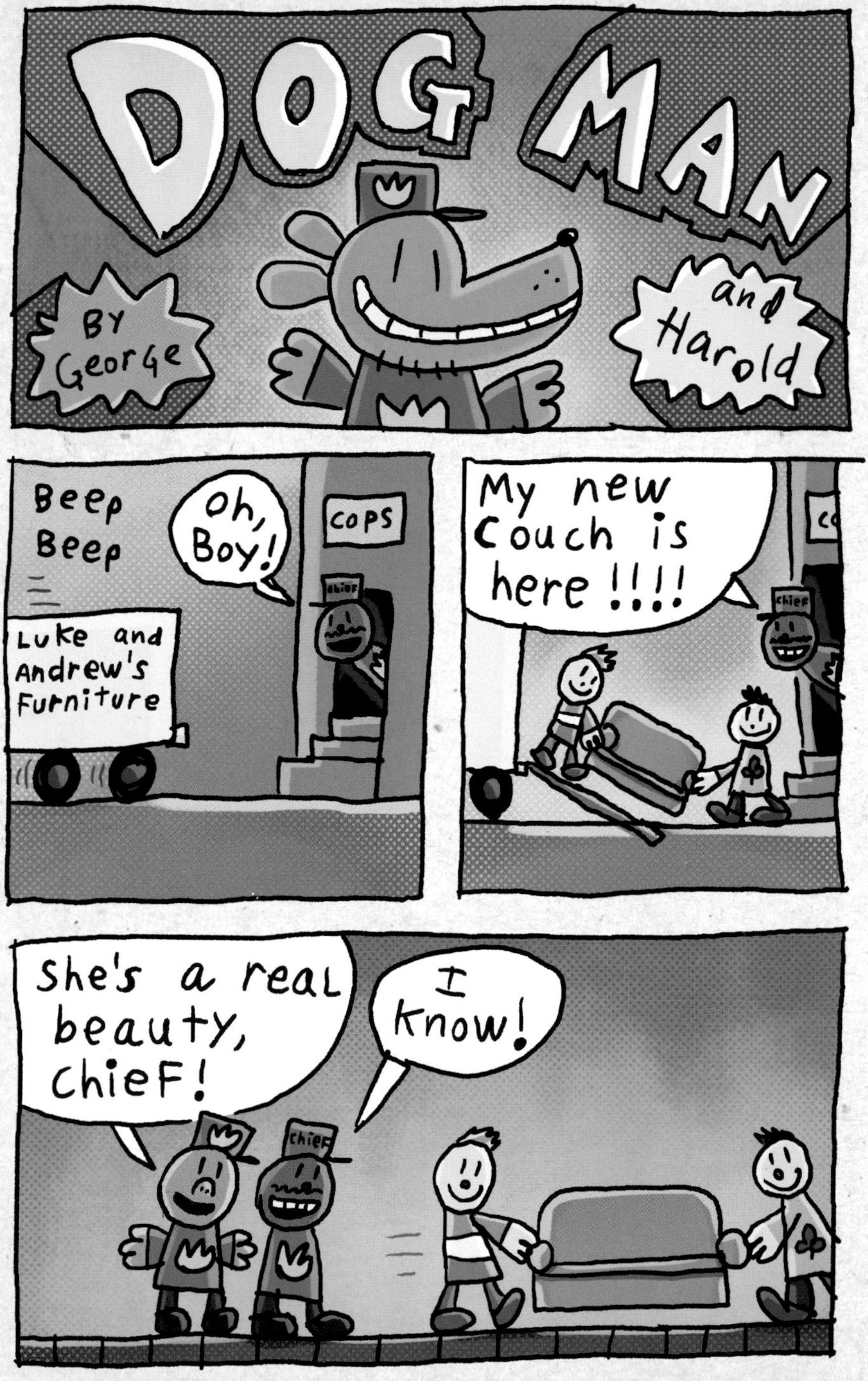
DOG MAN
BY George
and Harold
Beep Beep
Oh, Boy!
COPS
Luke and Andrew's Furniture
My new Couch is here!!!!
She's a real beauty, ChieF!
I know!

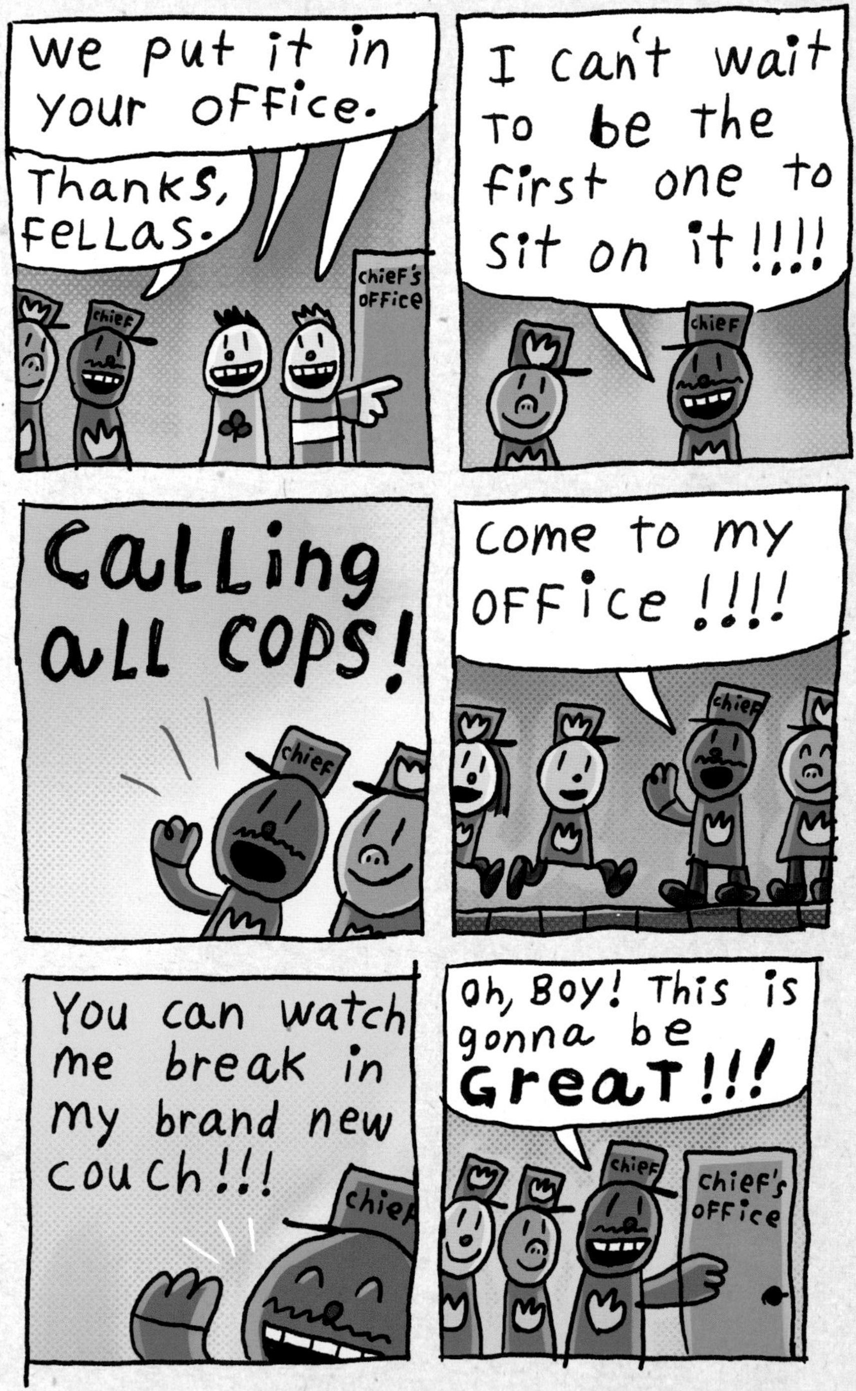
We put it in your office.
Thanks, fellas.
chief
chief's office
I can't wait to be the first one to sit on it!!!!
chief
Calling all cops!
chief
Come to my office!!!!
chief
You can watch me break in my brand new couch!!!
Oh, boy! This is gonna be GREAT!!!
chief
chief's office

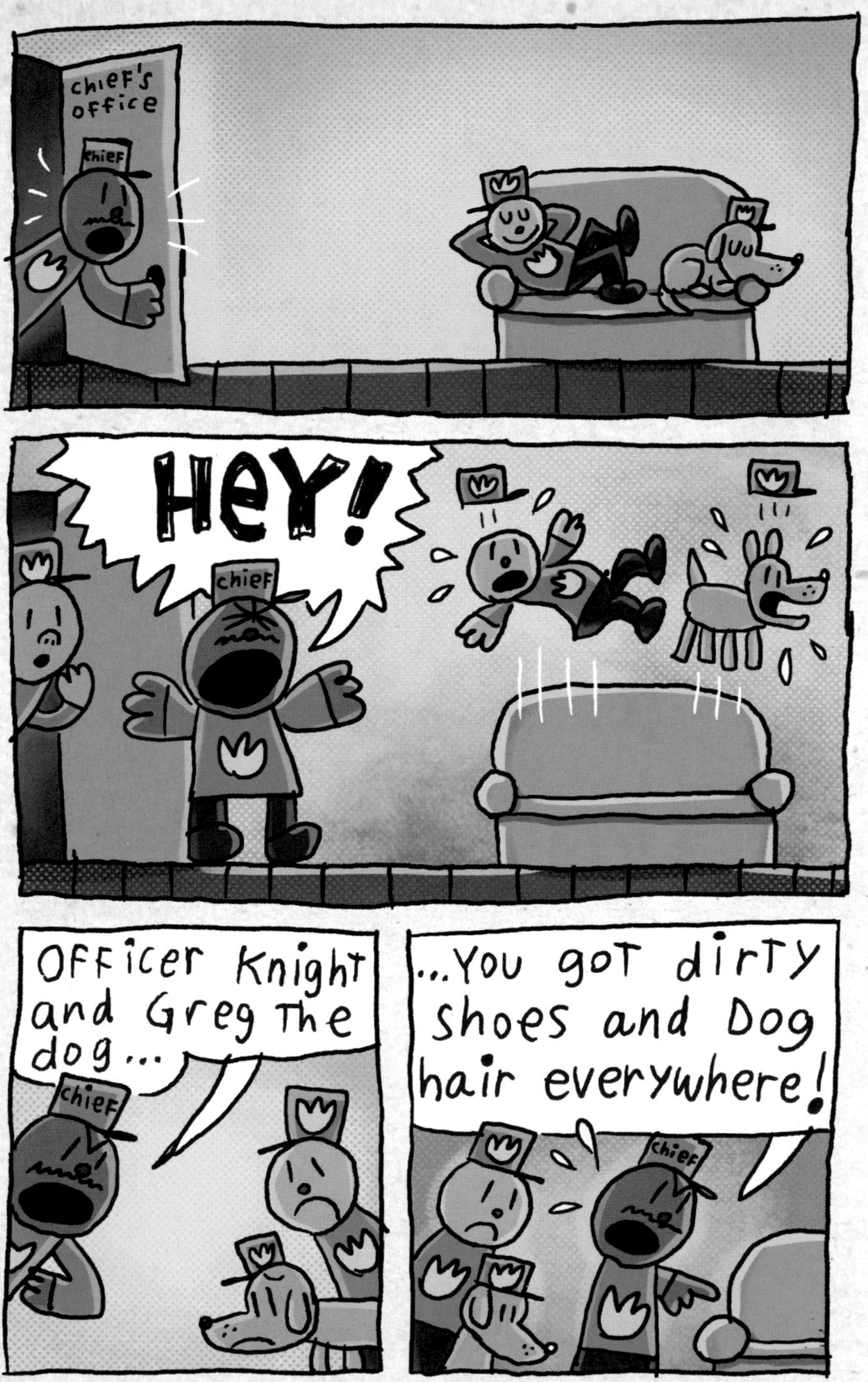
chief's office
chief
HEY!
chief
Officer Knight and Greg the dog...
chief
...You got dirty shoes and Dog hair everywhere!
chief

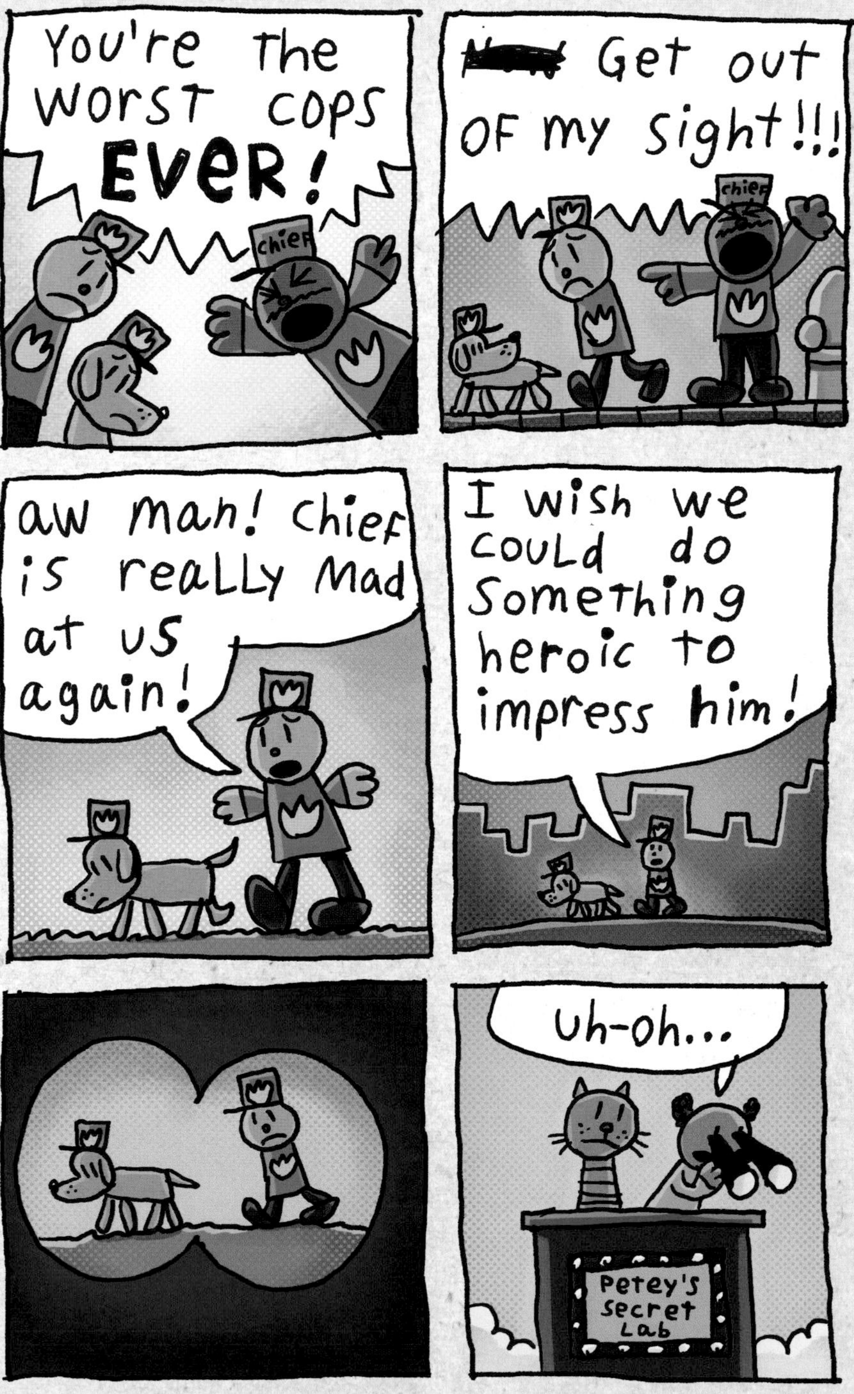
You're the worst cops EVER!
chief
Get out OF my sight!!!
chief
aw man! chief is really Mad at us again!
I wish we could do Something heroic to impress him!
Uh-oh...
Petey's Secret Lab

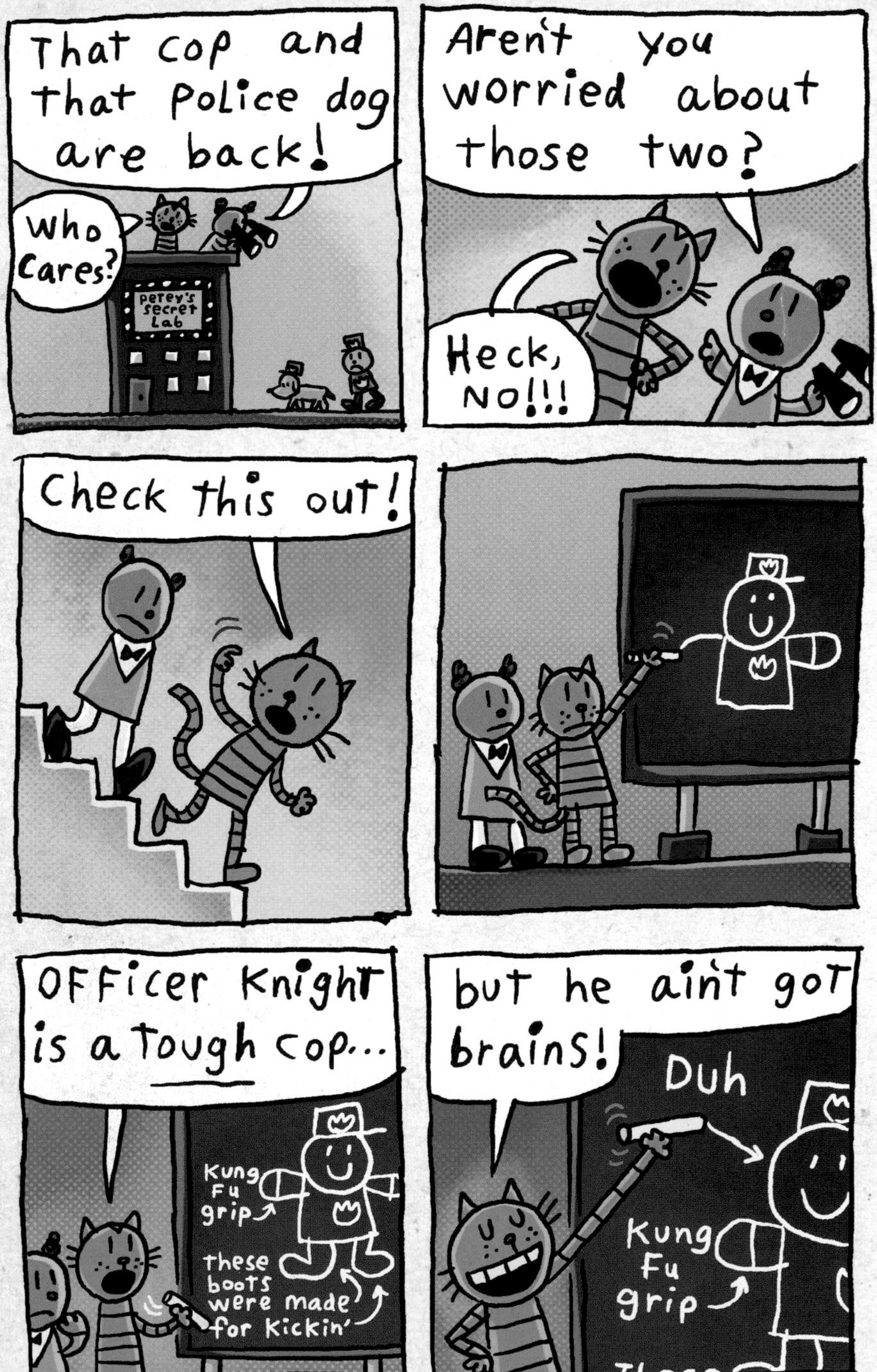
That cop and that Police dog are back!
Who Cares?
petey's secret Lab
Aren't you worried about those two?
Heck, No!!!
Check this out!
OFFicer Knight is a Tough cop...
Kung Fu grip
these boots were made for Kickin'
but he ain't got brains!
Duh
Kung Fu grip

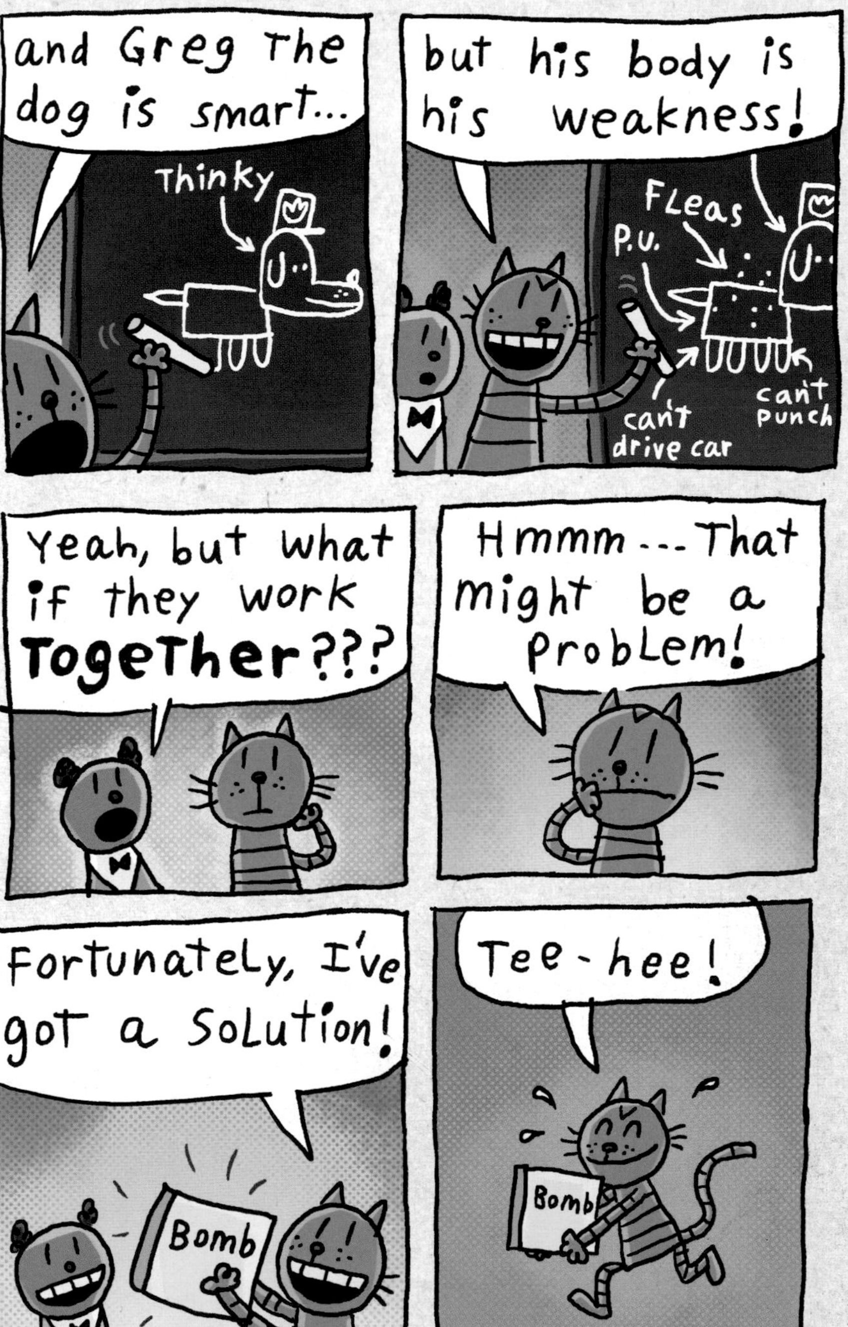
and Greg the dog is smart...
Thinky
but his body is his weakness!
Fleas
P.U.
can't drive car
can't punch
Yeah, but what if they work **TOGETHER???**
Hmmm... That might be a problem!
Fortunately, I've got a solution!
Bomb
Tee-hee!
Bomb

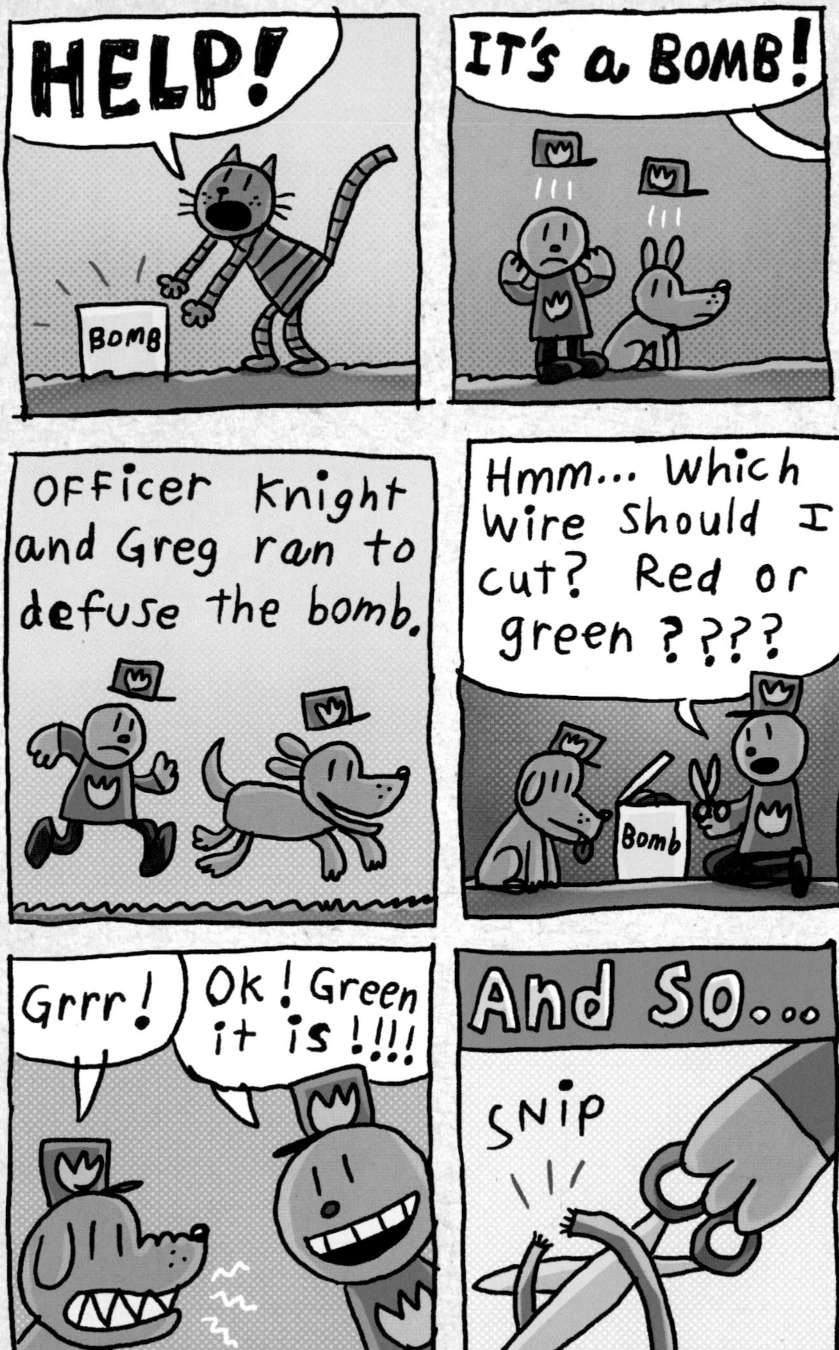
HELP!
BOMB
IT's a BOMB!
Officer Knight and Greg ran to defuse the bomb.
Hmm... Which wire should I cut? Red or green????
Bomb
Grrr!
Ok! Green it is!!!!
And so...
SNIP

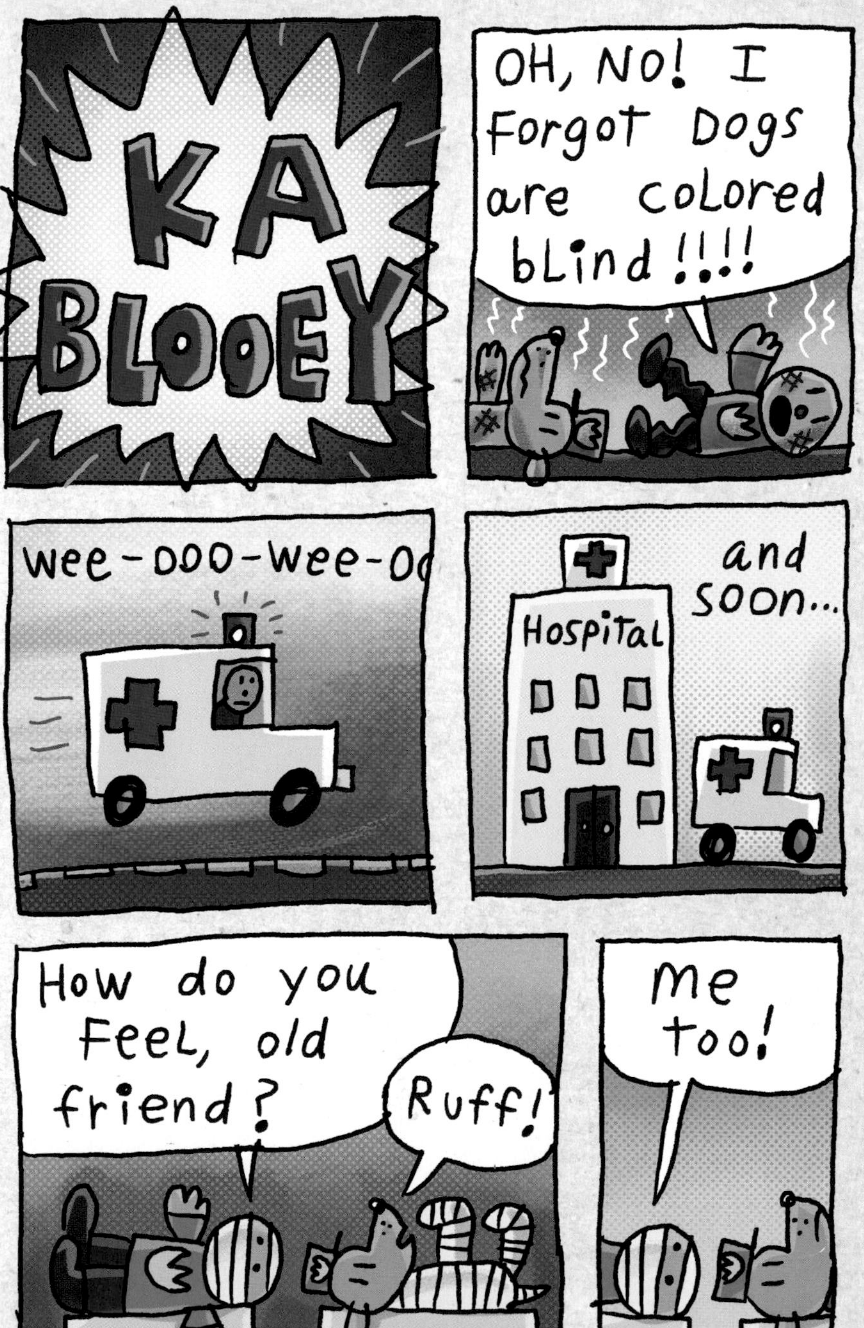
KA BLOOEY
OH, NO! I Forgot Dogs are colored bLind!!!!
wee-DOO-wee-Oo
and soon...
Hospital
How do you FeeL, old friend?
Ruff!
me too!

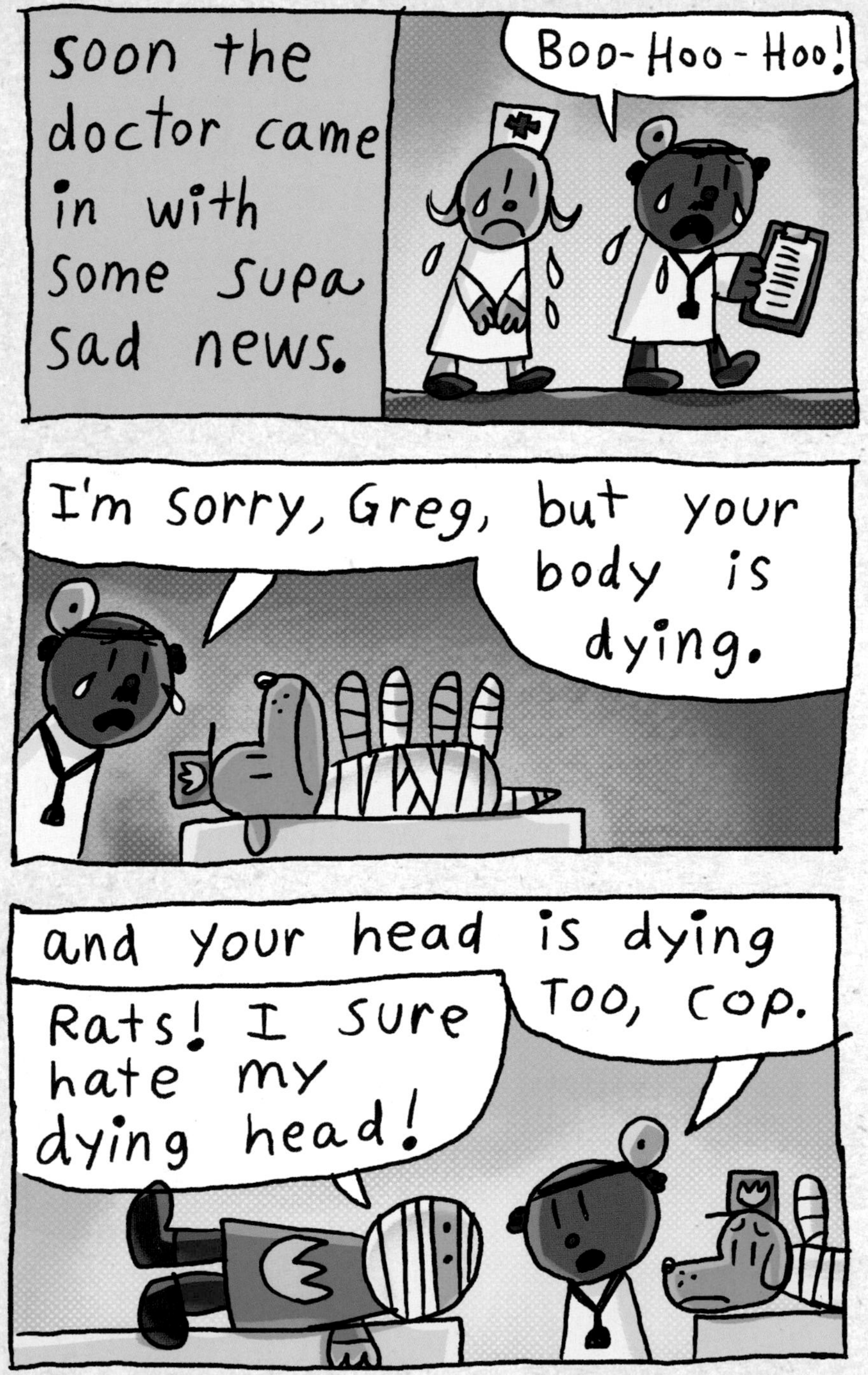
Soon the doctor came in with some supa sad news.
BOO-HOO-HOO!
I'm sorry, Greg, but your body is dying.
and your head is dying too, cop.
Rats! I sure hate my dying head!

But just when all seemed lost...

HEY!

← nurse Lady

Why don't we sew Greg's head onto cop's body?

Good idea, nurse Lady! You're a genius!!!

Hooray!

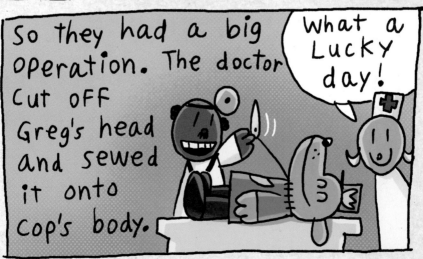

So they had a big operation. The doctor cut off Greg's head and sewed it onto cop's body.

What a lucky day!

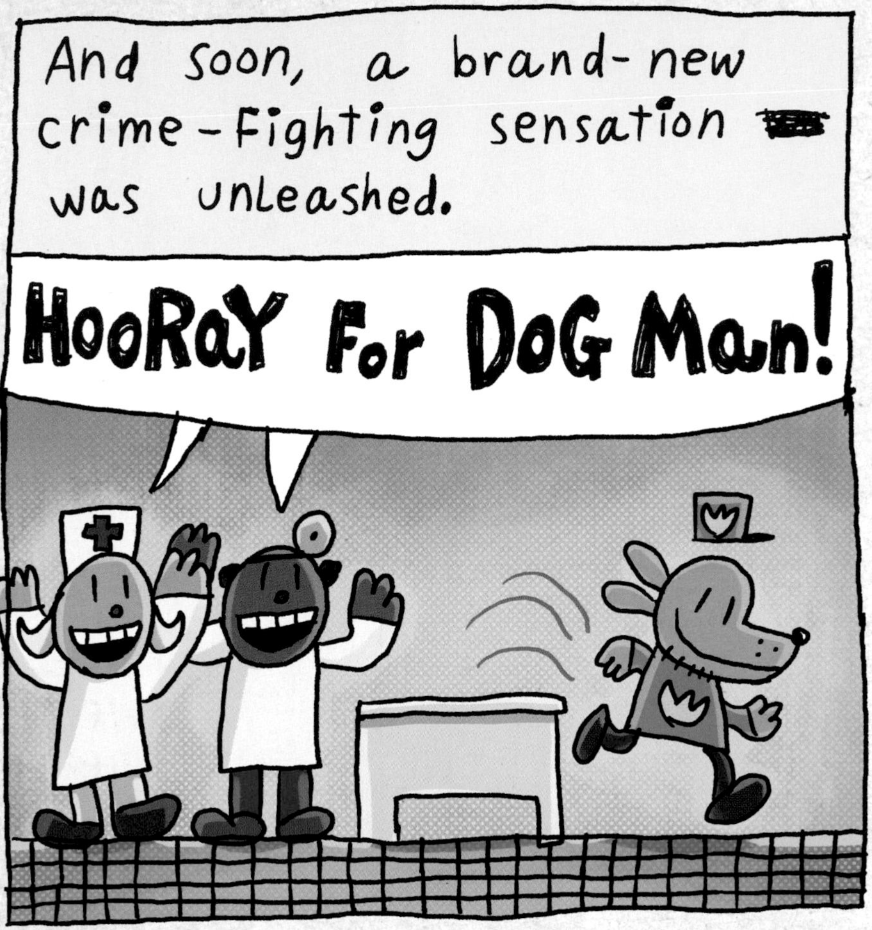
And soon, a brand-new crime-Fighting sensation was unleashed.
HOORAY For DOG Man!

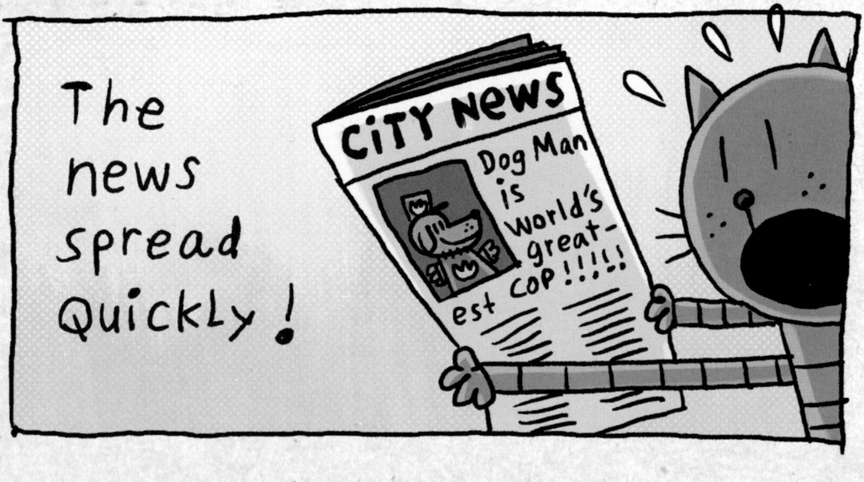
The news spread Quickly!
CITY NEWS
Dog Man is World's great-est COP!!!!!

21

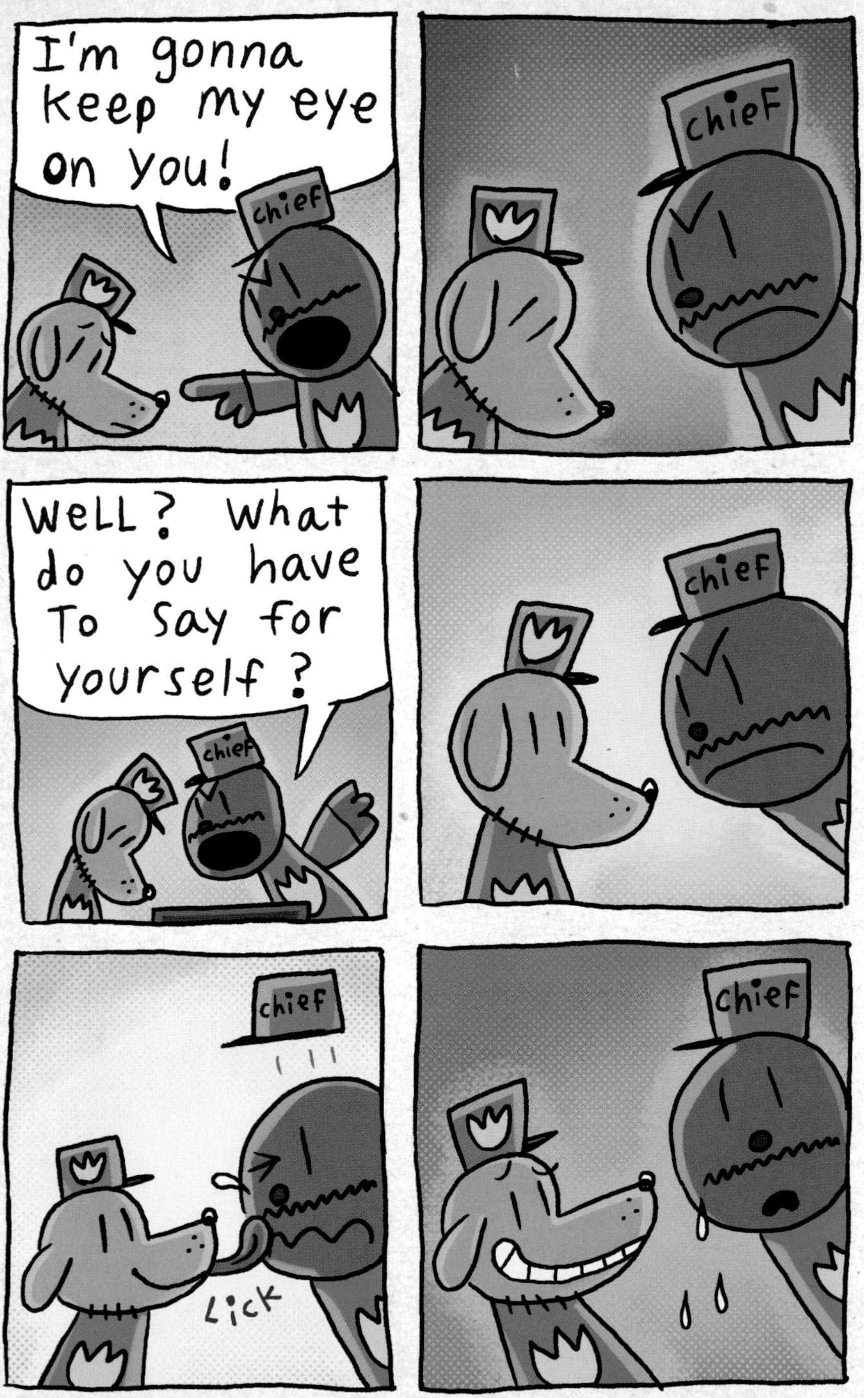
I'm gonna keep my eye on you!
chief
chief
WELL? What do you have To say for yourself?
chief
chief
chief
Lick
chief

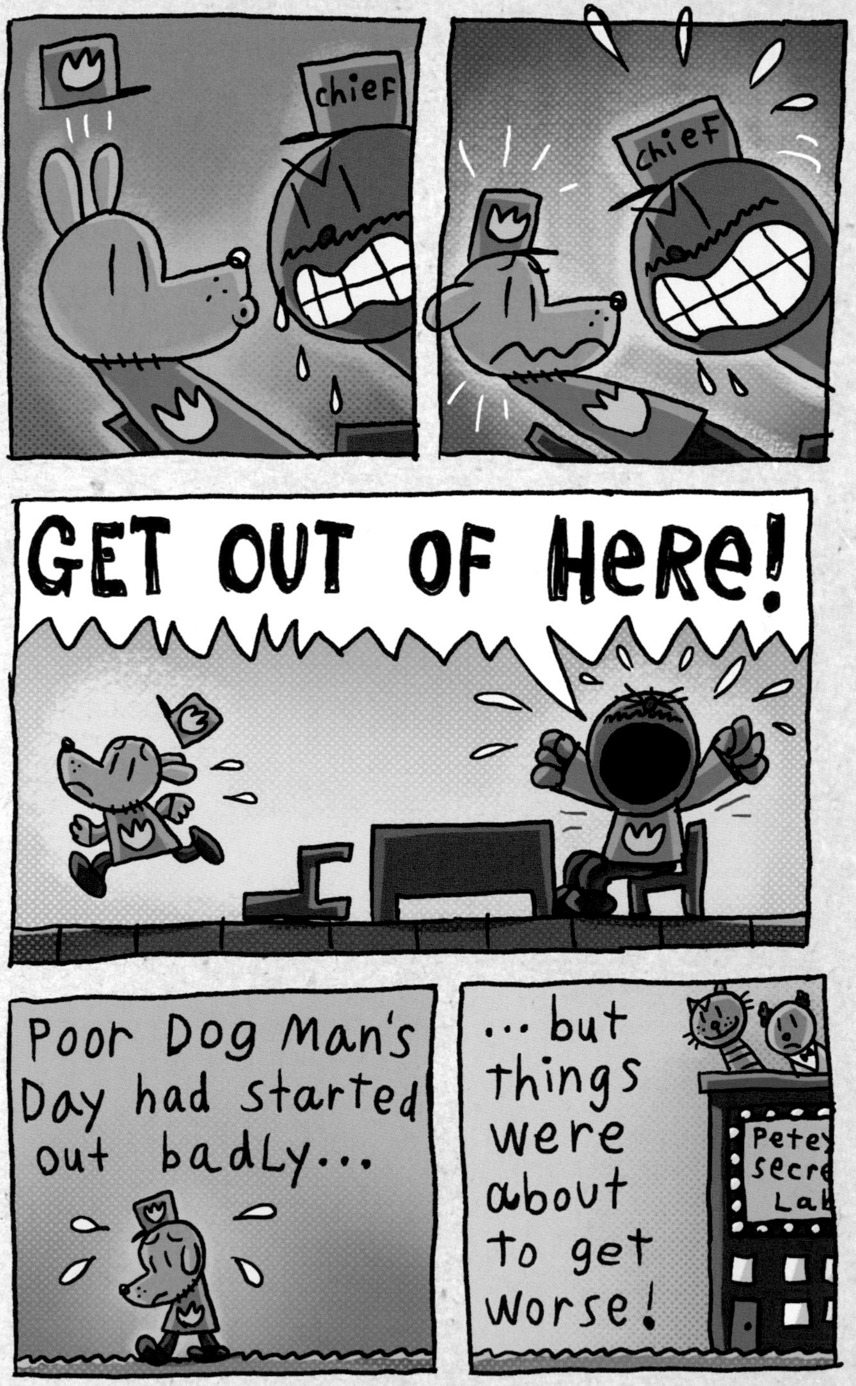
chief
chief
GET OUT OF HERE!
Poor Dog Man's Day had started out badly...
... but things were about to get worse!

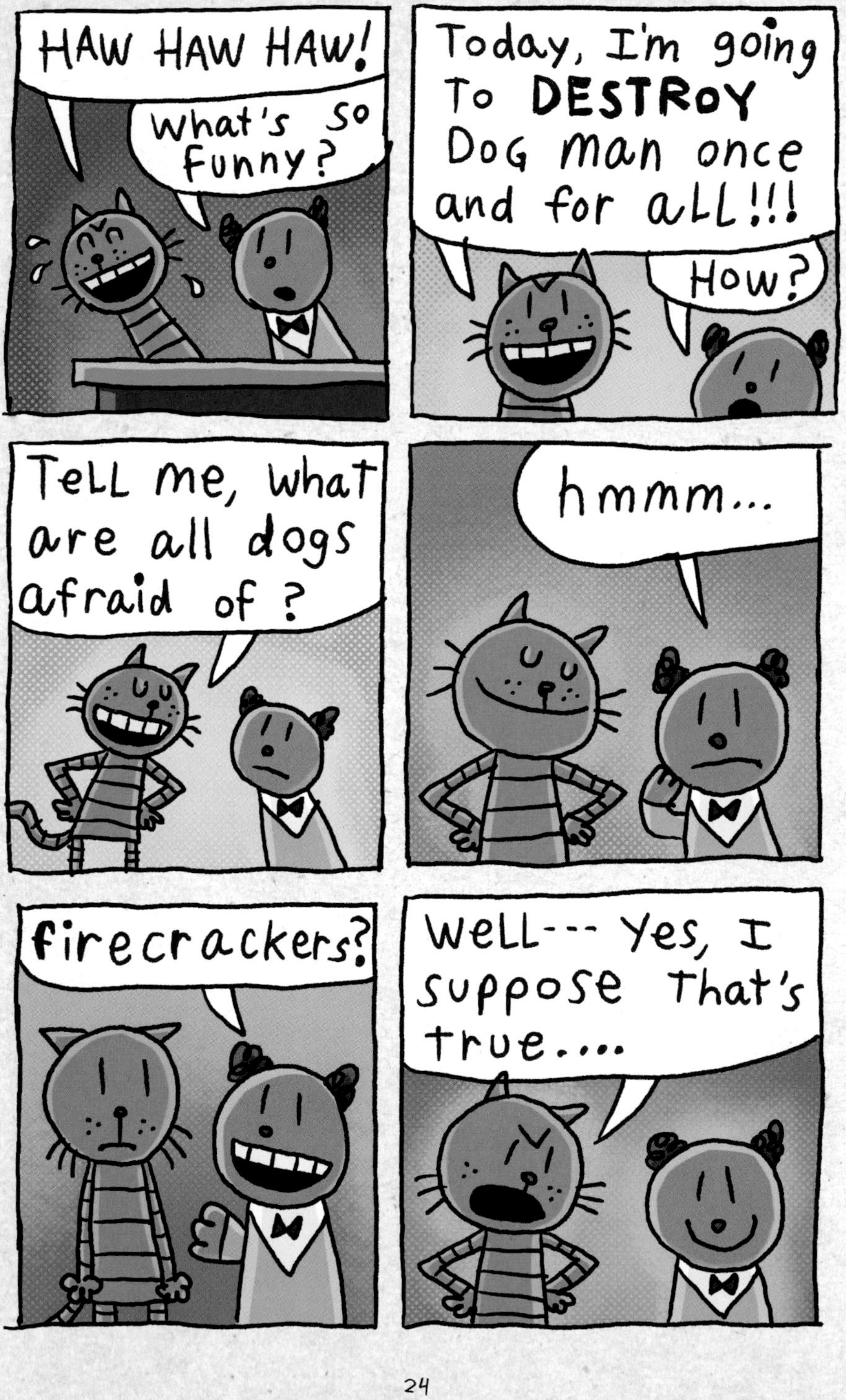
HAW HAW HAW!
What's so Funny?
Today, I'm going To DESTROY Dog man once and for aLL!!!
How?
TeLL me, what are all dogs afraid of?
hmmm...
firecrackers?
WeLL--- Yes, I suppose That's true....

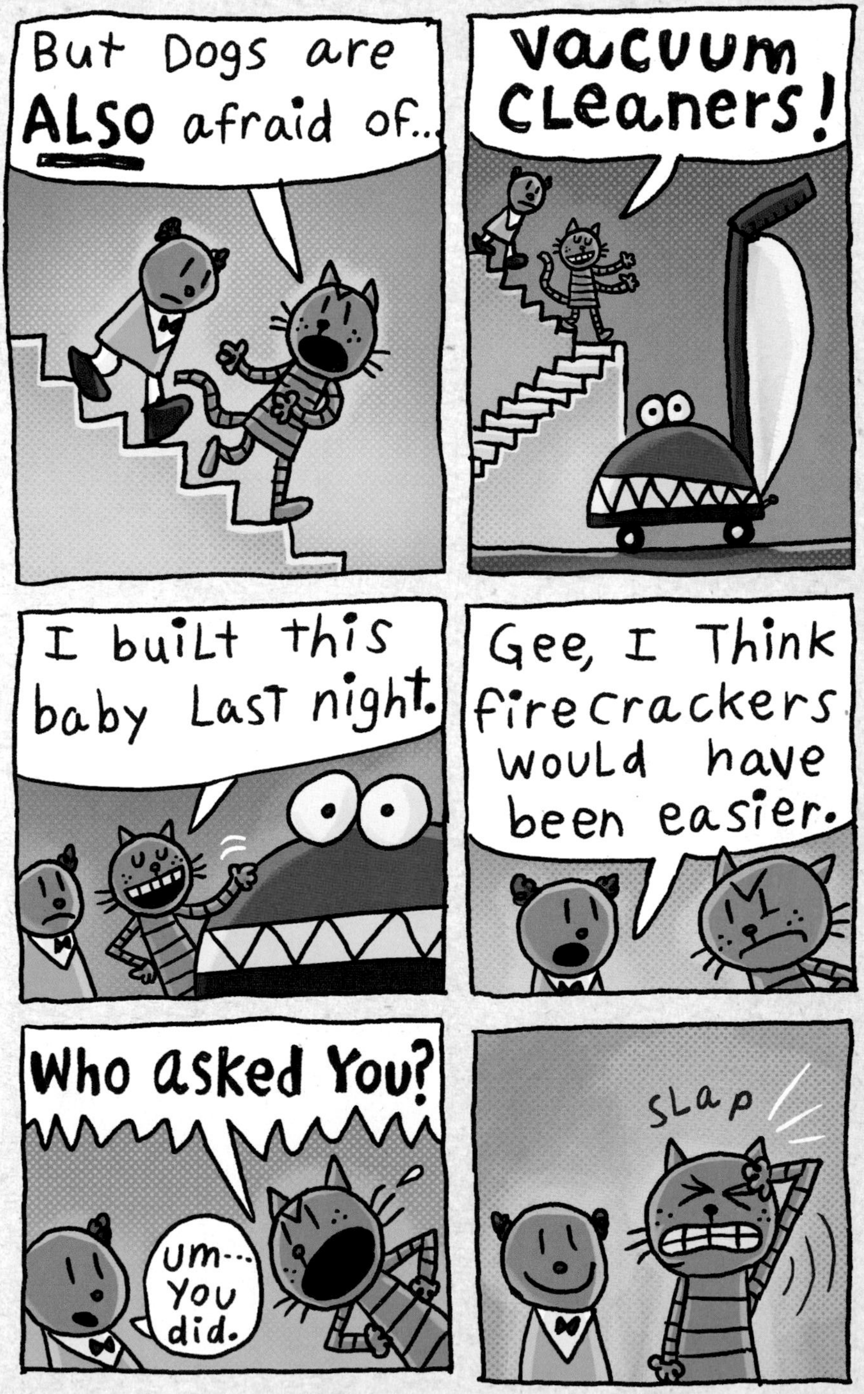
But Dogs are ALSO afraid of...
Vacuum Cleaners!
I built this baby Last night.
Gee, I Think firecrackers would have been easier.
Who asked You?
Um... You did.
SLap

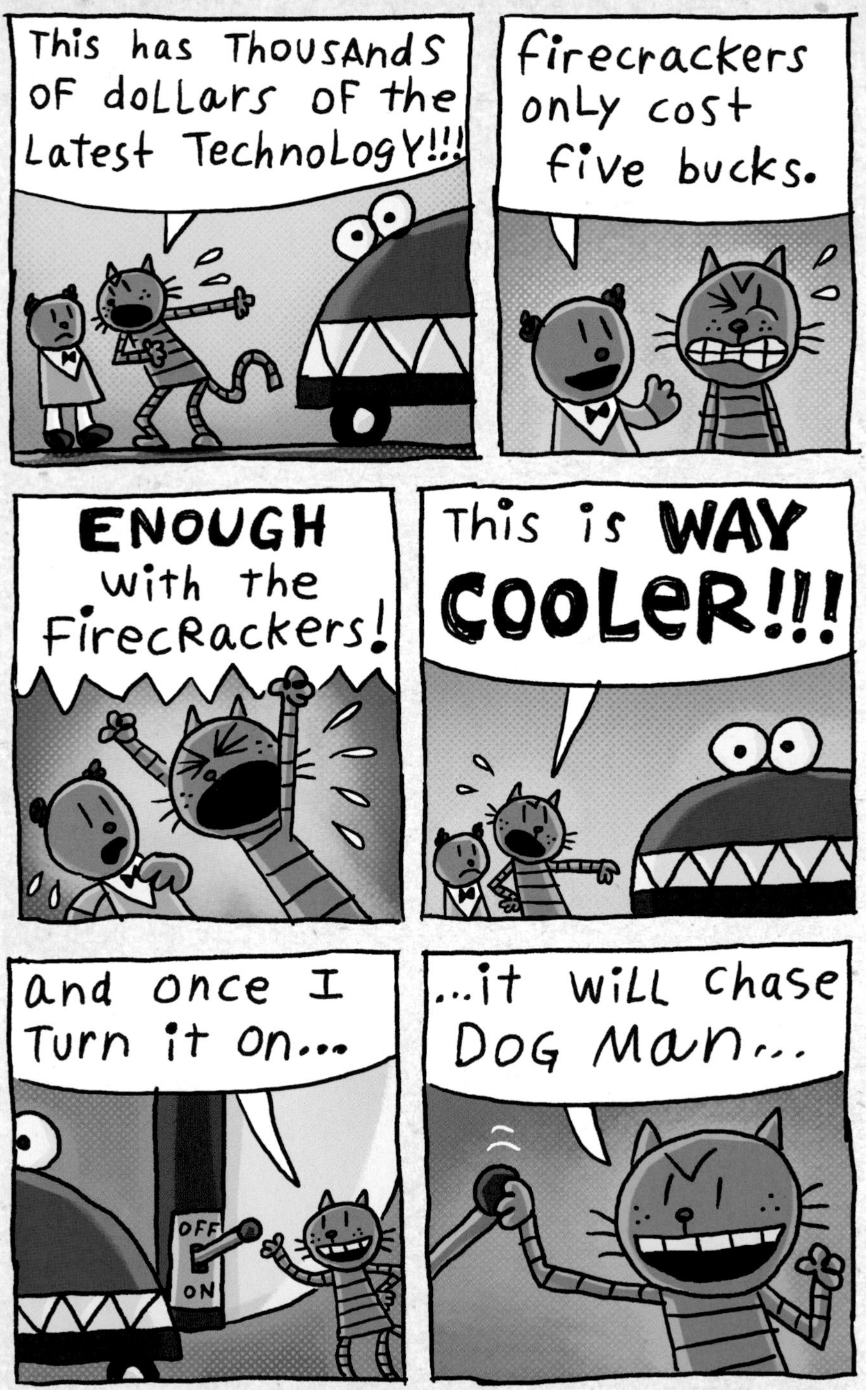
This has THOUSANDS OF doLLars OF the Latest TechnoLogY!!!
firecrackers onLy cost five bucks.
ENOUGH with the FirecRackers!
This is WAY COOLER!!!
and once I Turn it on...
...it WiLL chase DOG Man...
OFF
ON

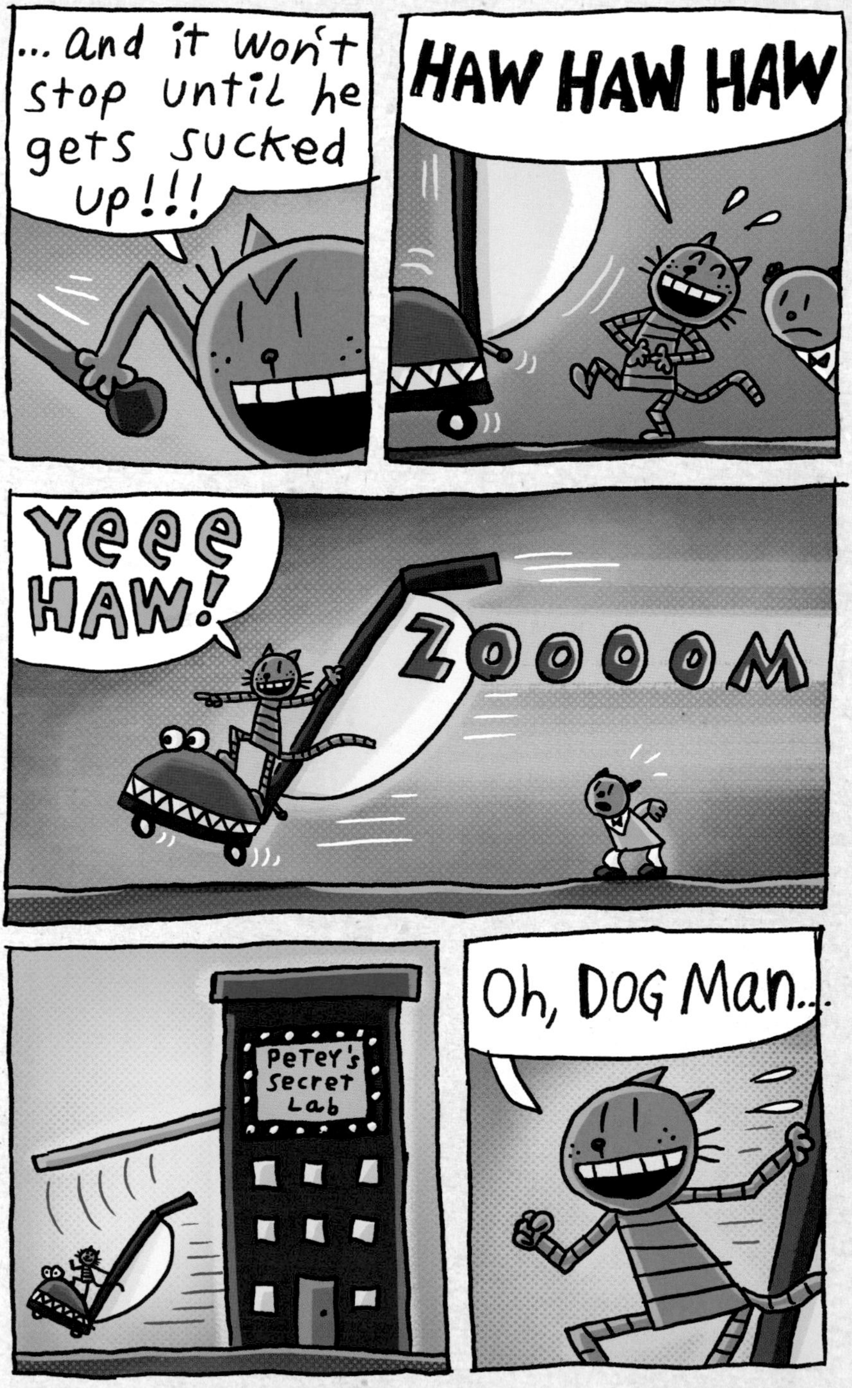
...and it won't stop until he gets sucked up!!!
HAW HAW HAW
YEEE HAW!
ZOOOOM
Petey's Secret Lab
Oh, DOG Man...

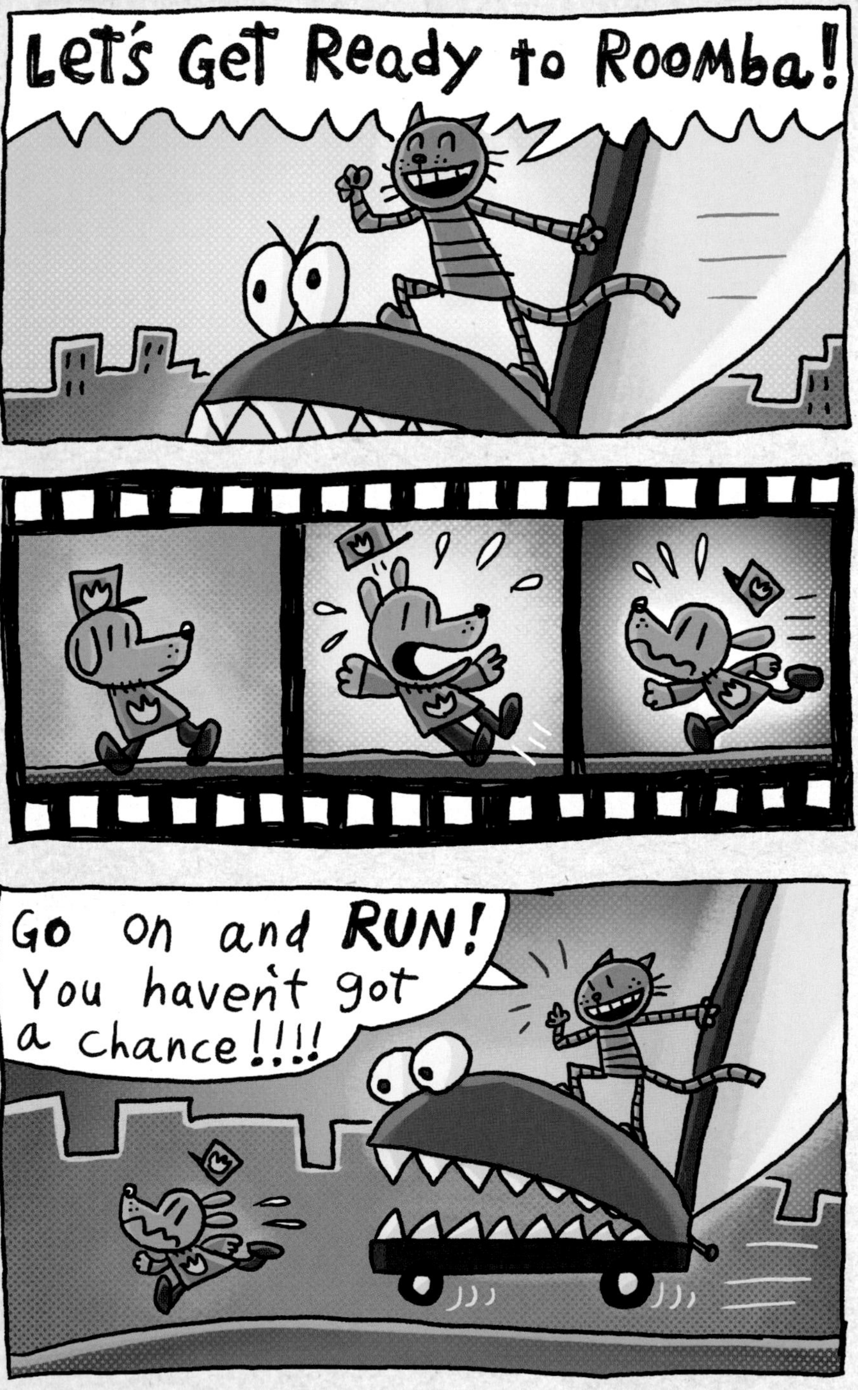
Let's Get Ready to Roomba!
Go on and RUN! You haven't got a chance!!!!

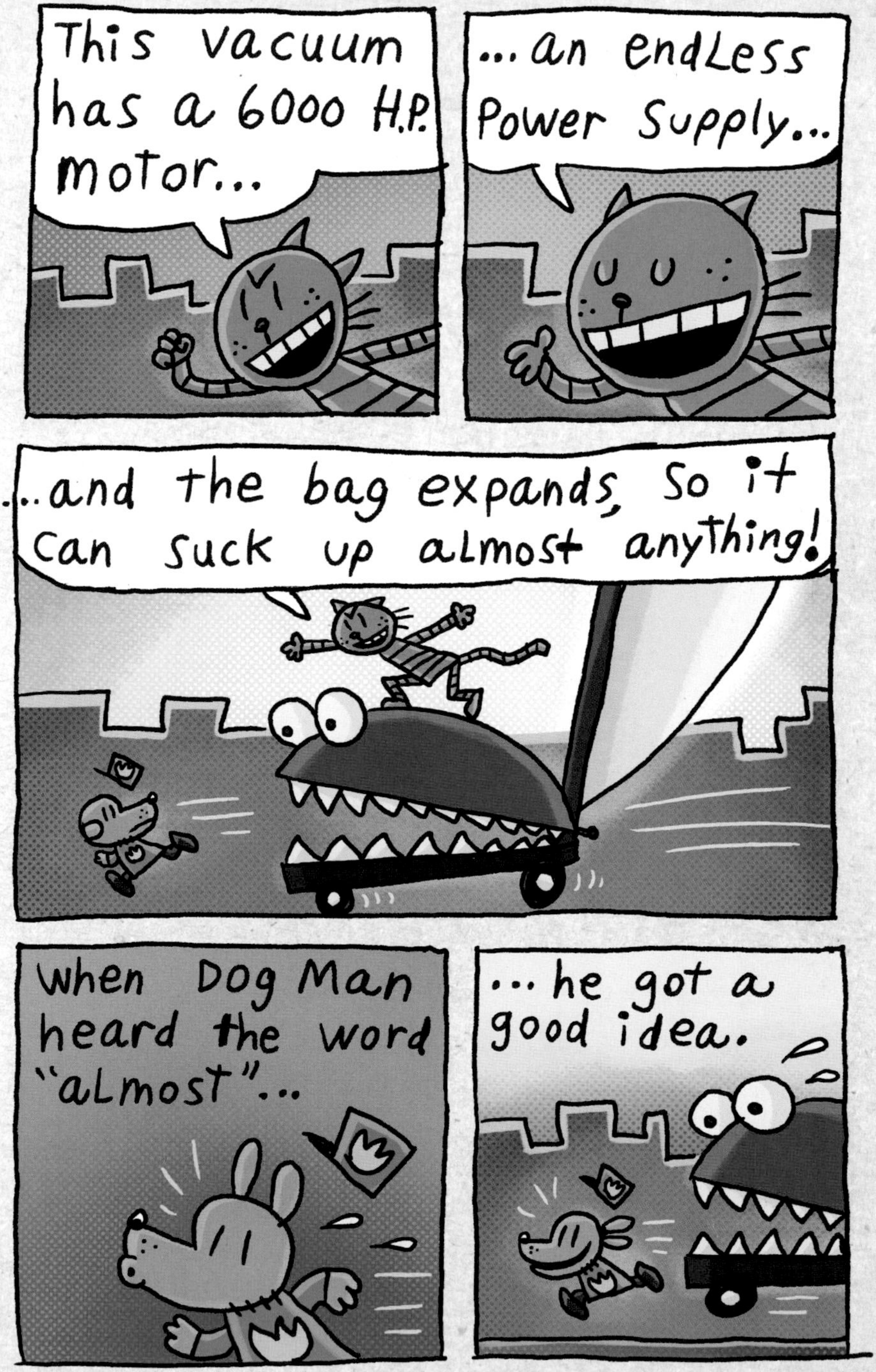
This vacuum has a 6000 H.P. motor...
...an endless Power Supply...
...and the bag expands, so it can suck up almost anything!
When Dog Man heard the word "almost"...
...he got a good idea.

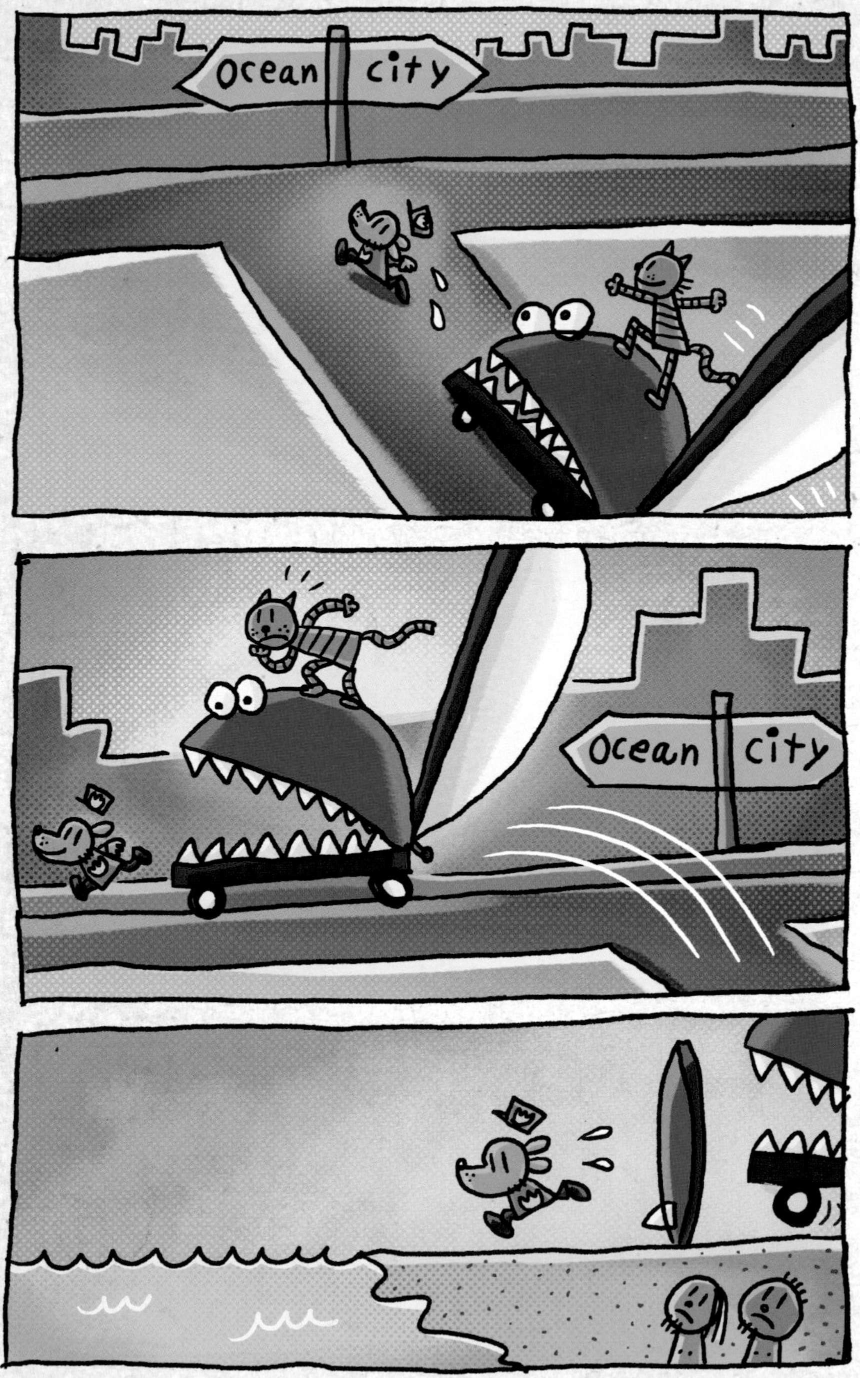
Ocean
city
Ocean
city

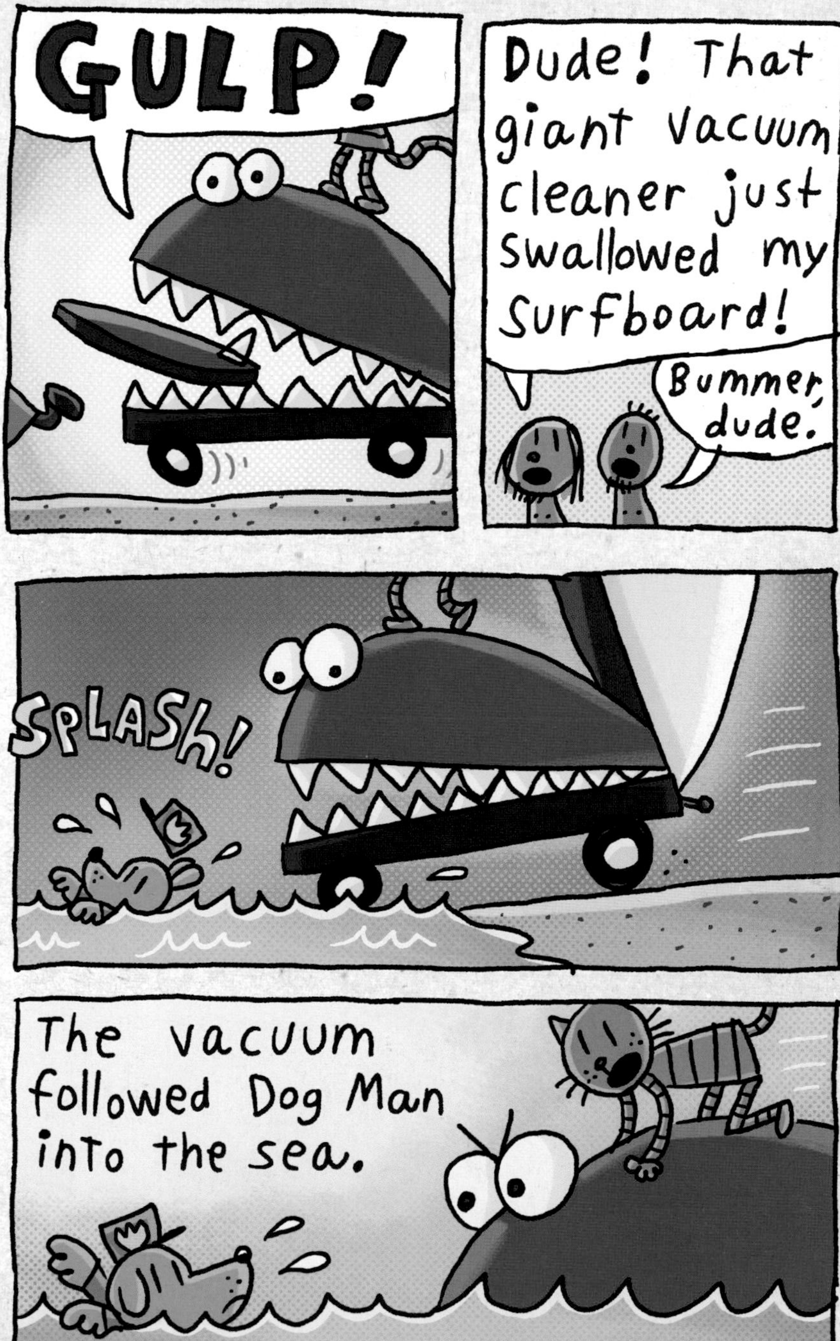
GULP!
Dude! That giant vacuum cleaner just swallowed my surfboard!
Bummer, dude.
SPLASH!
The vacuum followed Dog Man into the sea.

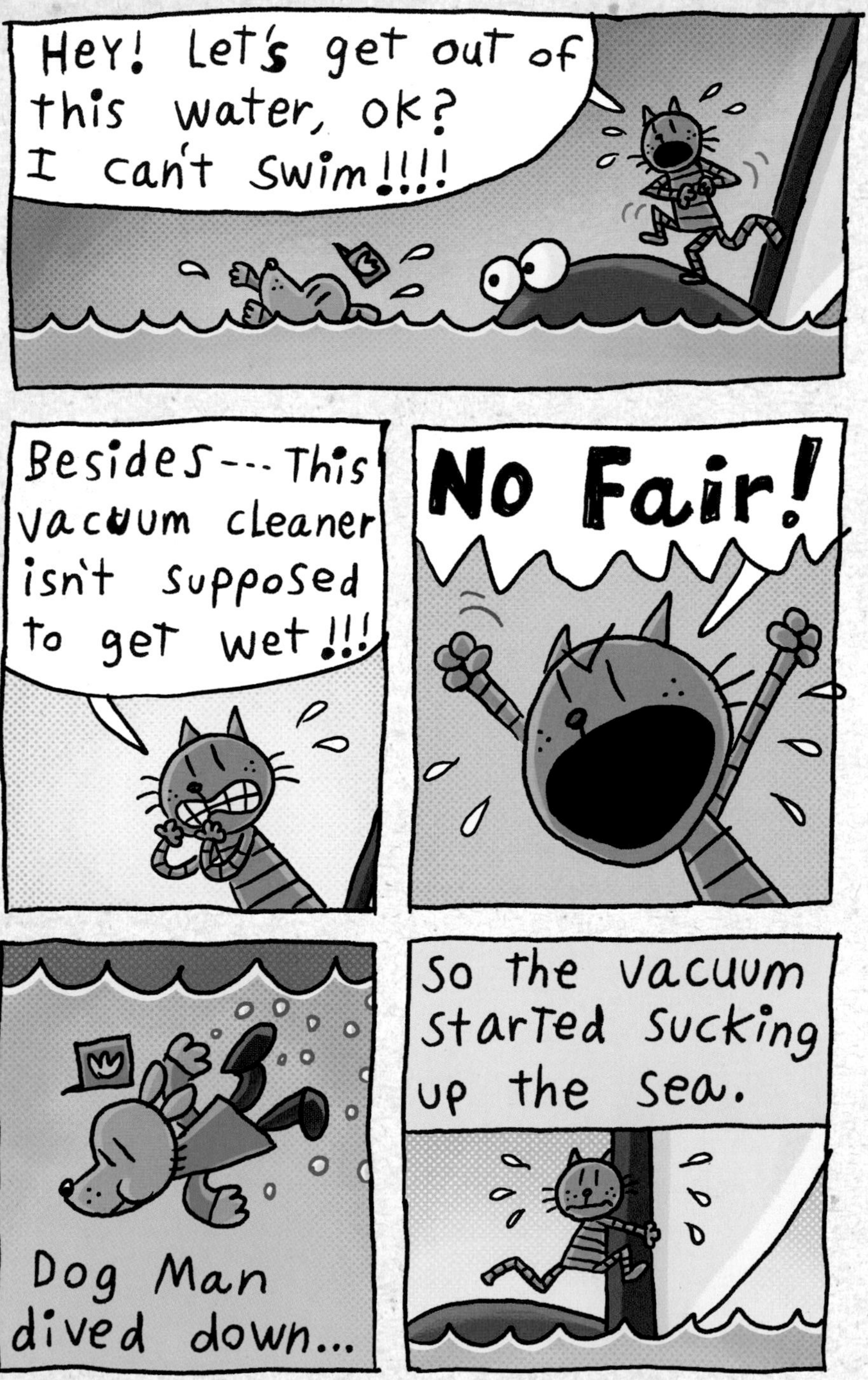
HEY! Let's get out of this water, OK? I can't swim!!!!
Besides--- This vacuum cleaner isn't supposed to get wet!!!
No Fair!
Dog Man dived down...
So the vacuum started sucking up the sea.

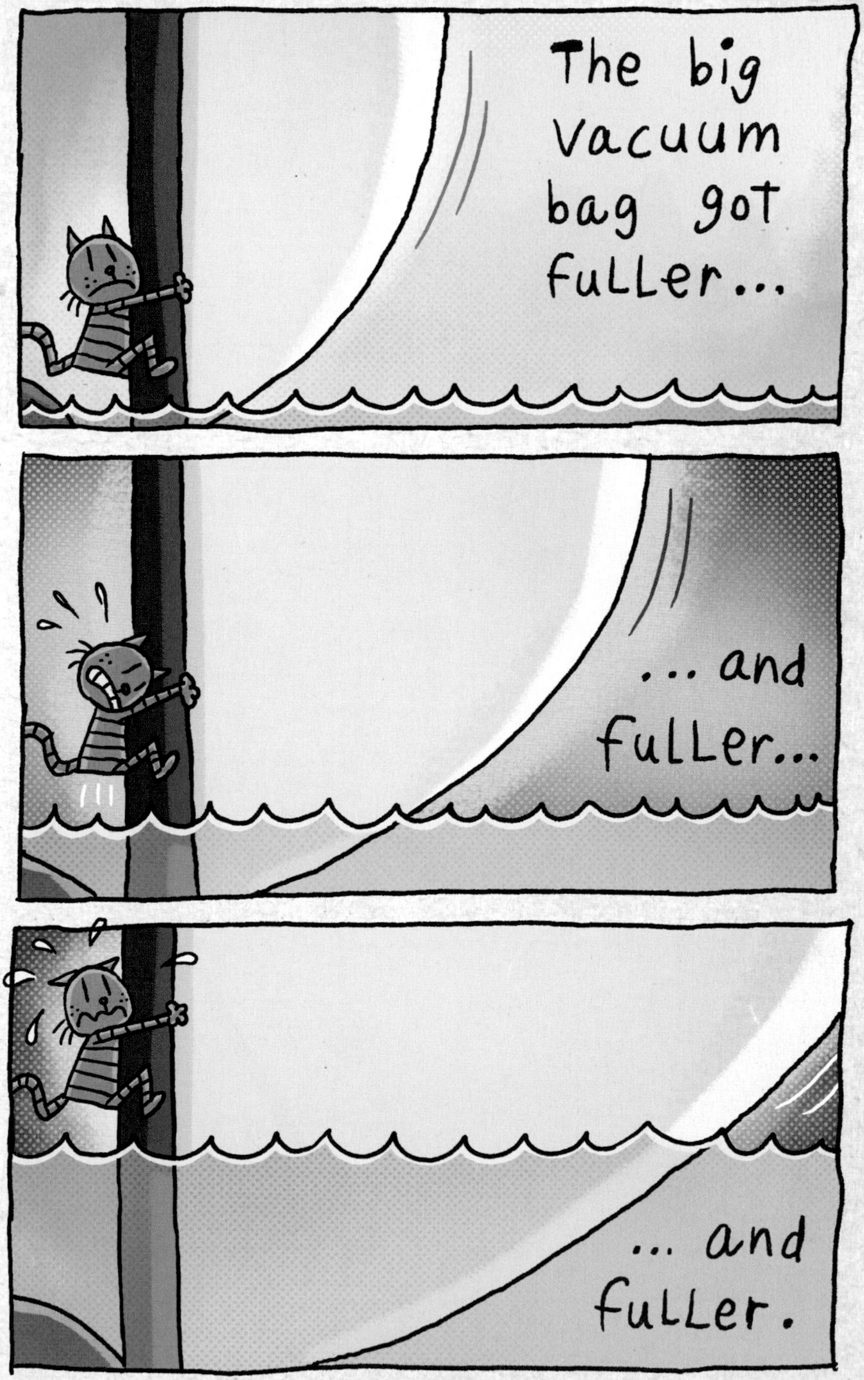
The big vacuum bag got fuller...
... and fuller...
... and fuller.

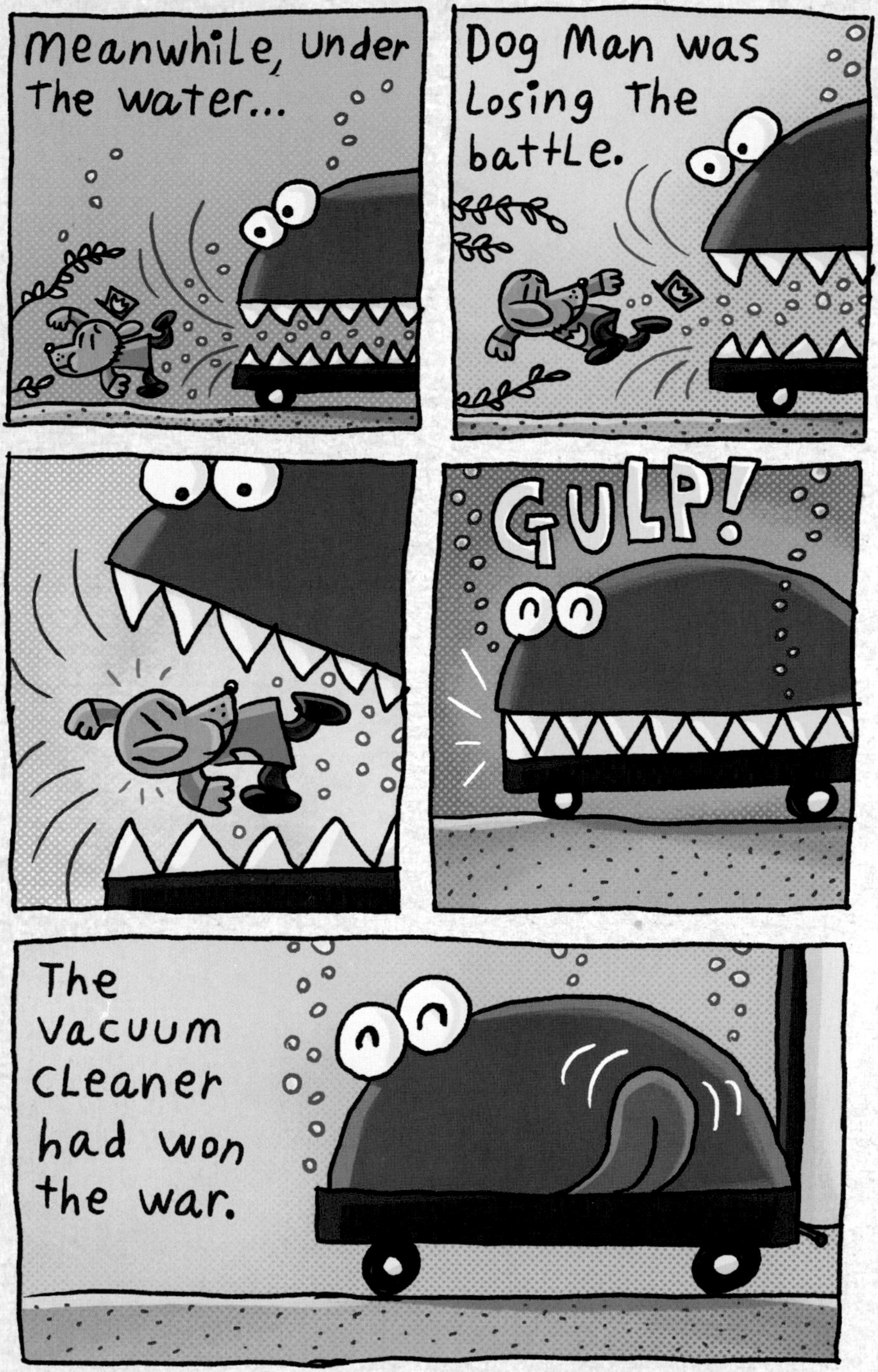
Meanwhile, under the water...
Dog Man was losing the battle.
GULP!
The vacuum cleaner had won the war.

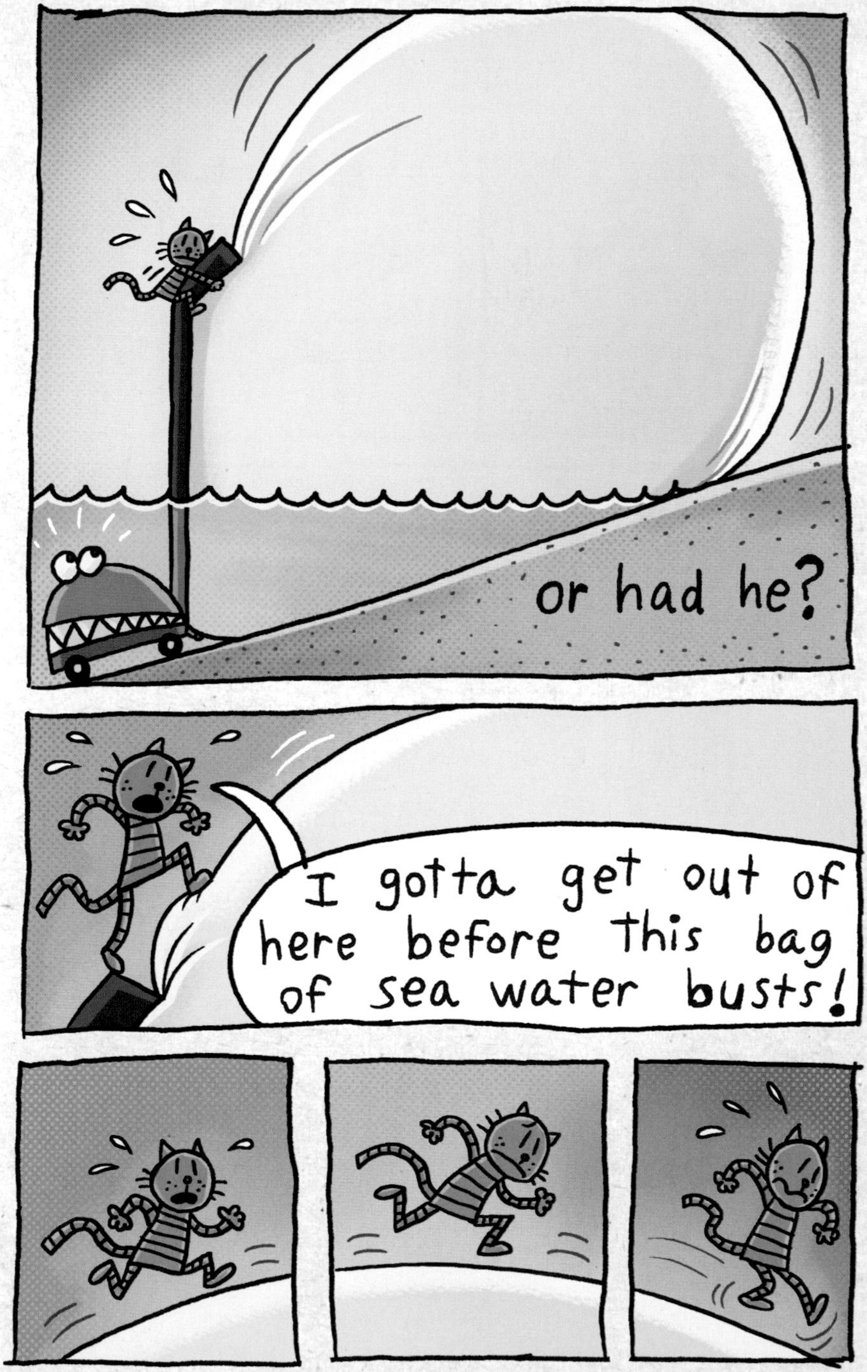
or had he?
I gotta get out of here before this bag of sea water busts!

WHOA!

Boing

Boing

Petey grabbed on with his claws.

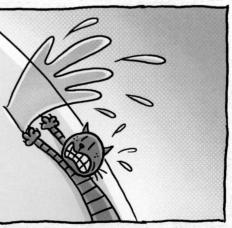

Suddenly, the vacuum bag began to rip.

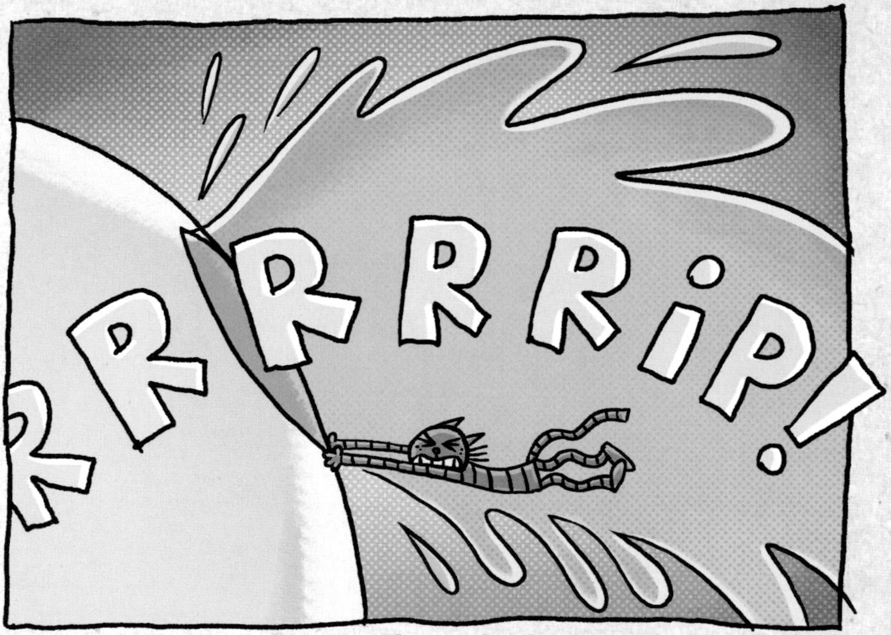
RRRRRIP!

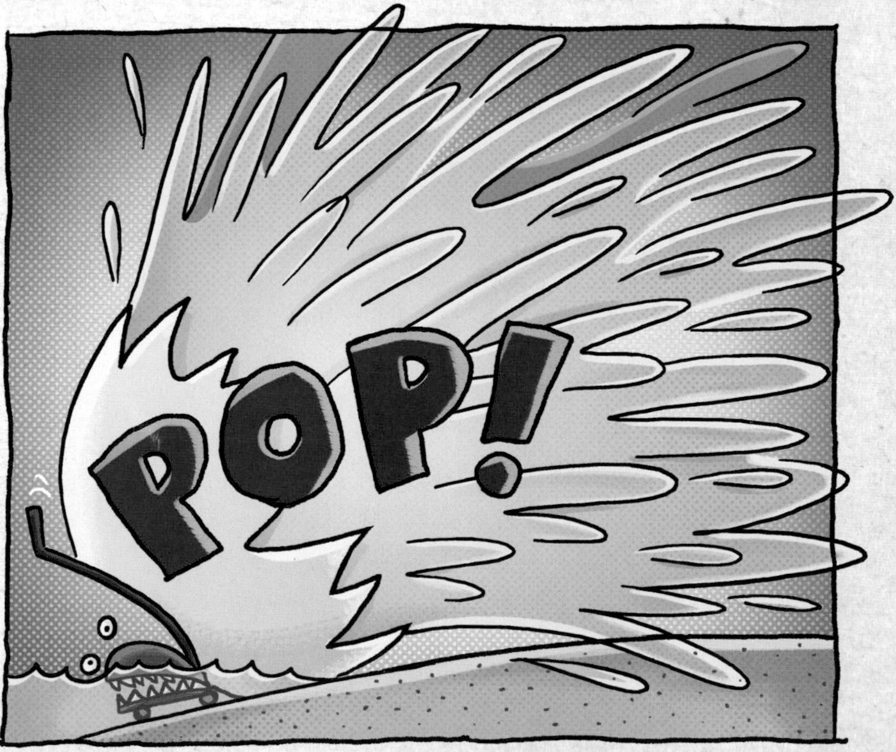
POP!

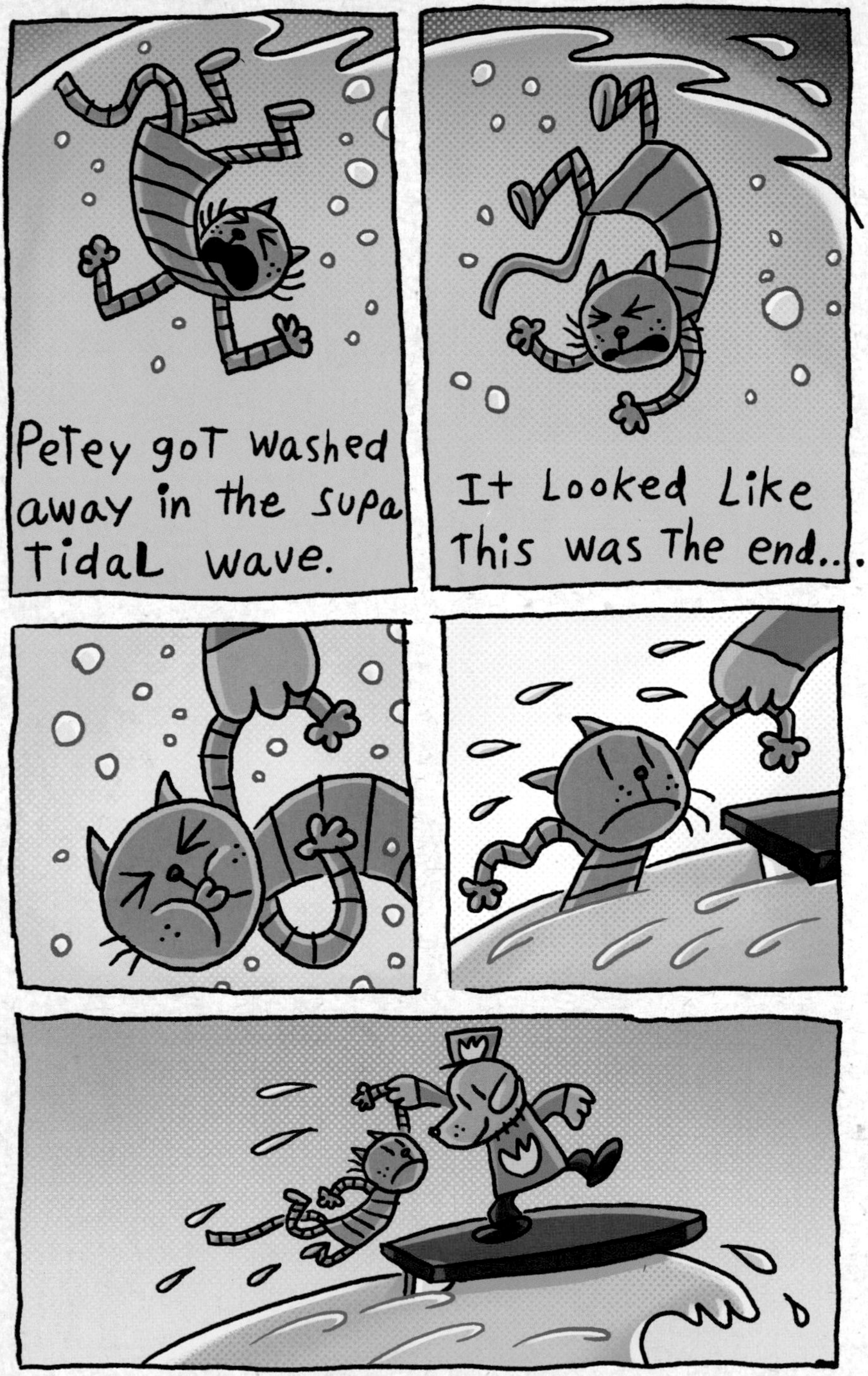
Petey goT washed away in the supa TidaL wave.
It Looked Like This was The end....

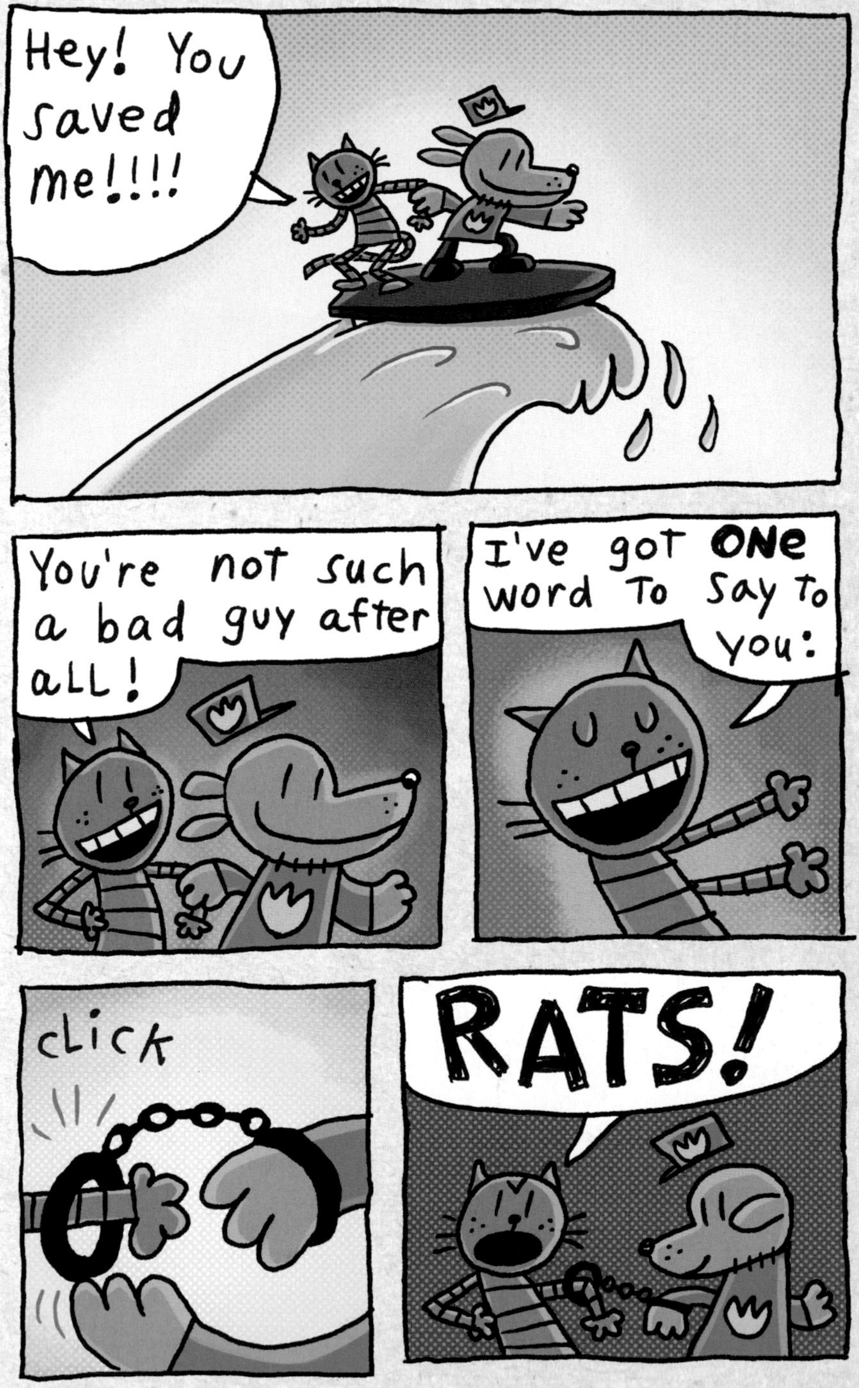
Hey! You saved me!!!!
You're not such a bad guy after all!
I've got ONE word to say to you:
click
RATS!

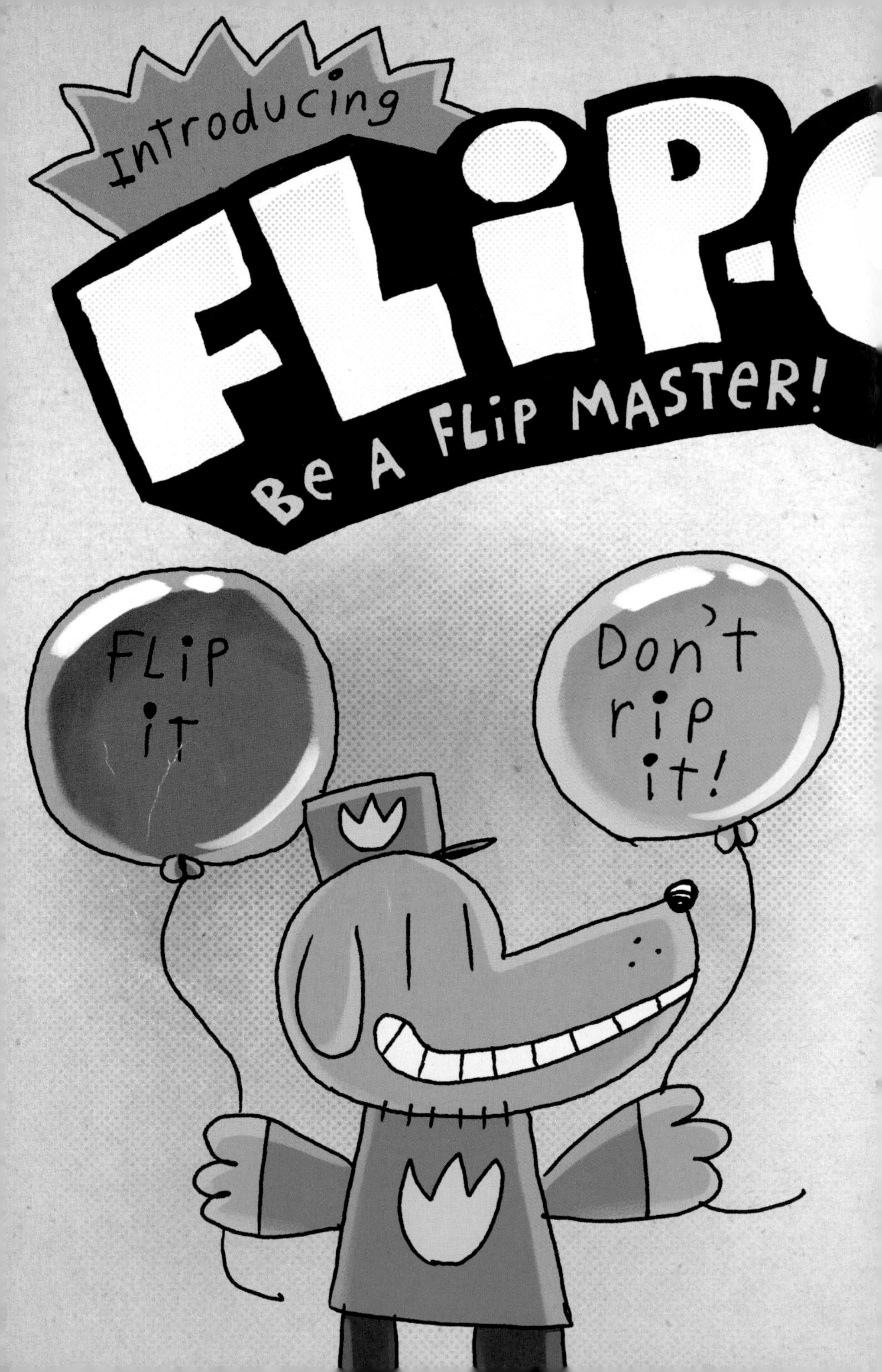
Introducing
FLIP-O
Be A FLIP MASTER!
FLIP it
Don't rip it!

O-RAMA

EXTRA cheesy

Here's How it WORKS:

STEP 1.
First, place your Left hand inside the dotted Lines marked "Left hand here". Hold The book open FLAT!

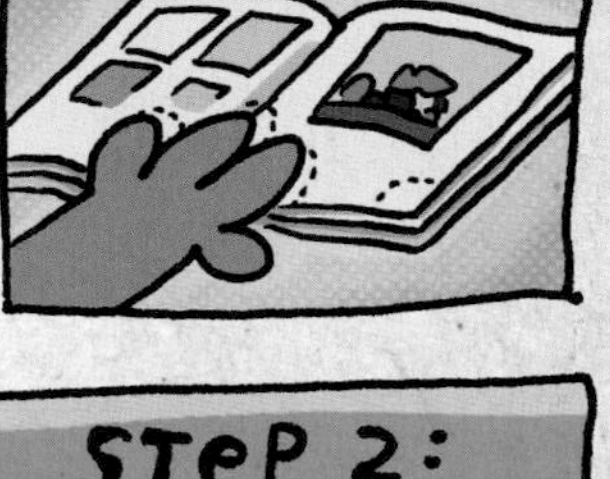

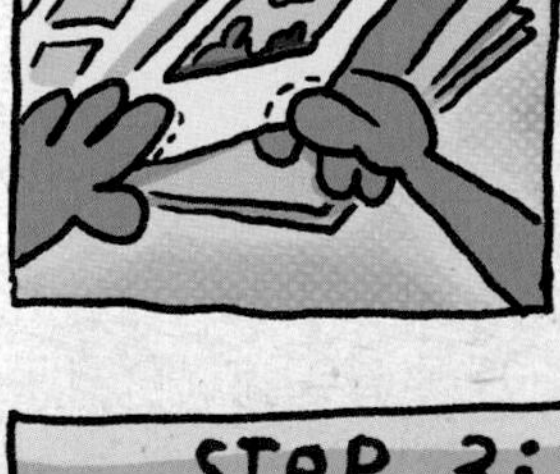

STEP 2:
Grasp the right-hand Page with your Thumb and index finger (inside the dotted Lines marked "Right Thumb Here").

STEP 3:
Now QUICKLY flip the right-hand page back and forth until the Picture appears to be Animated.

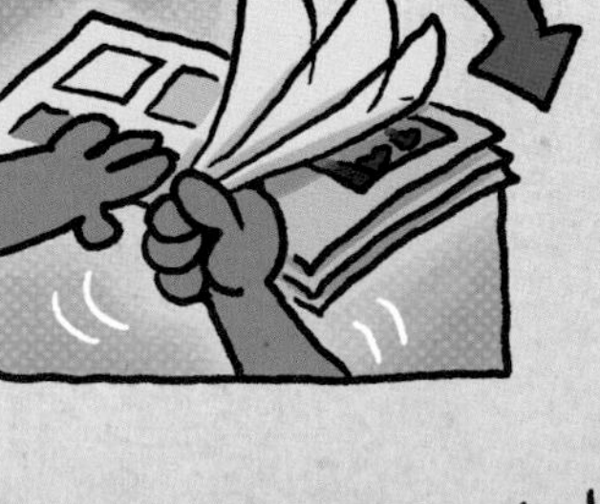

(For extra fun, try adding your own sound-effects!)

The Tidal wave got smaller and smaller...

...until it ended at just the right spot.

HEY COPS!!! Dog man captured Peter!!

This calls for a celebration!!!

Remember, flip only page 43. Be sure you can see the picture on page 43 **AND** the one on page 45 while you flip.

Left hand here.

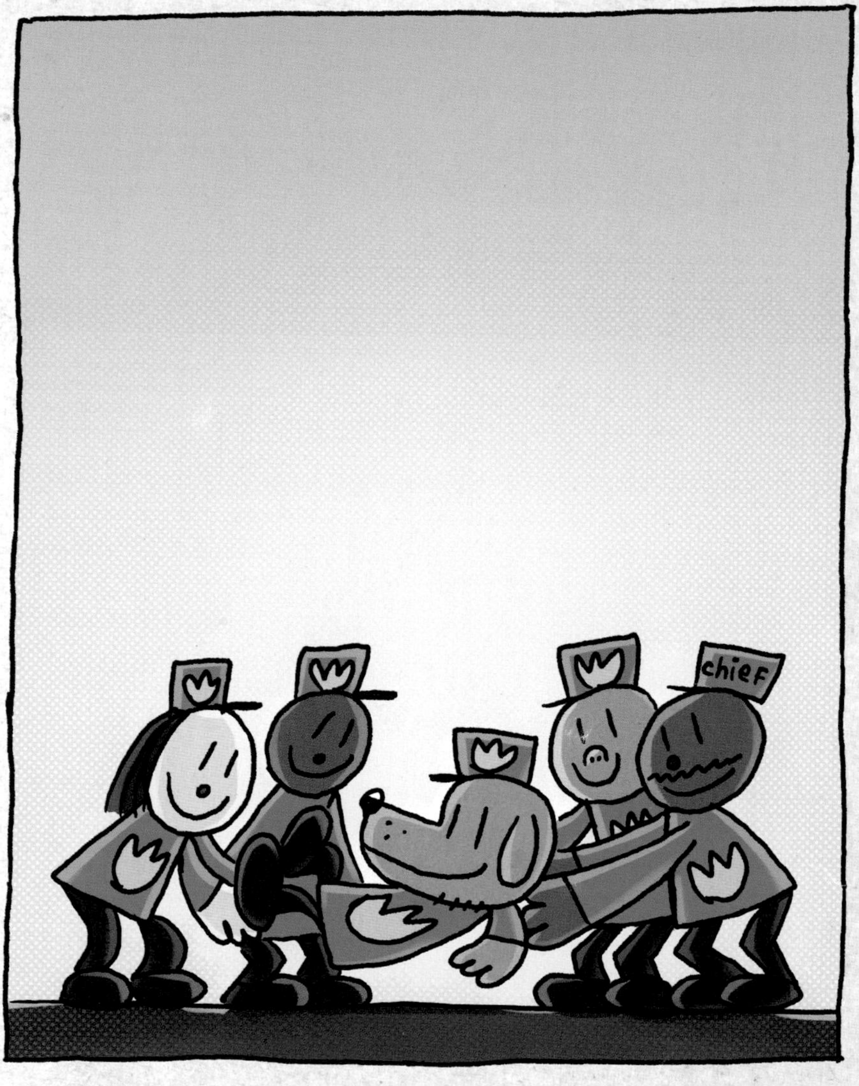
chief

For he's a
JoLLy good
doggy!

Right
Thumb
here.

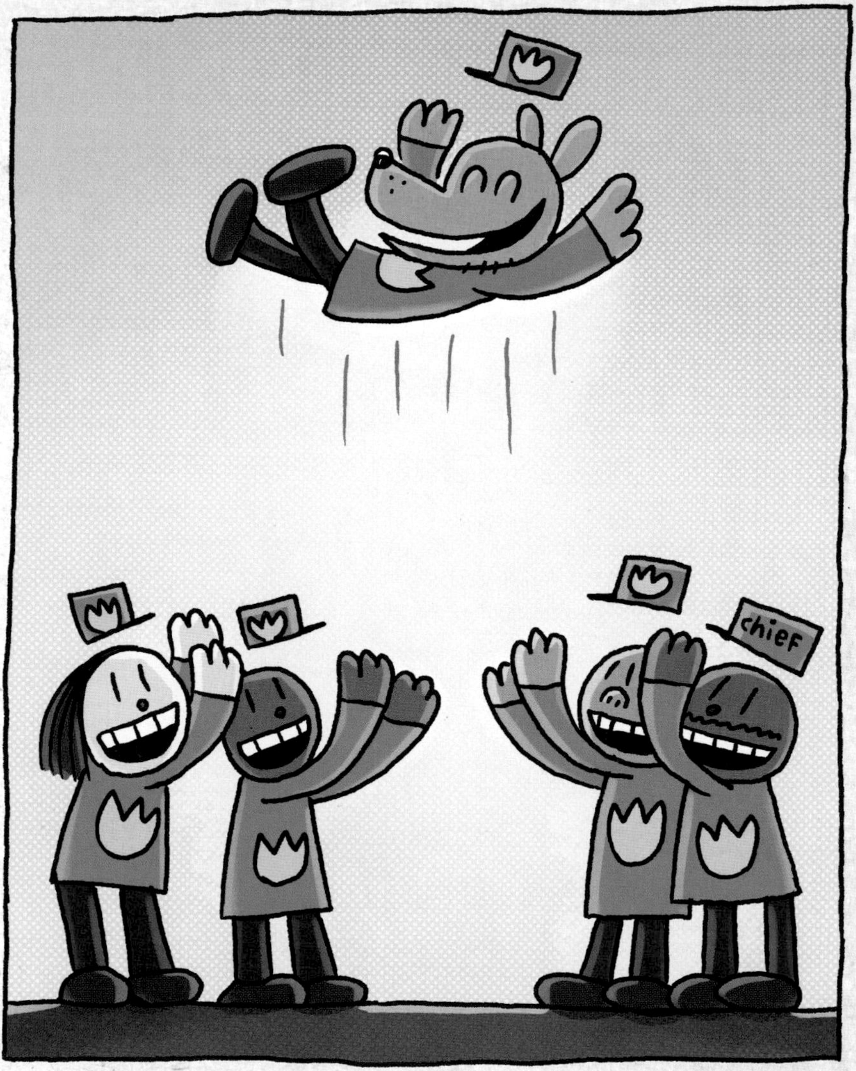
chief

For he's a
JoLLy good
doggy!

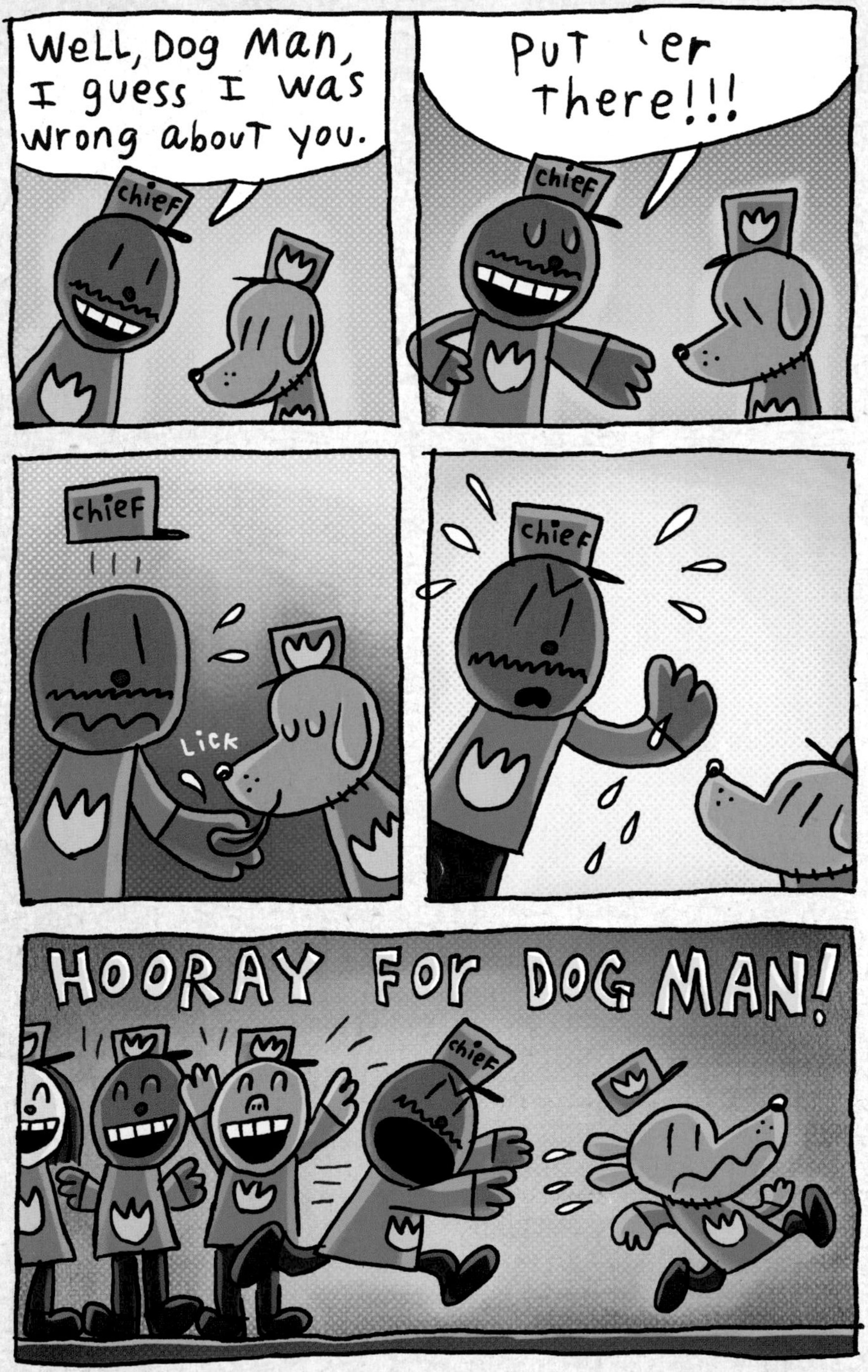
WeLL, Dog Man, I guess I was wrong about you.
chief
PuT 'er there!!!
chief
chief
Lick
chief
HOORAY FOr DOG MAN!
chief

CHAPTER 2
ROBO-CHIEF

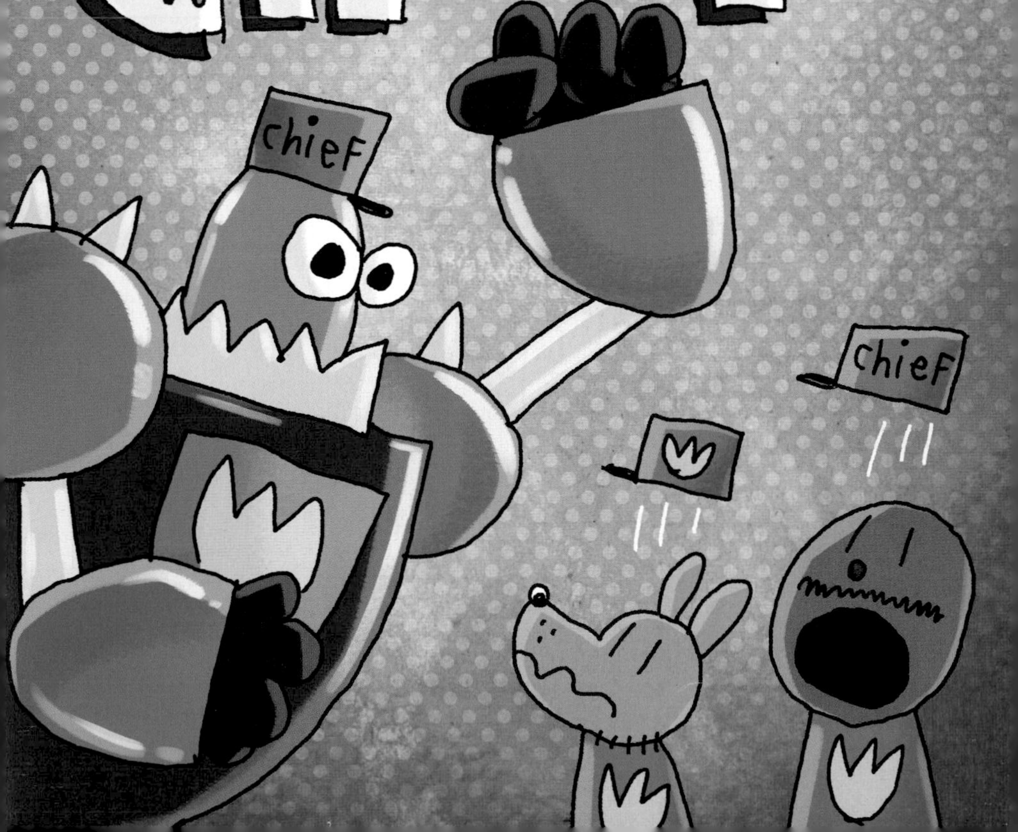
chief
chief

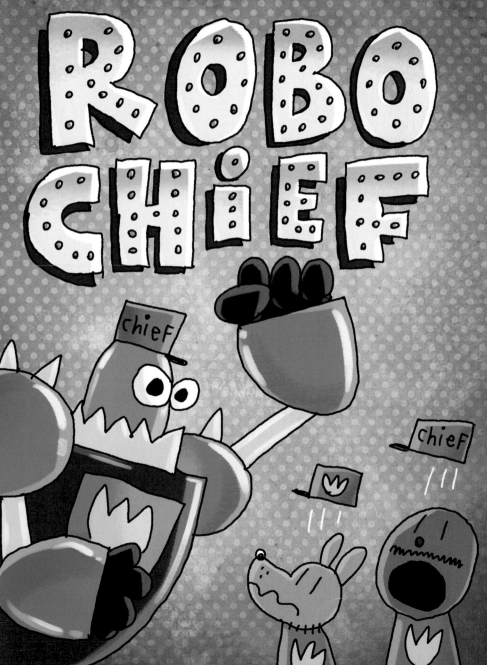

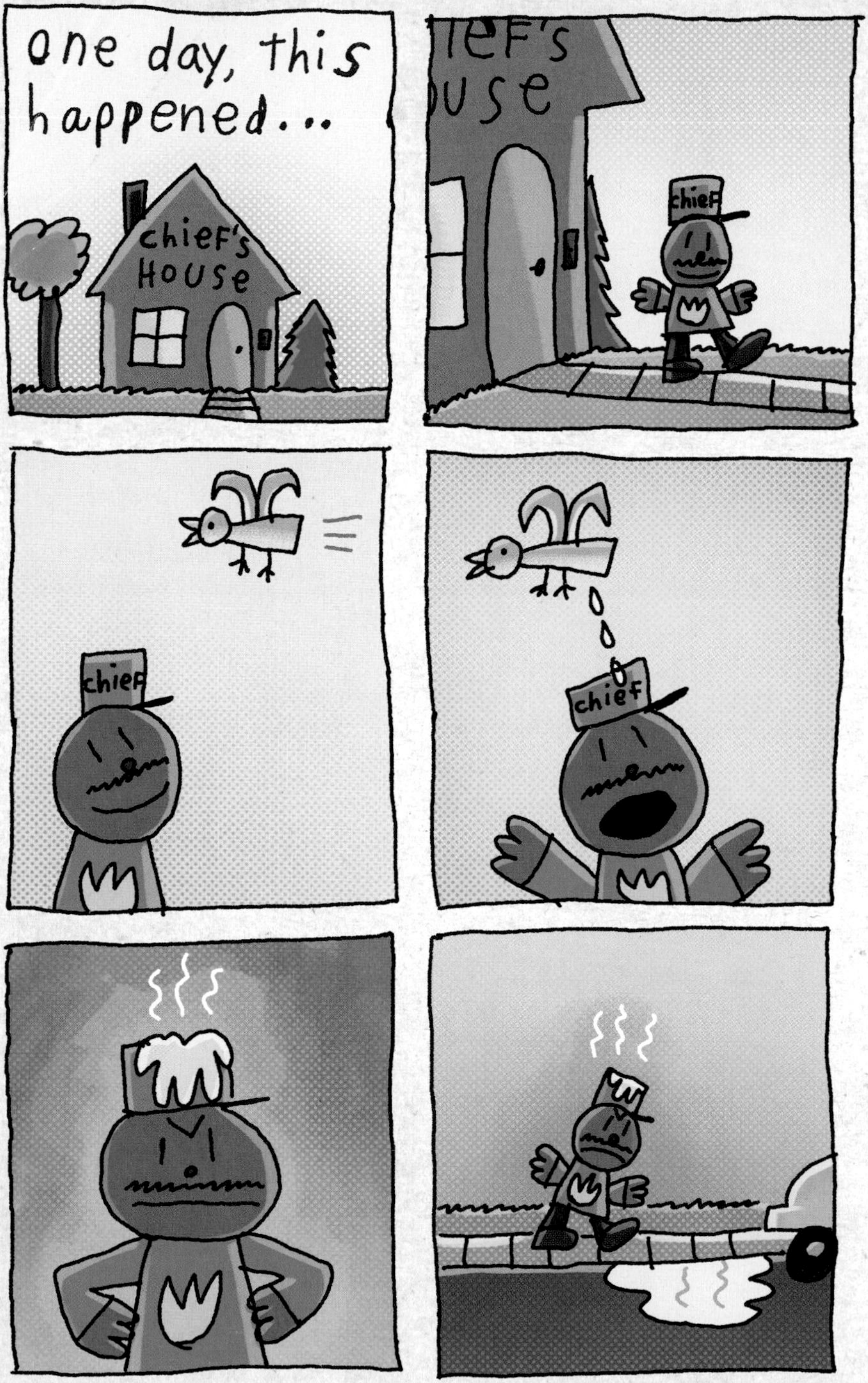
one day, this happened...
CHIEF'S HOUSE
chief
chief
chief

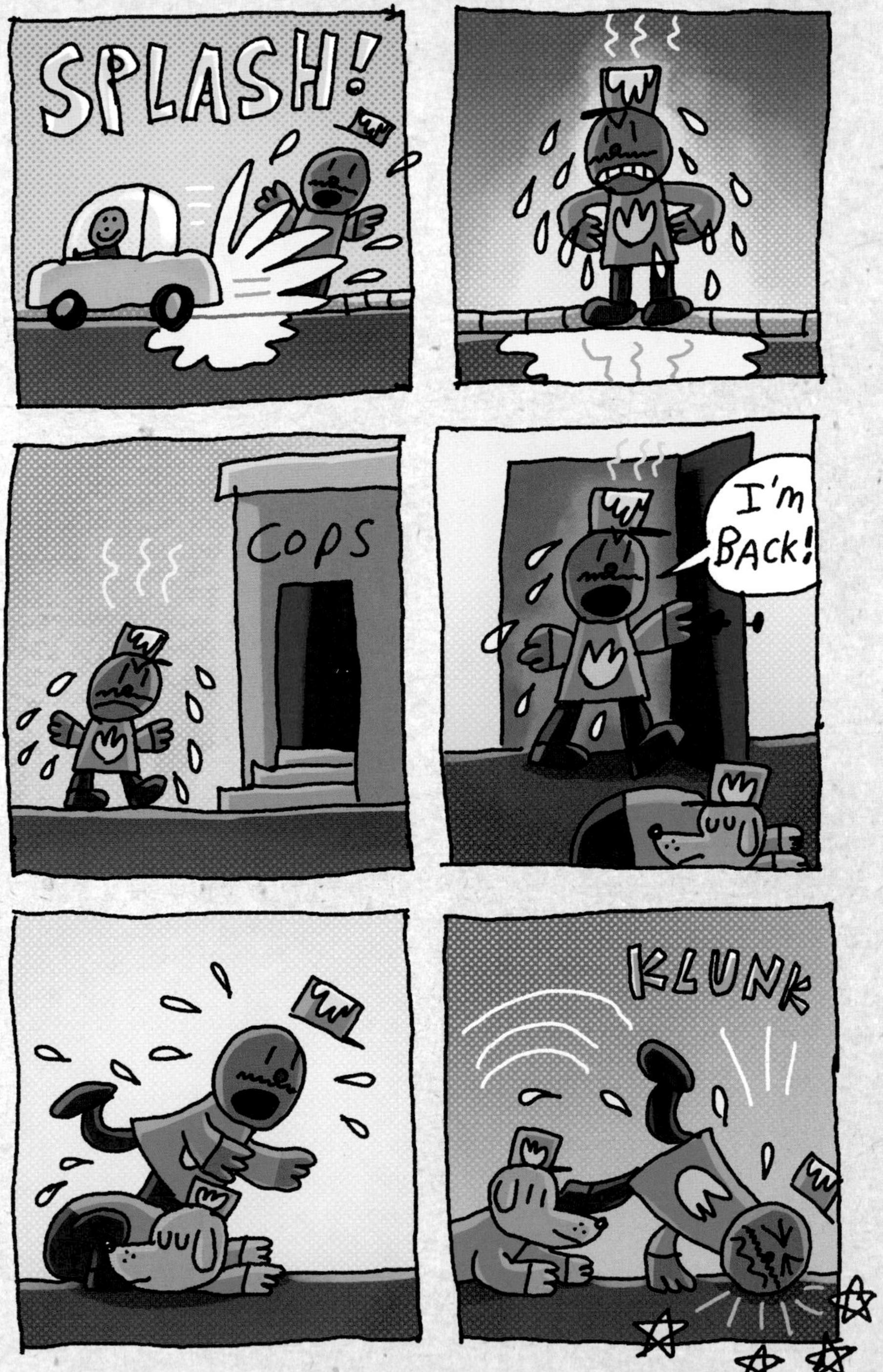
SPLASH!
COPS
I'm BACK!
KLUNK

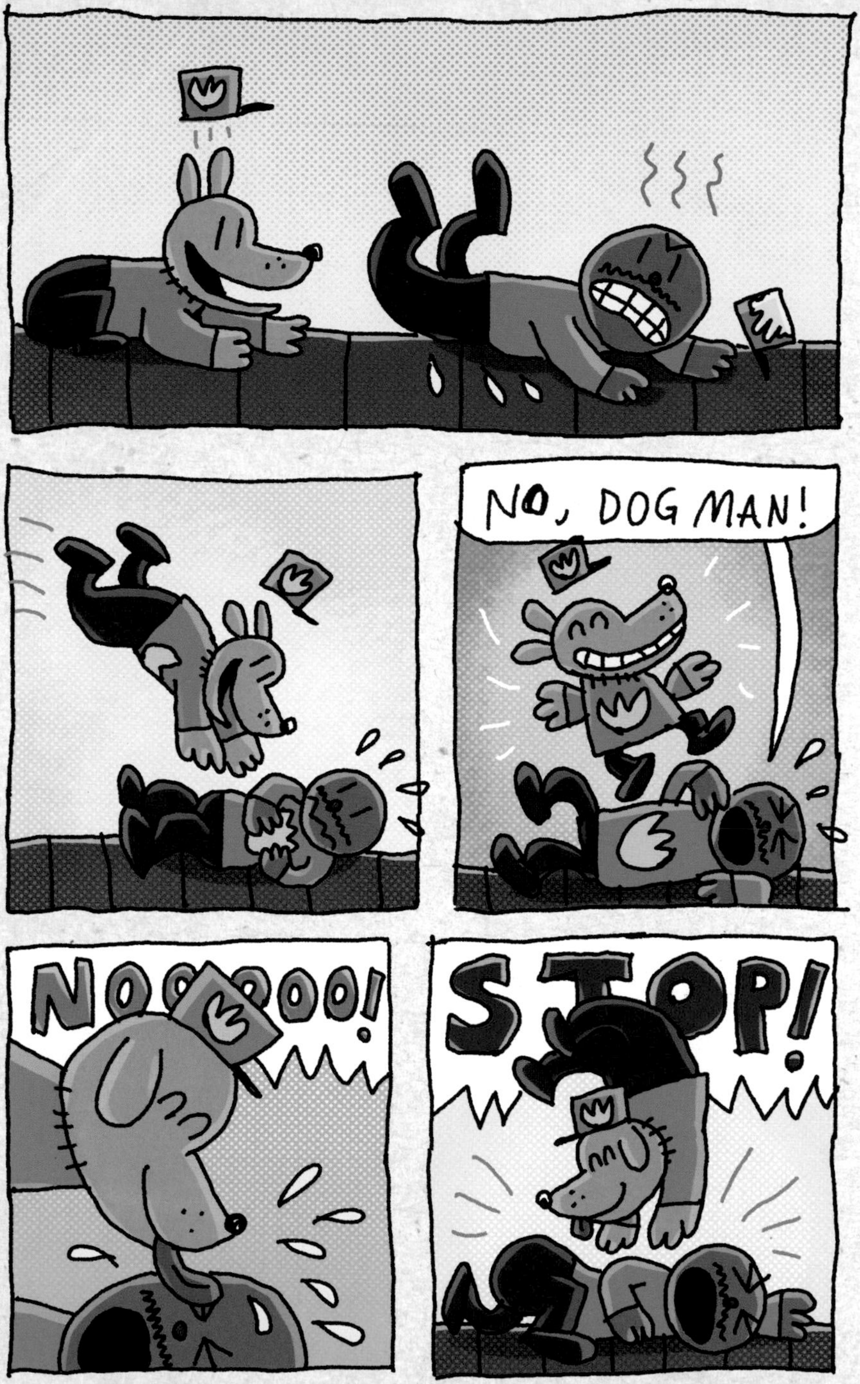
NO, DOG MAN!
NOOOOOO!
STOP!

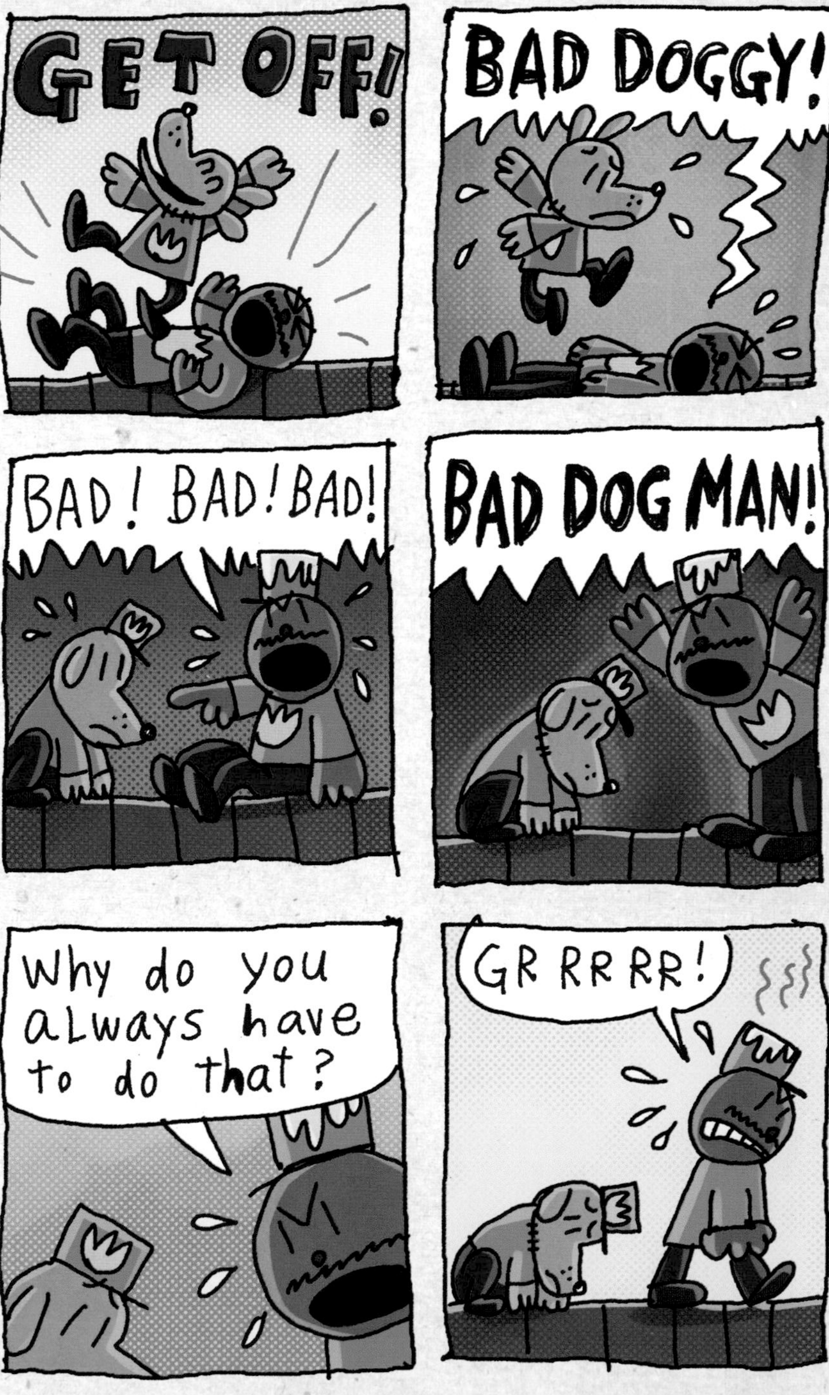
GET OFF!
BAD DOGGY!
BAD! BAD! BAD!
BAD DOG MAN!
Why do you always have to do that?
GRRRRR!

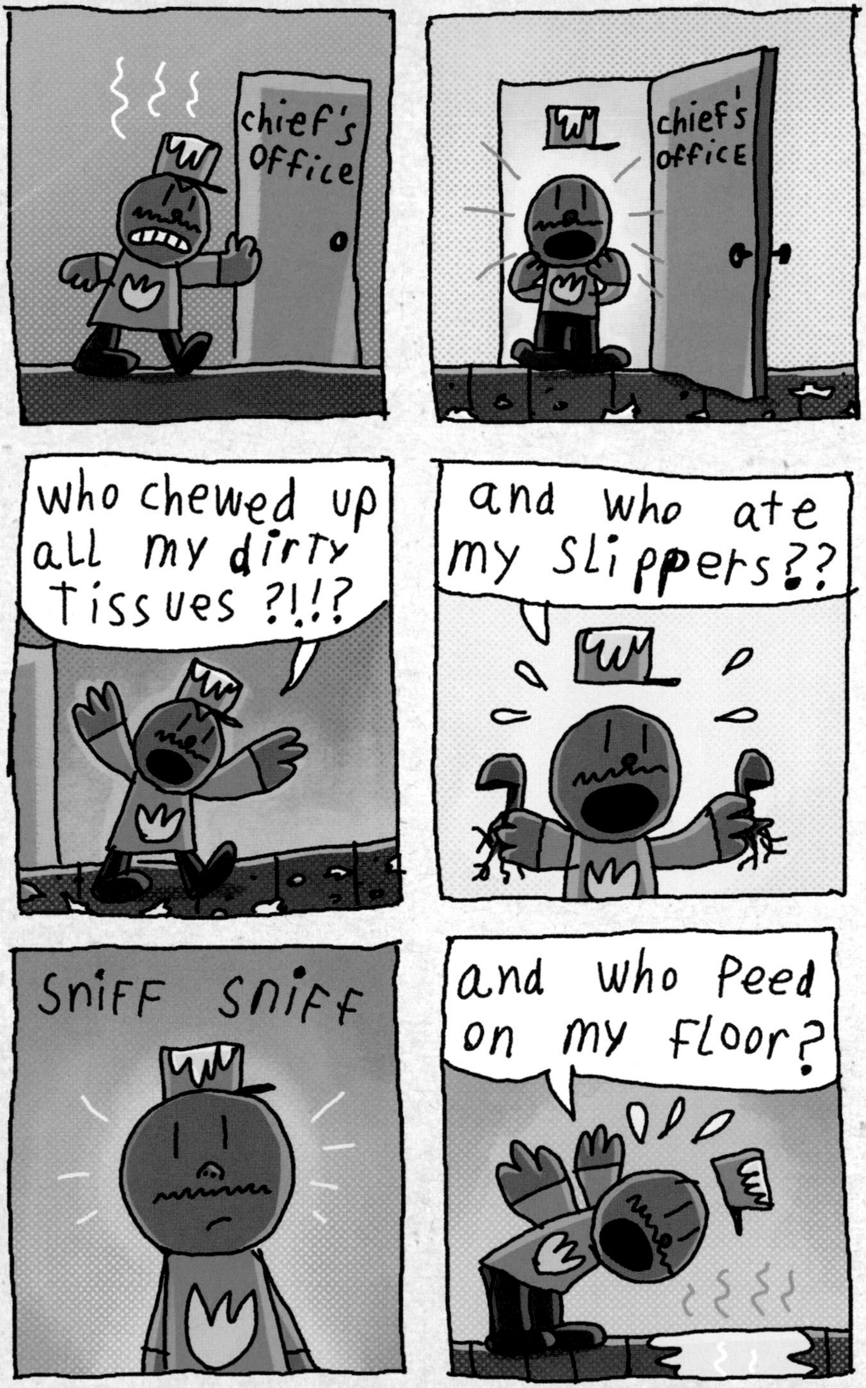
chief's office
chief's office
who chewed up all my dirty Tissues ?!!?
and who ate my Slippers??
Sniff Sniff
and who Peed on my Floor?

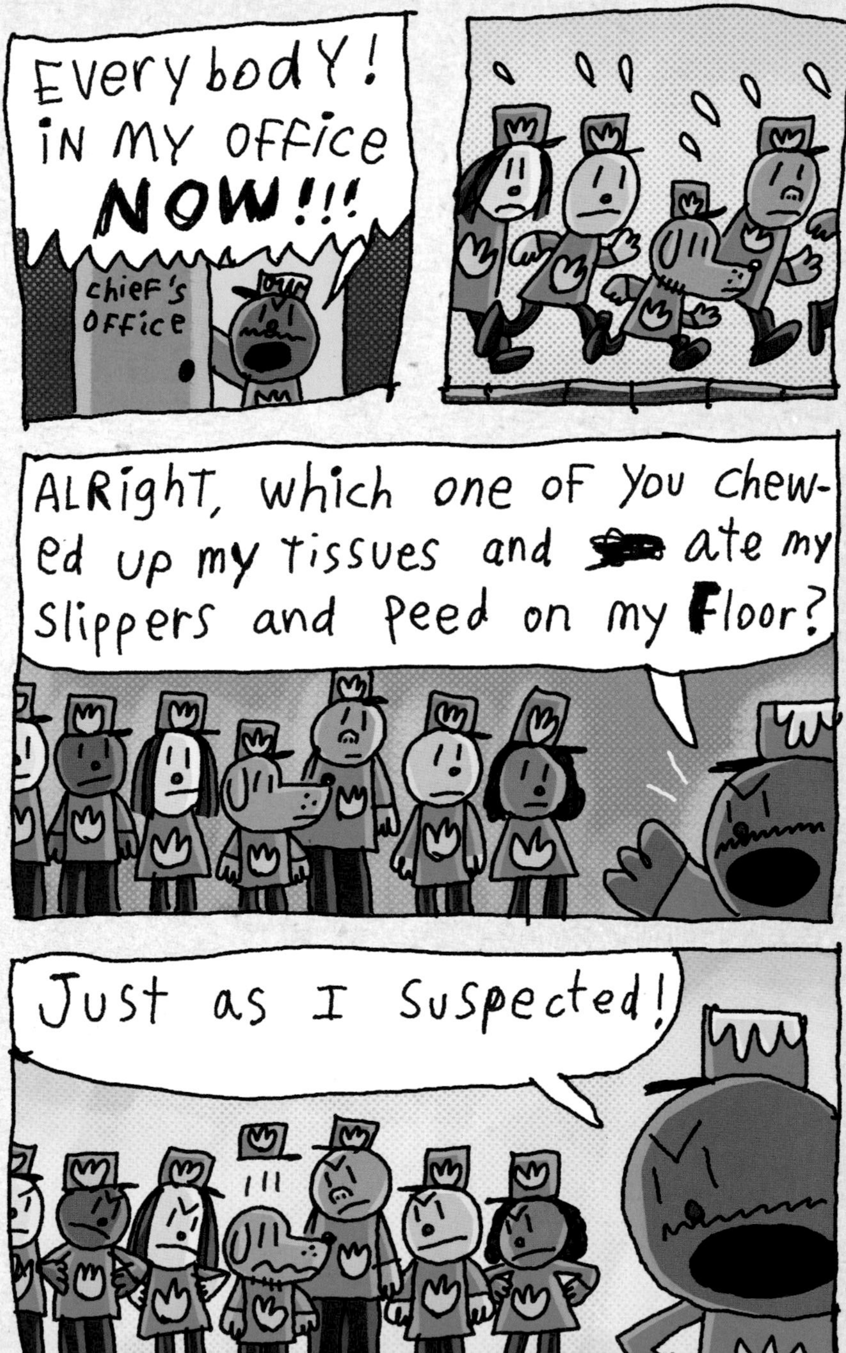

Everybody! in my office NOW!!!
chief's office
ALRight, which one of you chew-ed up my tissues and ate my slippers and peed on my Floor?
Just as I Suspected!

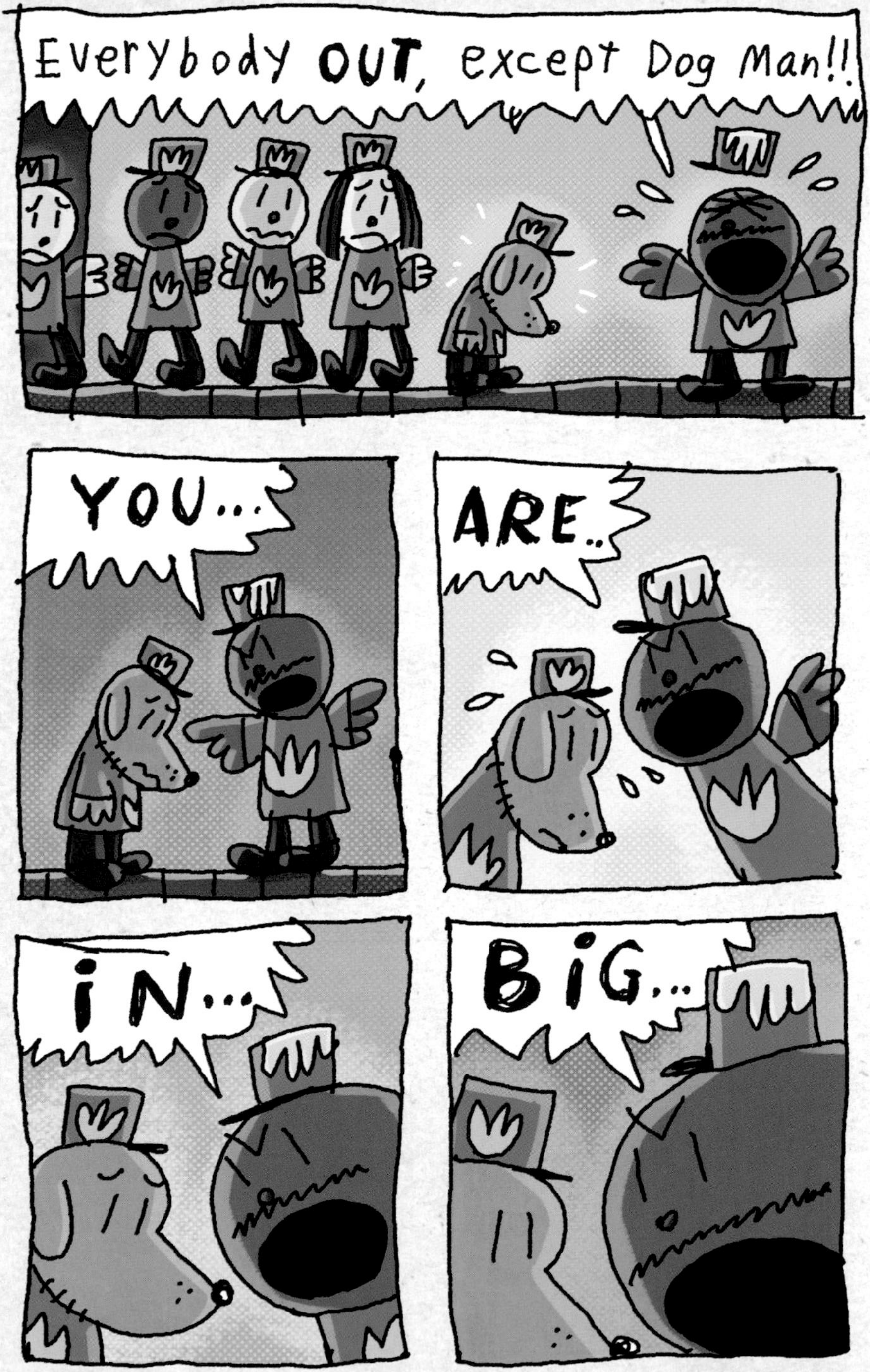
Everybody OUT, except Dog Man!!
YOU...
ARE...
IN...
BIG...

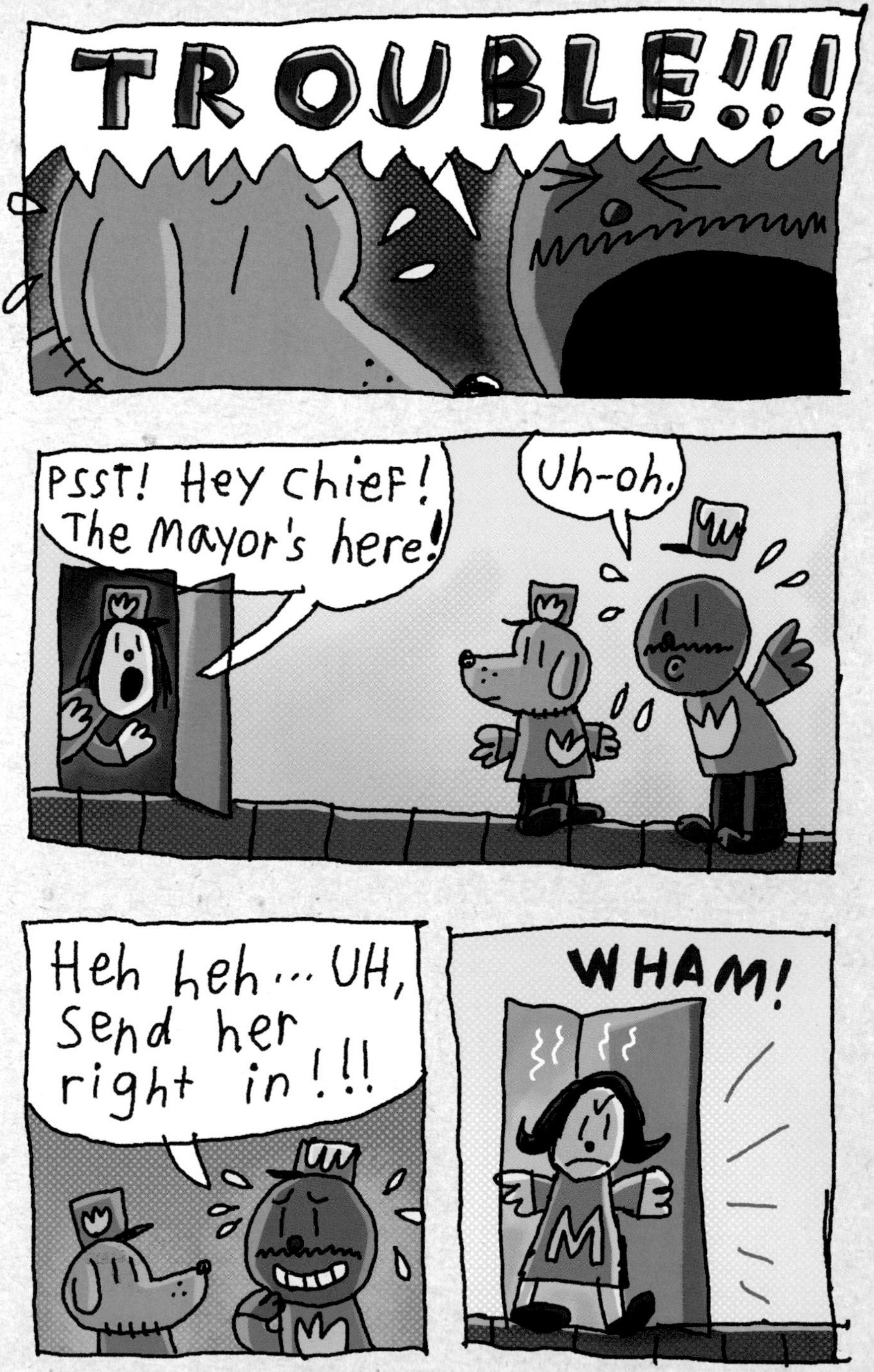
TROUBLE!!!
PSST! Hey chief! The mayor's here!
Uh-oh.
Heh heh... UH, Send her right in!!!
WHAM!

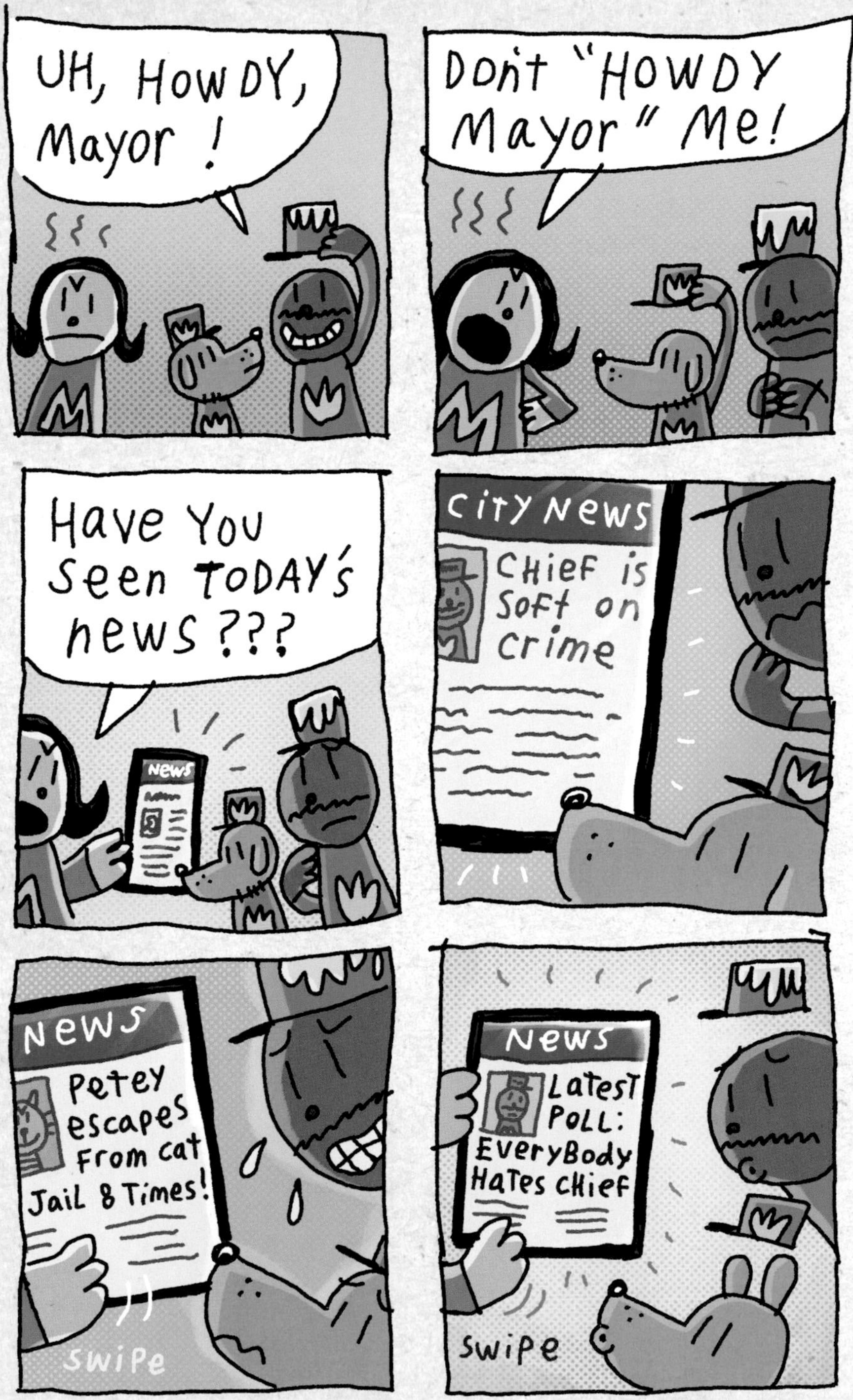
UH, HOWDY, Mayor!
Don't "HOWDY Mayor" Me!
Have You seen TODAY's news???
City News
Chief is Soft on crime
News
News
Petey escapes From cat Jail 8 Times!
SWIPE
News
Latest Poll: EveryBody Hates Chief
SWIPE

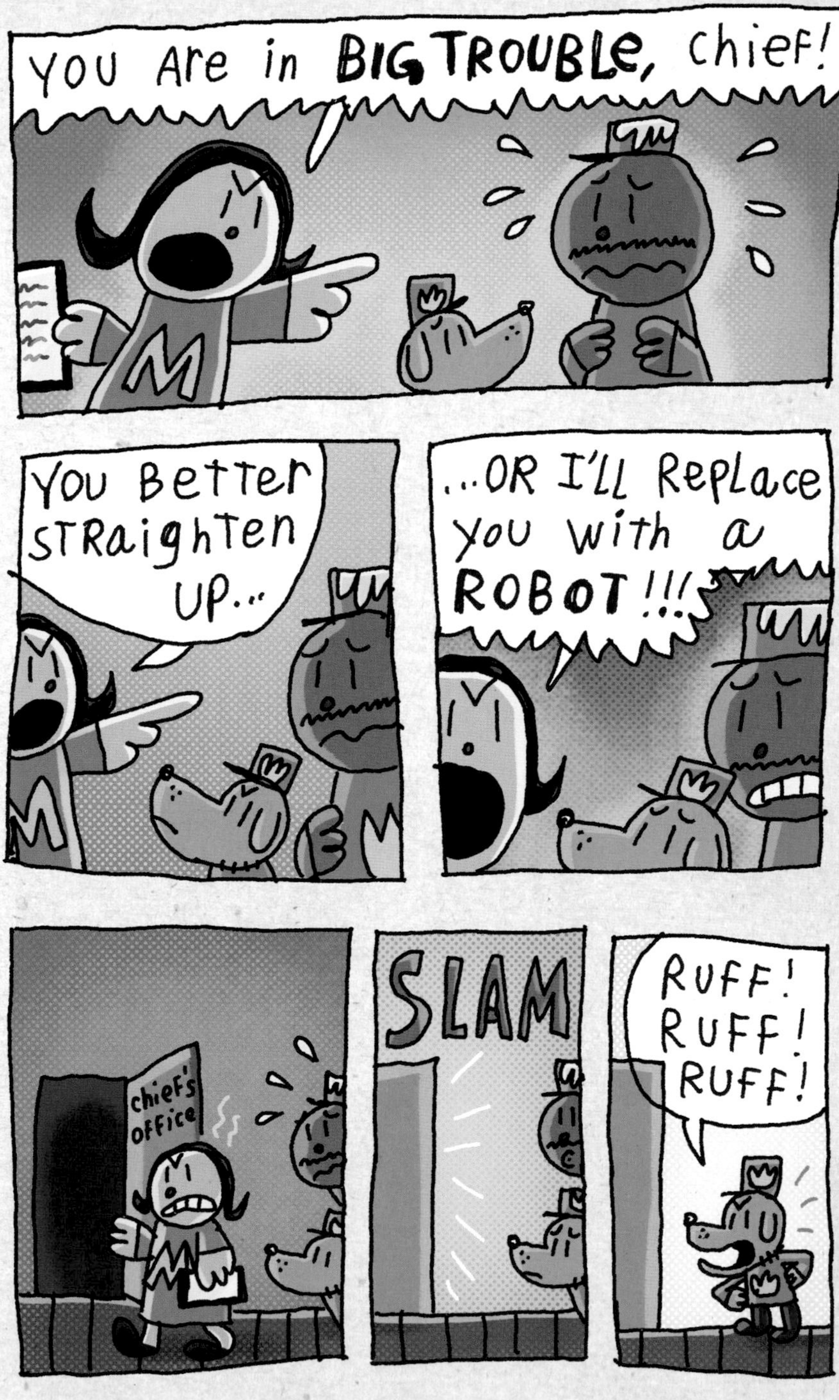
YOU ARE in BIG TROUBLE, chief!
YOU BETTER STRAighTEN UP...
...OR I'LL Replace you with a ROBOT!!!
chief's office
SLAM
RUFF! RUFF! RUFF!

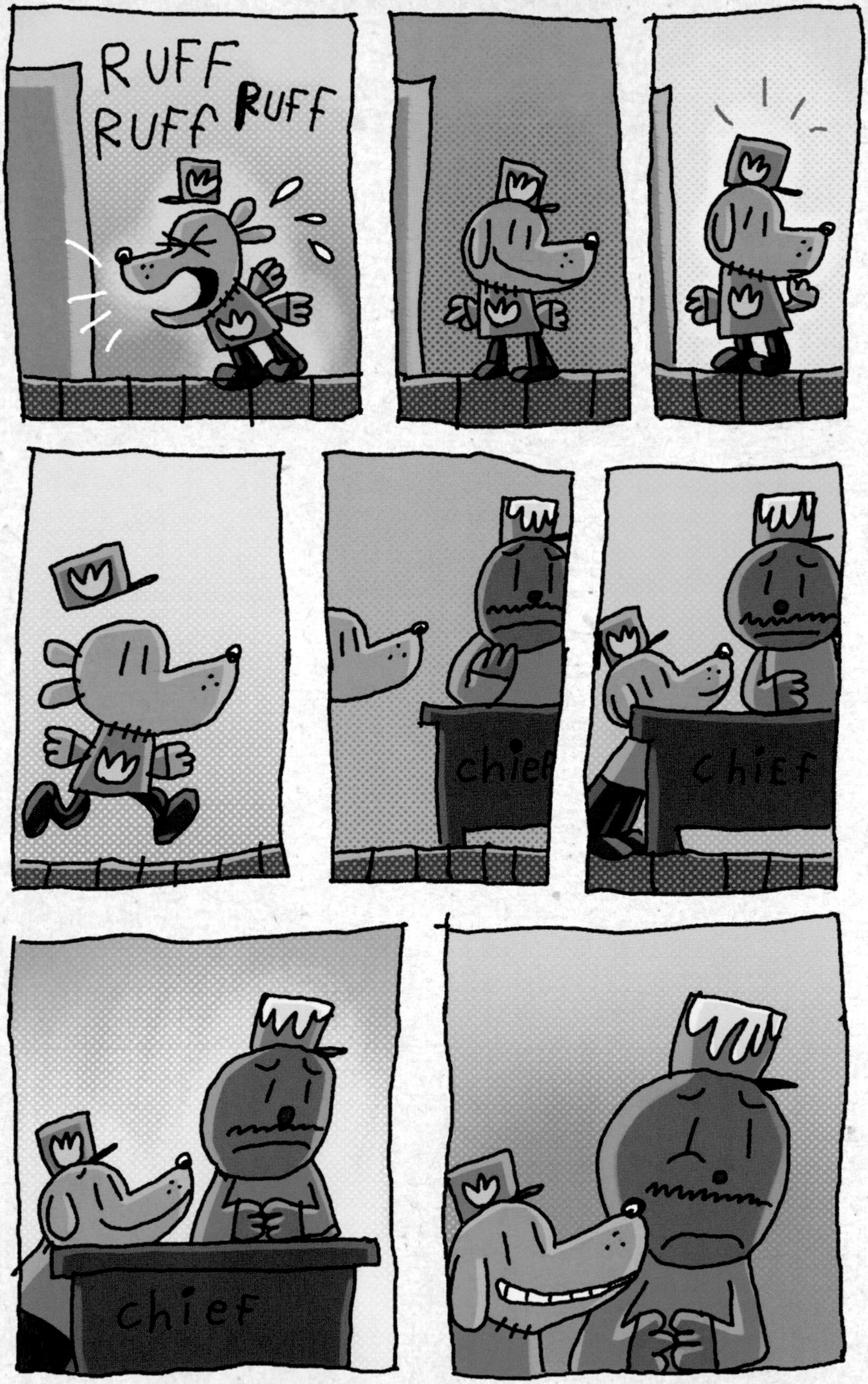

RUFF
RUFF RUFF
chief
CHIEF
chief

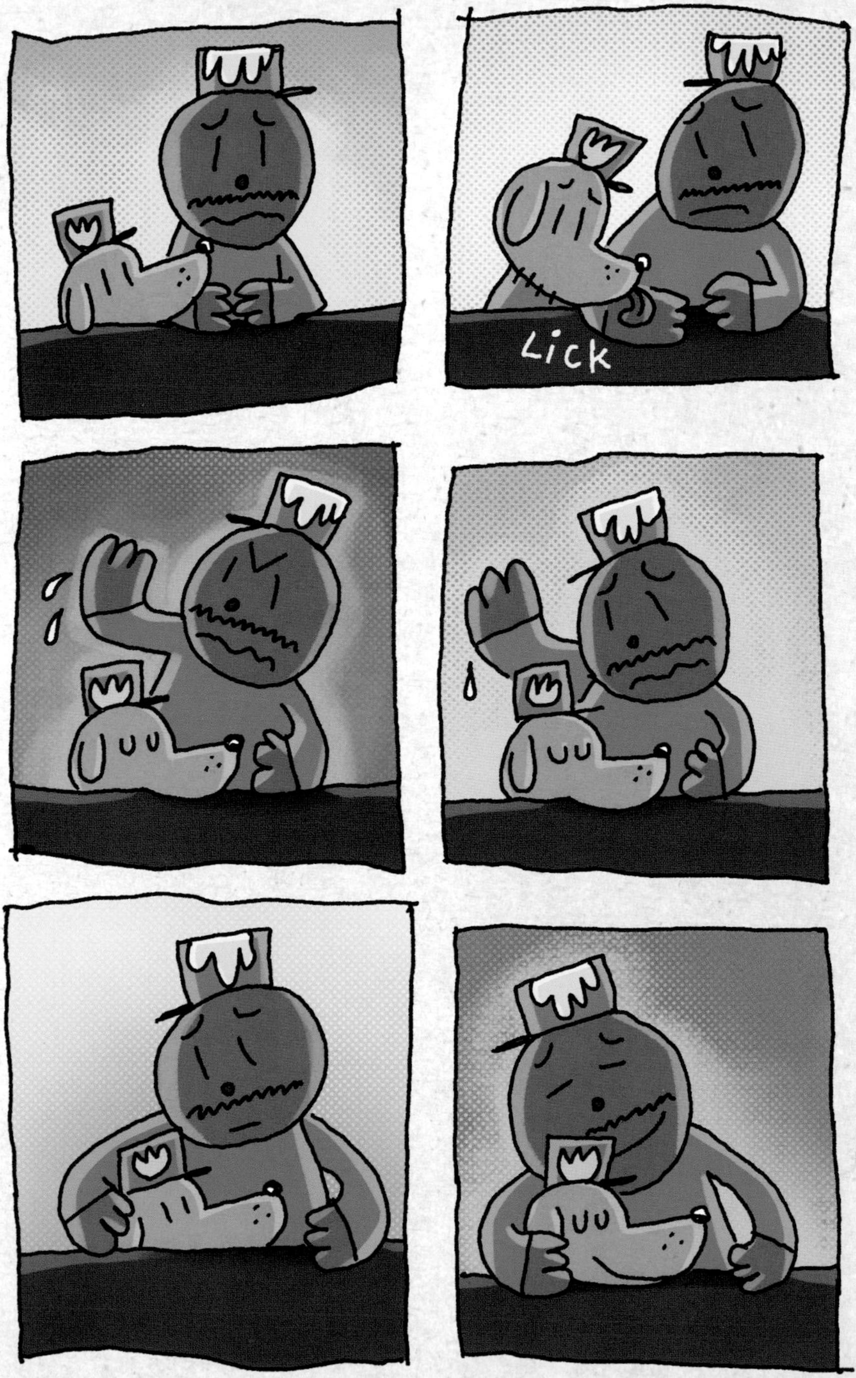
Lick

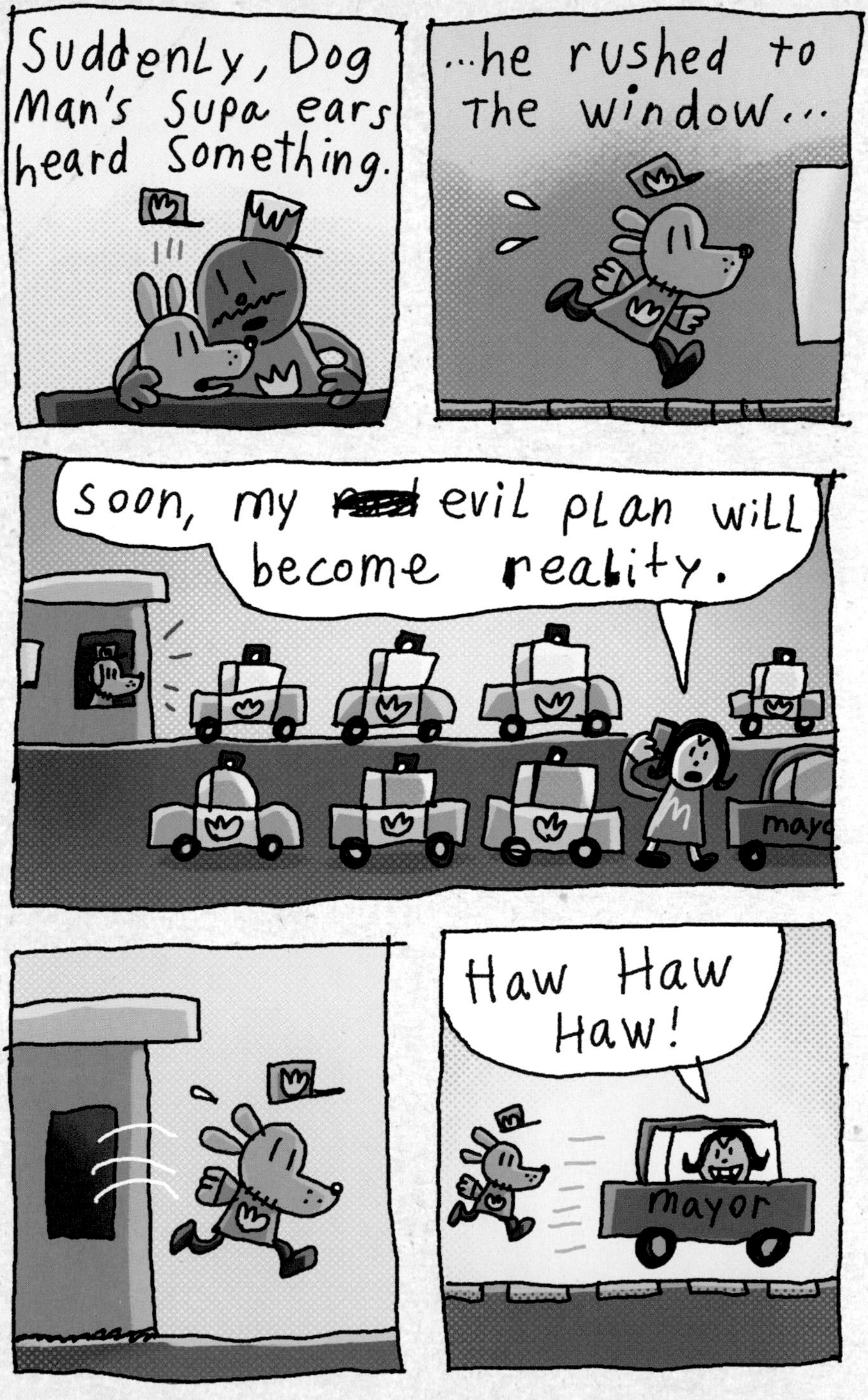
SuddenLy, Dog Man's Supa ears heard Something.
...he rushed to the window...
soon, my evil pLan wiLL become reality.
mayo
Haw Haw Haw!
mayor

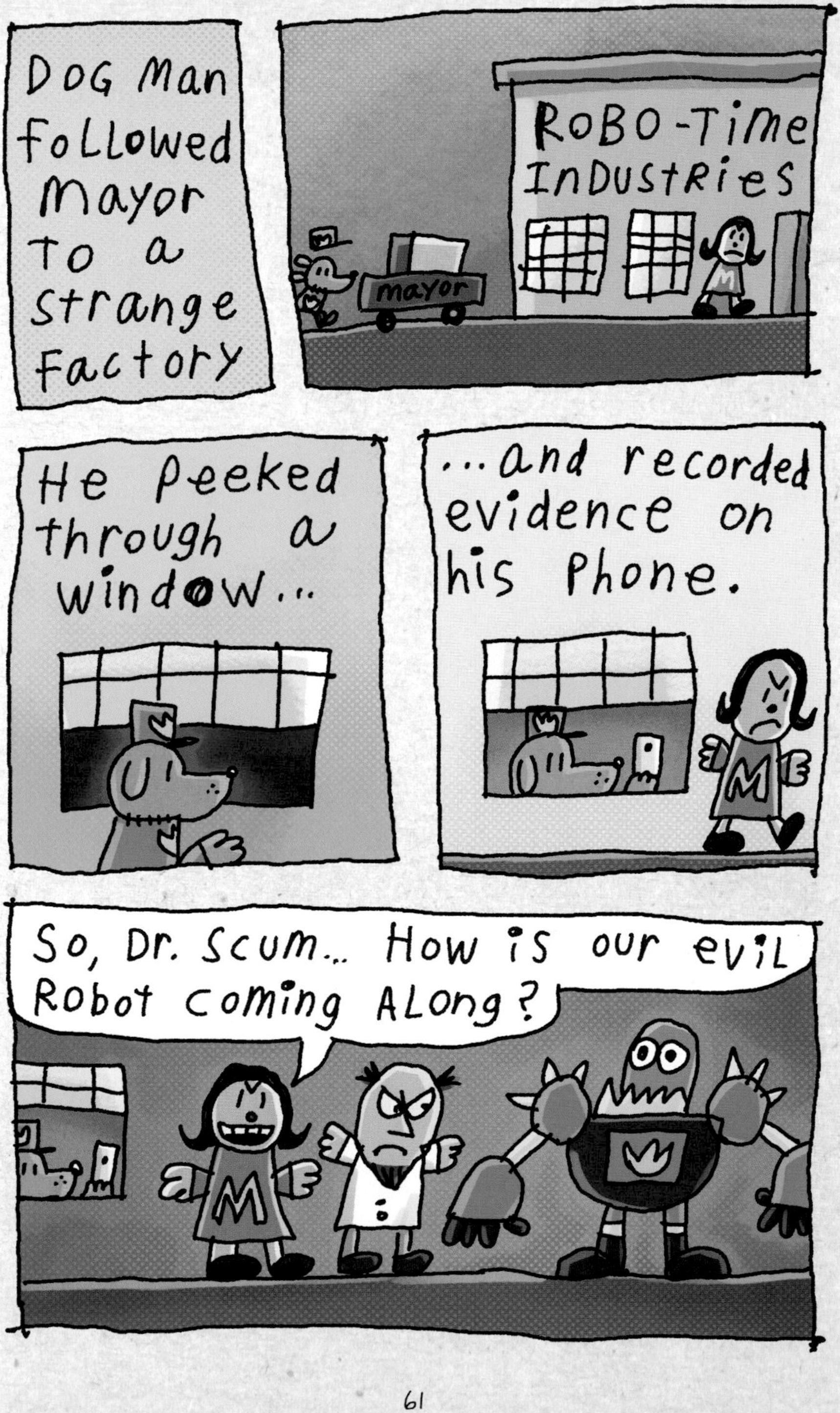
Dog Man followed mayor to a strange Factory
ROBO-Time INDUSTRIES
mayor
He peeked through a window...
...and recorded evidence on his Phone.
So, Dr. Scum... How is our evil Robot coming Along?

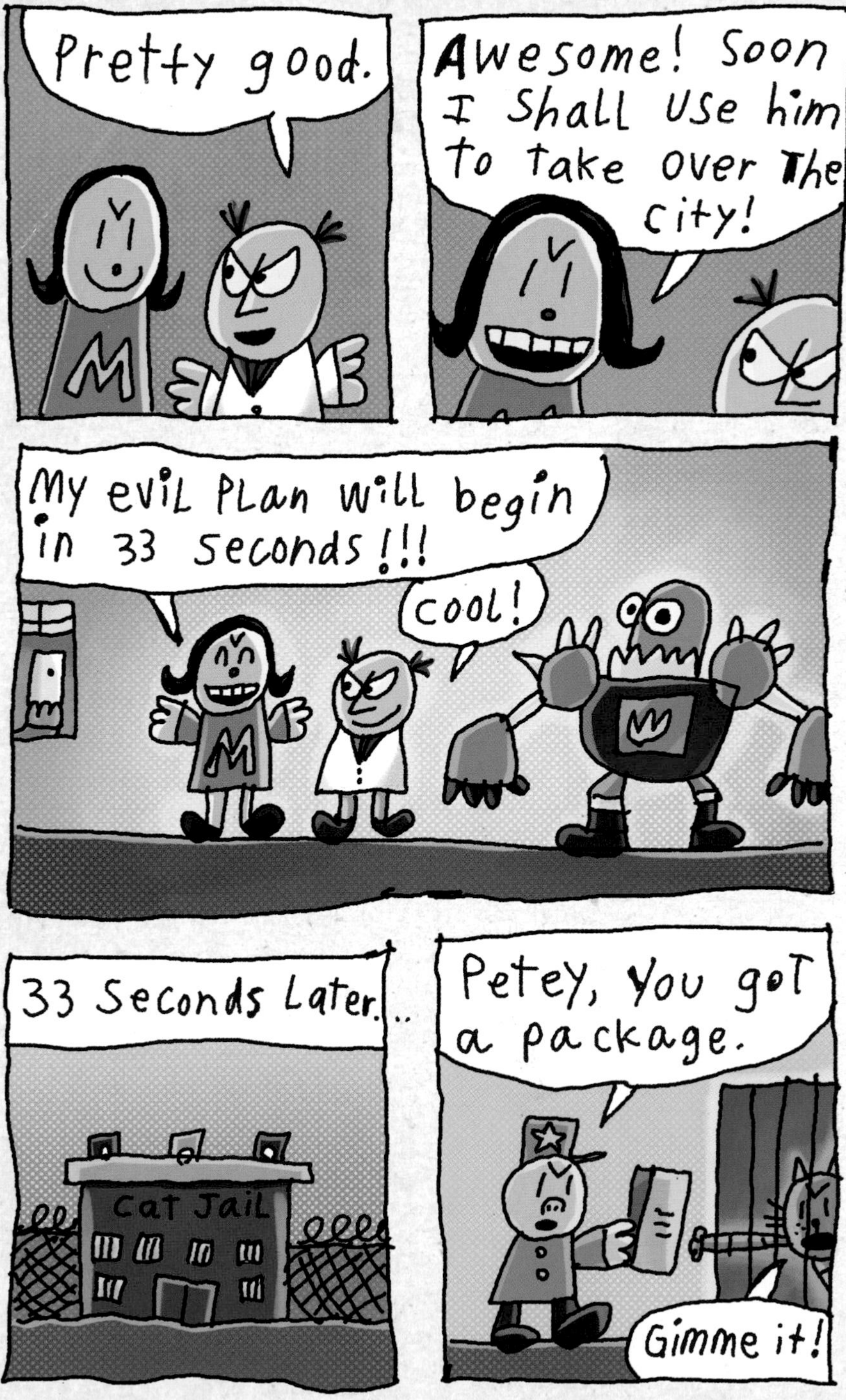
Pretty good.
Awesome! Soon I Shall Use him to take over The city!
My evil Plan will begin in 33 seconds!!!
cool!
33 Seconds Later...
Cat Jail
Petey, You got a package.
Gimme it!

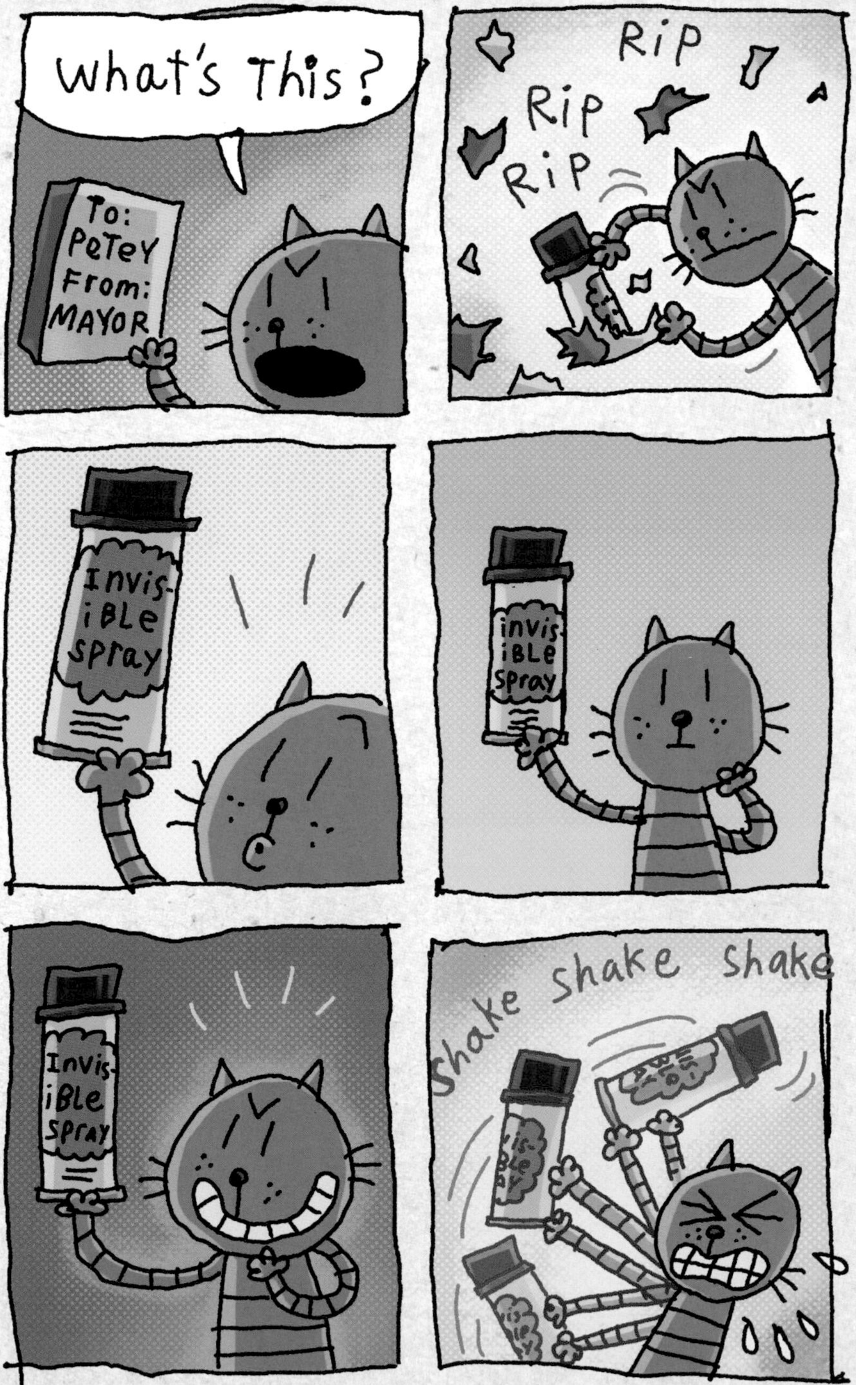
What's This?
To: PeTeY From: MAYOR
RiP
Rip
RiP
Invis-iBLe spray
invis-iBLe spray
Invis-iBle SPRAY
Shake shake shake

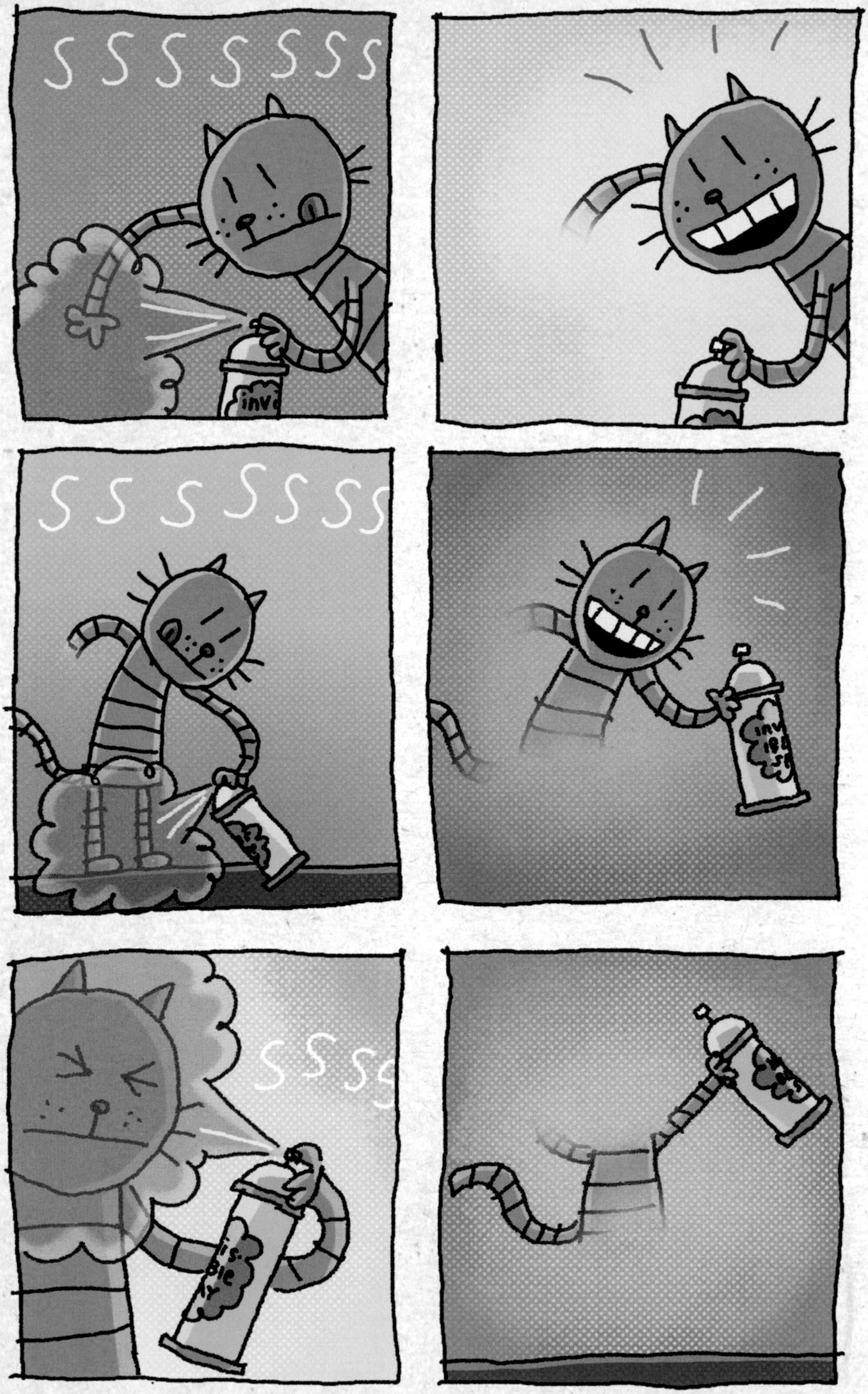
SSSSSSS
SSSSSSS
SSSS

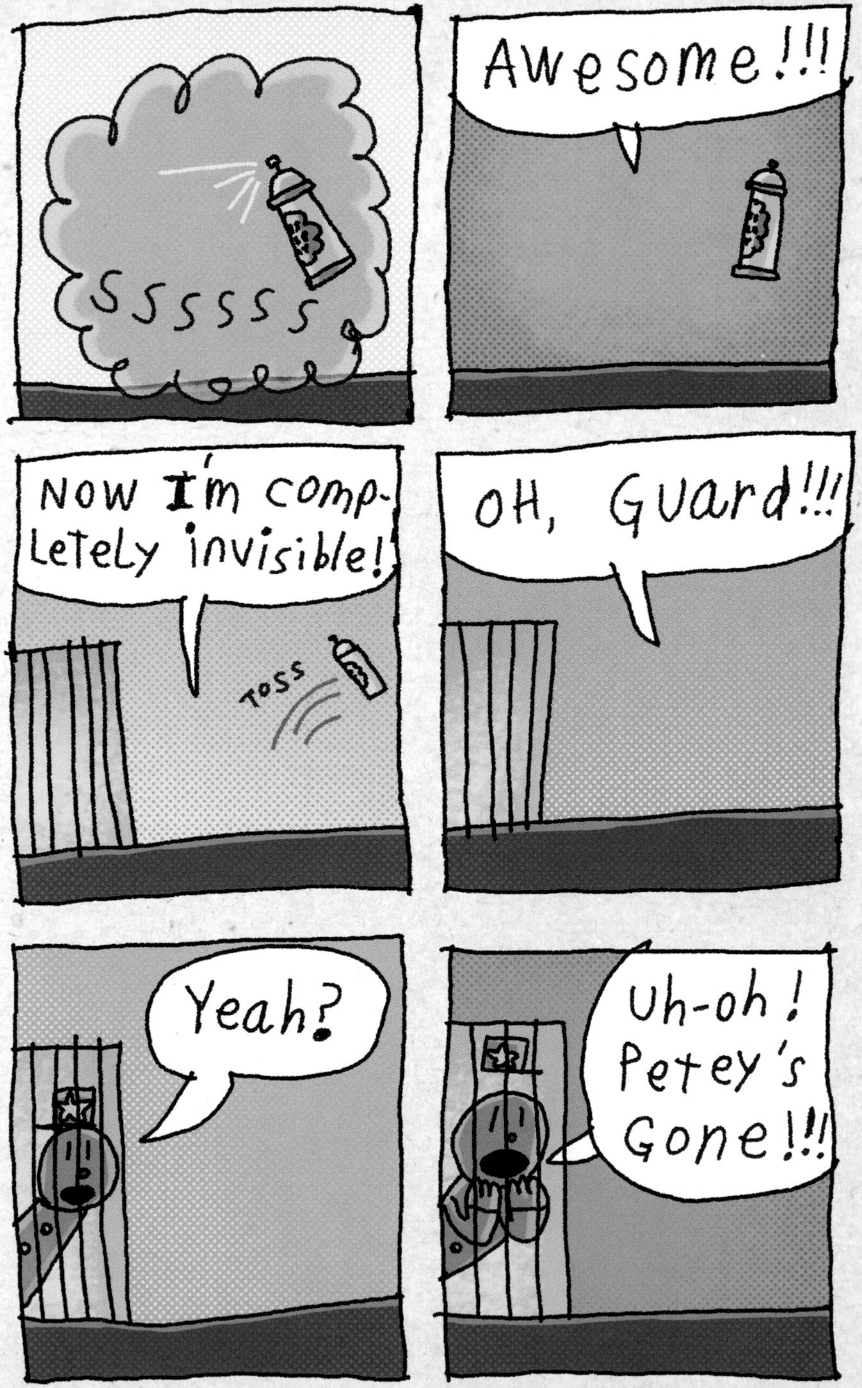
SSSSSS
Awesome!!!
Now I'm comp-
letely invisible!
TOSS
OH, Guard!!!
Yeah?
Uh-oh!
Petey's
Gone!!!

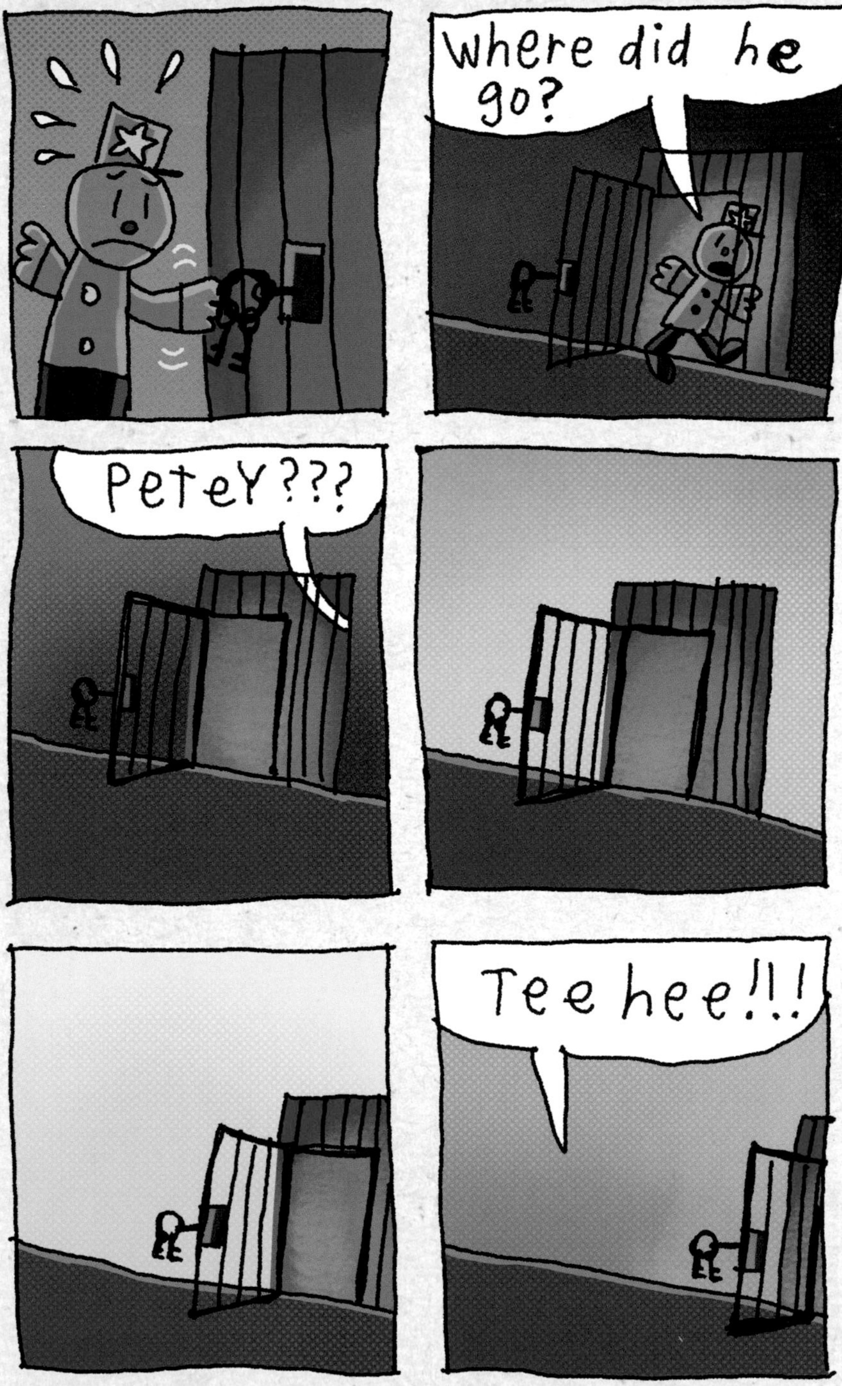
where did he go?
PeteY???
Teehee!!!

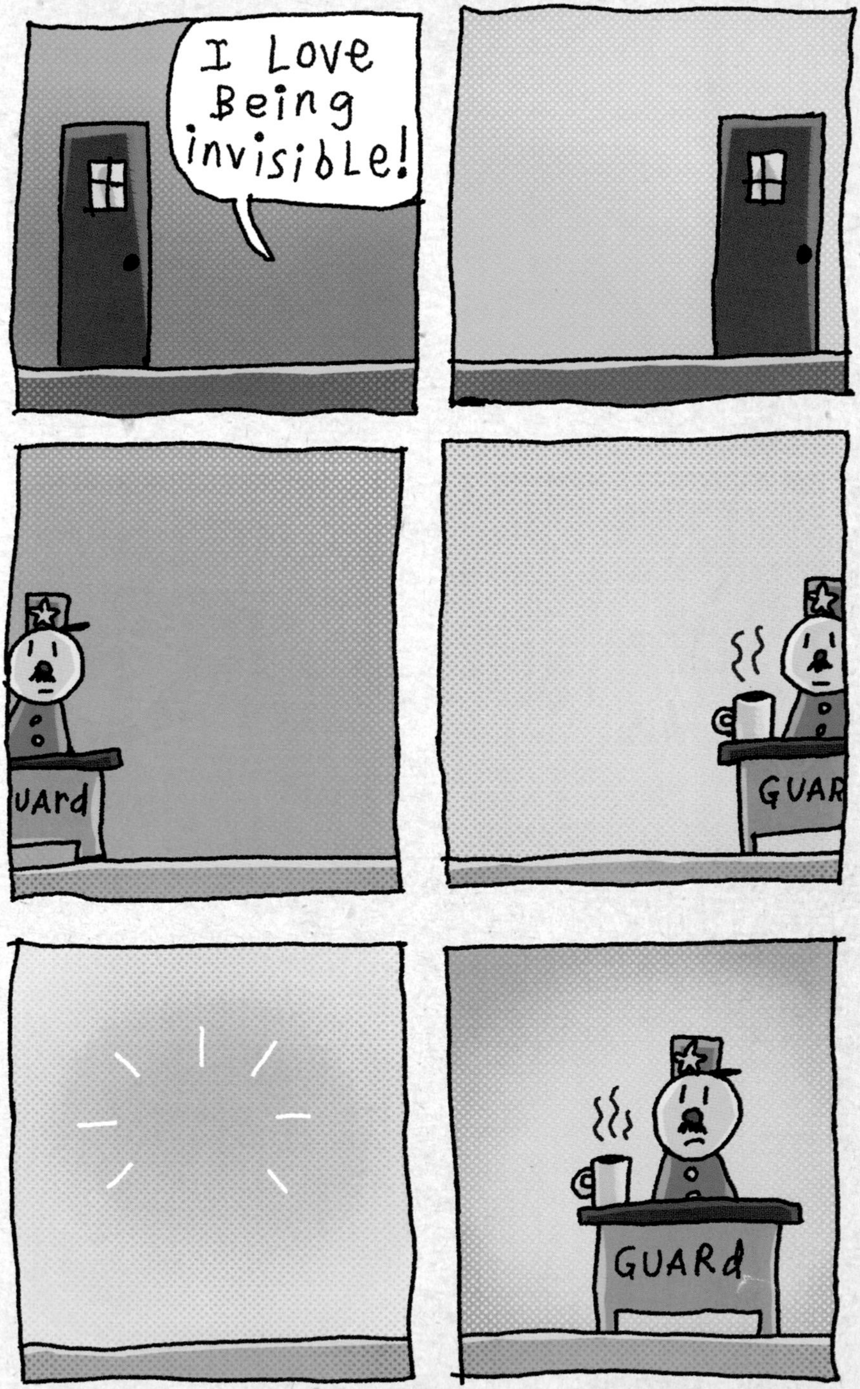
I Love Being invisible!
uard
GUAR
GUARd

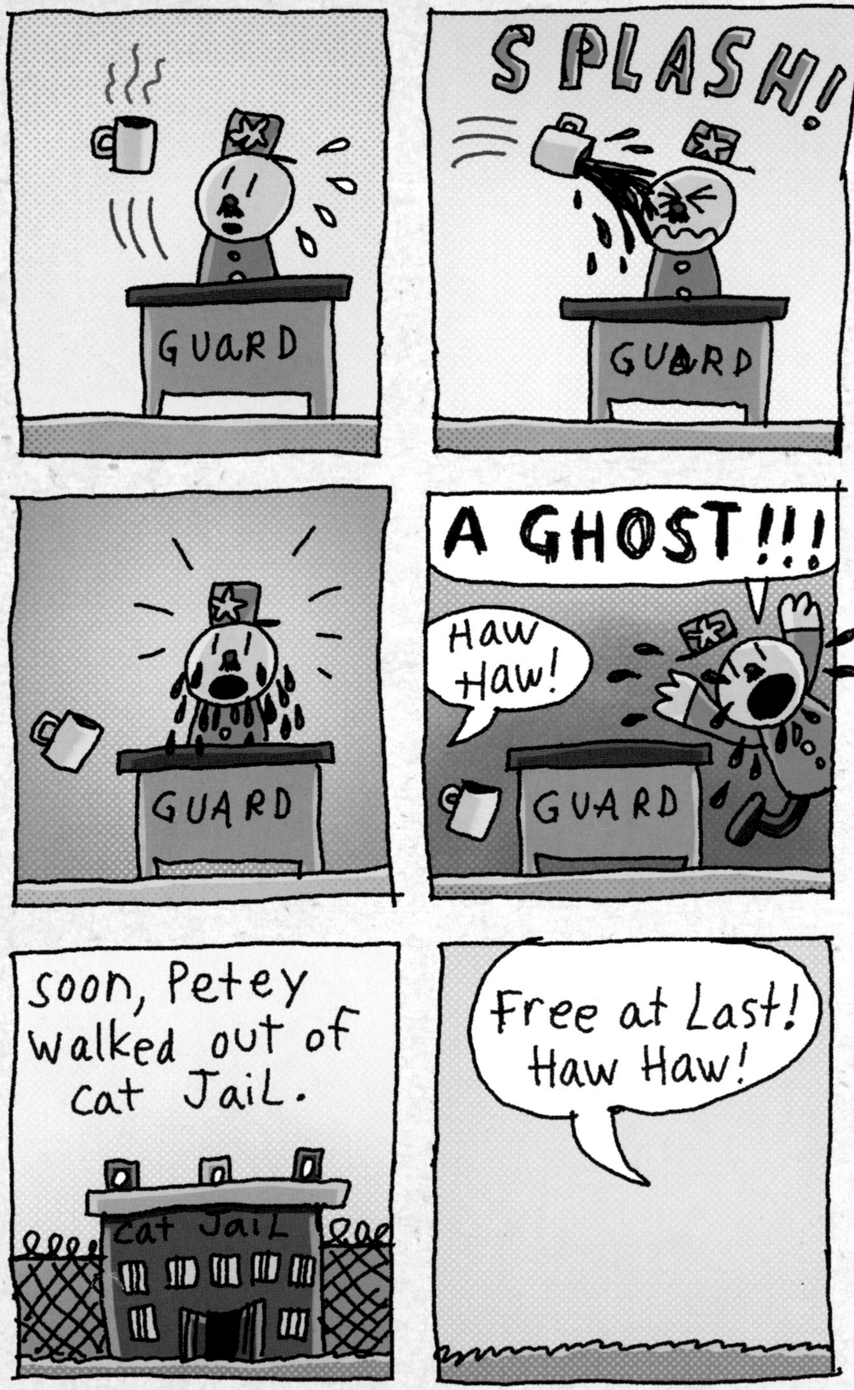
GUARD
SPLASH!
GUARD
GUARD
A GHOST!!!
Haw Haw!
GUARD
soon, Petey walked out of cat Jail.
Cat Jail
Free at Last! Haw Haw!

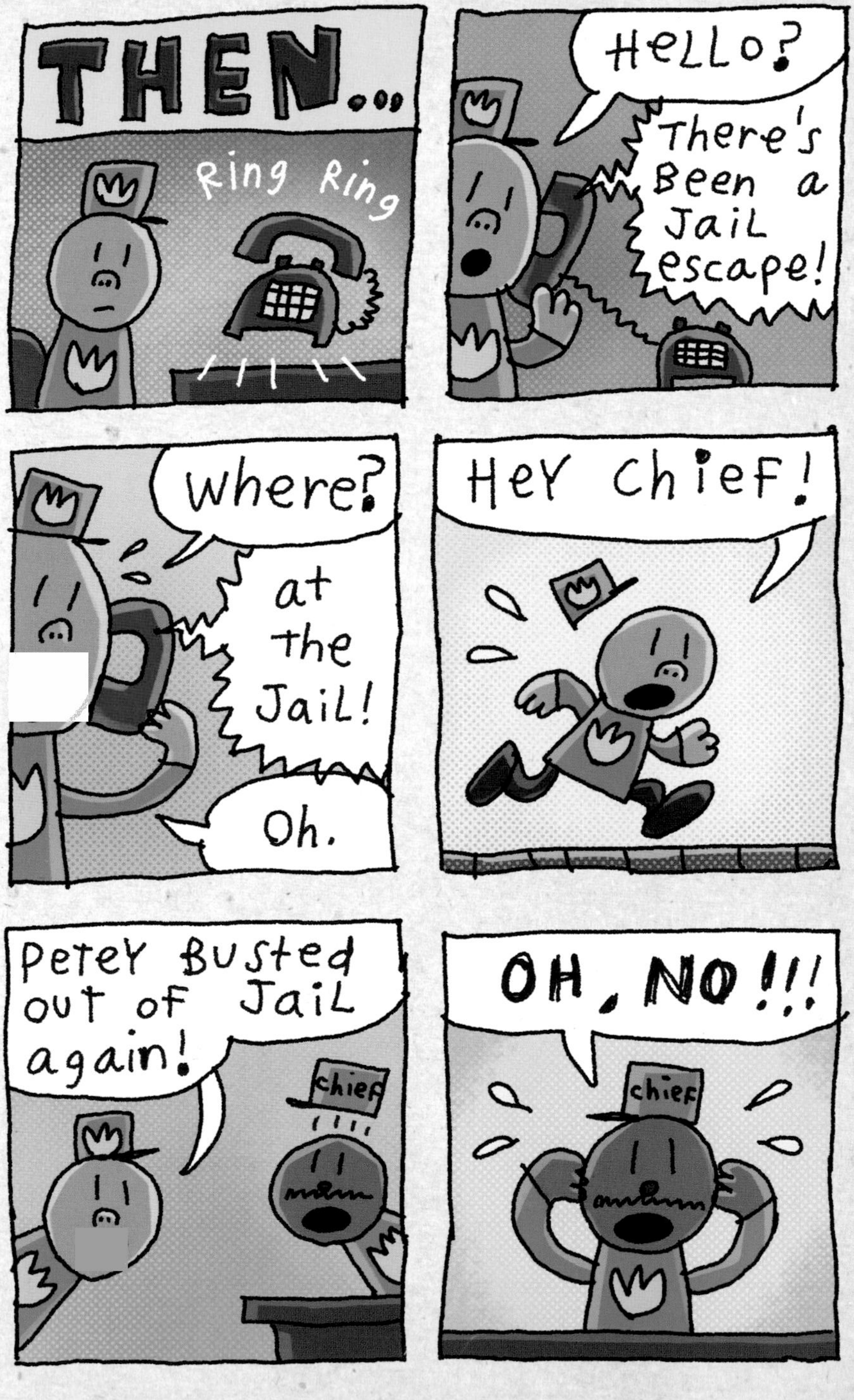
THEN...
Ring Ring
HeLLo?
There's Been a JaiL escape!
Where?
at the JaiL!
Oh.
HeY ChieF!
PeteY BuSted out of JaiL again!
chief
OH, NO!!!
chief

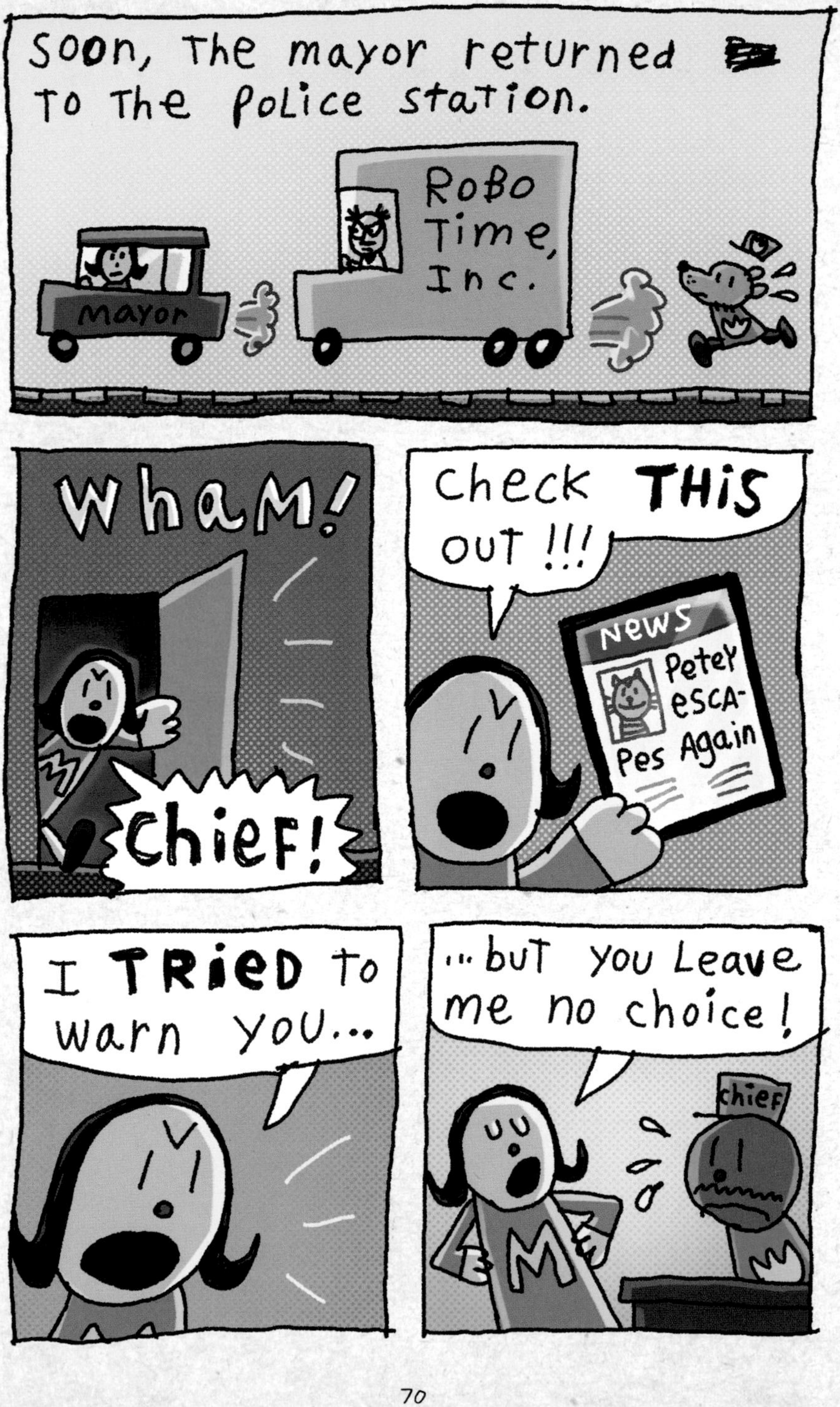
Soon, The mayor returned to The police station.
mayor
RoBo Time, Inc.
WhaM!
Chief!
Check THIS out!!!
News
Petey ESCA-Pes Again
I TRIED to warn you...
...but you Leave me no choice!
chief

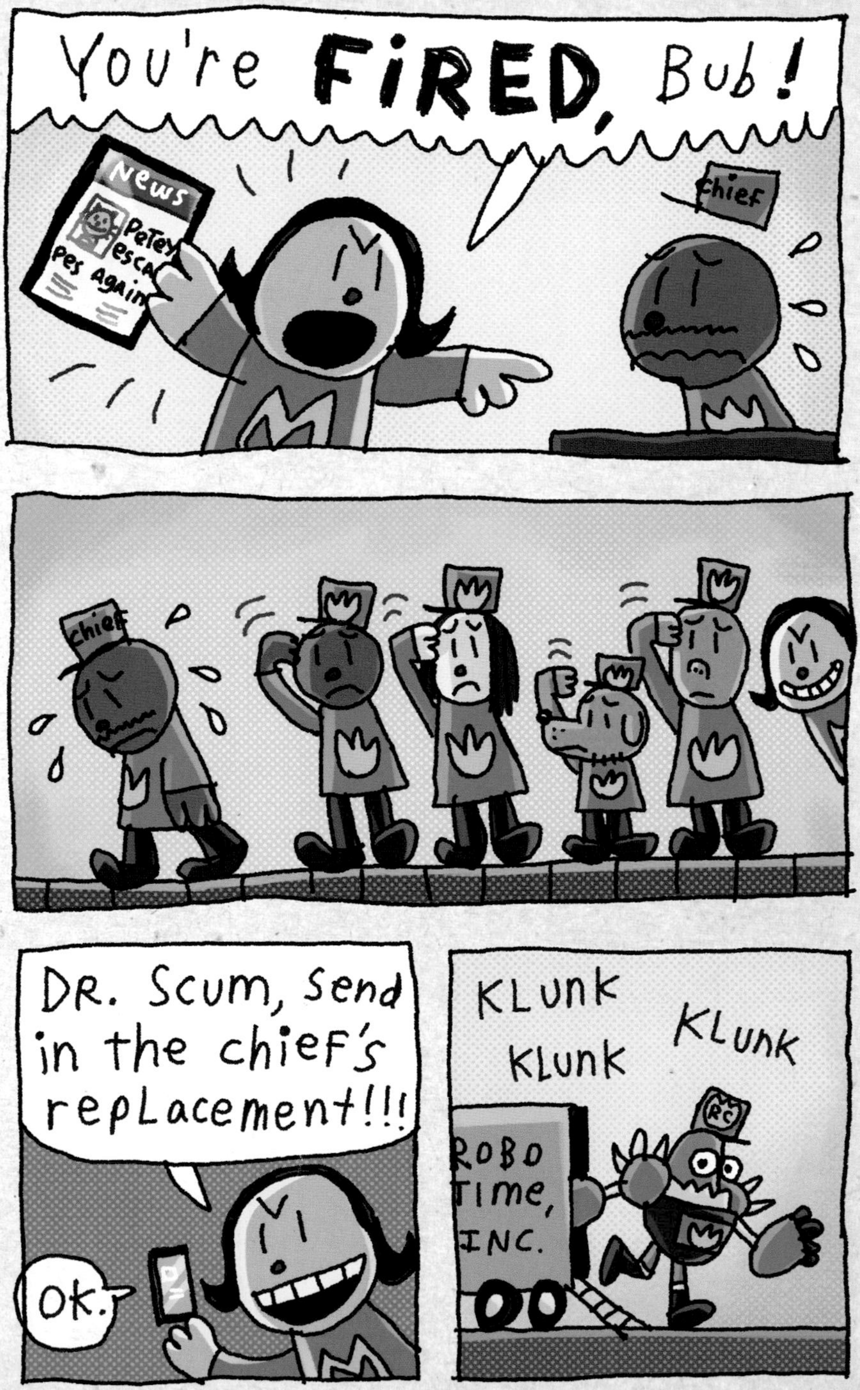
You're FIRED, Bub!
News
PeTey
escA
pes Again
chief
chief
DR. Scum, send in the chief's replacement!!!
OK.
KLUNK
KLUNK
KLUNK
ROBO Time, INC.
RC

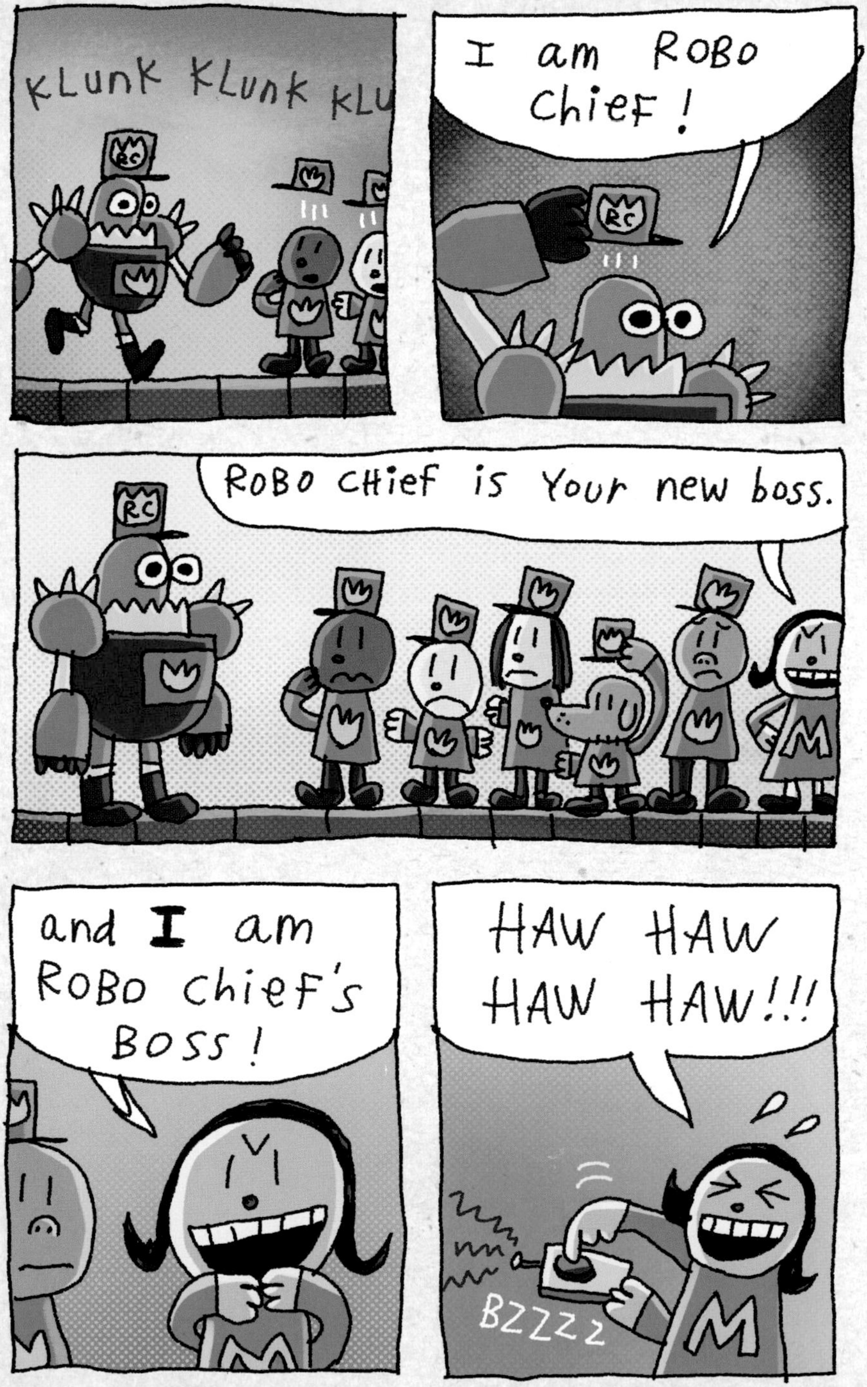
KLUNK KLUNK KLU
I am ROBO CHIEF!
ROBO CHIEF is Your new boss.
and I am ROBO chief's BOSS!
HAW HAW HAW HAW!!!
BZZZZ

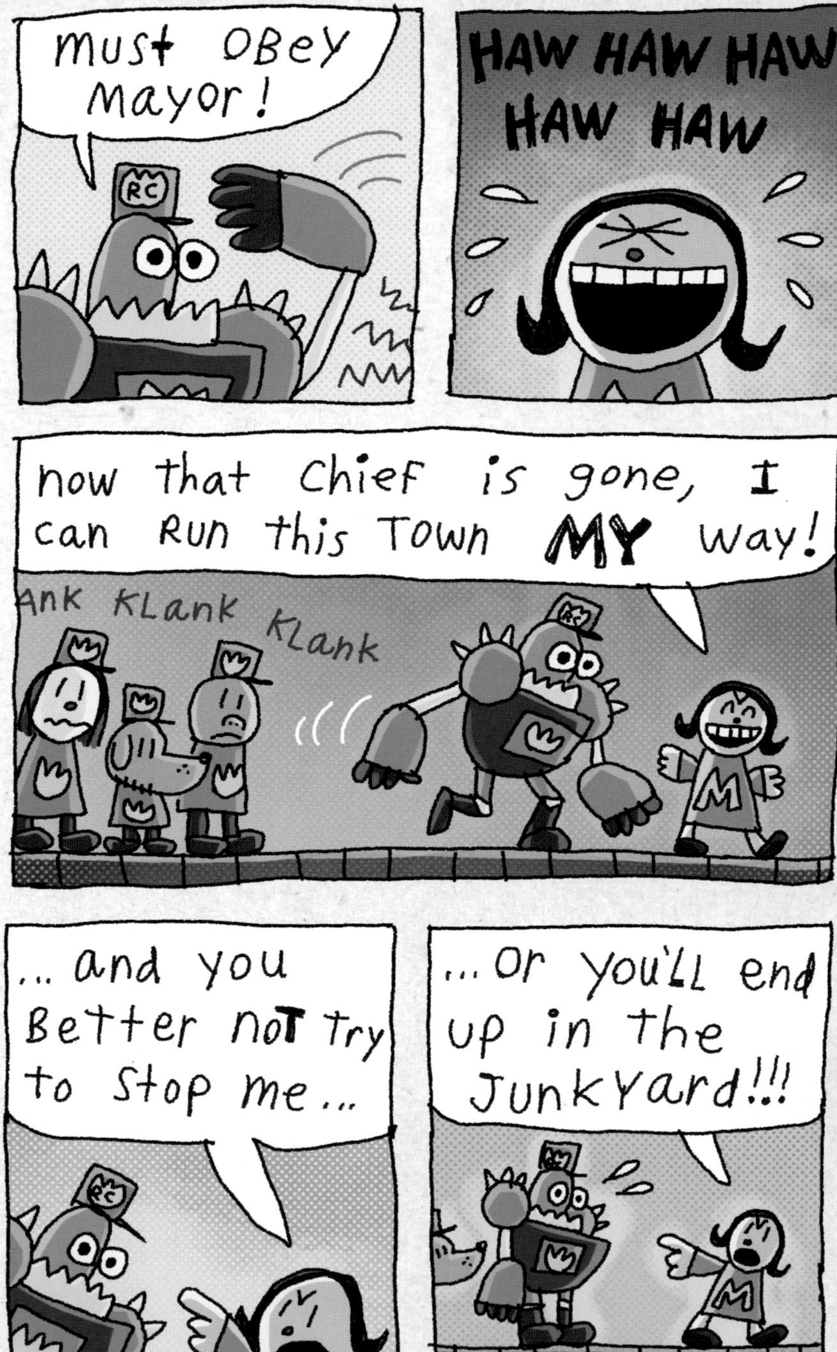
must OBey Mayor!
RC
HAW HAW HAW HAW HAW
now that Chief is gone, I can RUN this Town MY way!
Ank KLank KLank
RC
M
...and you Better noT try to Stop me...
RC
...or you'LL end up in the JunkYard!!!
M

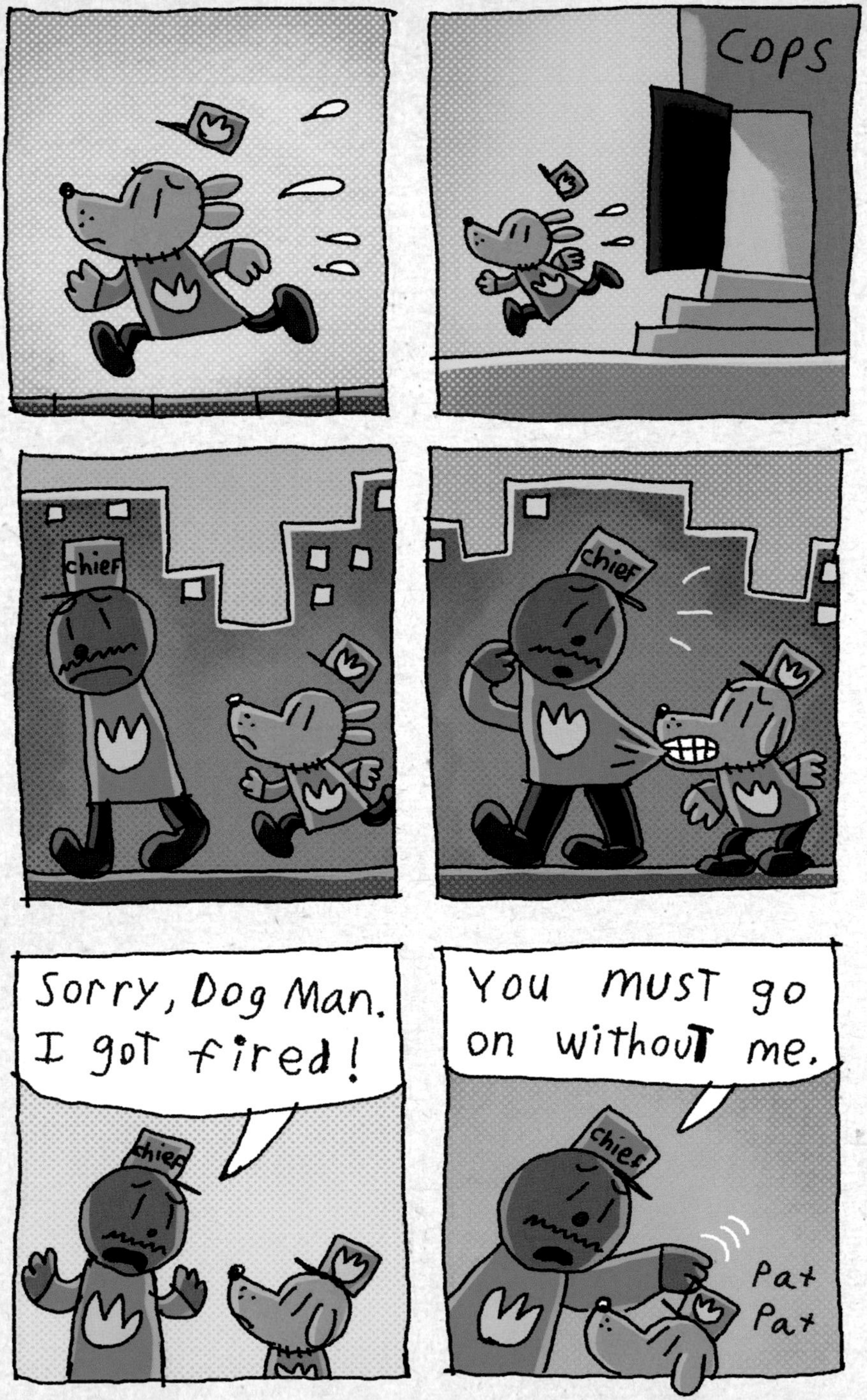
COPS
chief
chief
Sorry, Dog Man. I got fired!
chief
You MUST go on without me.
chief
Pat Pat

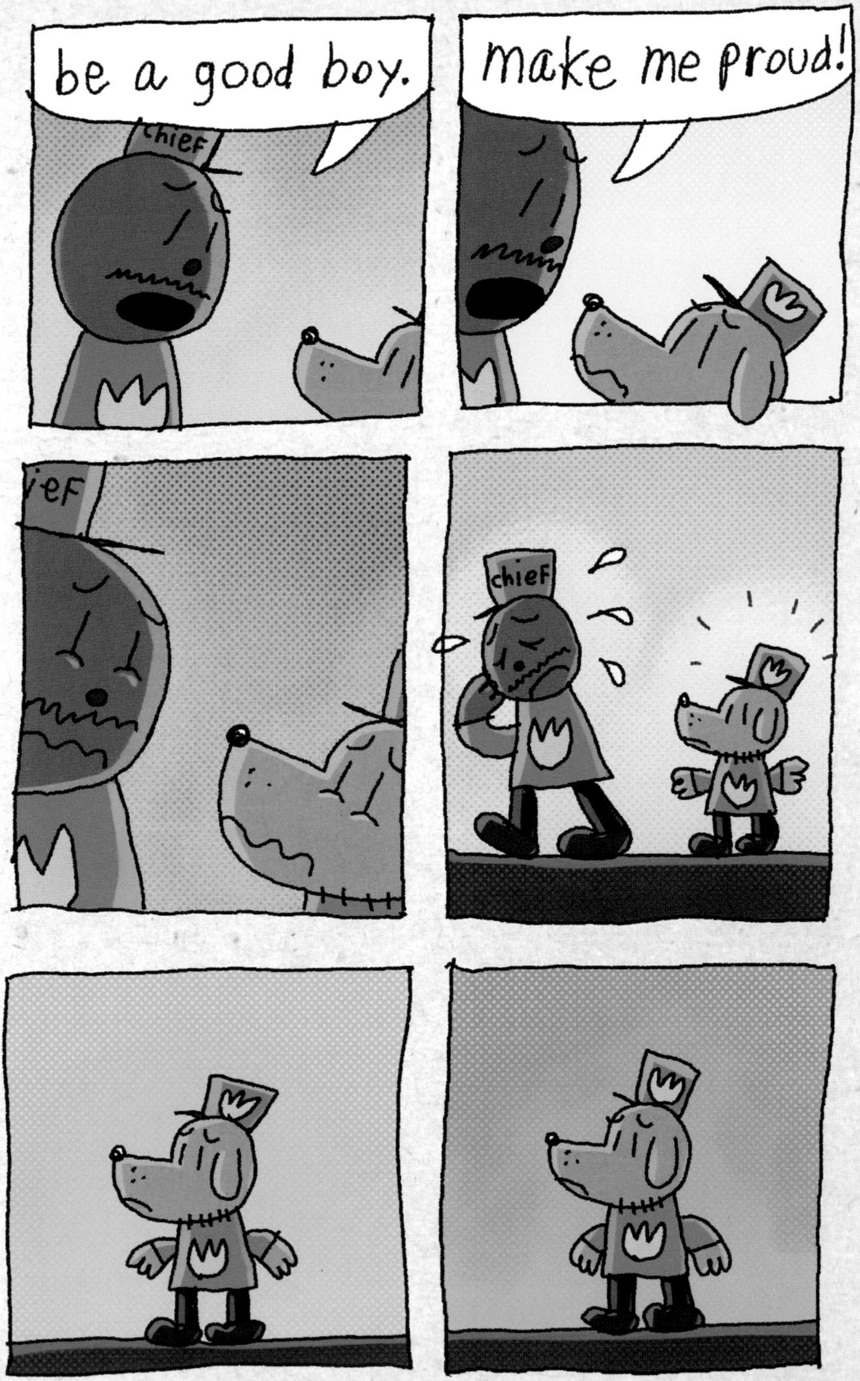
be a good boy.
chief
make me proud!
ieF
chieF

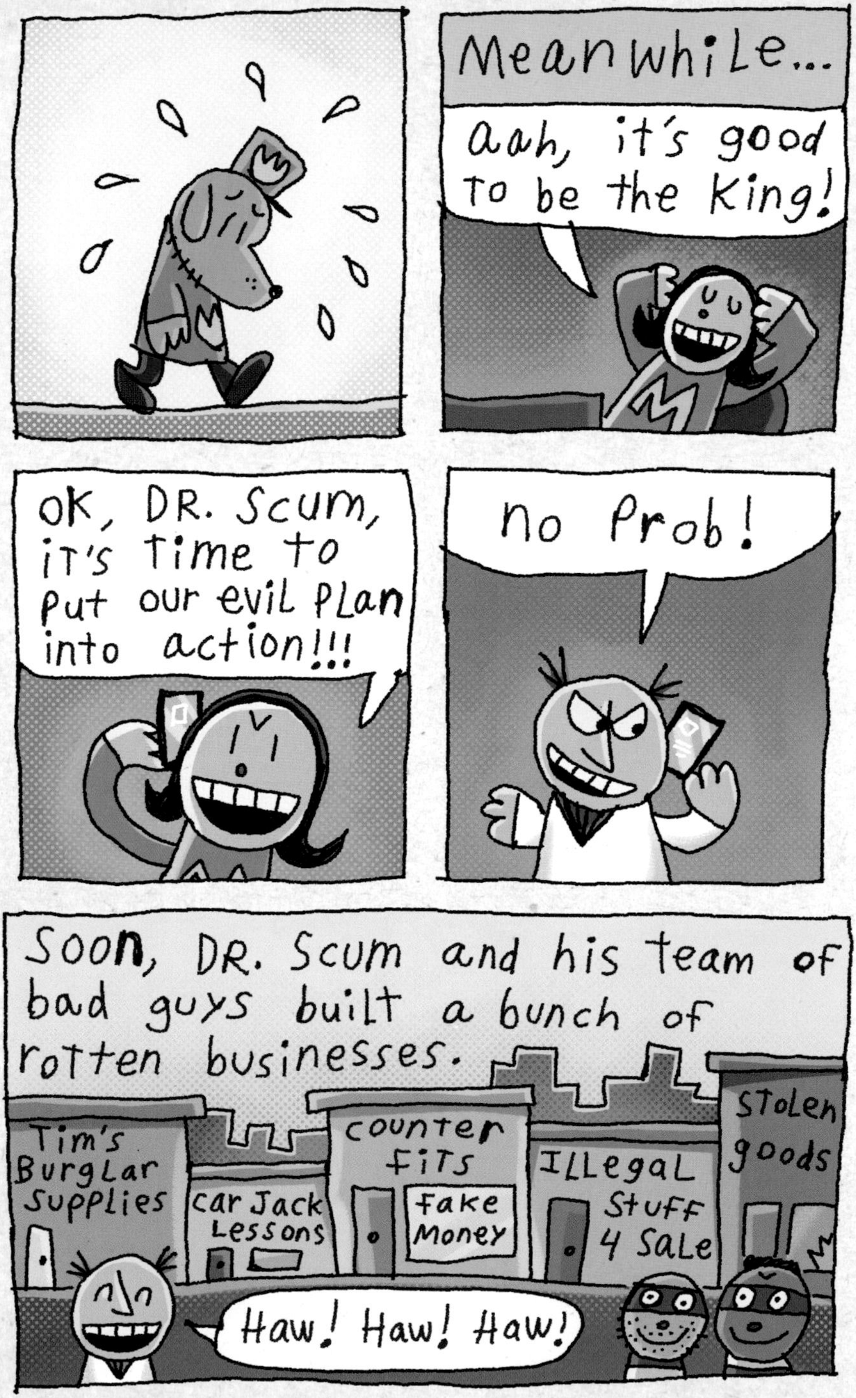

Meanwhile...
aah, it's good to be the King!
OK, DR. Scum, it's time to put our evil PLan into action!!!
no Prob!
Soon, DR. Scum and his team of bad guys built a bunch of rotten businesses.
Tim's Burglar Supplies
car Jack Lessons
counter fits
Fake Money
ILLegaL Stuff 4 SaLe
StoLen goods
Haw! Haw! Haw!

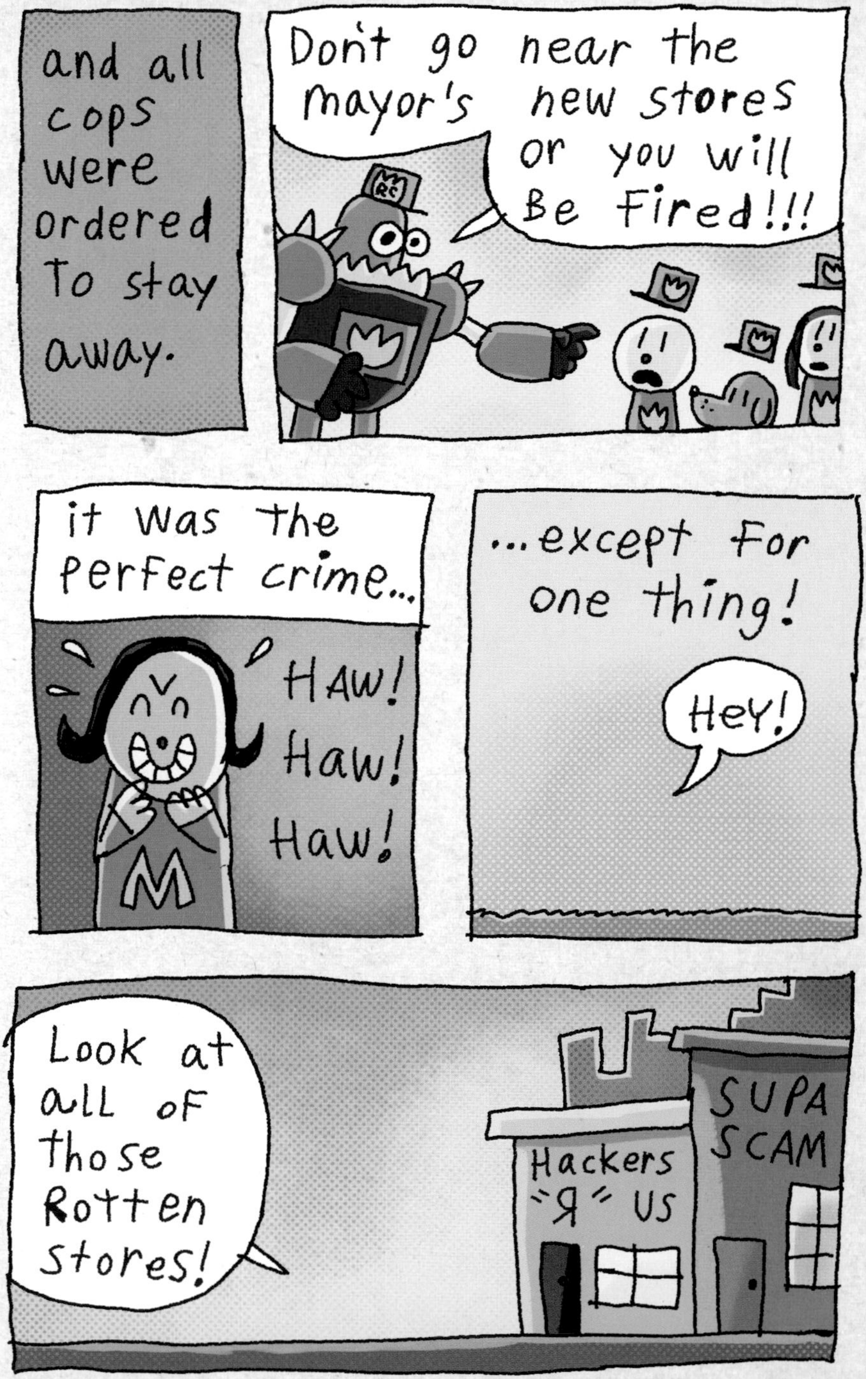
and all cops were ordered To stay away.
Don't go near the mayor's new stores or you will Be Fired!!!
MRC
it was the perfect crime...
HAW! Haw! Haw!
...except For one thing!
HEY!
Look at all of those Rotten stores!
Hackers Я US
SUPA SCAM

Invisible Petey was not Happy!

} } }

Grrr!

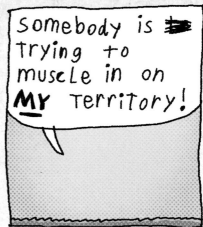

Somebody is ~~tr~~ trying to muscle in on **MY** Territory!

I have to Stop those evil Jerks!

There can only be **ONE** villain in This town!!!

Invisible Petey got right to work.

He Followed each customer into The rotten stores...

BiLL's Bombs

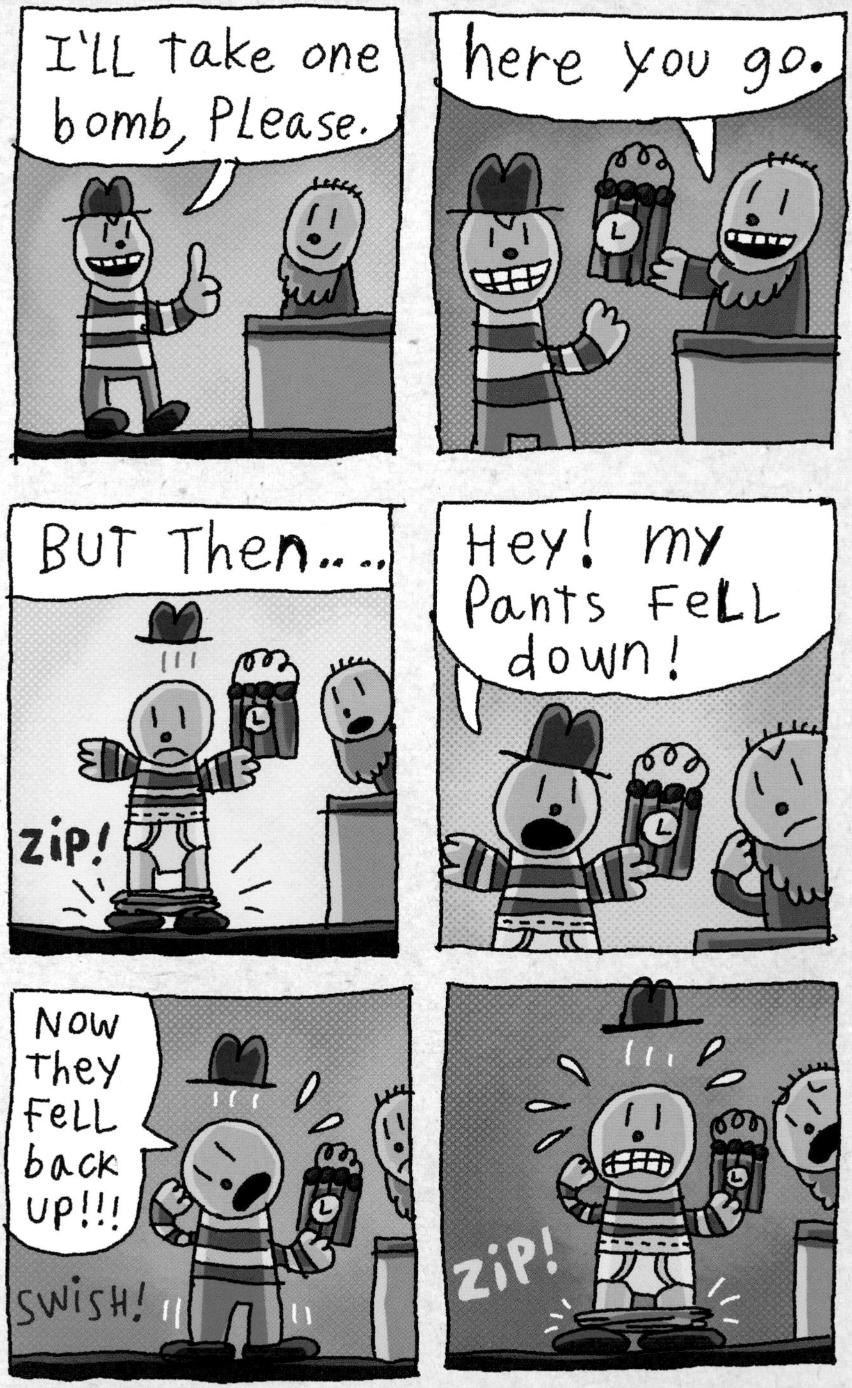
I'LL take one bomb, PLease.
here you go.
BUT Then....
ZIP!
Hey! my Pants FeLL down!
Now They FeLL back up!!!
SWISH!
ZIP!

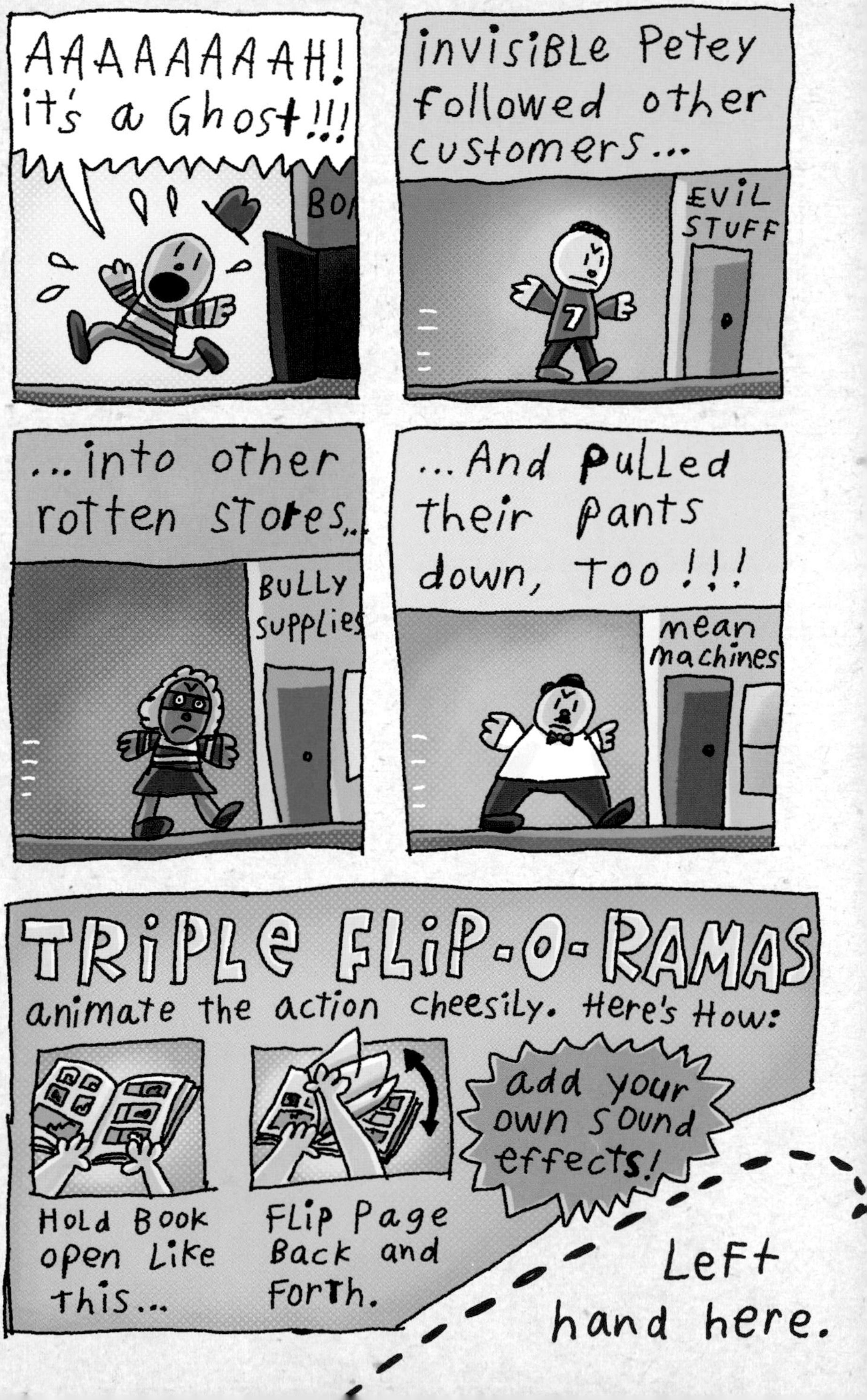

AAAAAAAAH! it's a Ghost!!!
invisiBLe Petey followed other customers...
EVIL STUFF
...into other rotten stores...
BULLY SUPPLIES
...And puLLed their pants down, Too!!!
mean machines
TRIPLE FLIP-O-RAMAS
animate the action cheesiLy. Here's How:
HoLd Book open Like this...
FLip Page Back and Forth.
add your own sound effects!
Left hand here.

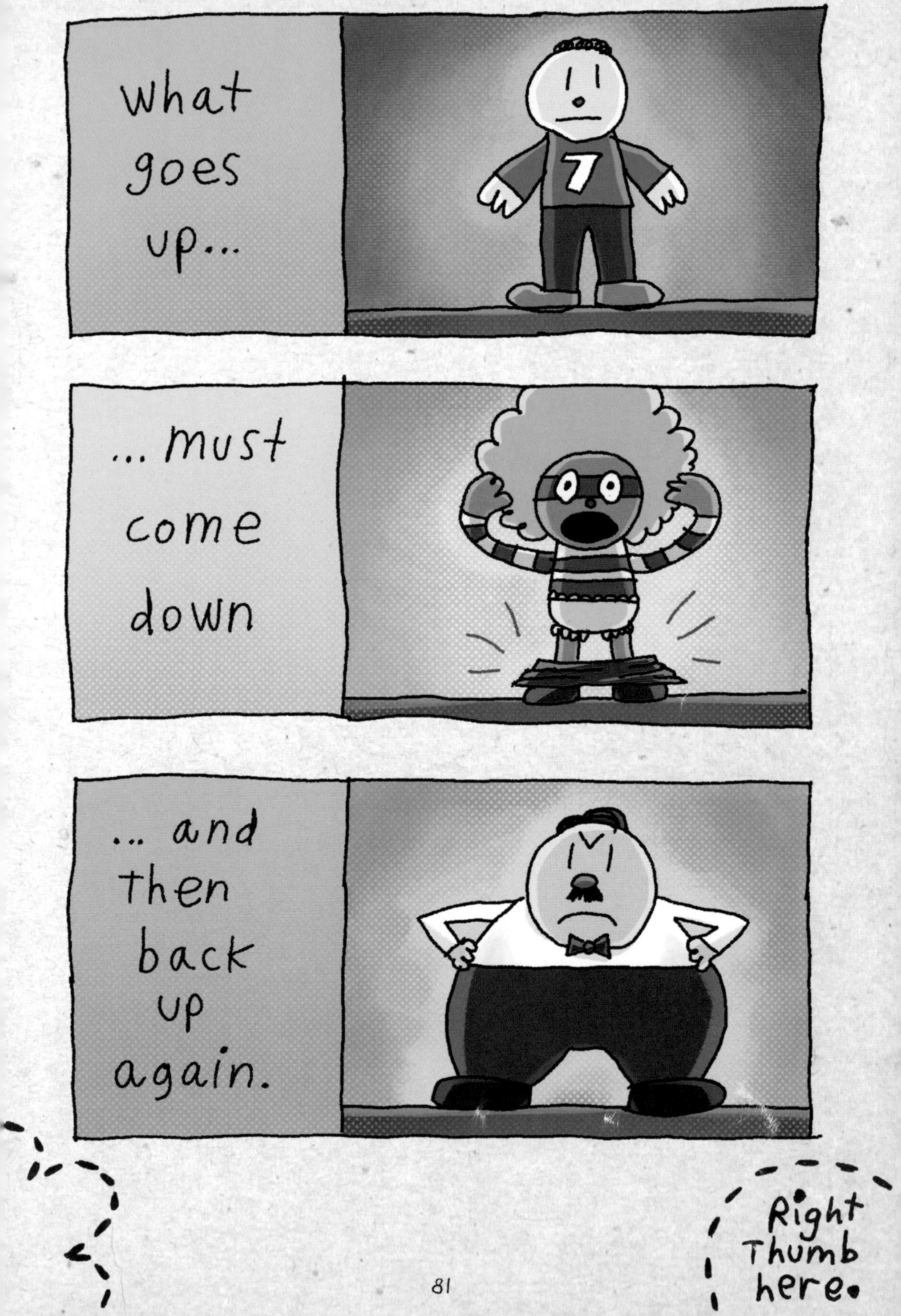
what goes up...
... must come down
... and then back up again.
Right Thumb here.

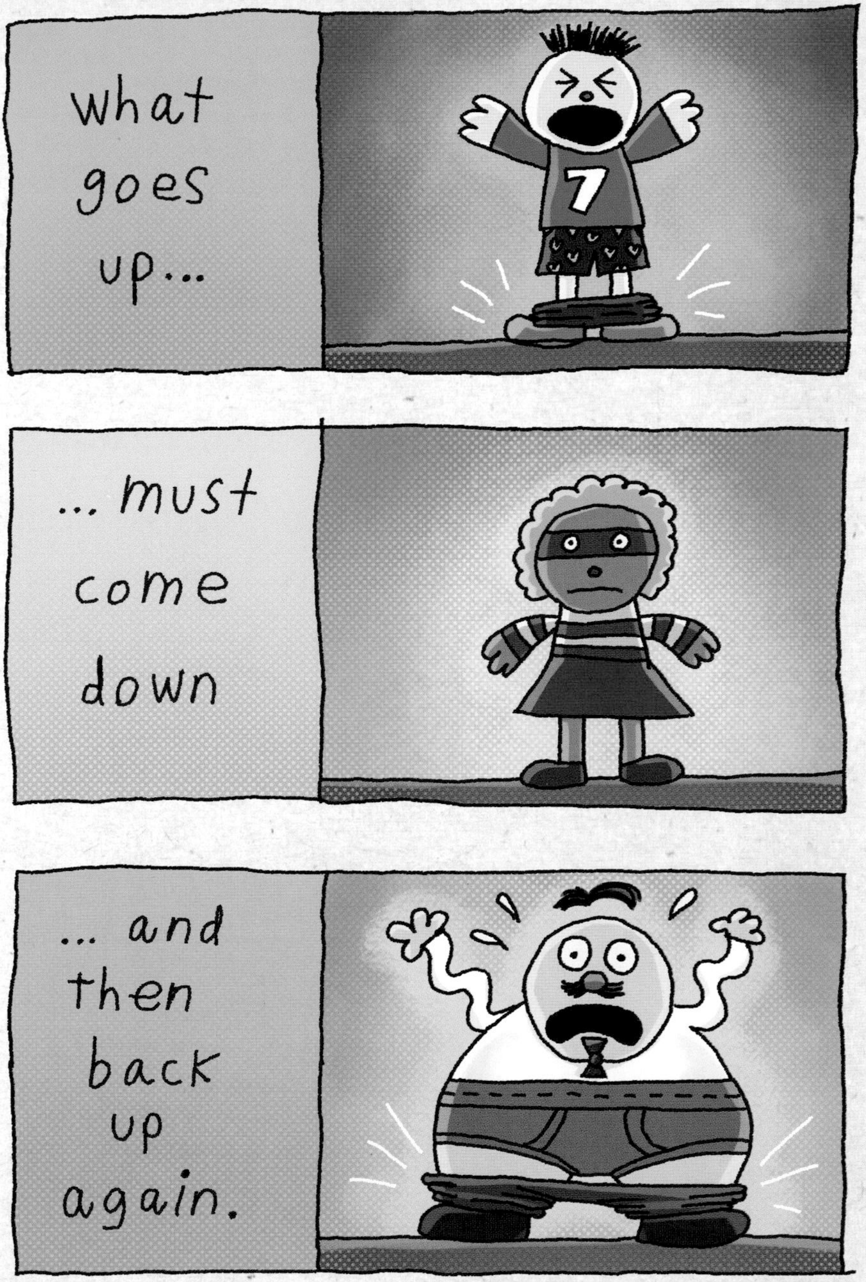

what goes up...
7
... must come down
... and then back up again.

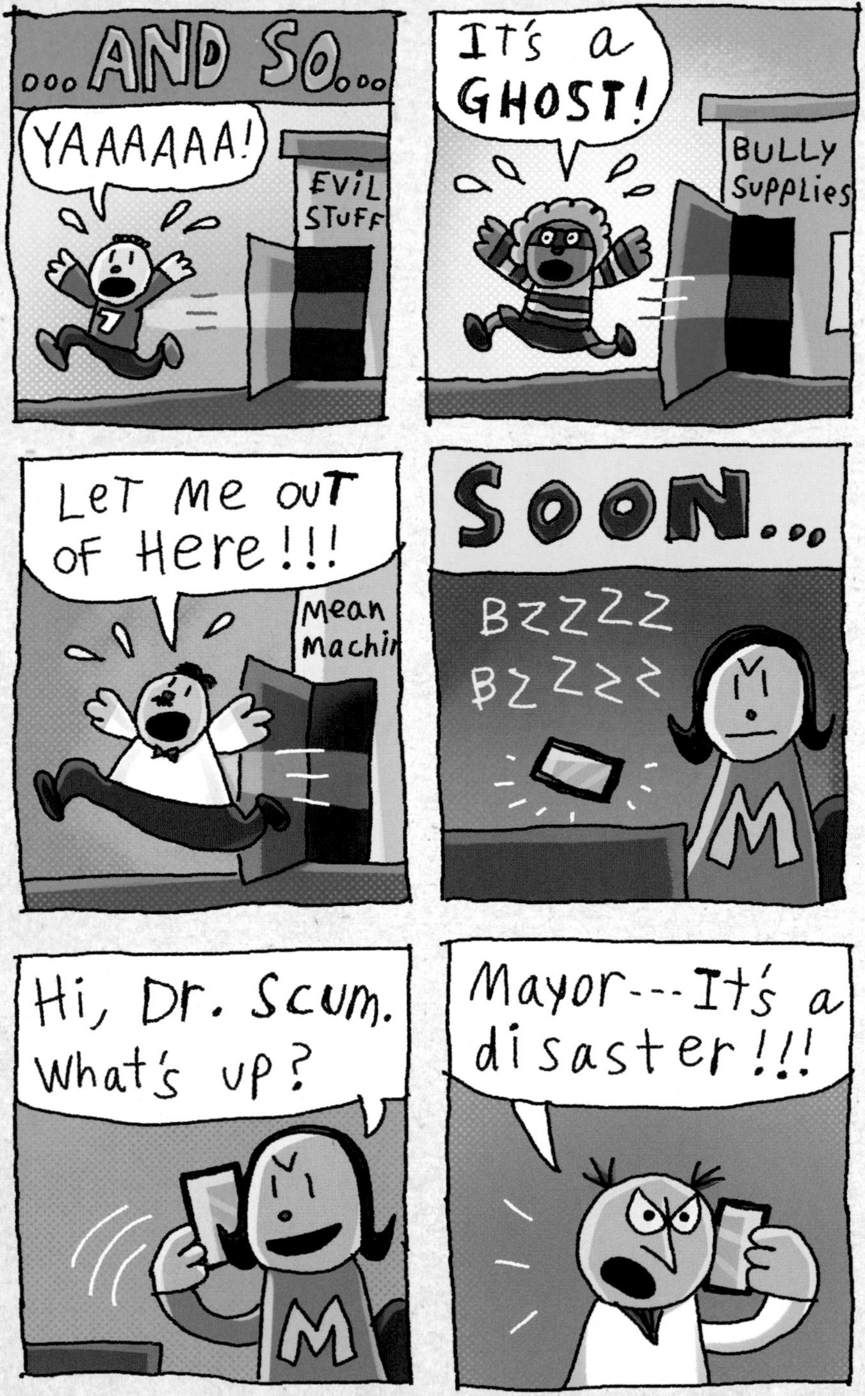
...AND SO...
YAAAAAA!
EVIL STUFF
It's a GHOST!
BULLY Supplies
Let me out of Here!!!
Mean Machi
SOON...
BZZZZ
BZZZZ
M
Hi, Dr. Scum. What's up?
M
Mayor---It's a disaster!!!

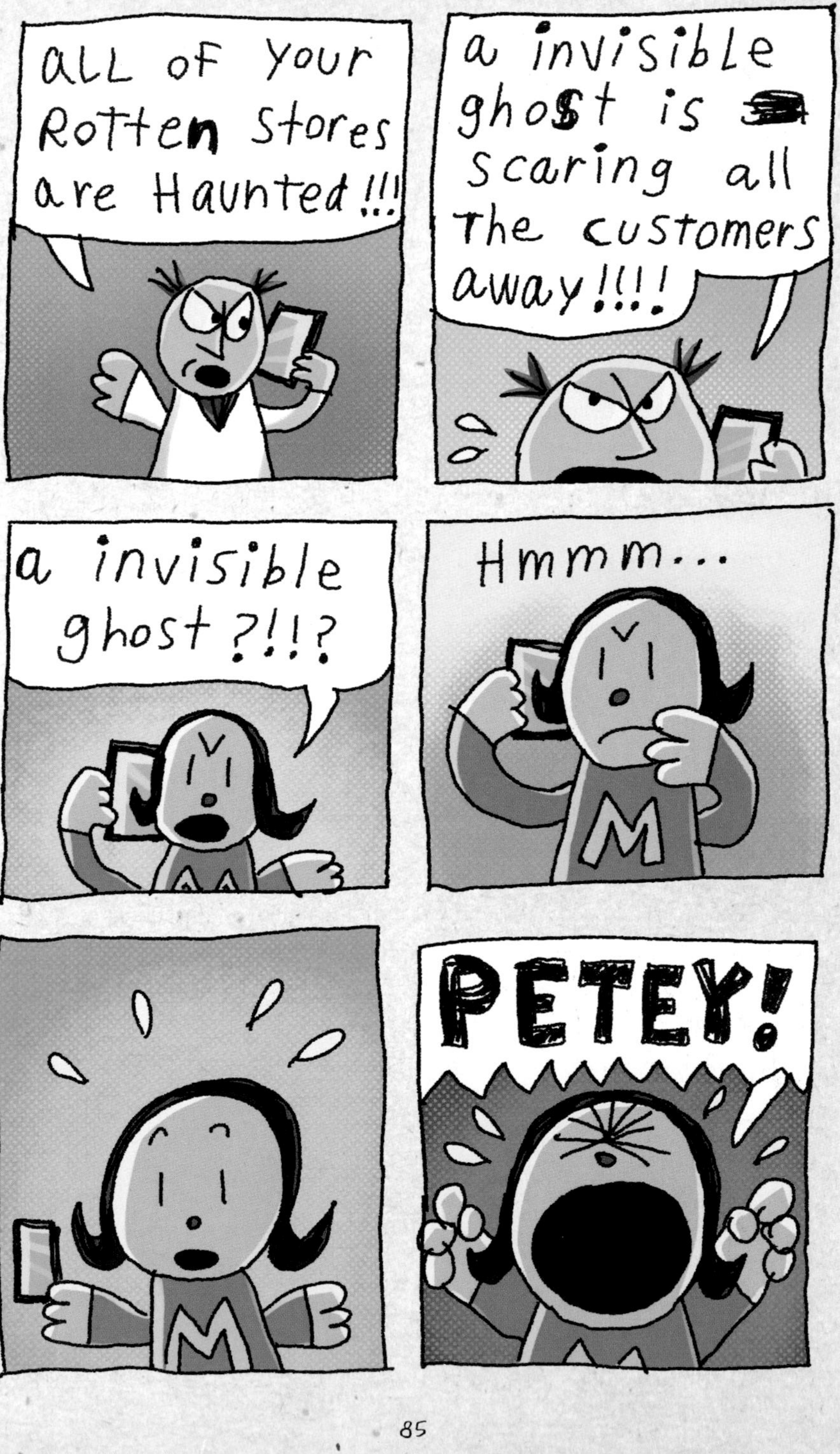
ALL of your Rotten Stores are Haunted!!!
a invisible ghost is scaring all The customers away!!!!
a invisible ghost?!!?
Hmmm...
PETEY!

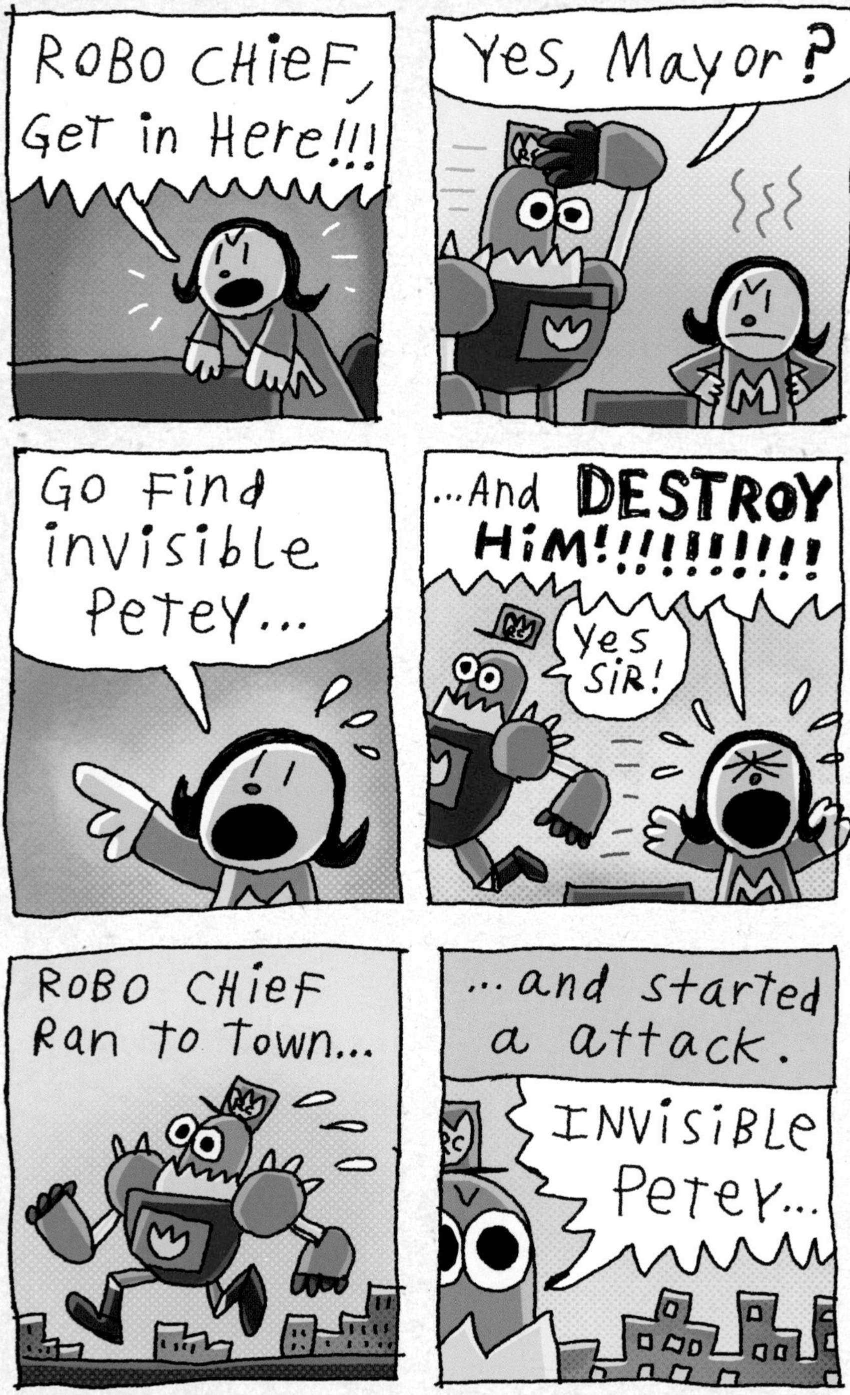
ROBO CHIEF, Get in Here!!!
Yes, Mayor?
Go Find invisible Petey...
...And DESTROY HiM!!!!!!!!!!!
Yes SiR!
ROBO CHIEF Ran to Town...
...and started a attack.
INVISIBLE Petey...

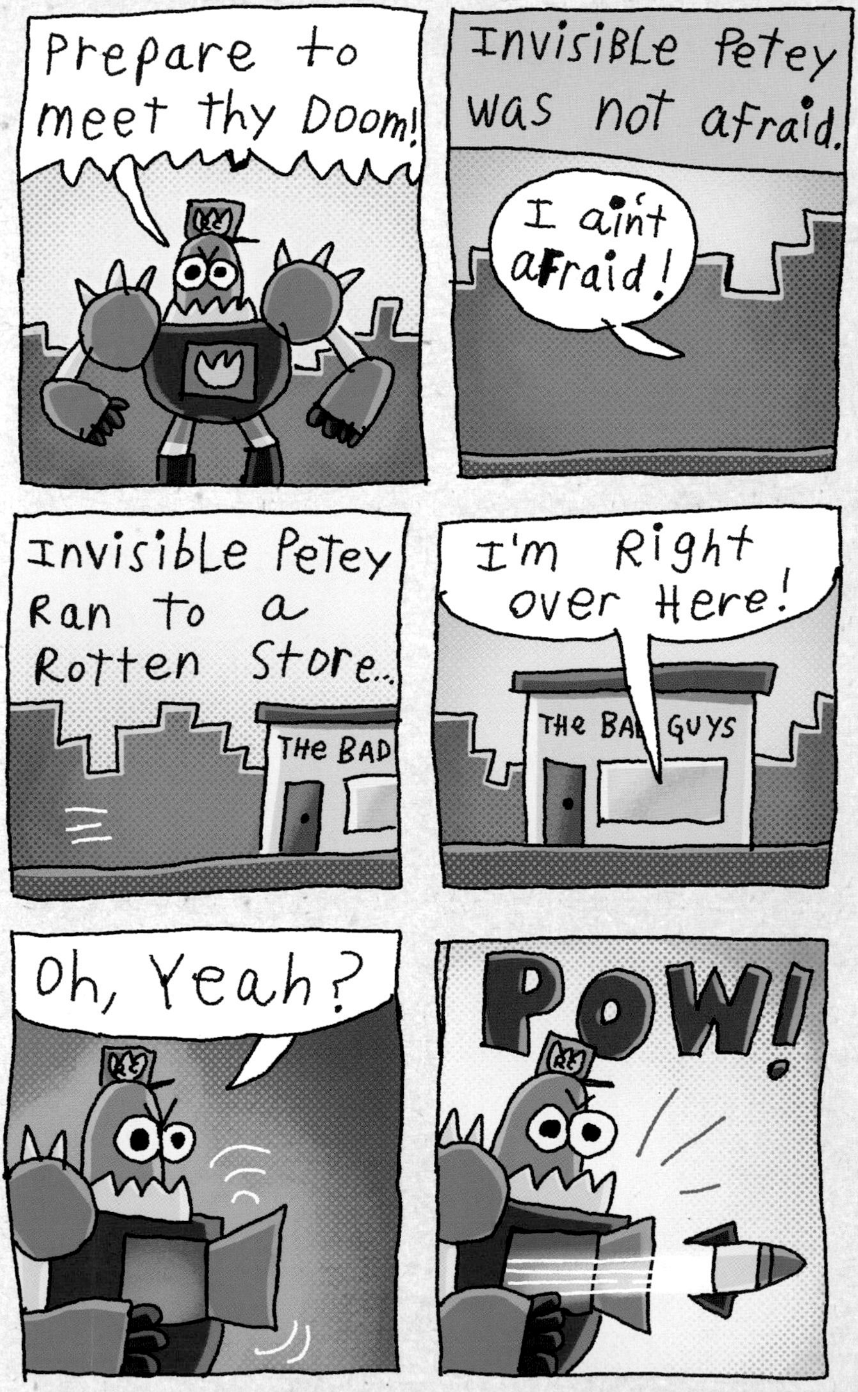

Prepare to meet thy Doom!
Invisible Petey was not afraid.
I ain't afraid!
Invisible Petey Ran to a Rotten Store...
THE BAD
I'm Right over Here!
THE BAD GUYS
Oh, Yeah?
POW!

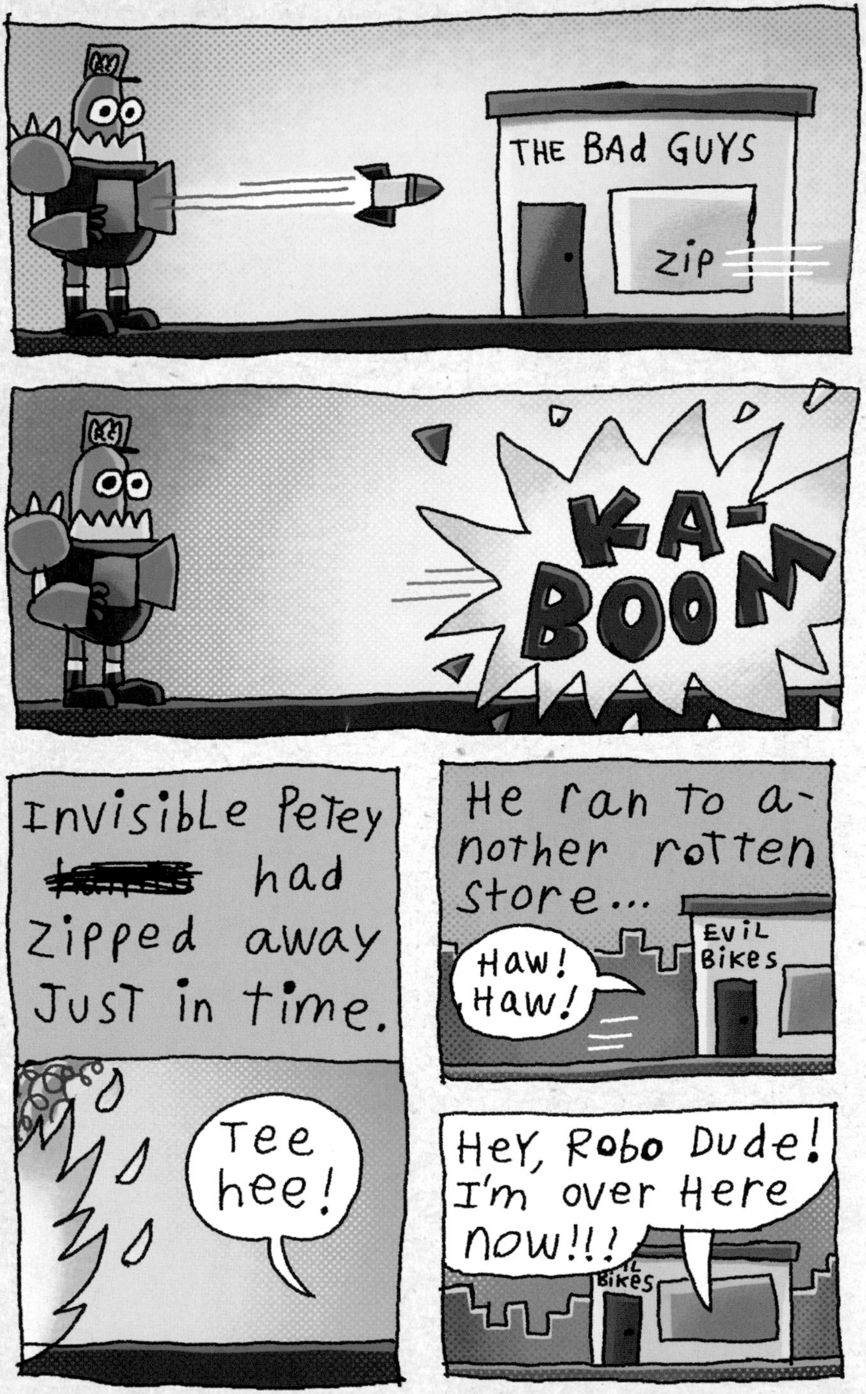
THE BAd GUYS
zip
KA-BOOM
Invisible Petey had zipped away just in time.
He ran to another rotten store...
Haw! Haw!
EVIL BIKES
Tee hee!
Hey, Robo Dude! I'm over Here now!!!
BIKES

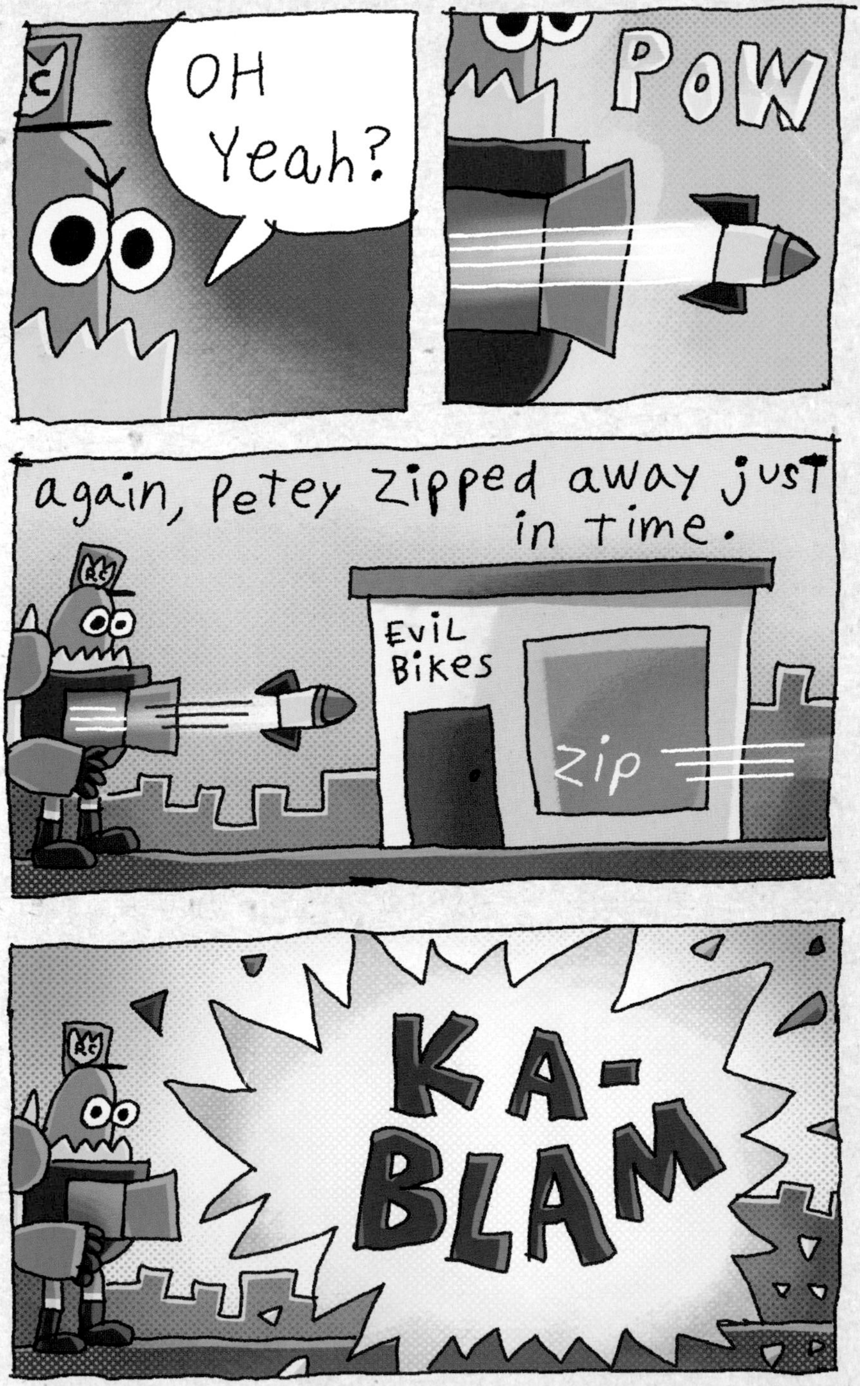
OH Yeah?
POW
again, Petey zipped away just in time.
EVIL Bikes
zip
KA-BLAM

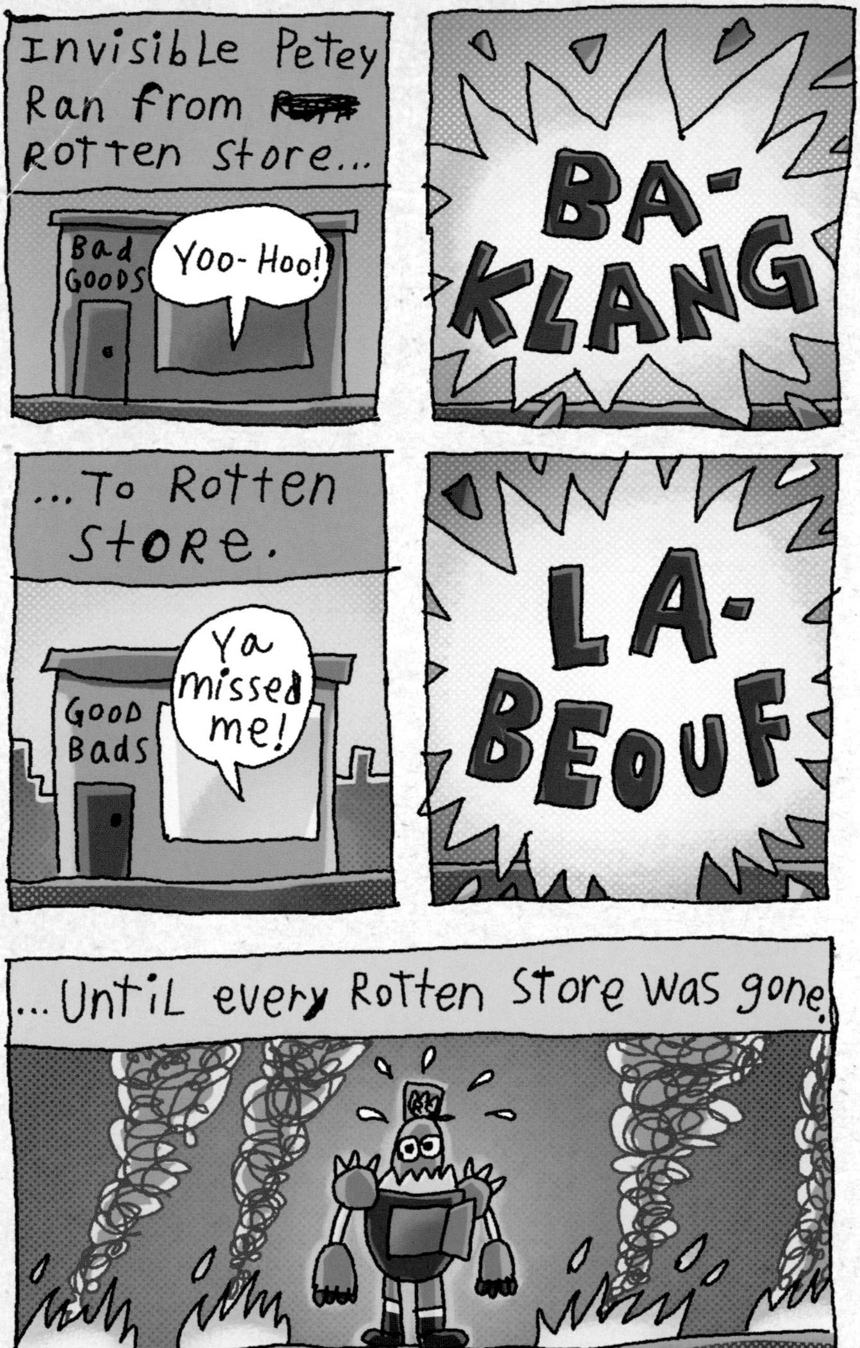
Invisible Petey Ran from Rotten Store...
Bad GOODS
Yoo-Hoo!
BA-KLANG
...To Rotten Store.
GOOD Bads
Ya missed me!
LA-BEOUF
...Until every Rotten Store was gone.

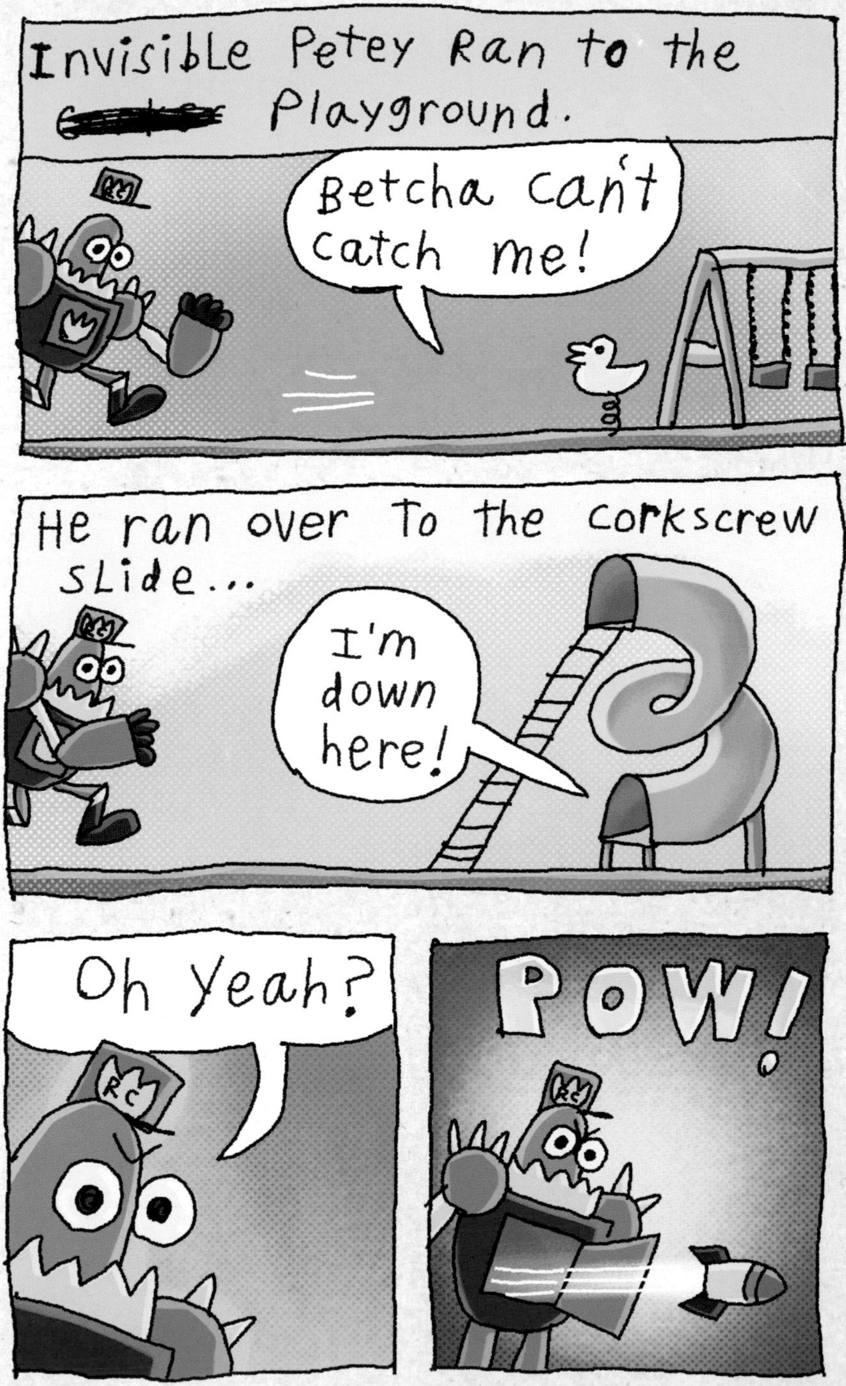
Invisible Petey Ran to the Playground.
Betcha can't catch me!
He ran over To the corkscrew sLide...
I'm down here!
Oh yeah?
POW!

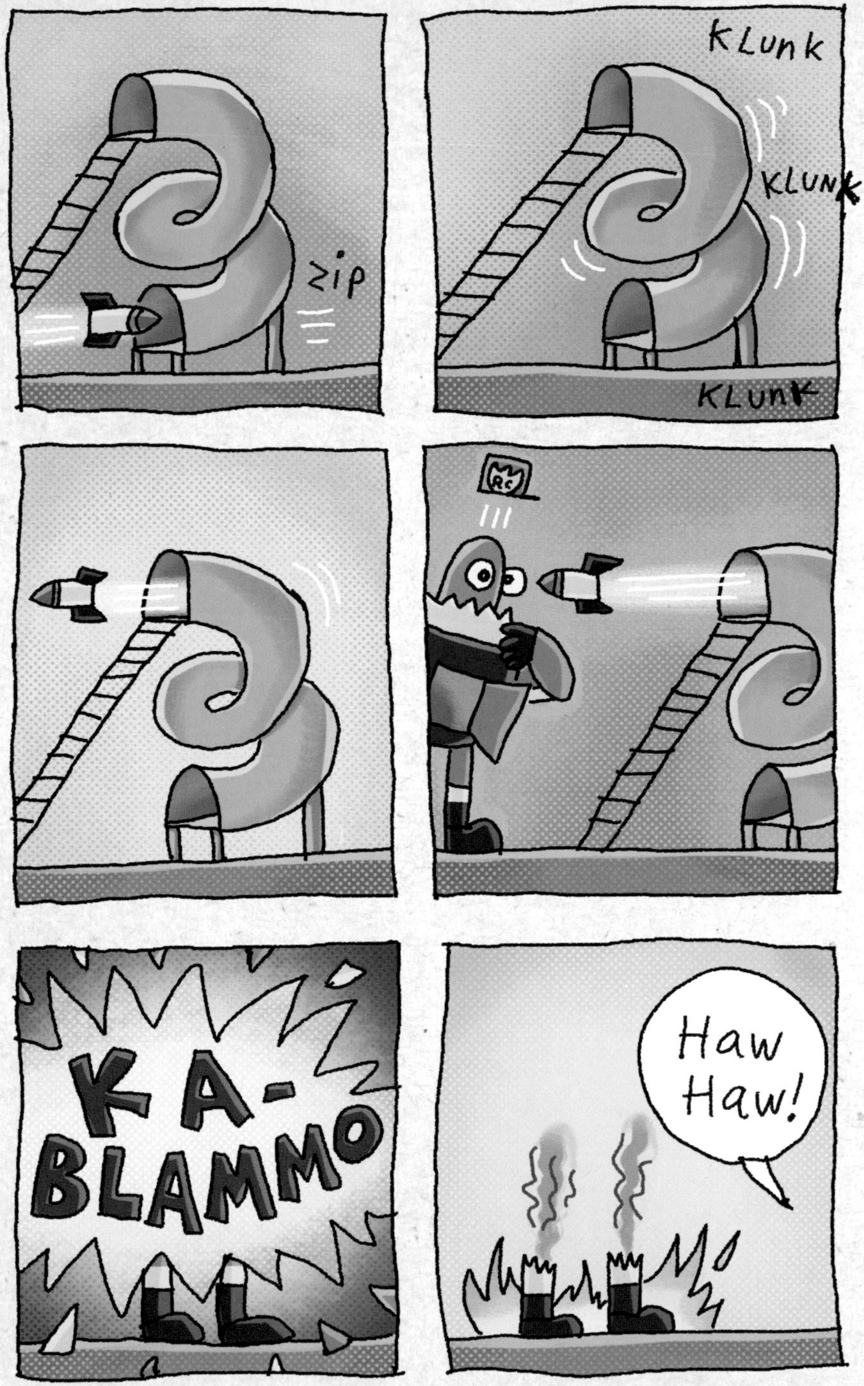
zip
KLunk
KLUNK
KLUNK
KA-BLAMMO
Haw Haw!

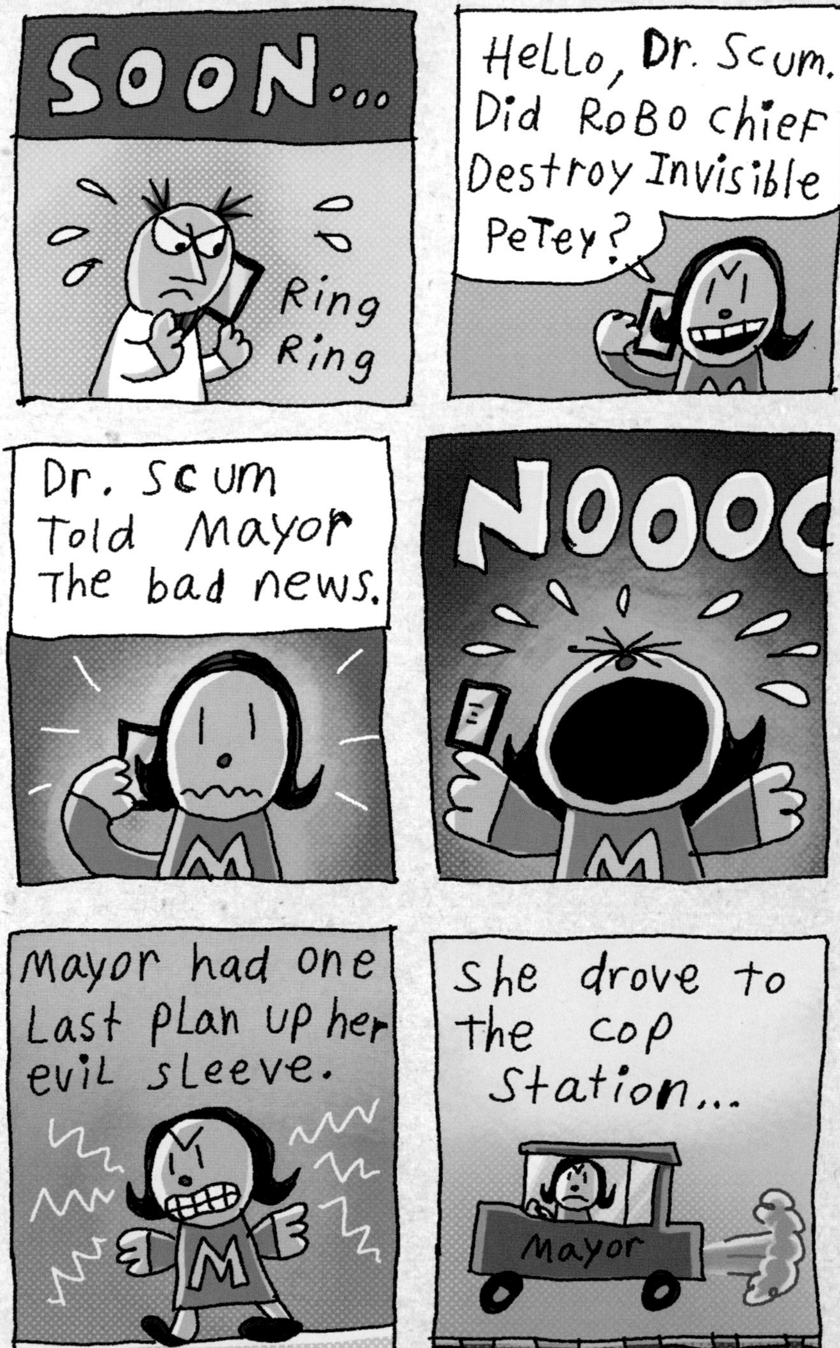
SOON...
Ring Ring
Hello, Dr. Scum. Did RoBo Chief Destroy Invisible Petey?
Dr. Scum Told Mayor The bad news.
NOOOO
Mayor had one Last plan up her evil sleeve.
She drove to the cop Station...
Mayor

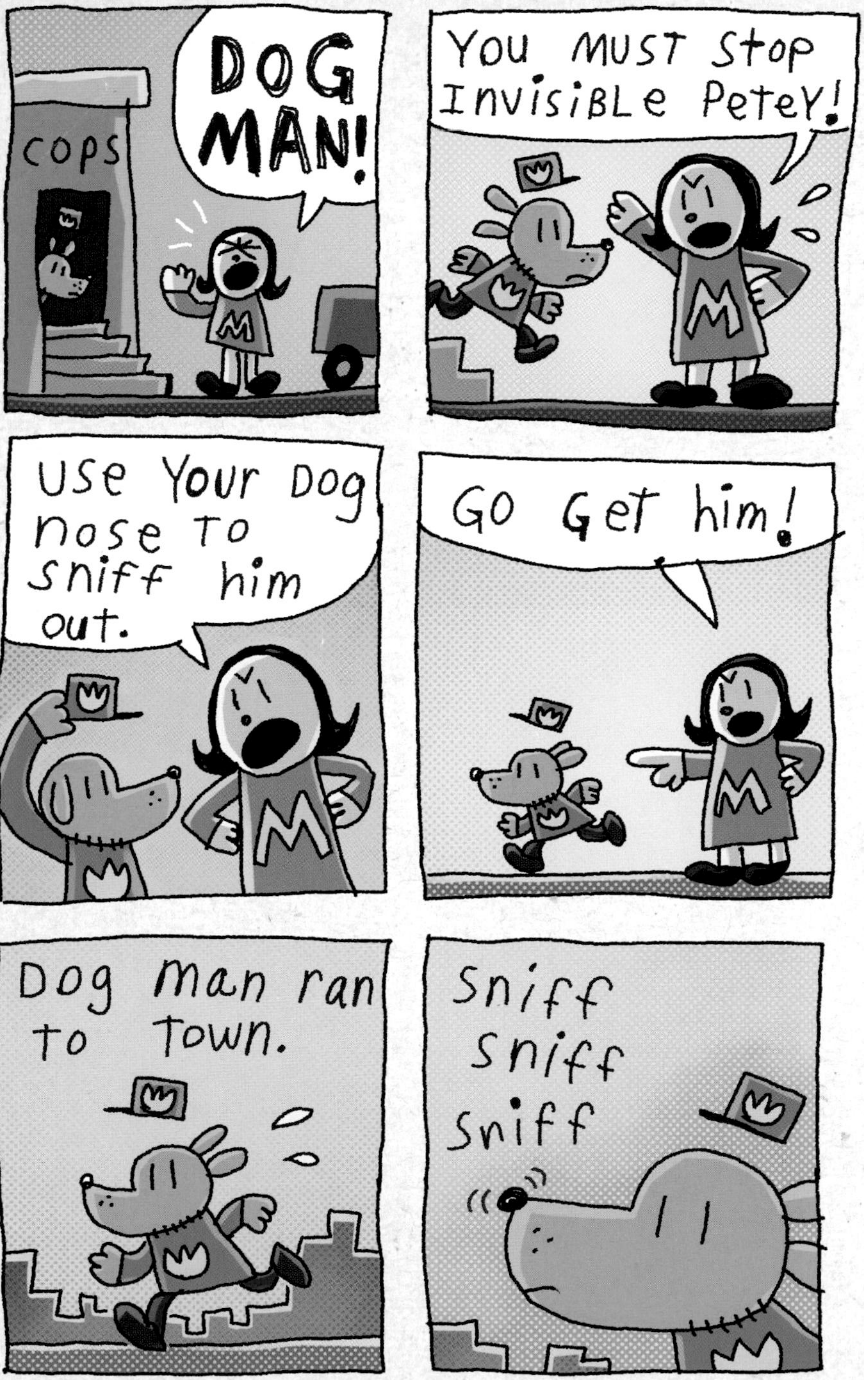

COPS
DOG MAN!
YOU MUST STOP INVISIBLE PETEY!
USE YOUR DOG NOSE TO SNIFF HIM OUT.
GO GET HIM!
DOG MAN RAN TO TOWN.
SNIFF SNIFF SNIFF

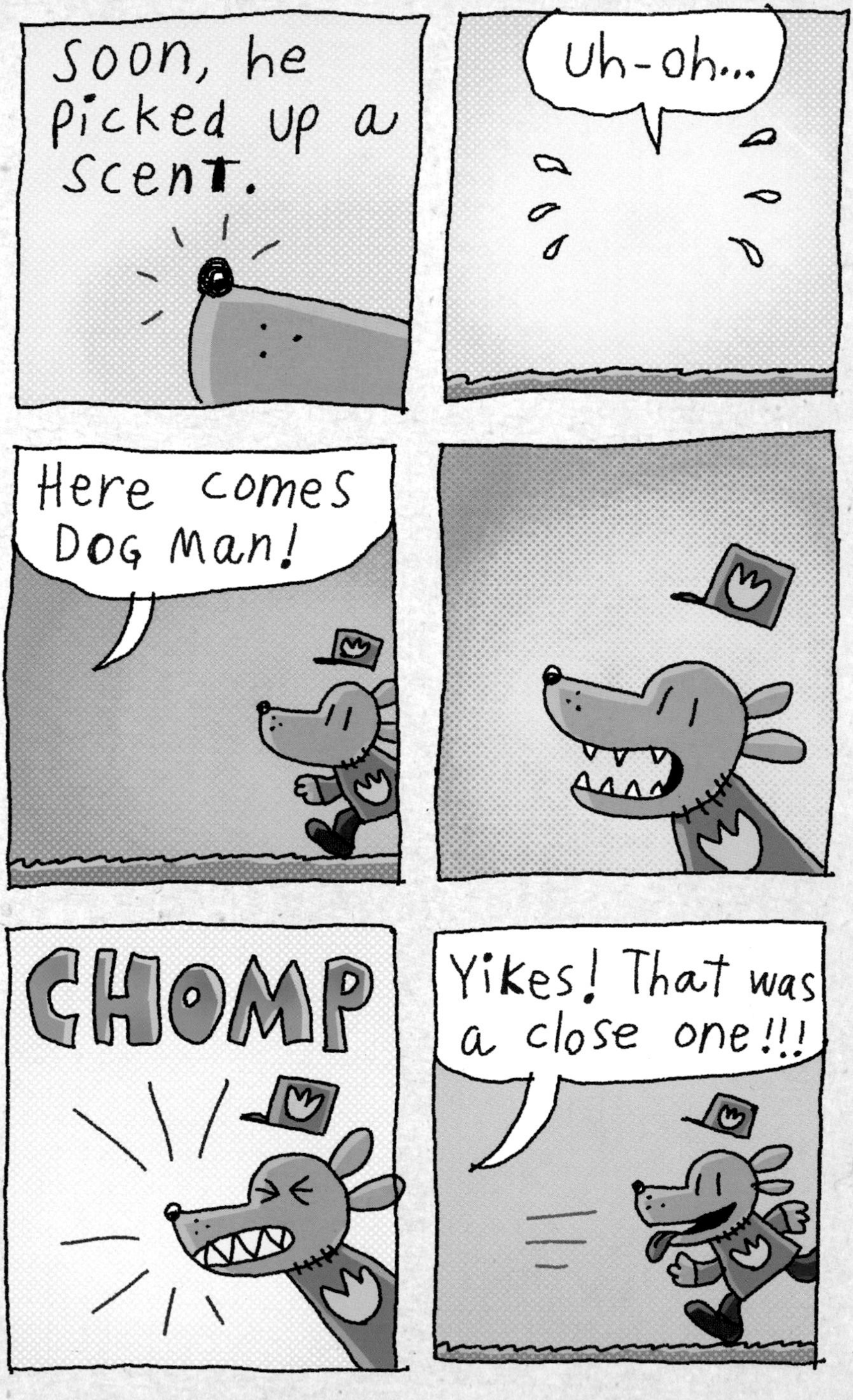
Soon, he picked up a scent.
Uh-oh...
Here comes DOG MAN!
CHOMP
Yikes! That was a close one!!!

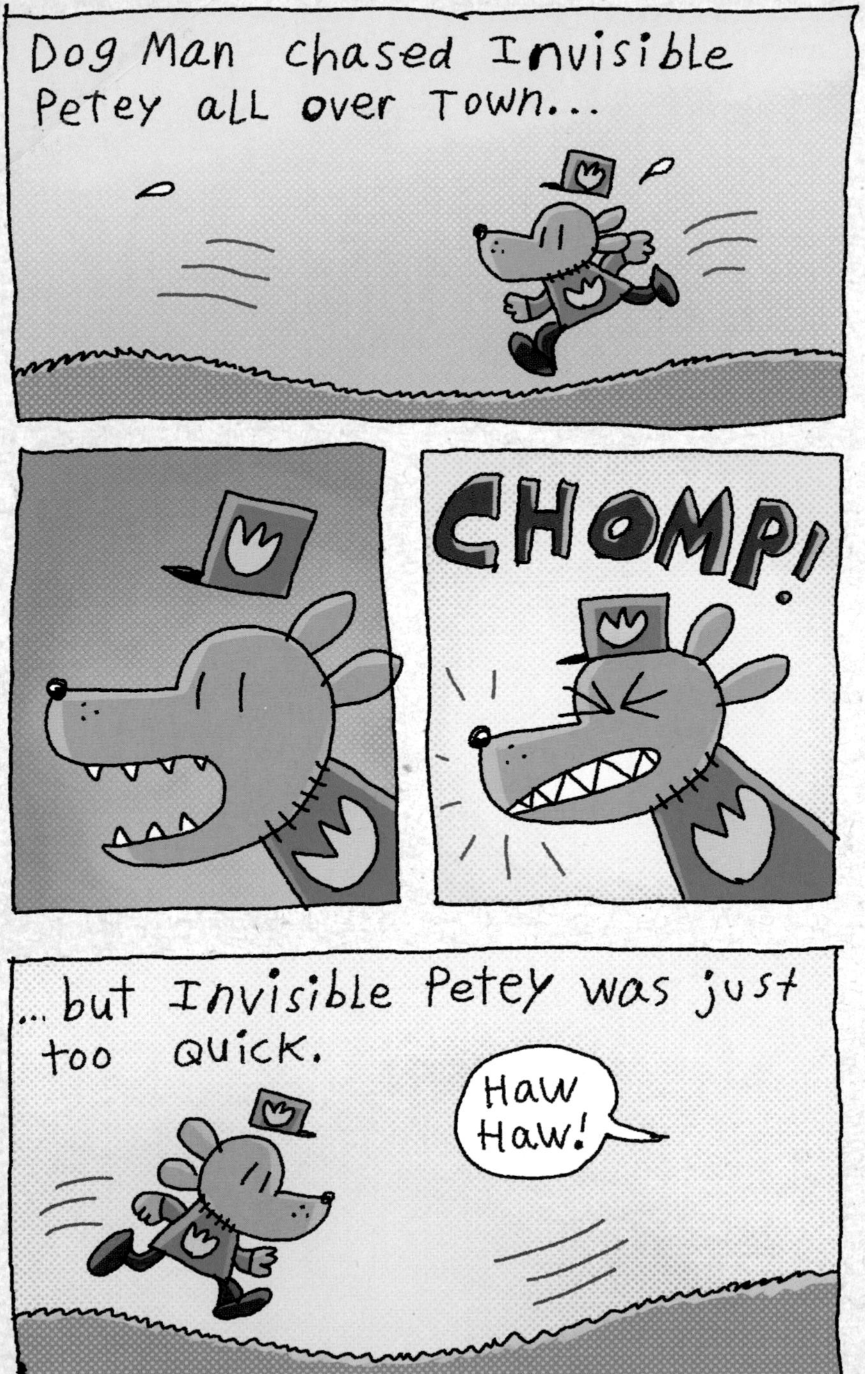
Dog Man chased Invisible Petey all over Town...
CHOMP!
...but Invisible Petey was just too quick.
Haw Haw!

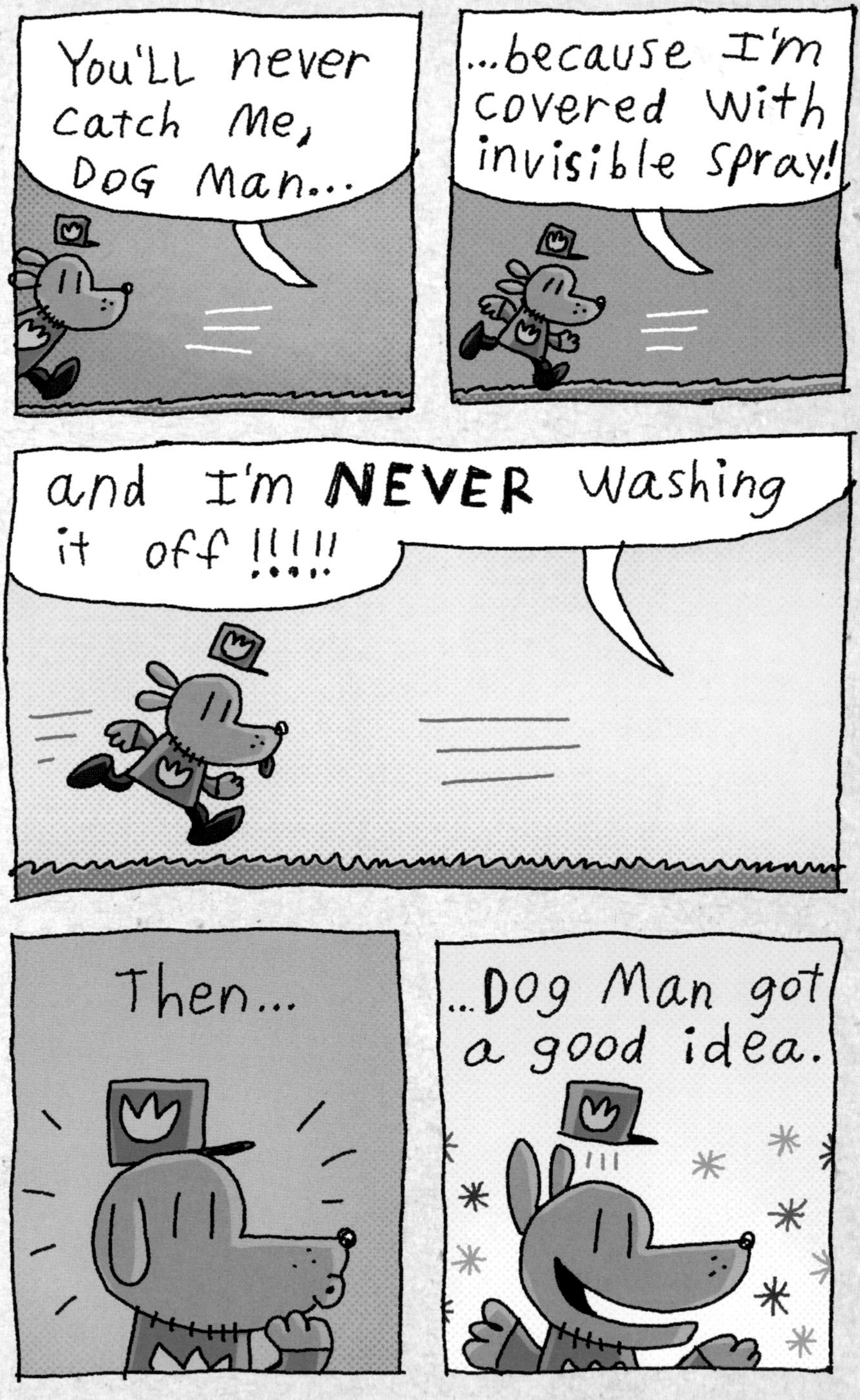
You'LL never catch me, DOG Man...
...because I'm covered with invisible spray!
and I'm NEVER washing it off!!!!!
Then...
...Dog Man got a good idea.

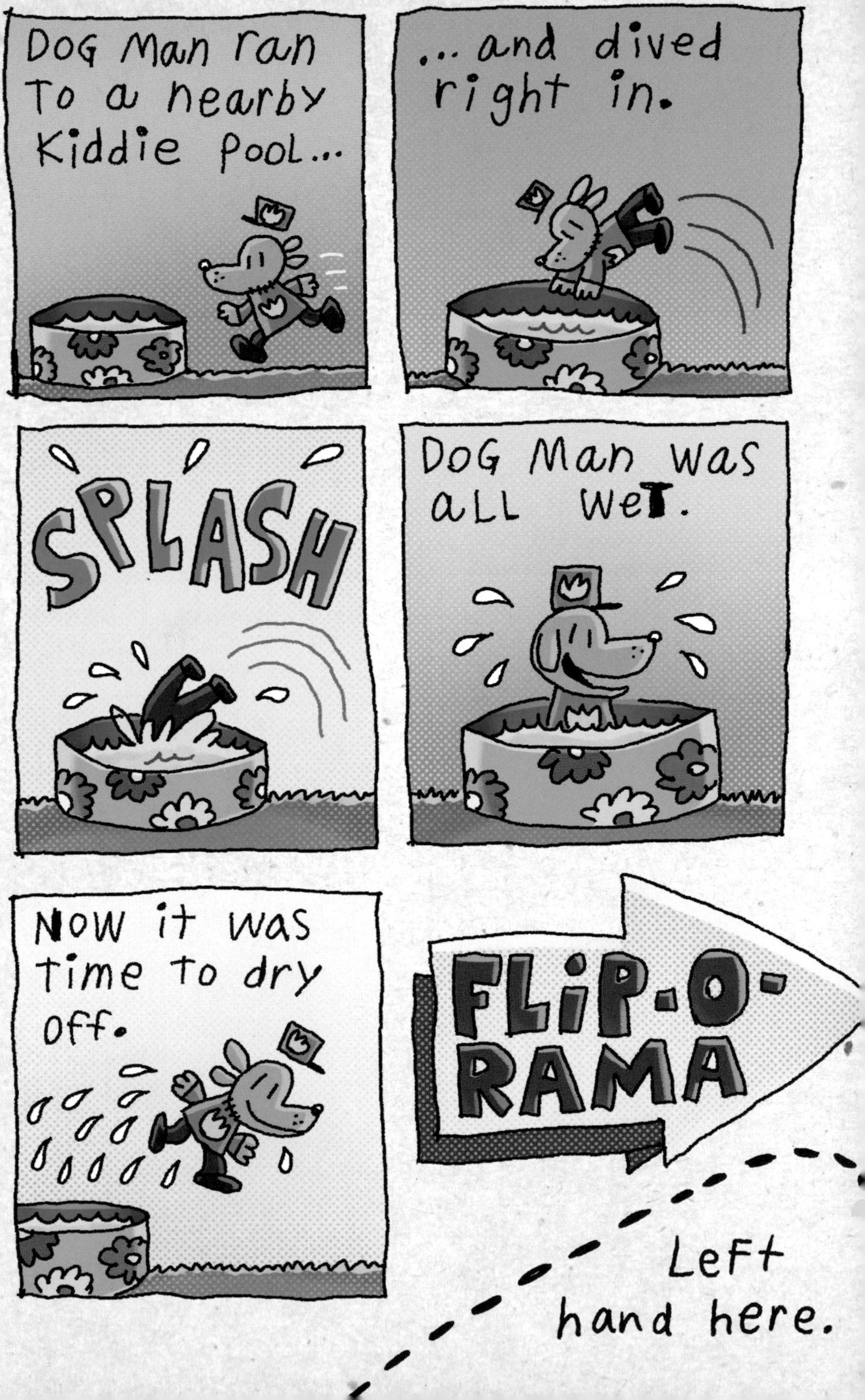
Dog Man ran To a nearby Kiddie pool...
... and dived right in.
SPLASH
Dog Man was all wet.
Now it was time to dry off.
FLIP-O-RAMA
Left hand here.

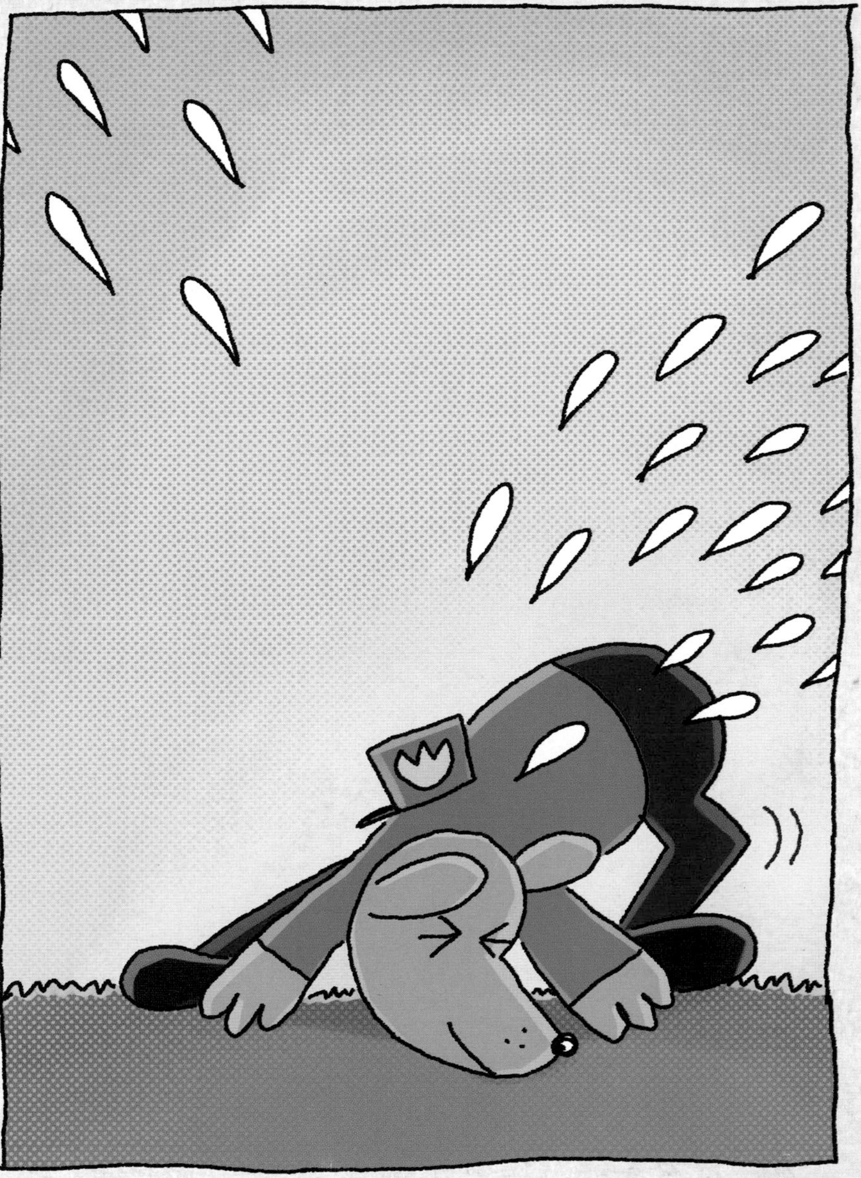

Supa
Soaker

Right
Thumb
here.

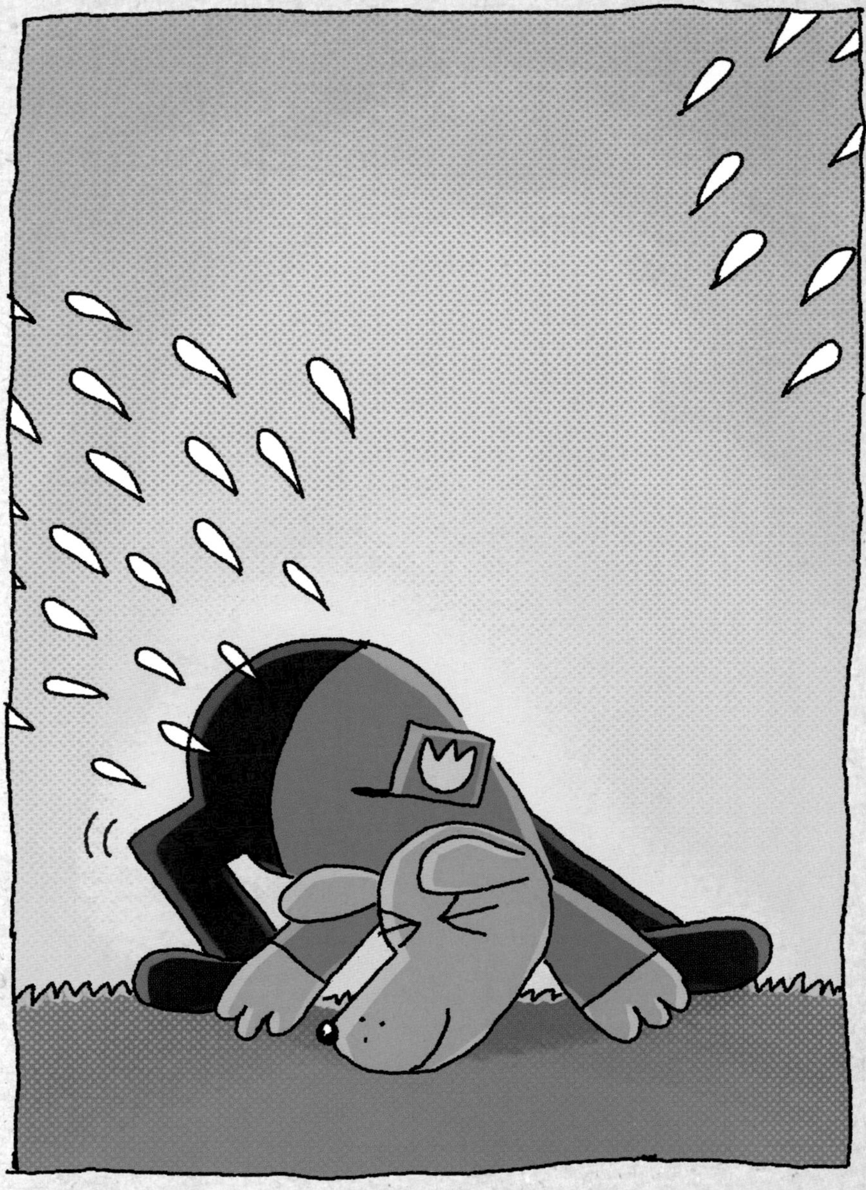

Supa
soaker

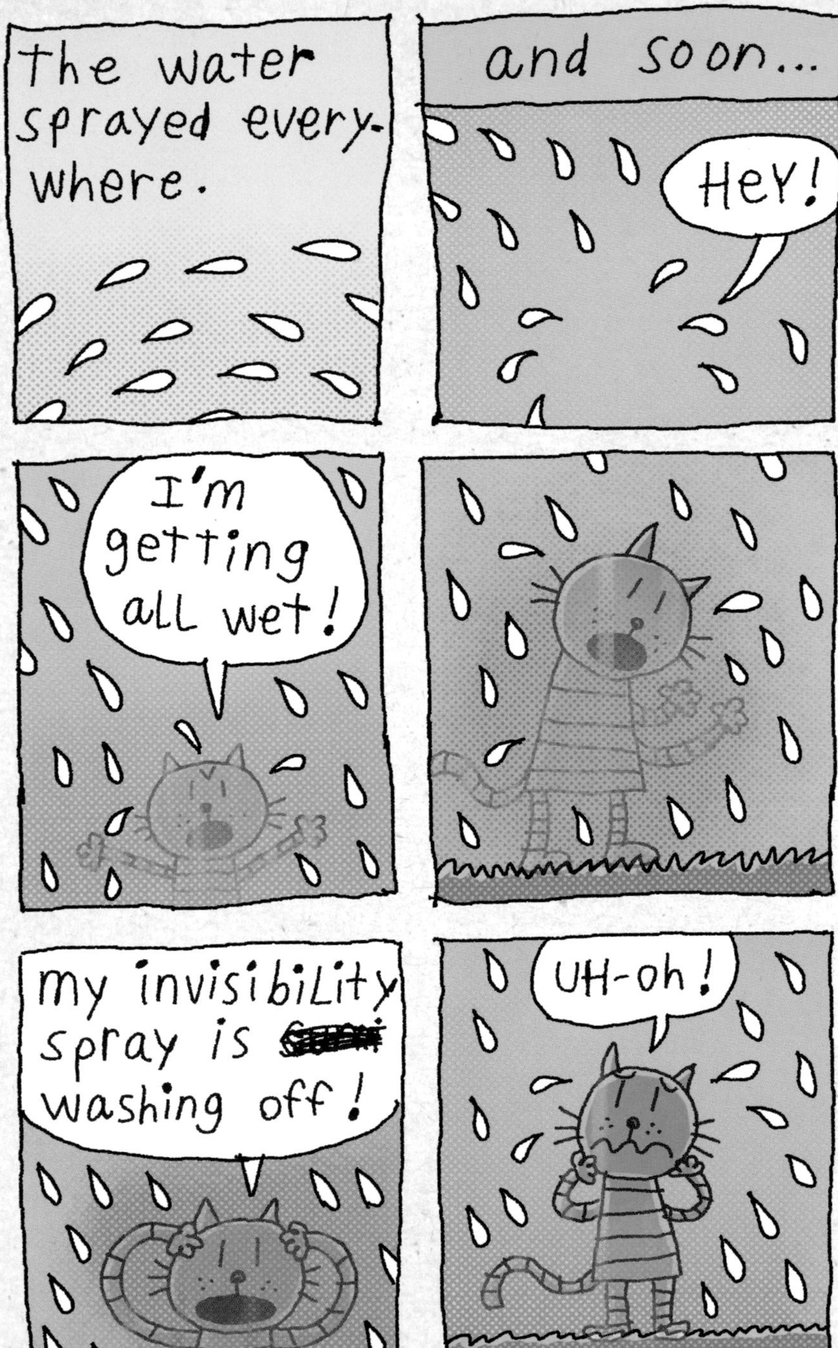
The water sprayed every-where.
and soon...
HEY!
I'm getting all wet!
my invisibility spray is washing off!
UH-oh!

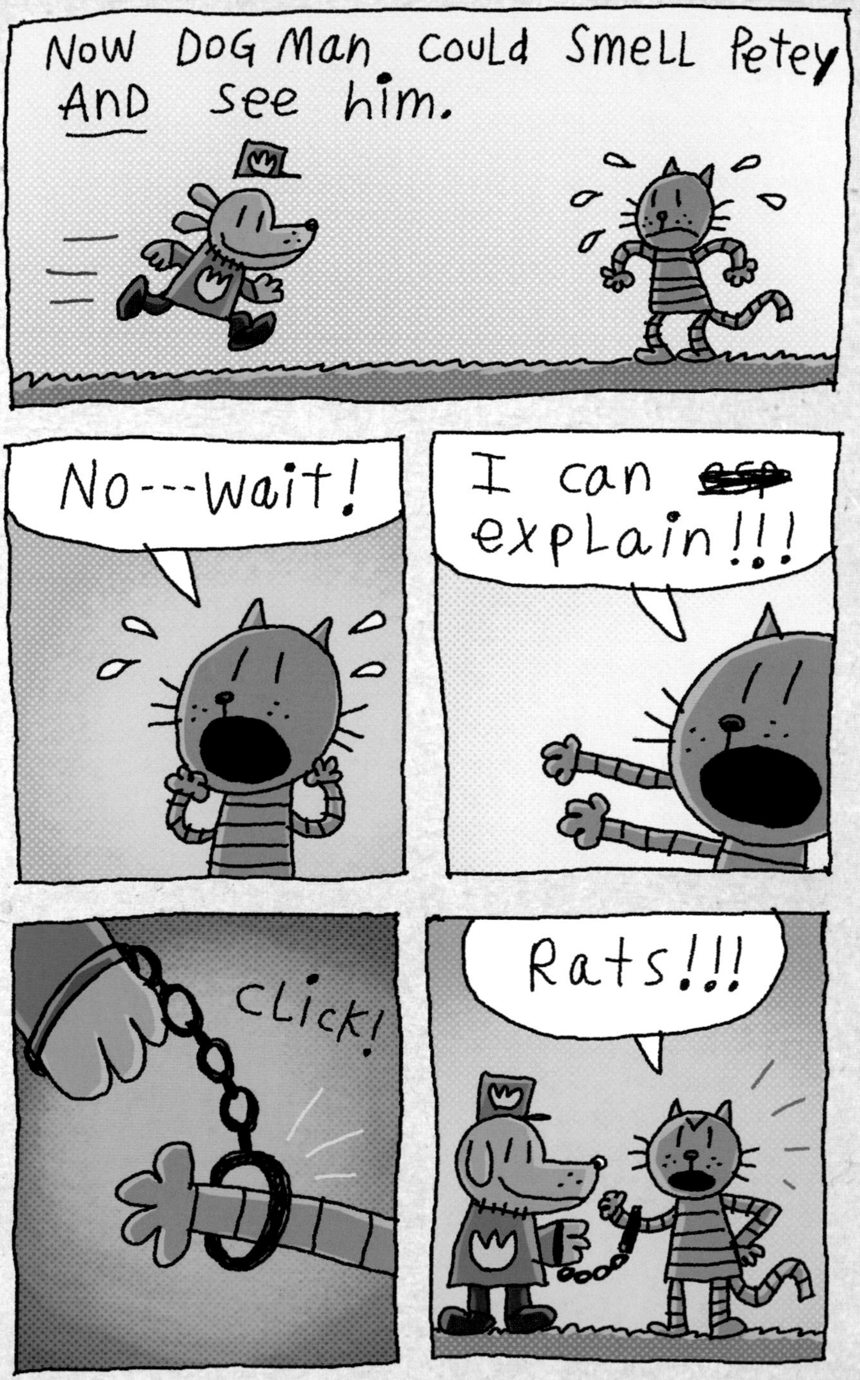
Now Dog Man could smell Petey AND see him.
No---wait!
I can explain!!!
Click!
Rats!!!

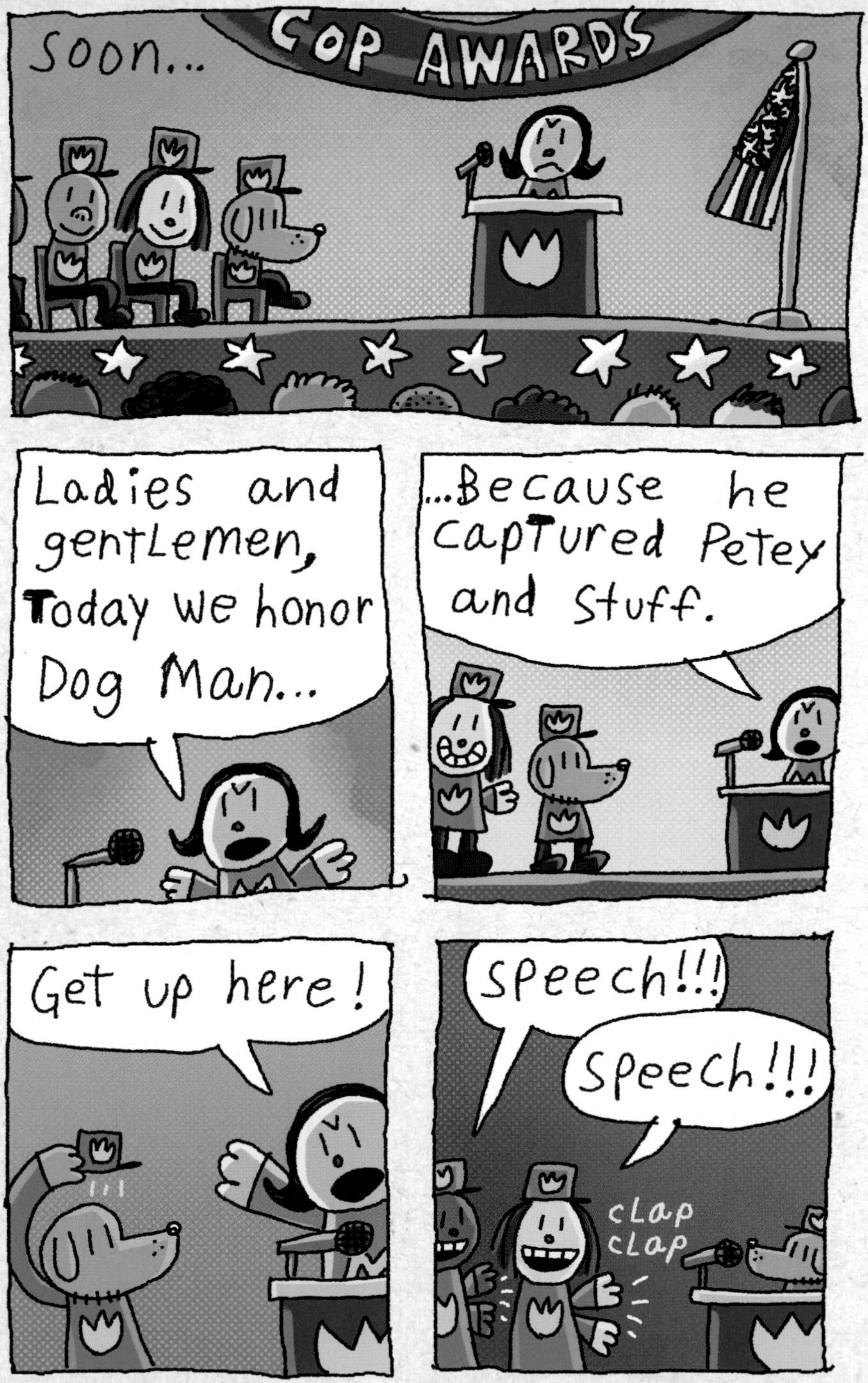
Soon...
COP AWARDS
Ladies and gentlemen, Today we honor Dog Man...
...Because he captured Petey and stuff.
Get up here!
Speech!!!
Speech!!!
clap clap

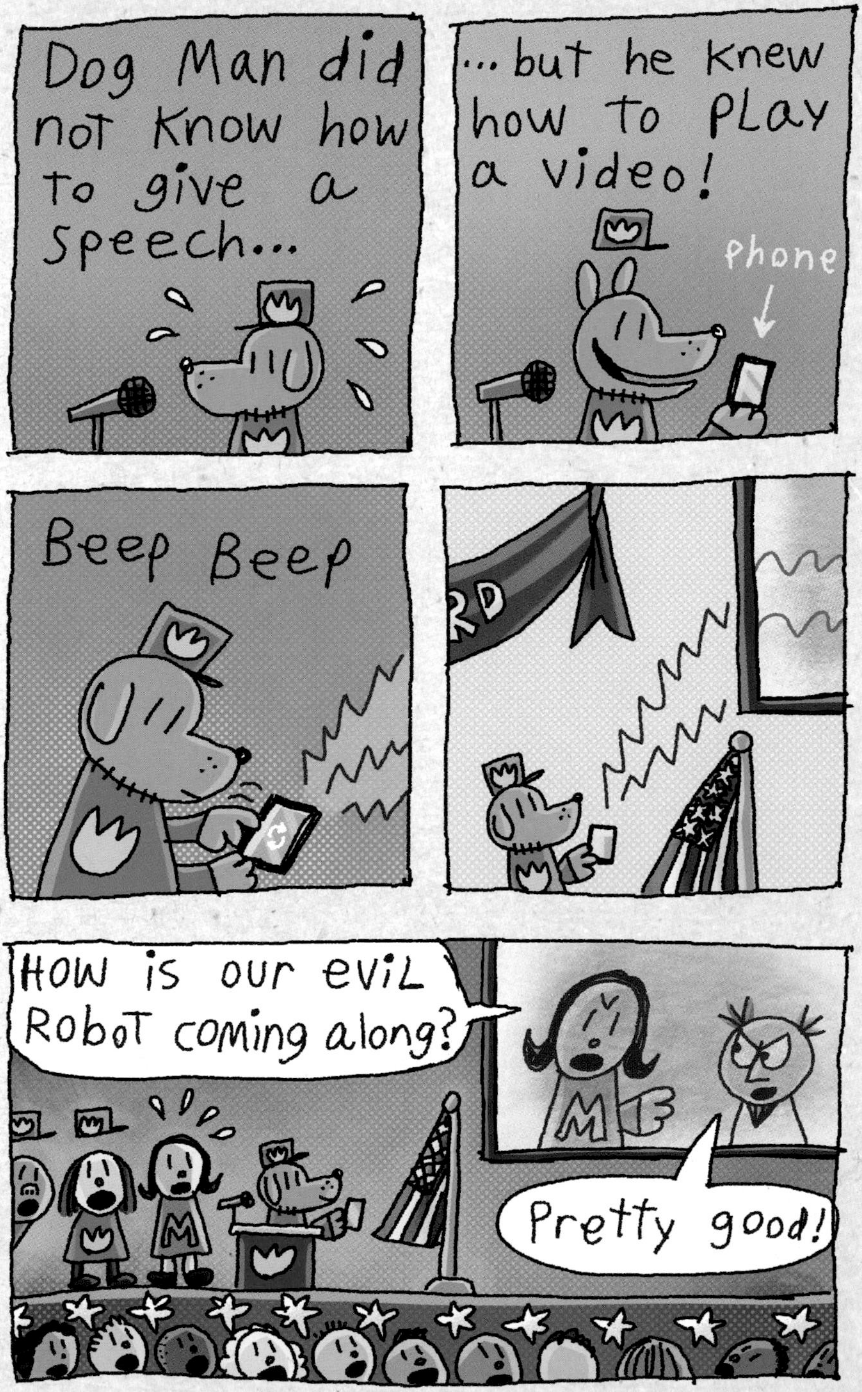
Dog Man did not know how to give a speech...
...but he knew how to play a video!
Phone
Beep Beep
RD
How is our evil Robot coming along?
Pretty good!

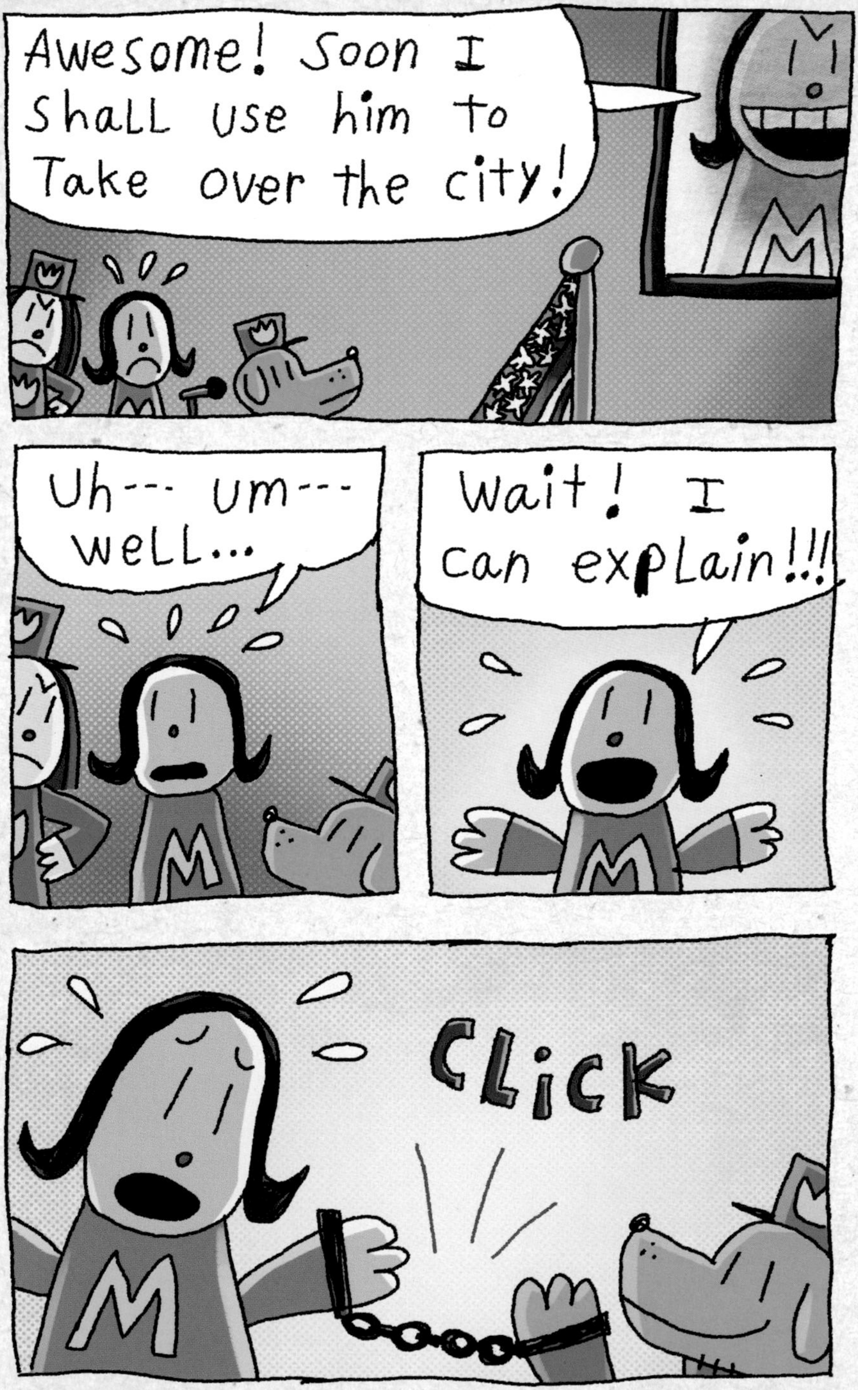
Awesome! Soon I shall use him to Take over the city!
Uh--- um--- well...
Wait! I can explain!!!
CLICK

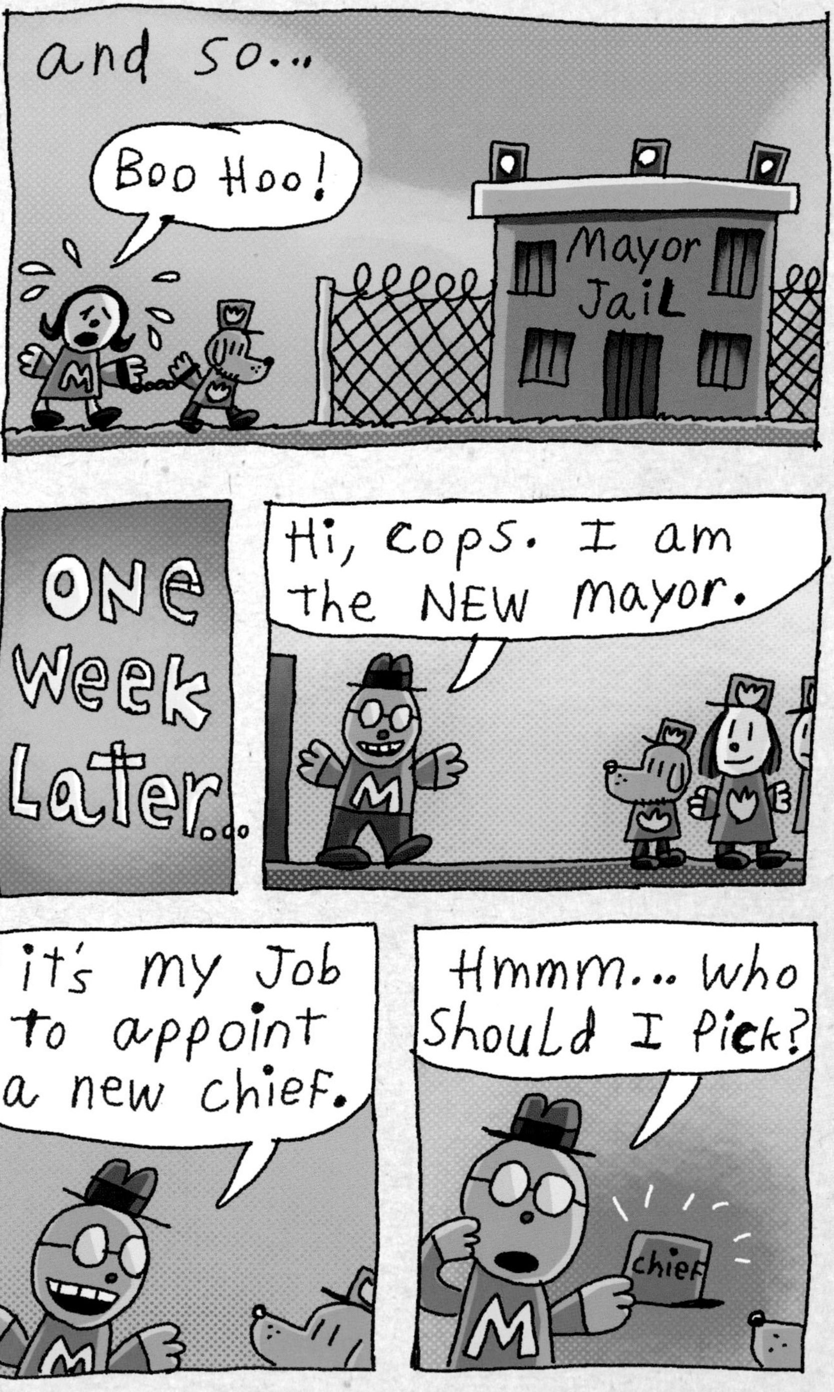
and so...
Boo Hoo!
Mayor Jail
One Week Later...
Hi, cops. I am the NEW mayor.
it's my Job to appoint a new chief.
Hmmm... who should I pick?
chief

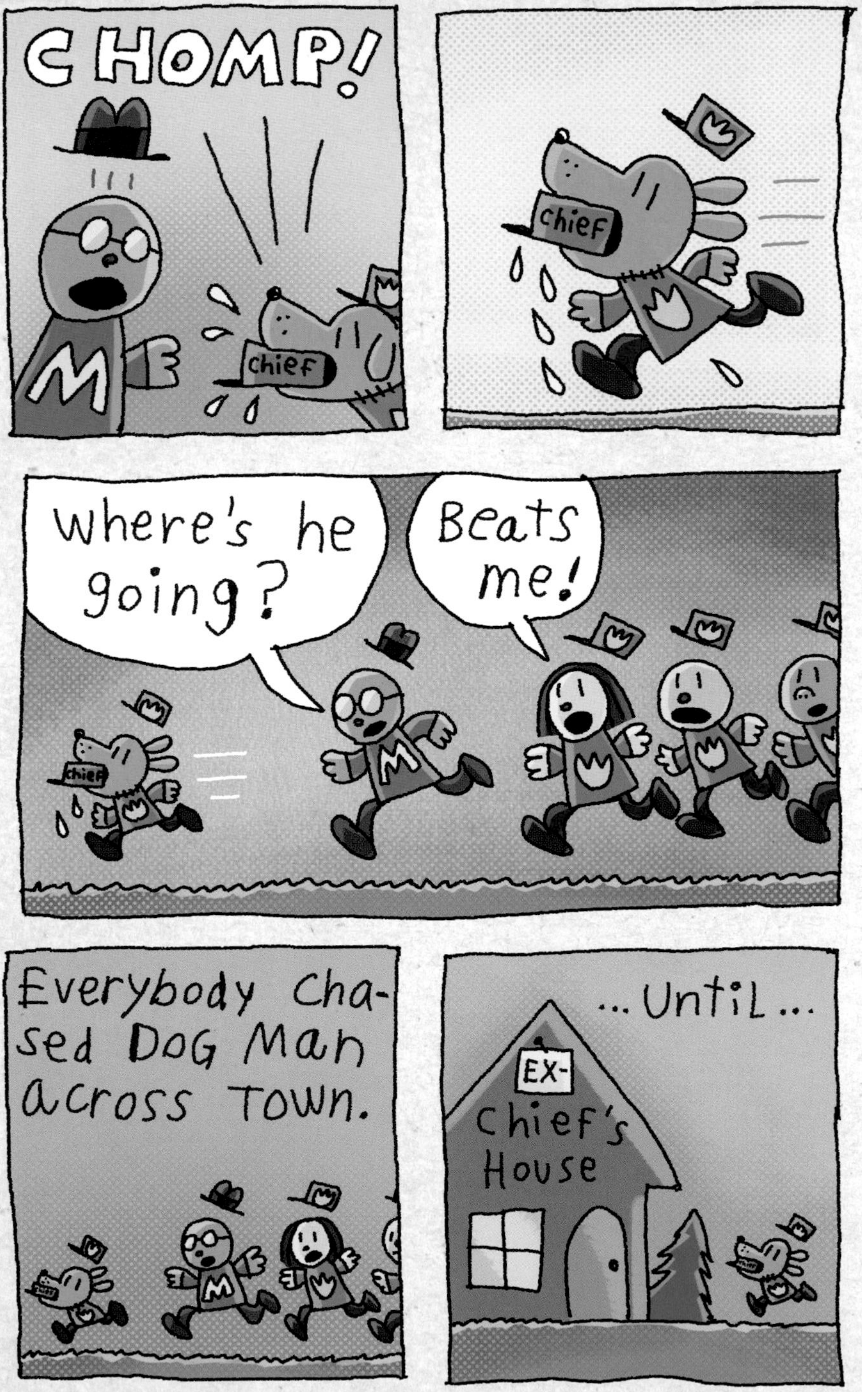
CHOMP!
chief
chief
Where's he going?
Beats me!
chief
Everybody Chased DoG Man across Town.
...UntiL...
EX-
Chief's House

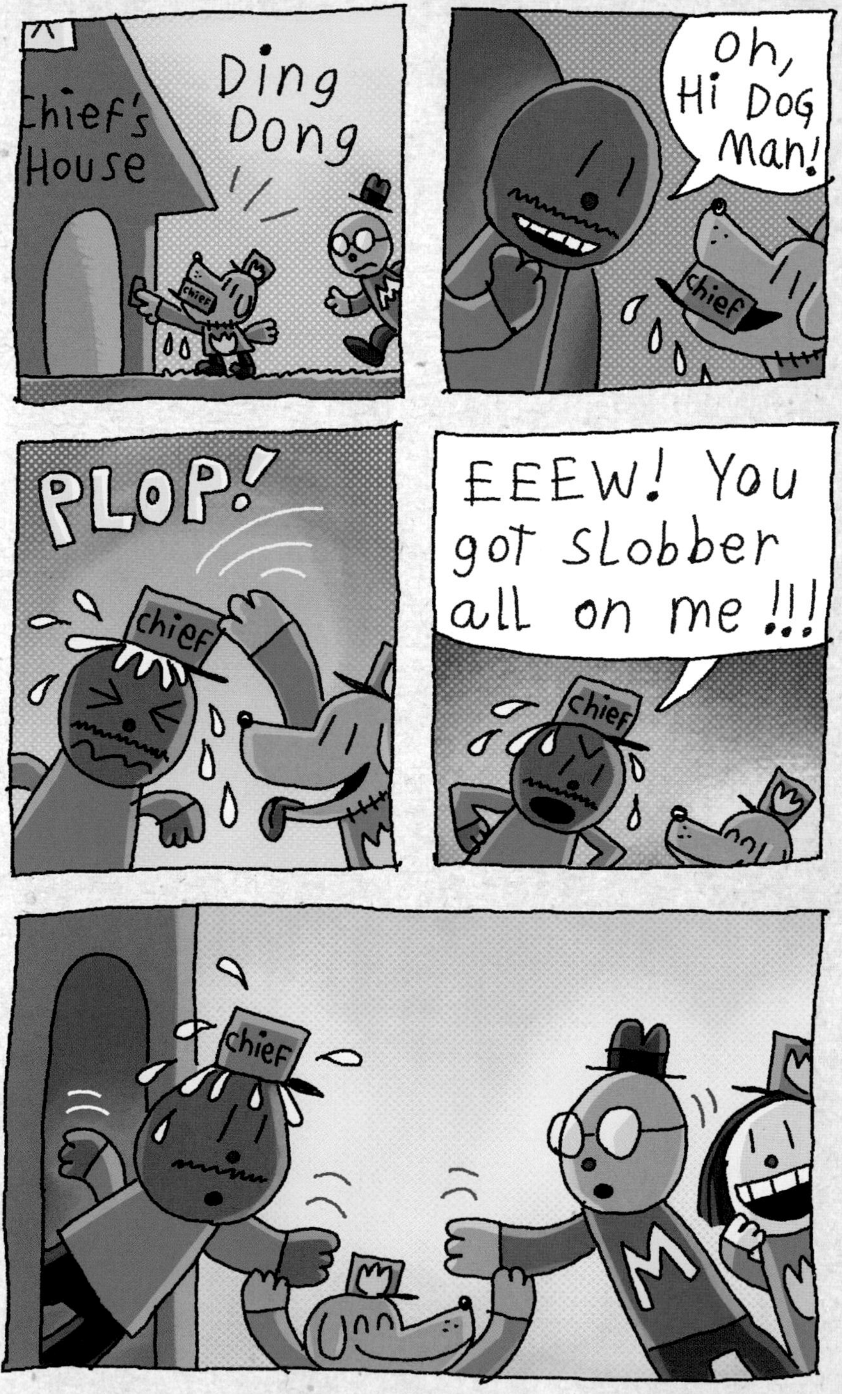
Chief's House
Ding Dong
Oh, Hi Dog Man!
chief
PLOP!
chief
EEEW! You got slobber all on me!!!
chief
chief

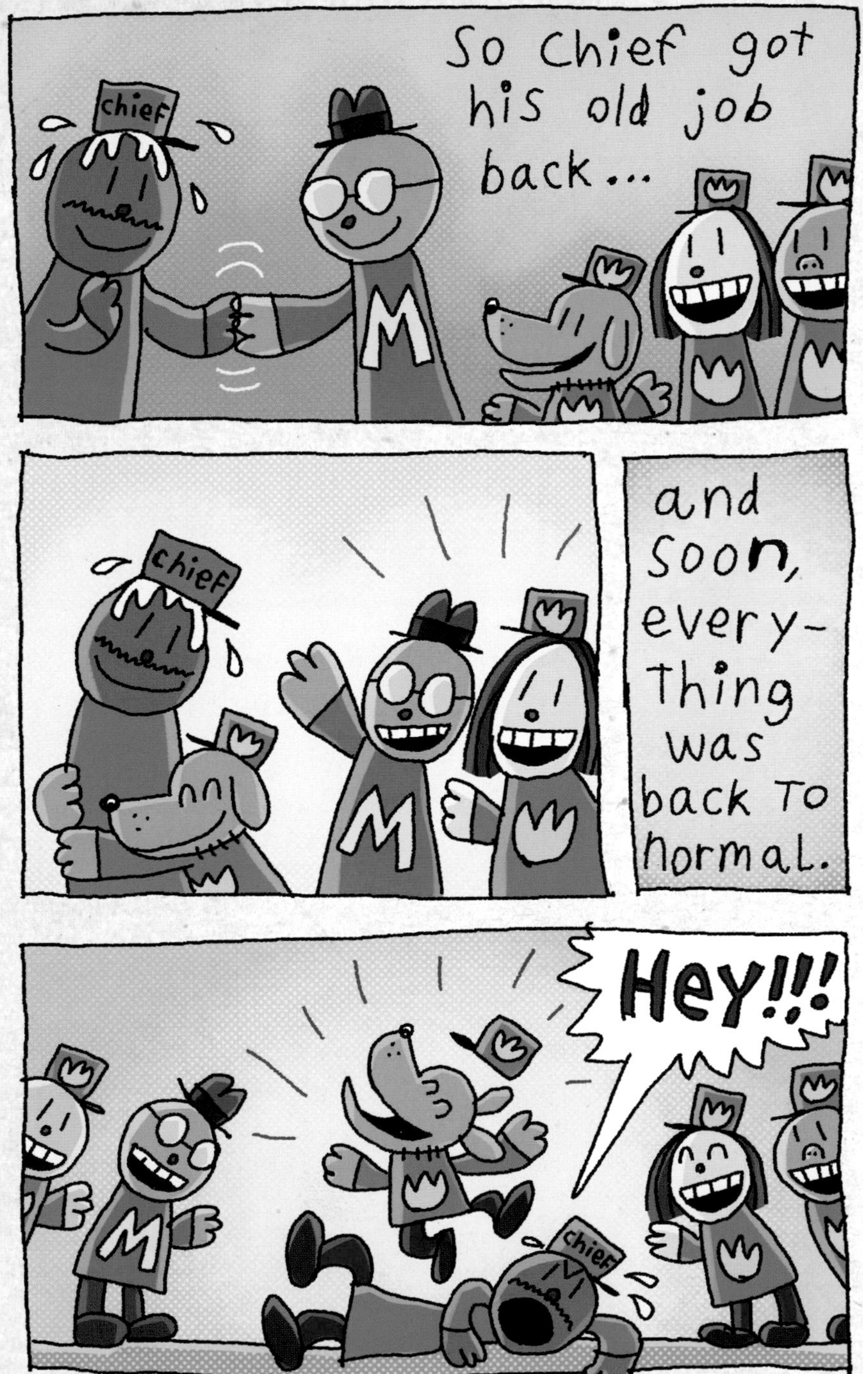
So Chief got his old job back...
chief
and soon, every-Thing was back To normal.
chief
Hey!!!
chief

CHAPTER 3

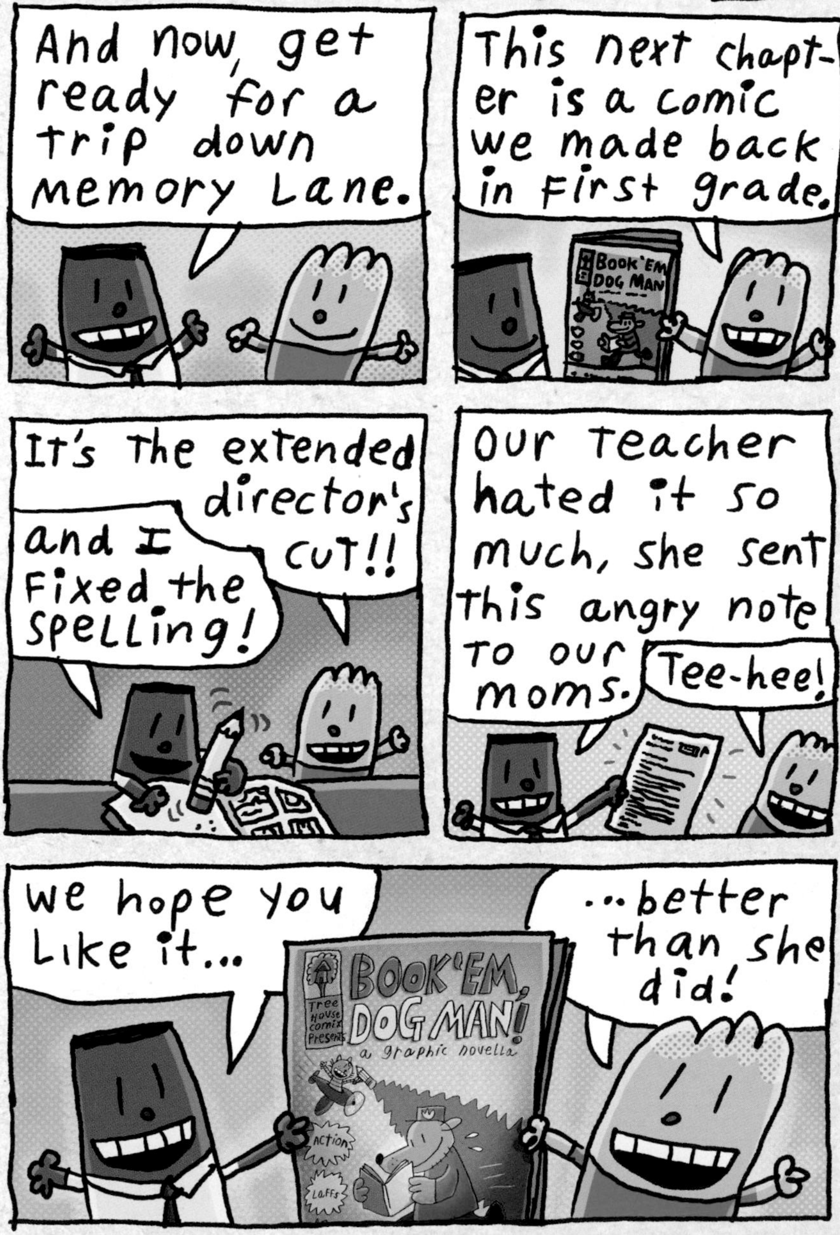
And now, get ready for a trip down memory Lane.
This next chapter is a comic we made back in First grade.
BOOK'EM DOG MAN
It's the extended director's CUT!!
and I Fixed the spelling!
Our Teacher hated it so much, she sent this angry note to our moms.
Tee-hee!
we hope you Like it...
Tree House Comix Presents
BOOK'EM, DOG MAN!
a graphic novella
ACTION
LAFFS
...better than she did!

Jerome Horwitz Elementary School

We put the "ow" in Knowledge

Dear Mr. and Mrs. Beard,

Once again I am writing to inform you of your son's disruptive activity in my classroom.

The assignment was to create a WRITTEN public service message to promote reading. Your son and his friend, Harold Hutchins (I am sending a nearly identical letter to Harold's mother), were specifically told NOT to make a comic book for this assignment.

As usual, they did exactly what they were told not to do (see attached comic book). When I confronted George about his disobedience, he claimed that this was not a comic book, but a "graphic novella." I am getting fed up with George's impudence.

I have told both boys on numerous occasions that the classroom is no place for creativity, yet they continue to make these obnoxious and offensive "comix." As you will see, this comic book contains multiple references to human and/or animal feces. It also features a very questionable scene of disregard for homeless/hungry individuals. There are scenes of smoking, violence, nudity, and don't get me started on the spelling and grammar. Frankly, I found the little trash bag "baby" at the end to be very disturbing. I mean, how is that even possible?!!?

George's silly, disruptive behavior, as well as these increasingly disgusting and scatological comic books, are turning my classroom into a zoo. I have spoken to Principal Krupp about Dog Man on numerous occasions. We both believe that you should consider psychological counseling for your son, or at the very least some kind of behavior modification drug to cure his "creative streak."

Regretfully,

Ms. Construde

Ms. Construde
Grade 1 Teacher

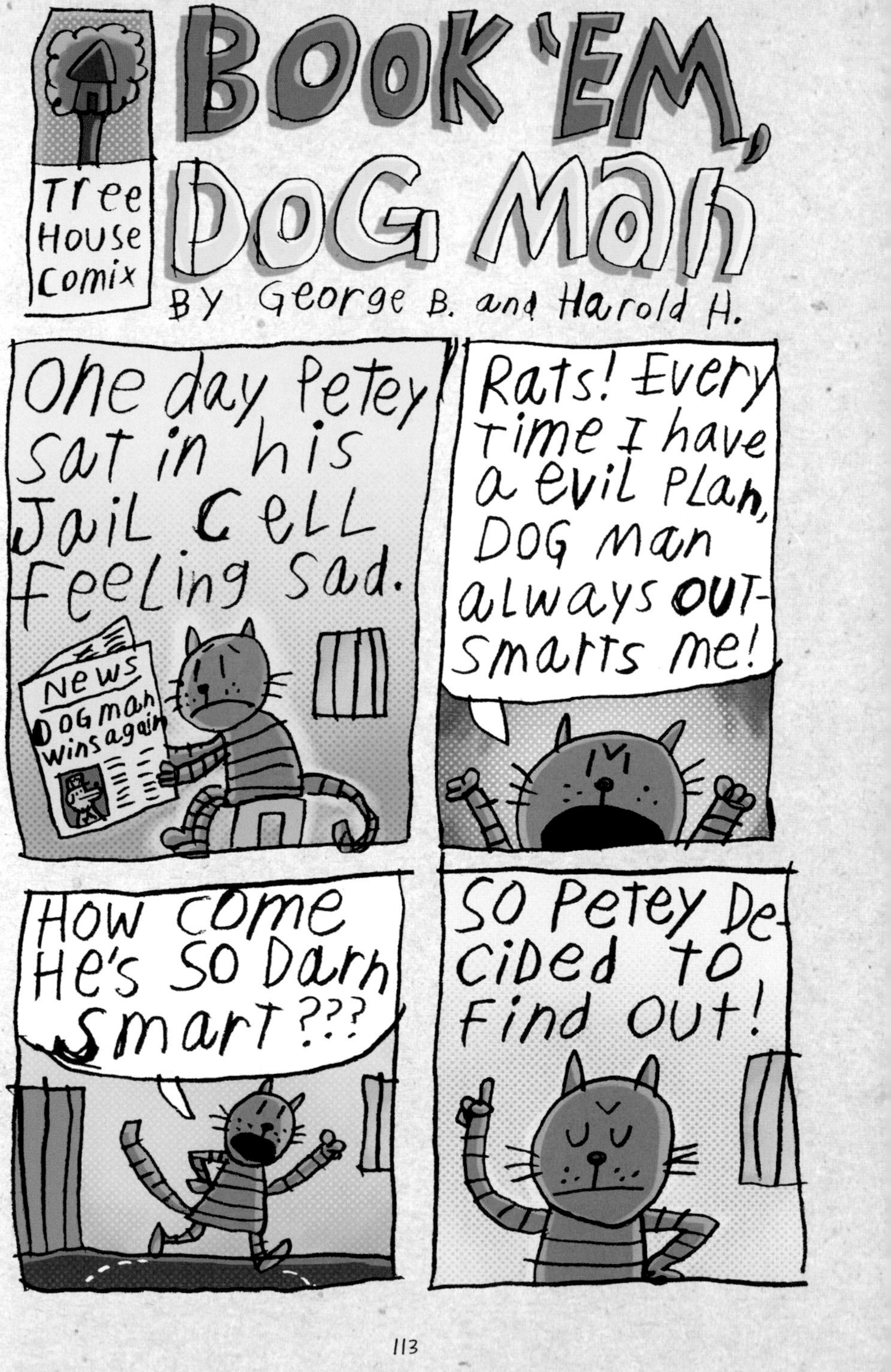
Tree House Comix
BOOK 'EM, DOG MAN
BY George B. and Harold H.
One day Petey sat in his Jail Cell Feeling sad.
News
DOG man wins again
Rats! Every time I have a evil Plan, DOG man always OUT-smarts me!
How come He's So Darn Smart???
So Petey De-cided to Find out!

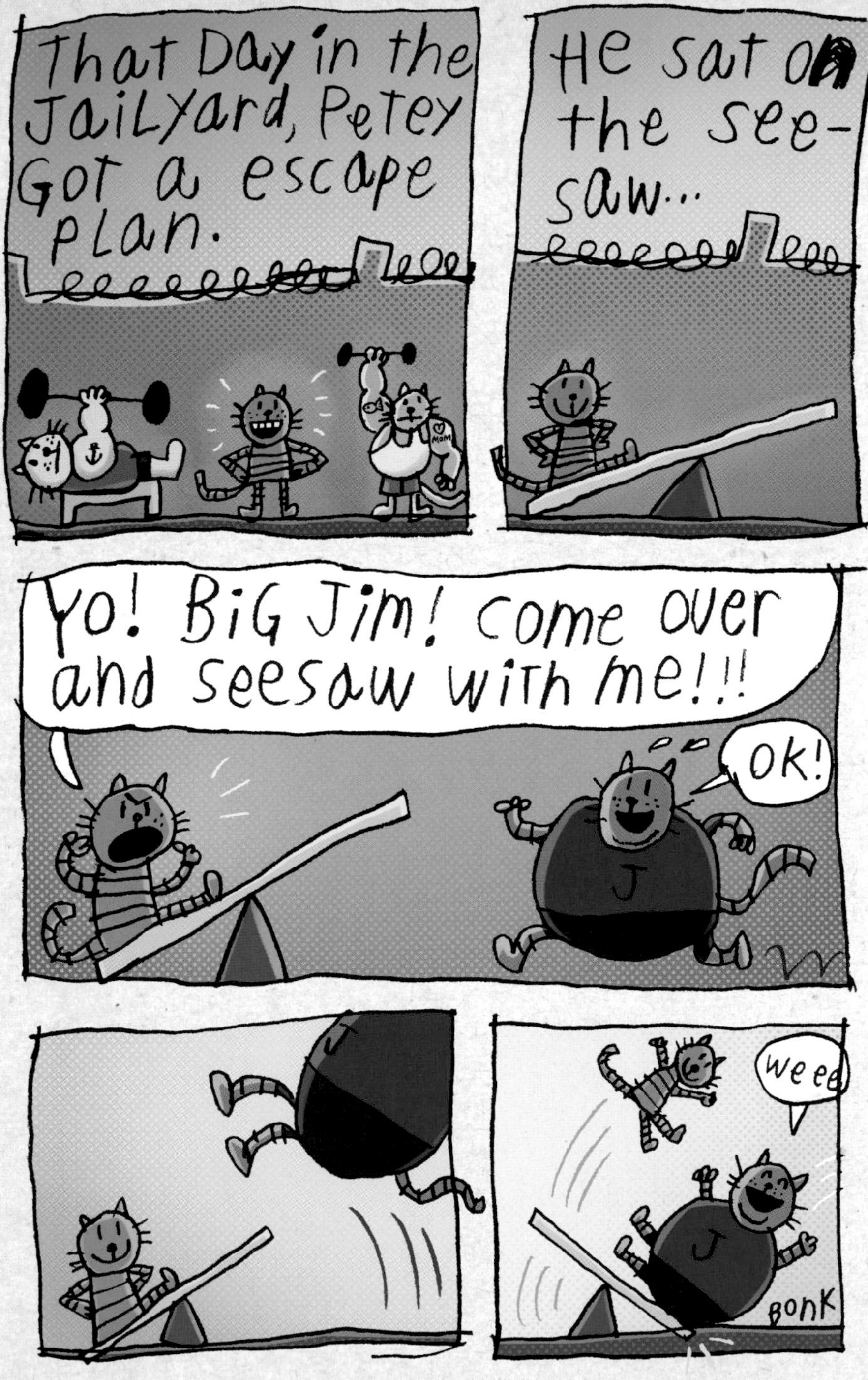
That Day in the JaiLyard, Petey Got a escape plan.
MOM
He sat o the see-saw...
Yo! BiG Jim! come over and seesaw with me!!!
OK!
weee
BONK

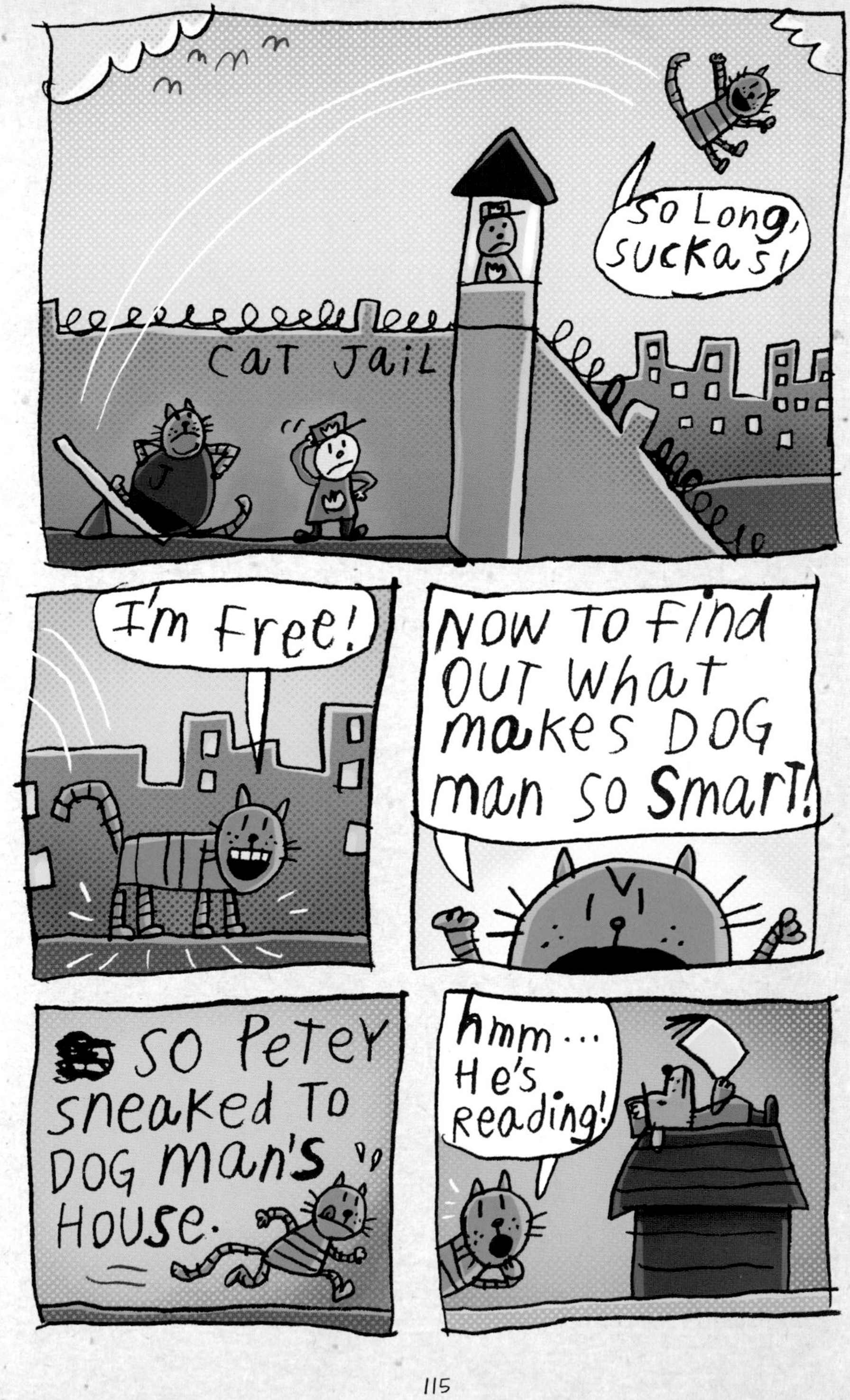
CAT JAIL
So Long, Suckas!
I'm Free!
Now To Find OUT What makes DOG man so SmarT!
So Petey sneaked To DOG man's House.
hmm... He's Reading!

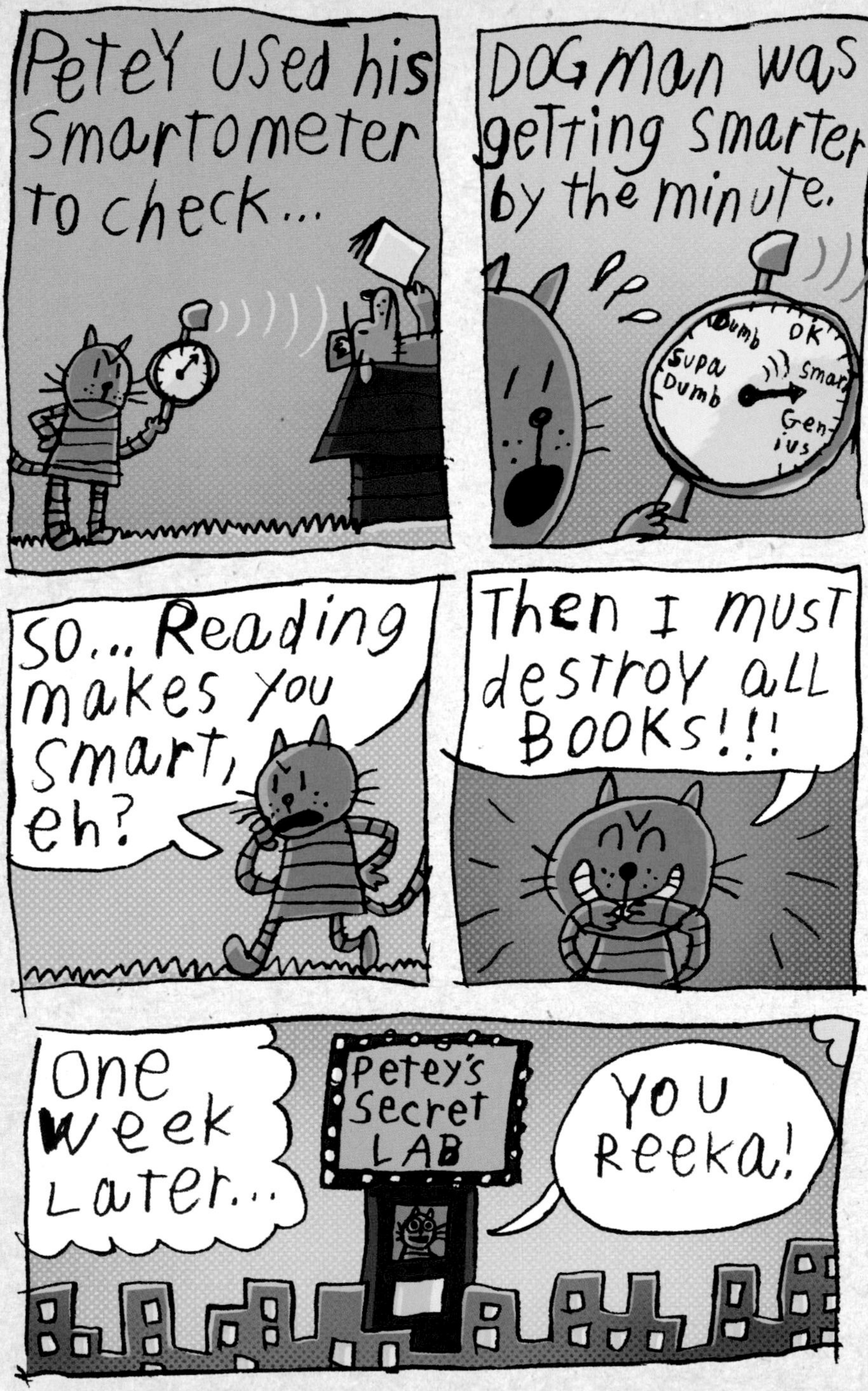
Petey used his Smartometer to check...
Dog Man was getting smarter by the minute.
Dumb
OK
Supa Dumb
Smart
Genius
So... Reading makes you smart, eh?
Then I must destroy all BOOKS!!!
One week later...
Petey's Secret LAB
You Reeka!

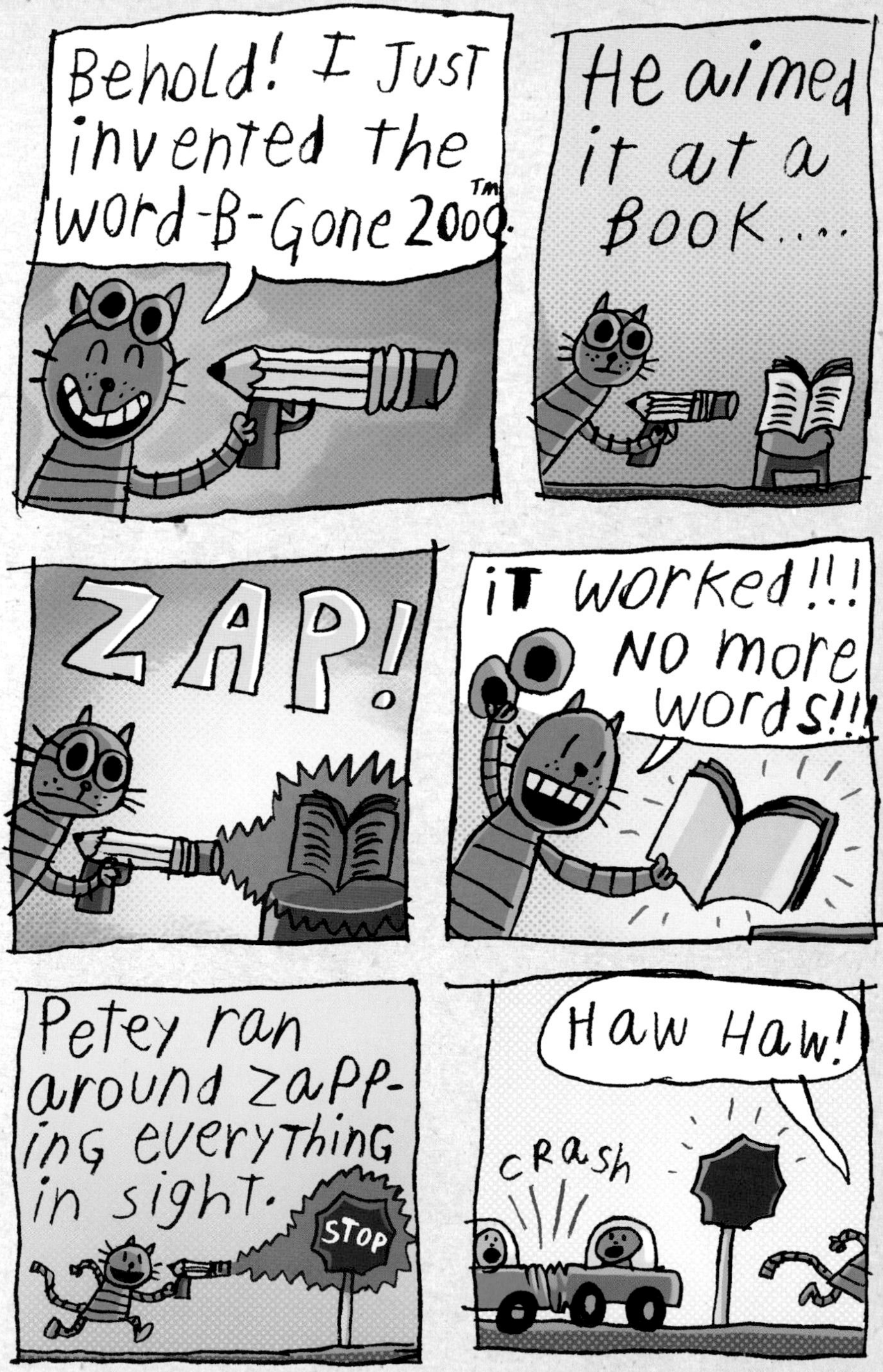
Behold! I JUST invented the word-B-Gone 2000™.
He aimed it at a BOOK....
ZAP!
iT worked!!! NO more words!!!
Petey ran around ZaPP-inG everyThinG in sight.
STOP
Haw Haw!
cRash

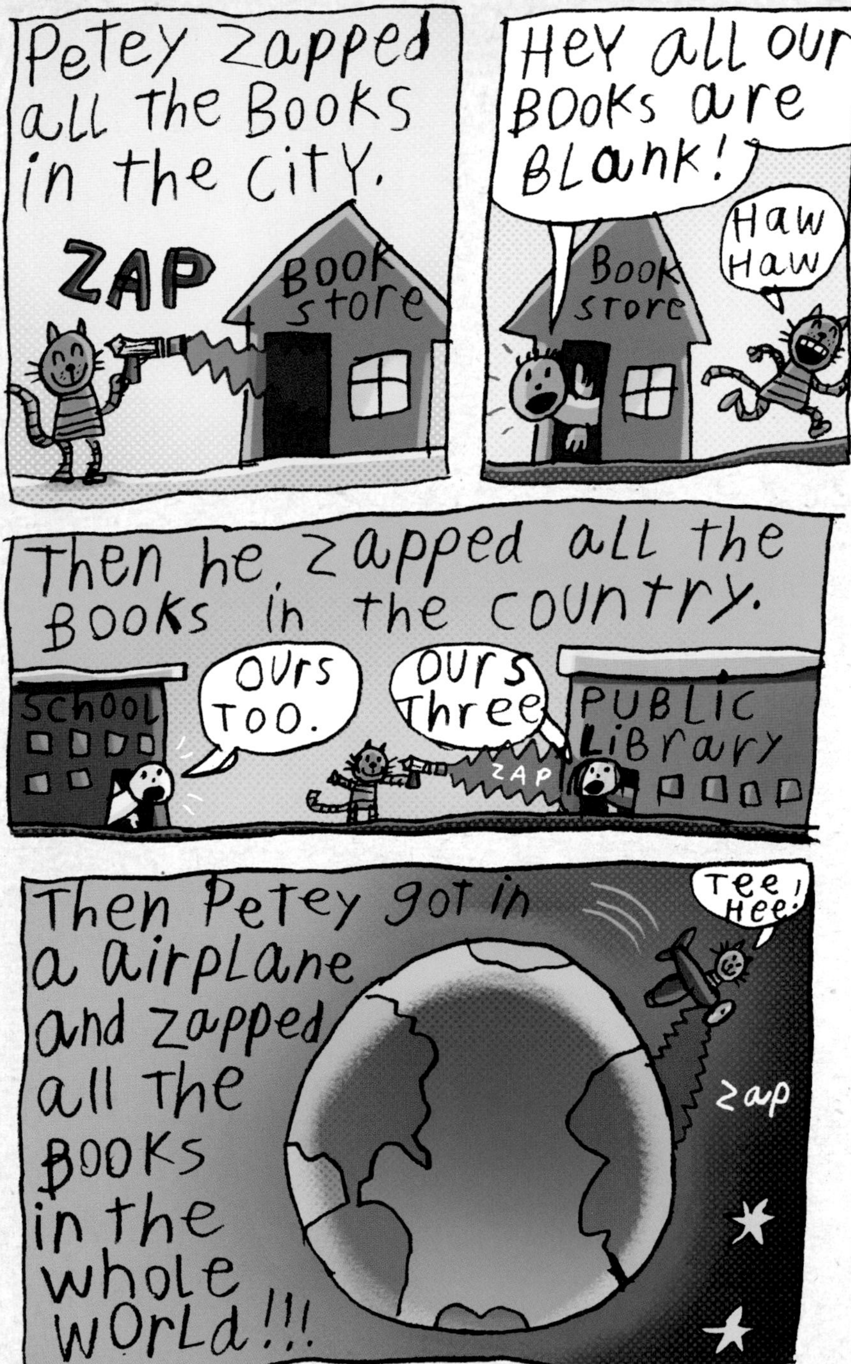
Petey zapped all the Books in the City.
ZAP
Book store
Hey all our Books are Blank!
Book store
Haw Haw
Then he zapped all the Books in the country.
School
Ours Too.
Ours Three
ZAP
PUBLIC Library
Then Petey got in a airplane and zapped all the Books in the whole World!!!
Tee! Hee!
Zap

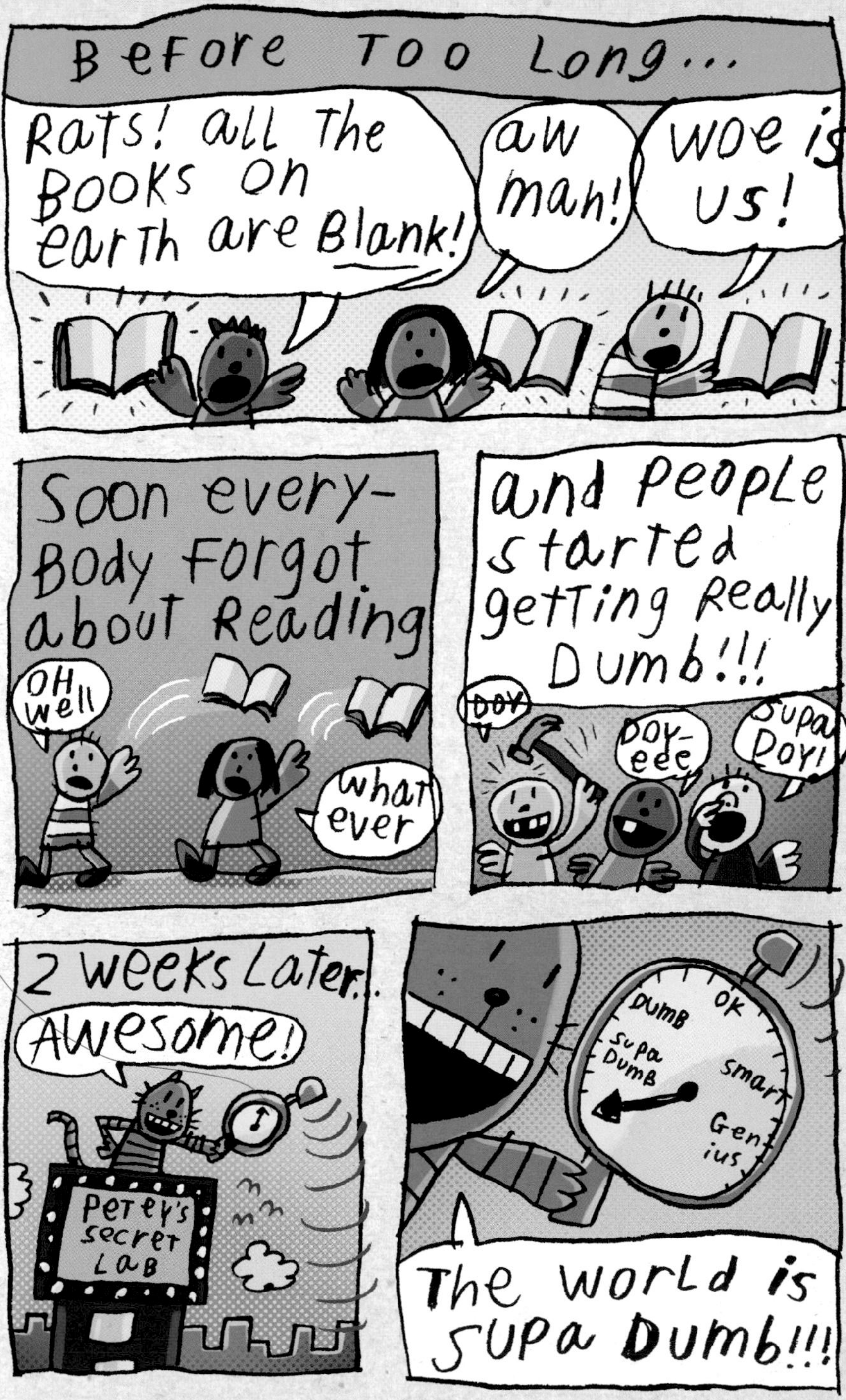
Before Too Long...
Rats! all The Books on earth are Blank!
aw man!
woe is us!
Soon every-Body Forgot about Reading
OH well
what ever
and People started getting Really Dumb!!!
DOY
DOY-eee
Supa DOY!
2 weeks Later...
Awesome!
Petey's Secret LAB
DUMB
OK
Supa DUMB
Smart
Genius
The world is Supa Dumb!!!

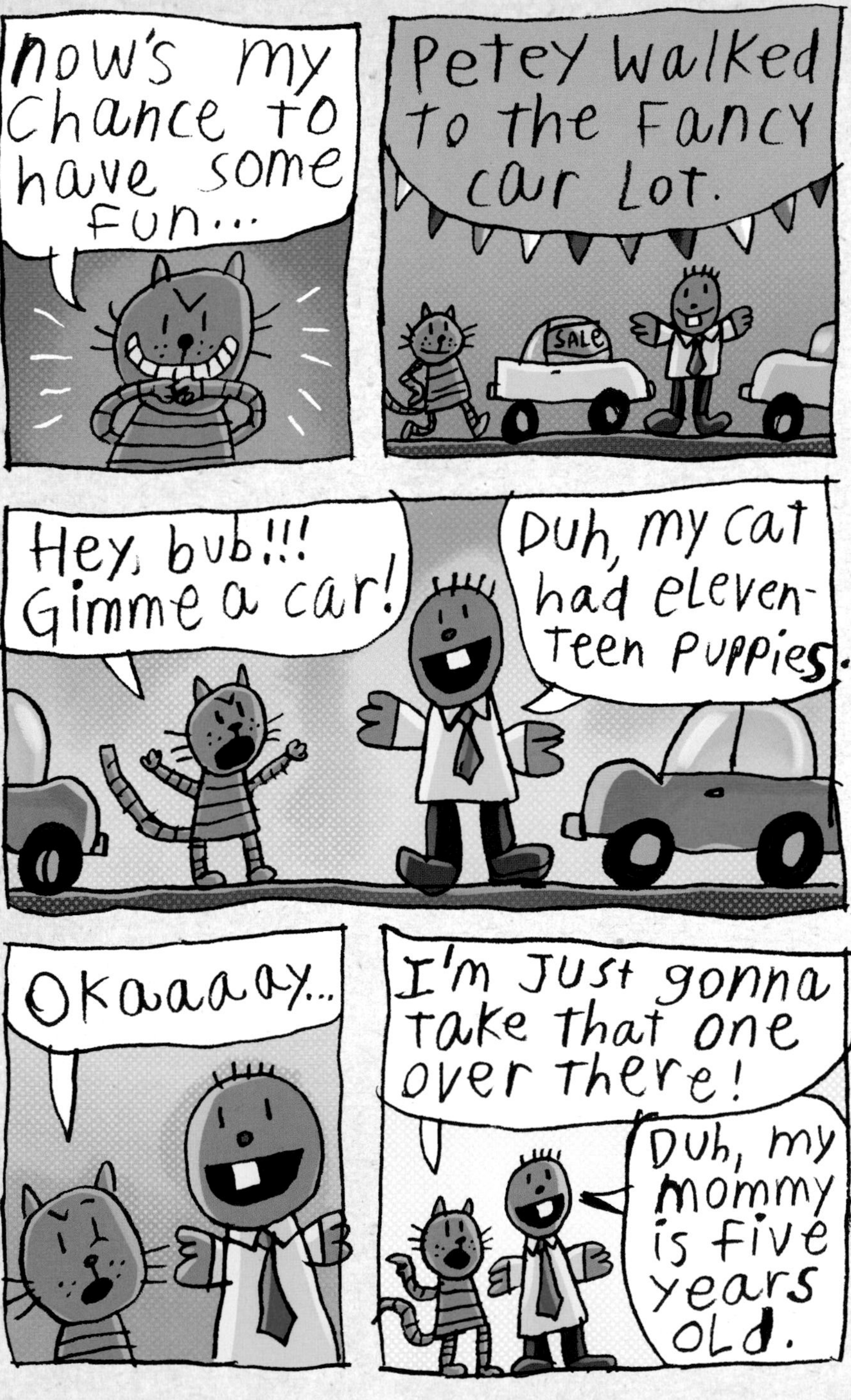
Now's my Chance to have some Fun...
Petey walked to the Fancy car Lot.
SALE
Hey, bub!!! Gimme a car!
Duh, my cat had eleven-teen puppies.
Okaaaay...
I'm just gonna take that one over there!
Duh, my mommy is five years old.

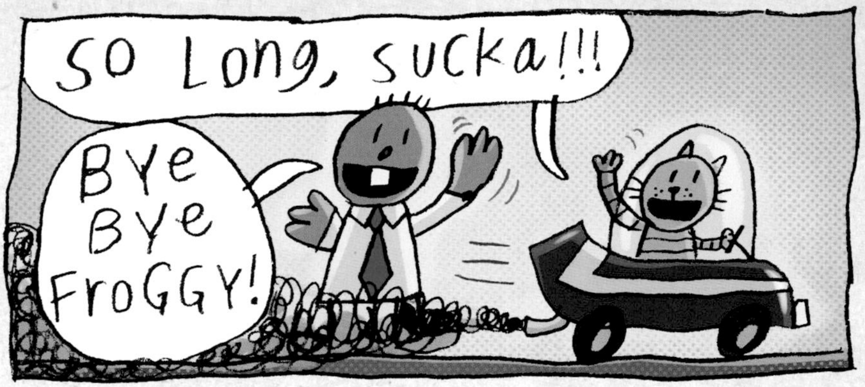
SO LONG, SUCKA!!!
BYE BYE FROGGY!

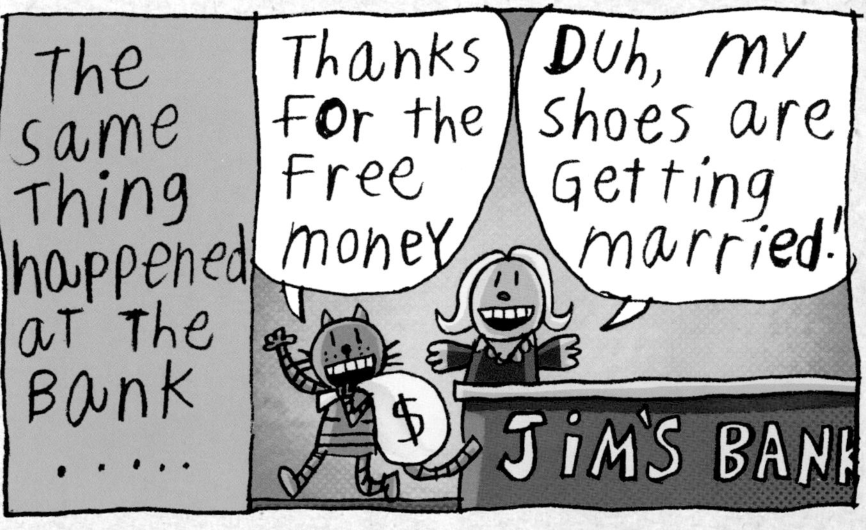
The same Thing happened at The Bank . . . . .
Thanks FOr the Free money
DUh, my shoes are Getting married!
JIM'S BANK

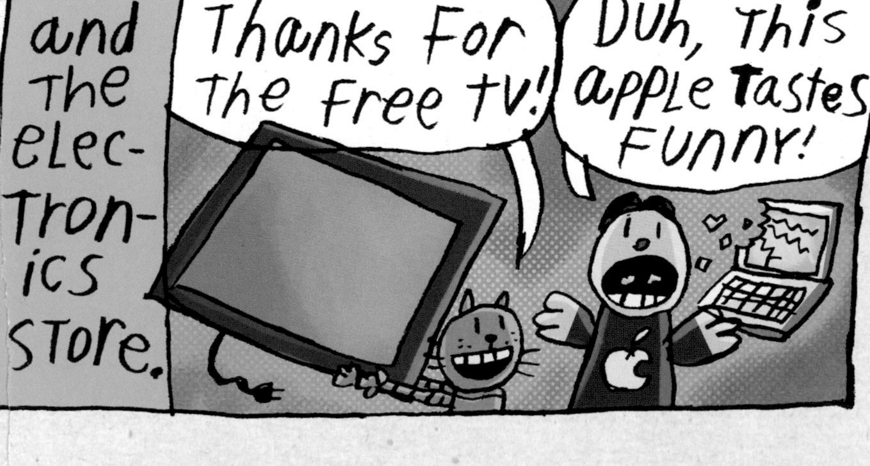
and The elec-Tron-ics sTore.
Thanks For The Free TV!
DUh, This apple Tastes FUNNY!

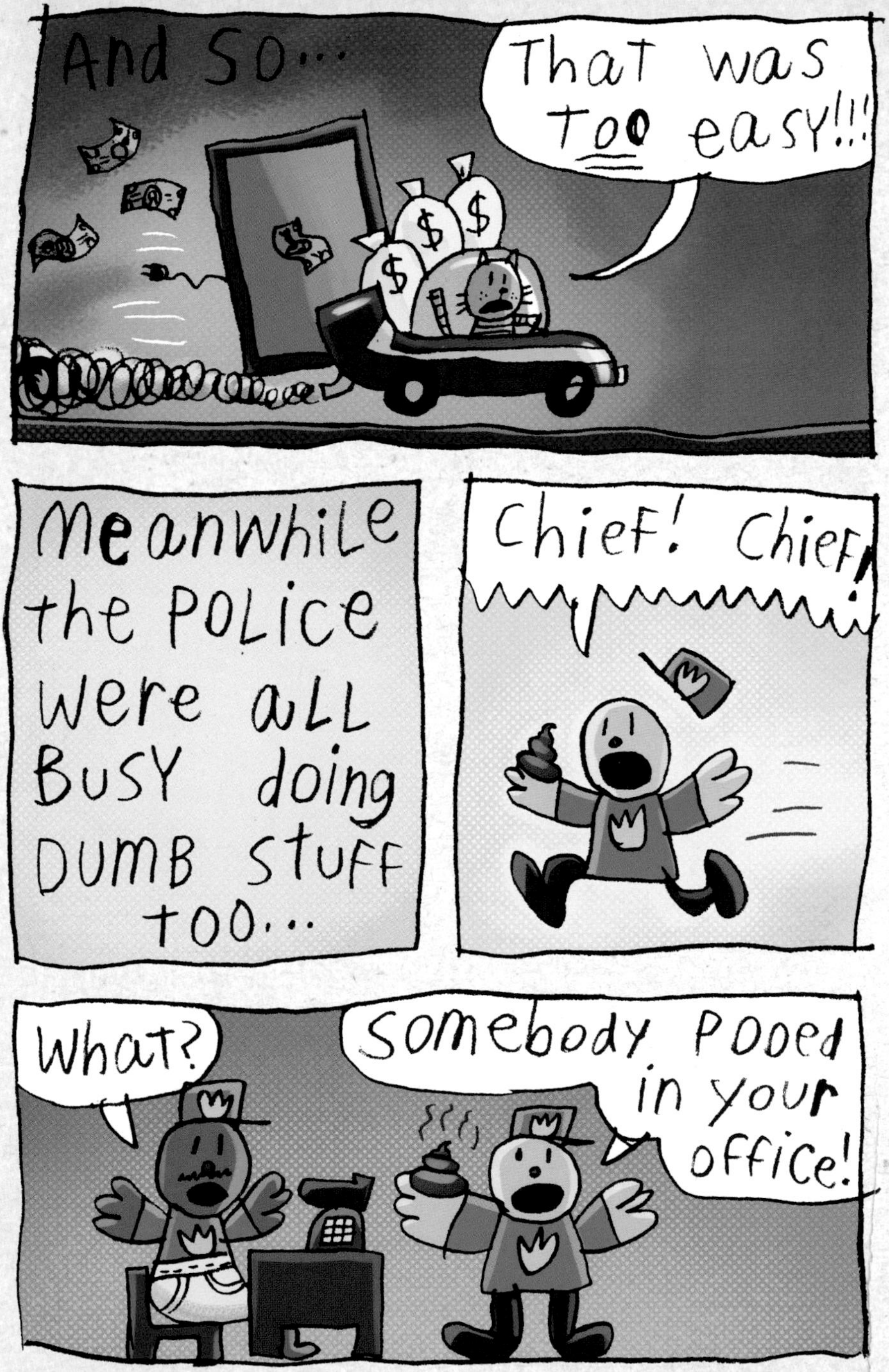
And so...
That was TOO easy!!!
Meanwhile the POLICE were all BUSY doing DUMB STUFF too...
Chief! Chief!
What?
Somebody pooed in your office!

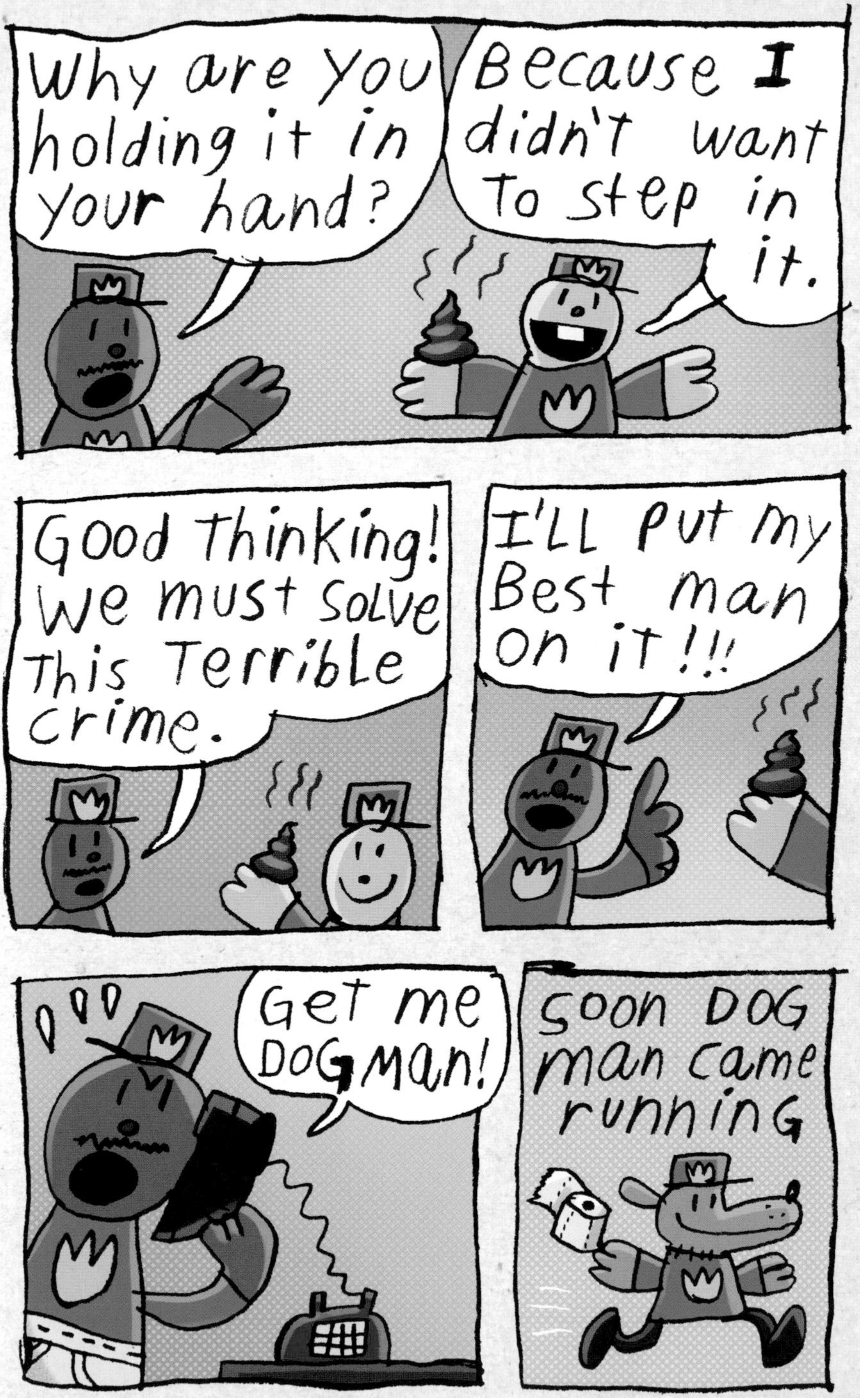
Why are you holding it in your hand?
Because I didn't want To step in it.
Good Thinking! We must solve This Terrible crime.
I'LL Put my Best man on it!!!
Get me DOG MAN!
Soon DOG man came running

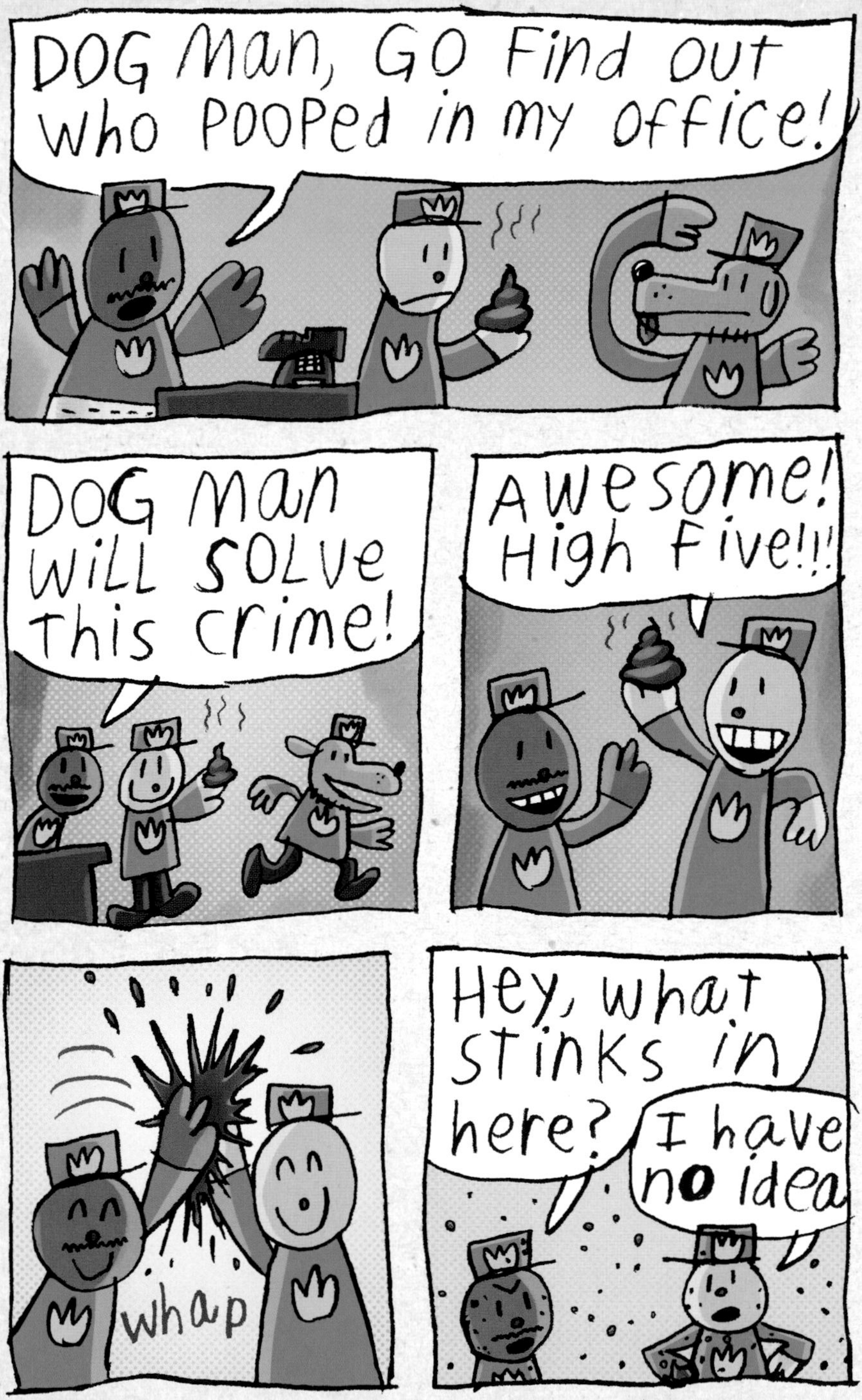
DOG Man, GO Find out who POOPed in my office!
DOG Man WiLL SOLVe This crime!
Awesome! High Five!!!
whap
Hey, what stinks in here?
I have no idea

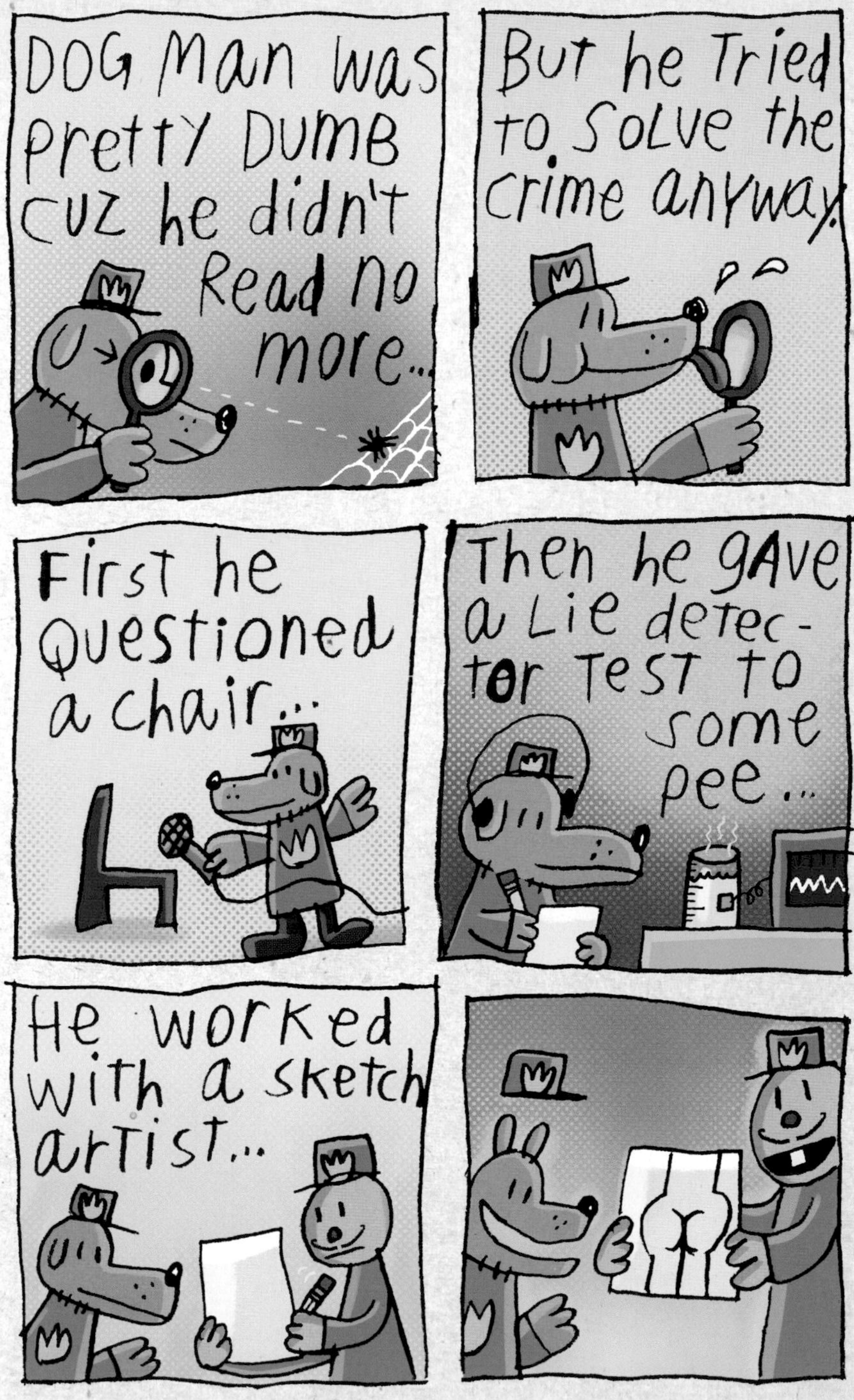
DOG Man was pretty DUMB cuz he didn't Read no more...
But he Tried to Solve the crime anyway.
First he Questioned a chair...
Then he gAVe a Lie detector Test to some pee...
He worked with a sketch artist...

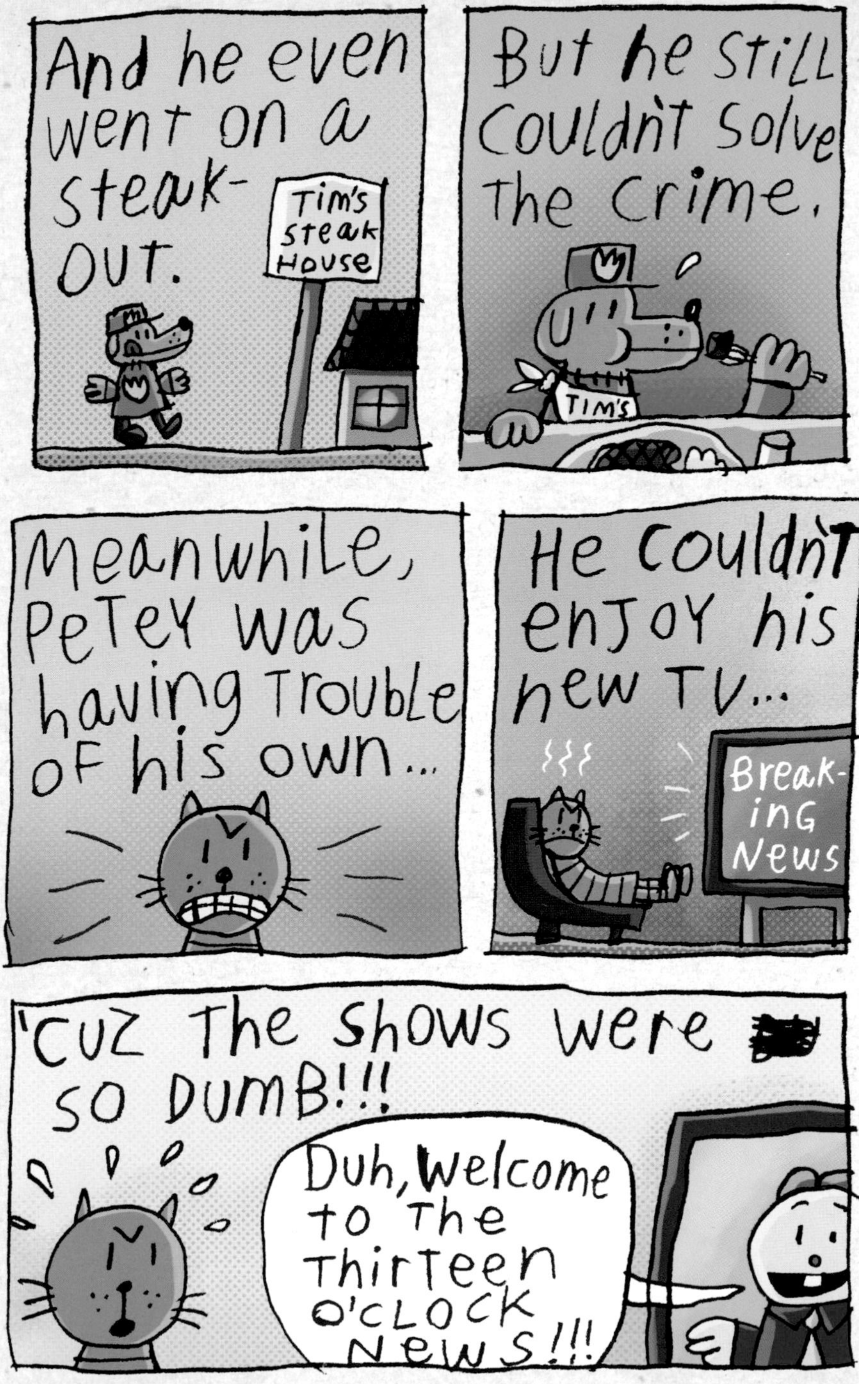
And he even went on a steak-out.
Tim's Steak House
But he still couldn't solve the crime.
Tim's
Meanwhile, Petey was having trouble of his own...
He couldn't enjoy his new TV...
Breaking News
'Cuz the shows were [redacted] so DUMB!!!
Duh, welcome to the Thirteen O'Clock News!!!

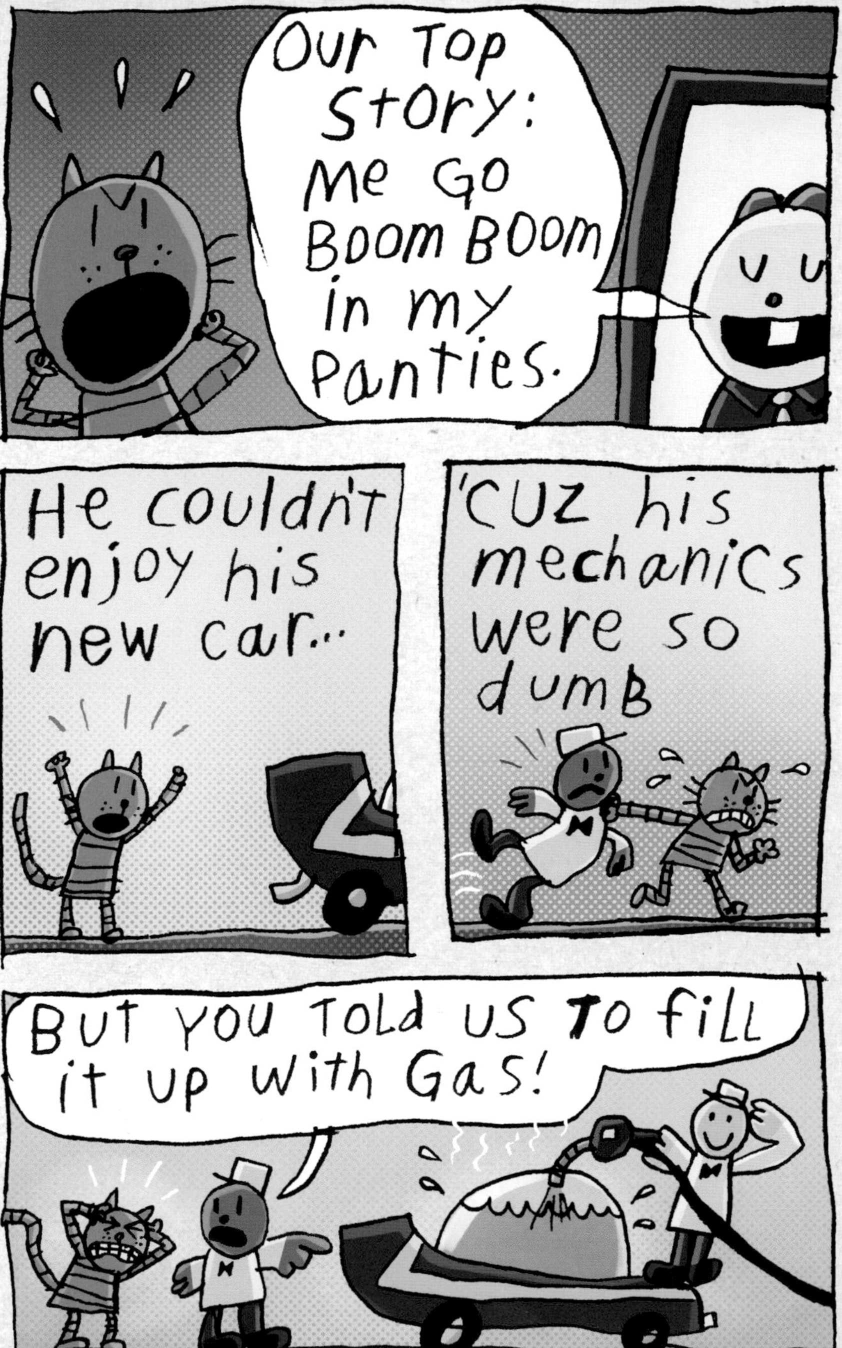
Our Top Story: Me Go Boom Boom in my Panties.
He couldn't enjoy his new car...
'Cuz his mechanics were so dumb
But you Told us To fill it up with Gas!

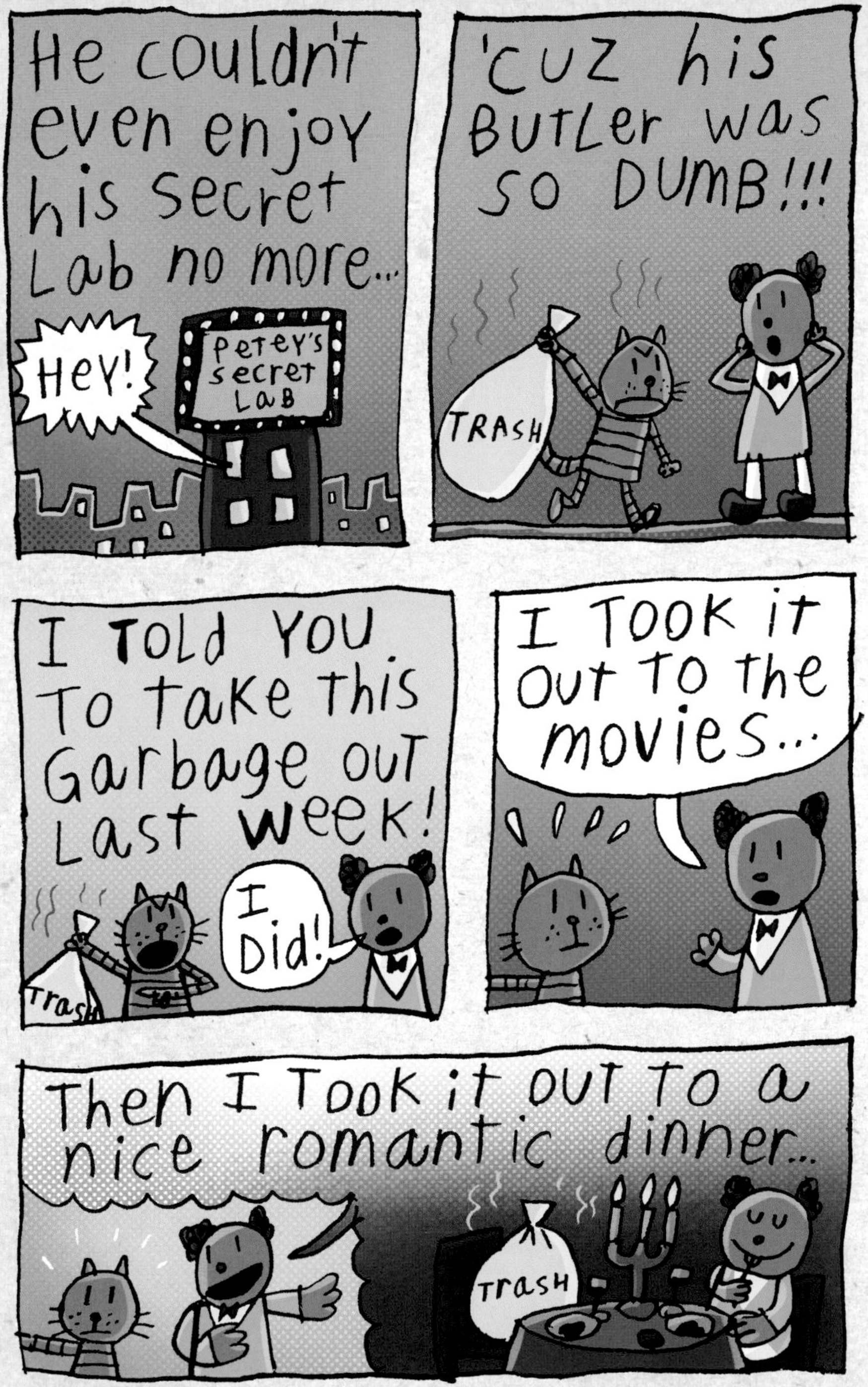
He couldn't even enjoy his secret Lab no more...
HEY!
Petey's secret Lab
'Cuz his Butler was so DUMB!!!
TRASH
I TOLd YOU To take this Garbage out Last week!
Trash
I Did!
I Took it out to the movies...
Then I Took it out to a nice romantic dinner...
Trash

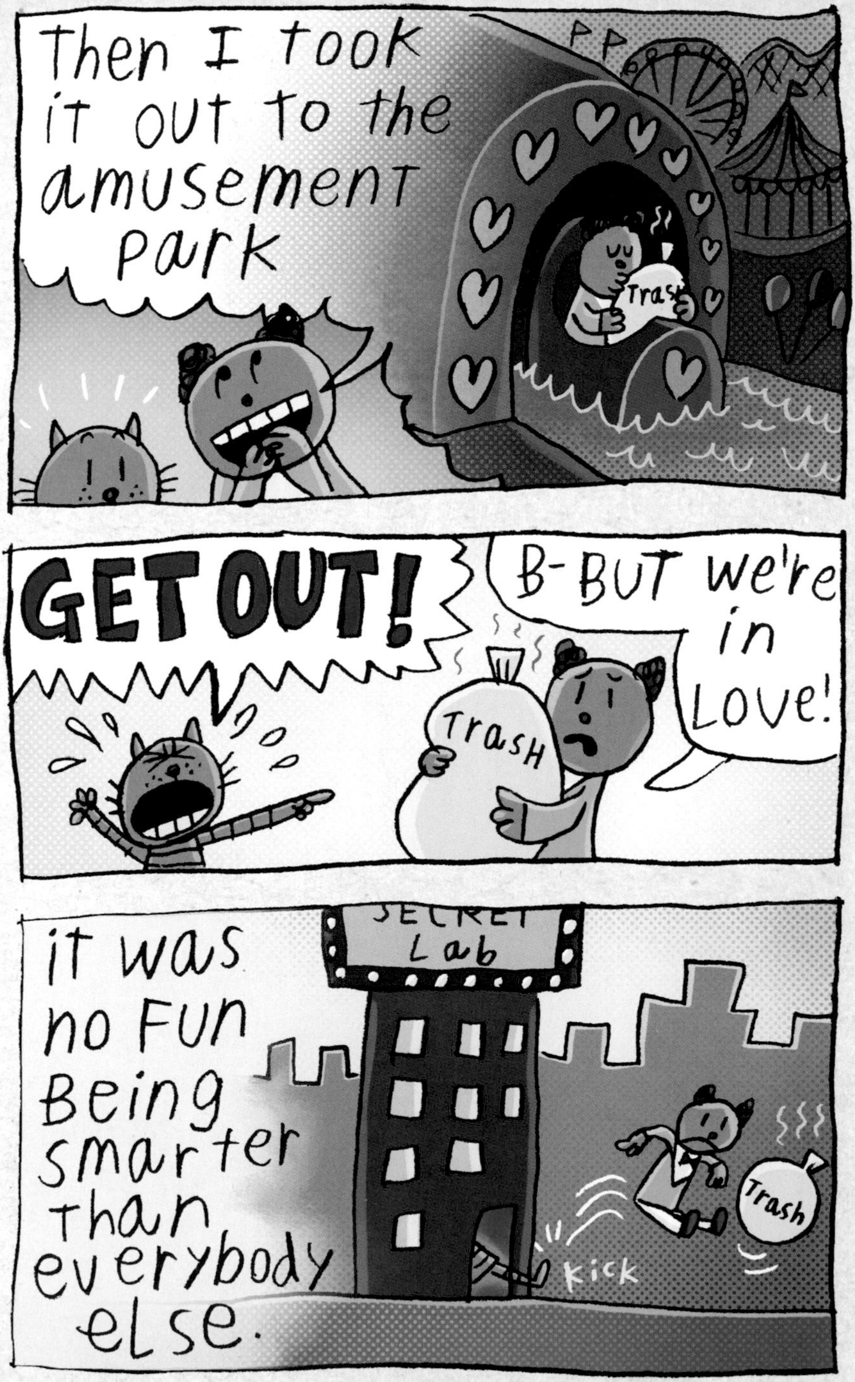
Then I took it out to the amusement park
GET OUT!
B-BUT we're in Love!
Trash
Lab
it was no Fun Being smarter than everybody else.
Kick
Trash

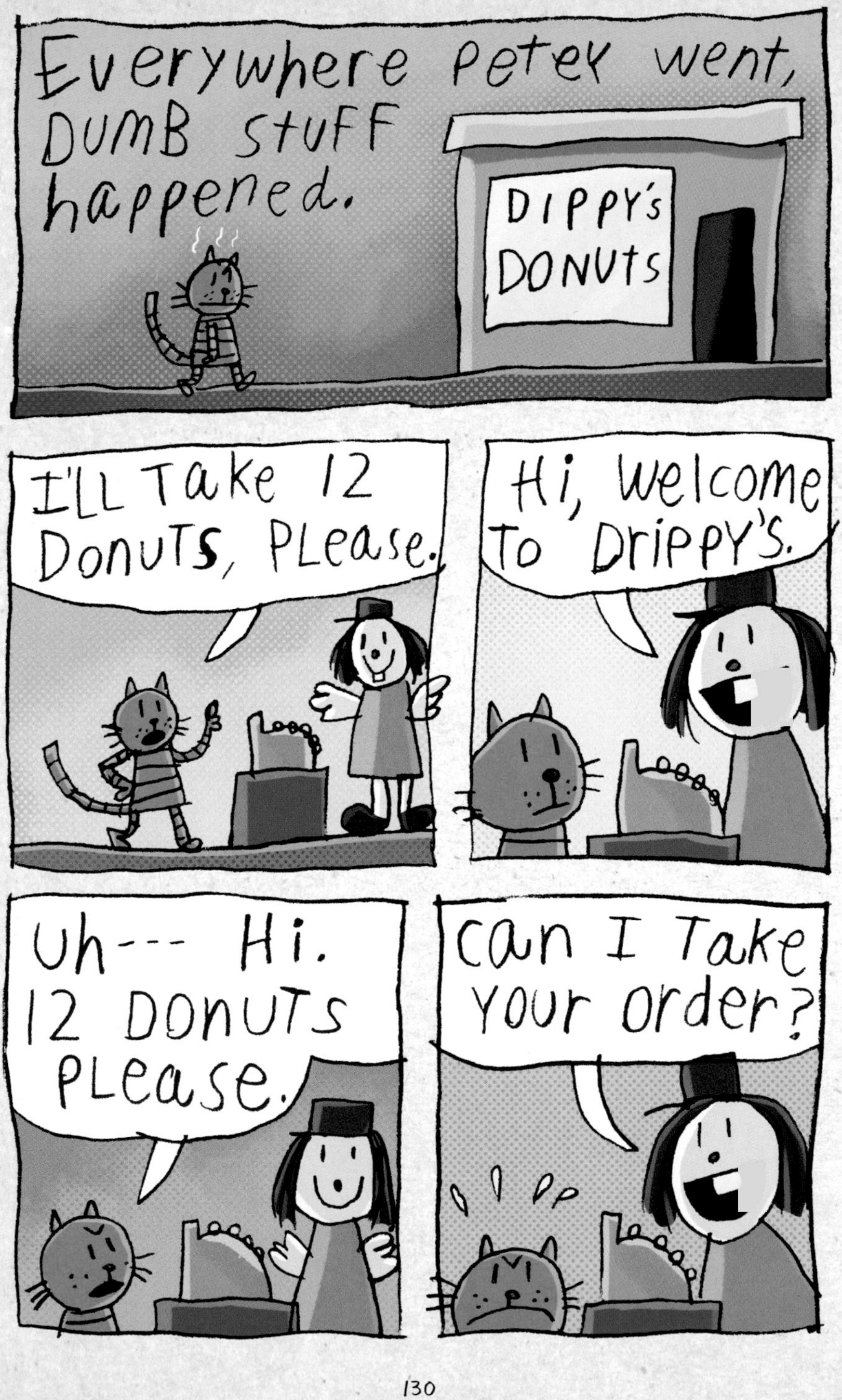
Everywhere Peter went, DUMB STUFF happened.
DIPPY'S DONUTS
I'LL Take 12 DonuTS, PLease.
Hi, Welcome To DriPPY'S.
Uh--- Hi. 12 DONUTS PLease.
Can I Take Your order?

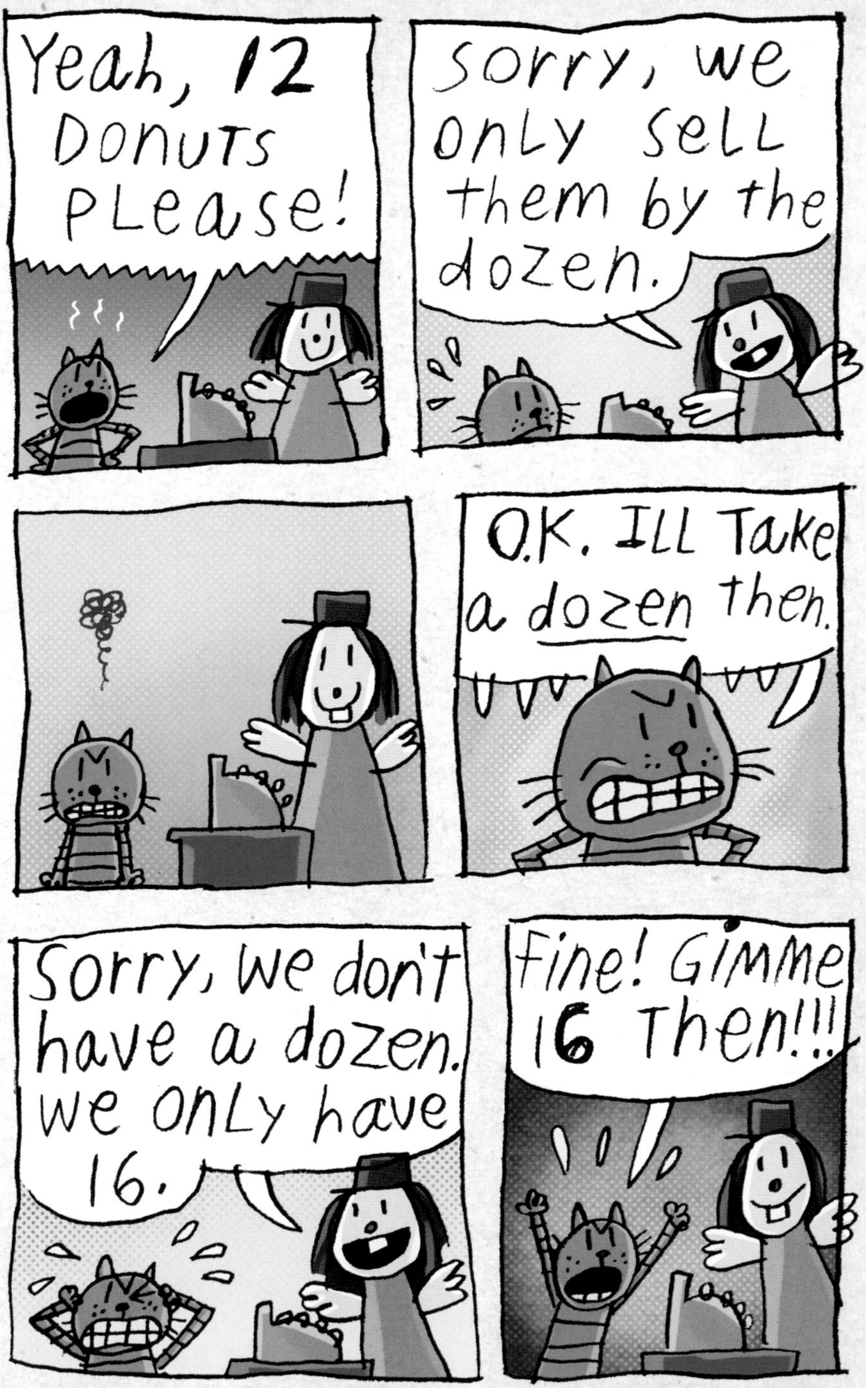
Yeah, 12 DONUTS PLEase!
Sorry, we only sell them by the dozen.
O.K. ILL Take a dozen then.
Sorry, we don't have a dozen. We ONLY have 16.
Fine! Gimme 16 Then!!!

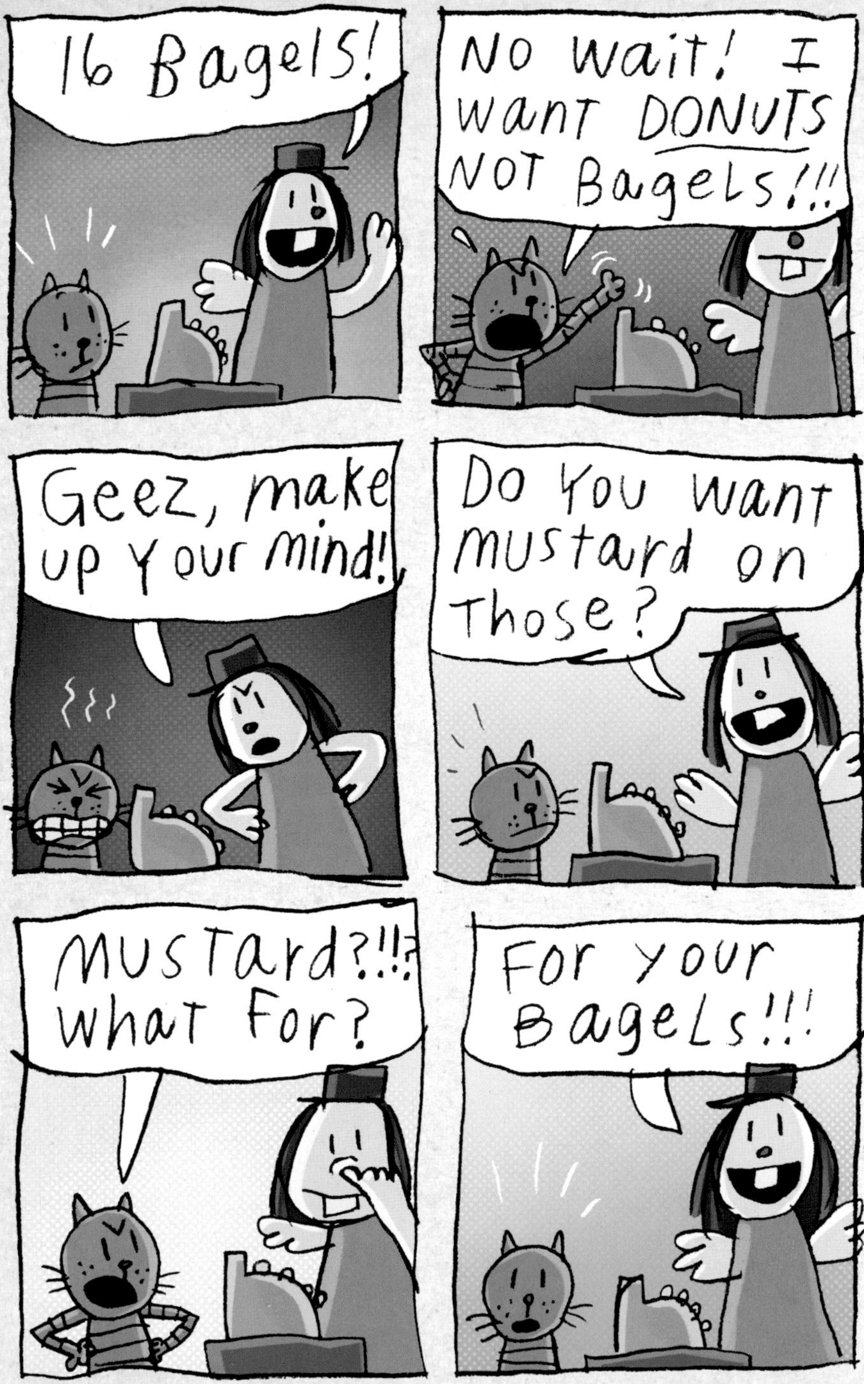
16 Bagels!
No wait! I want DONUTS NOT Bagels!!!
Geez, make up your mind!
Do you want mustard on Those?
MUSTard?!!? What For?
For your Bagels!!!

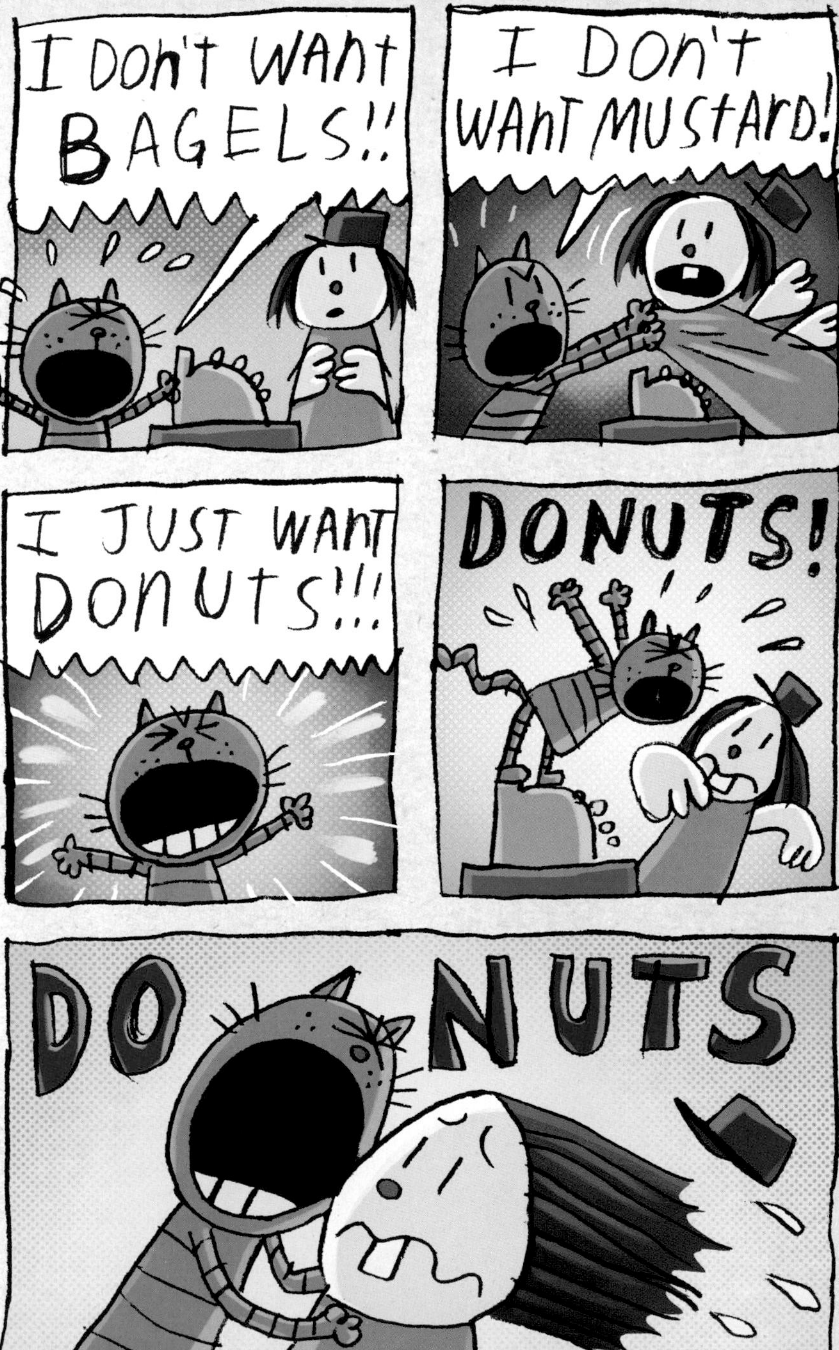
I DON'T WANT BAGELS!!
I DON'T WANT MUSTARD!
I JUST WANT DONUTS!!!
DONUTS!
DONUTS

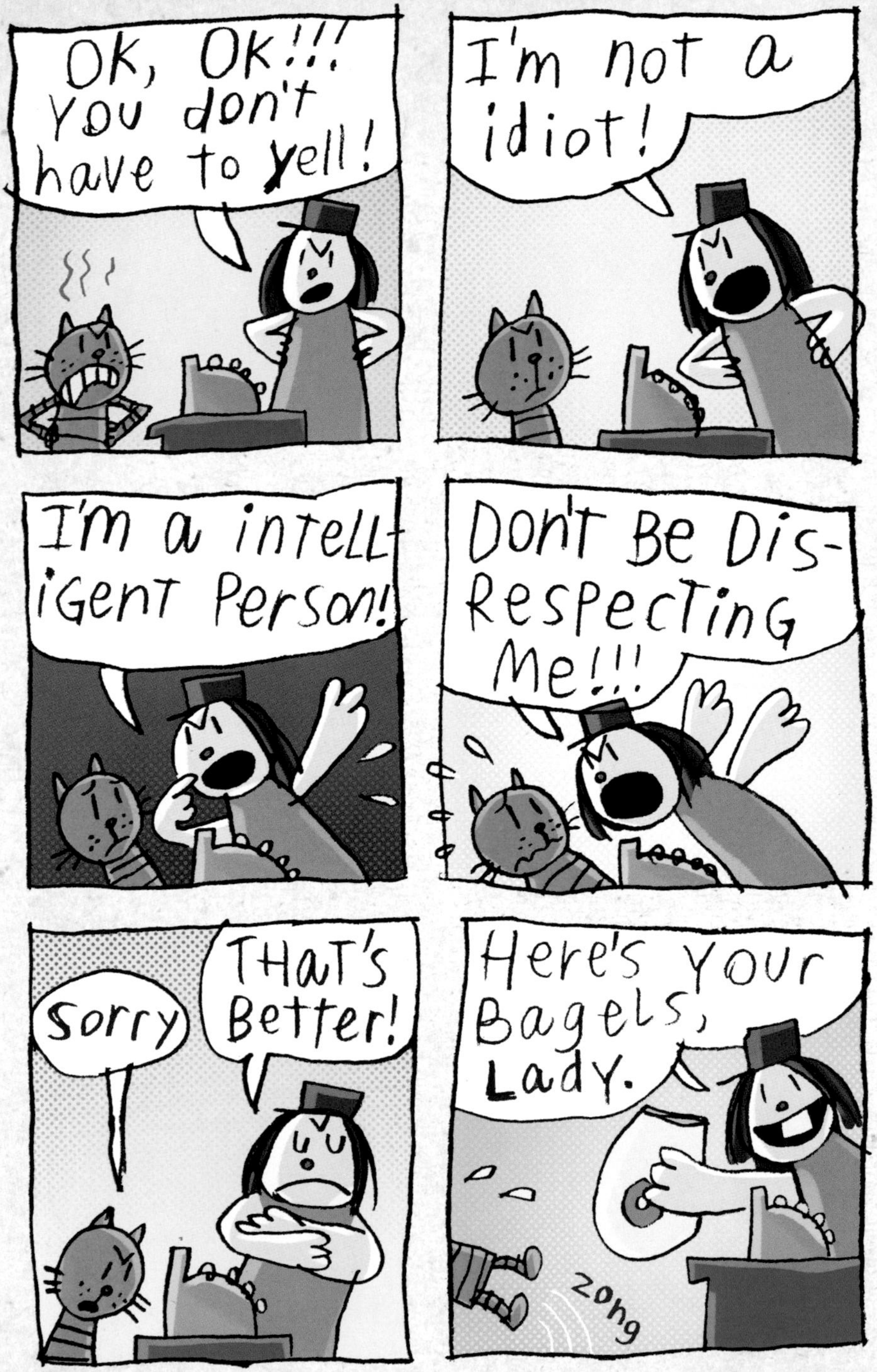
OK, OK!!! You don't have to yell!
I'm not a idiot!
I'm a intell-igent Person!
Don't Be Dis-Respecting Me!!!
Sorry
THAT'S Better!
Here's Your Bagels, Lady.
zohg

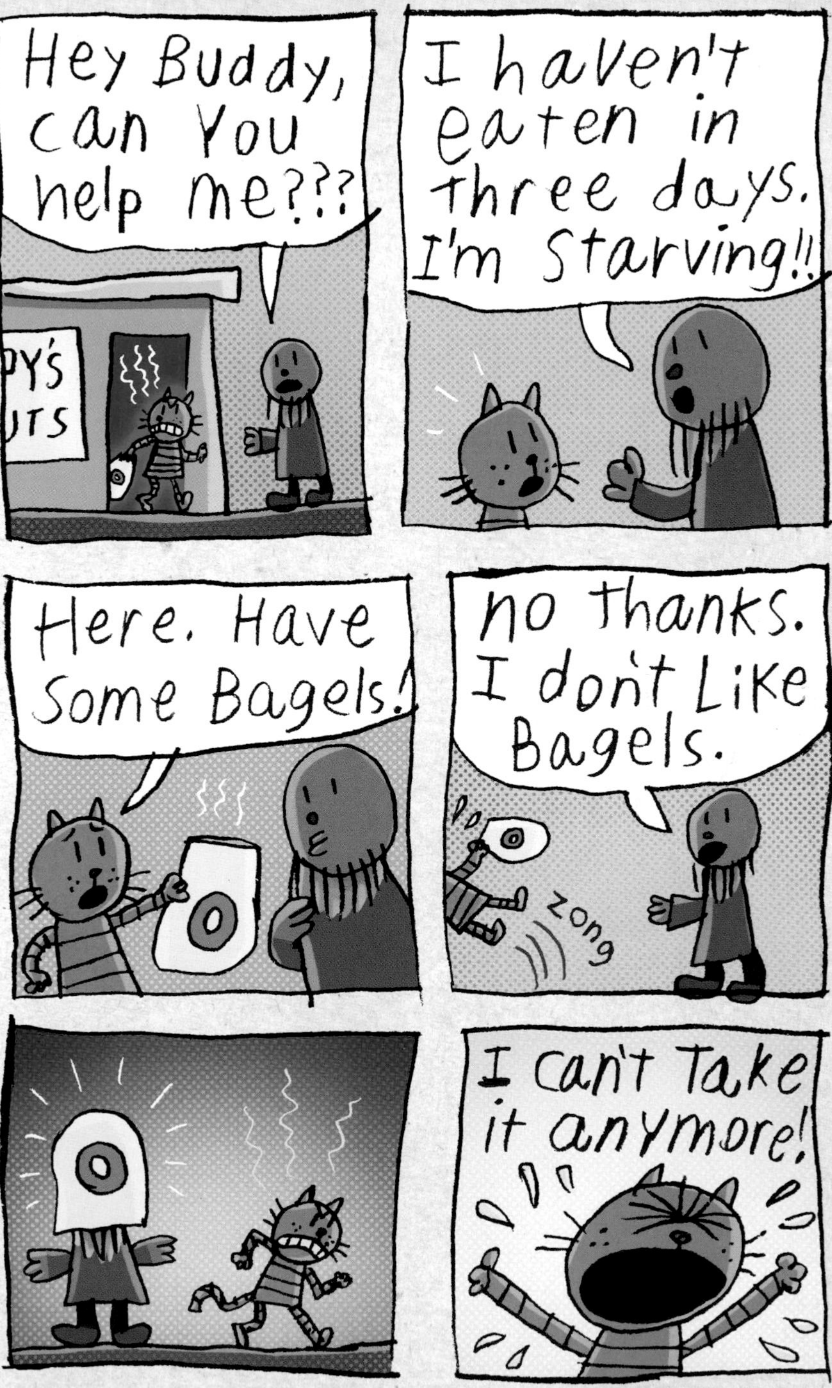
Hey Buddy, can You help me???
PY'S
UTS
I haven't eaten in three days. I'm Starving!!
Here. Have Some Bagels!
no thanks. I don't Like Bagels.
ZONG
I can't Take it anymore!

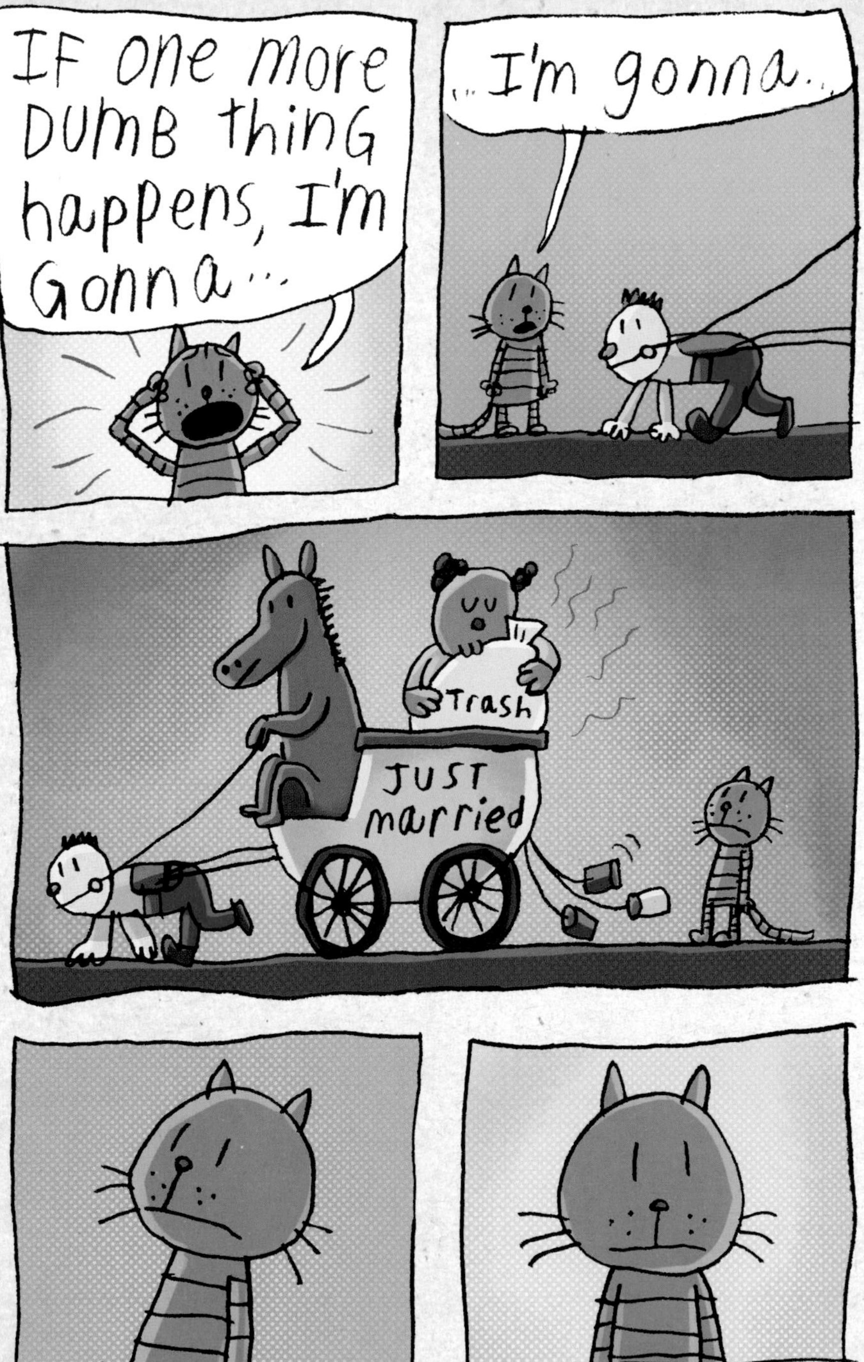
IF one more DUMB thinG happens, I'm Gonna...
...I'm gonna...
Trash
JUST married

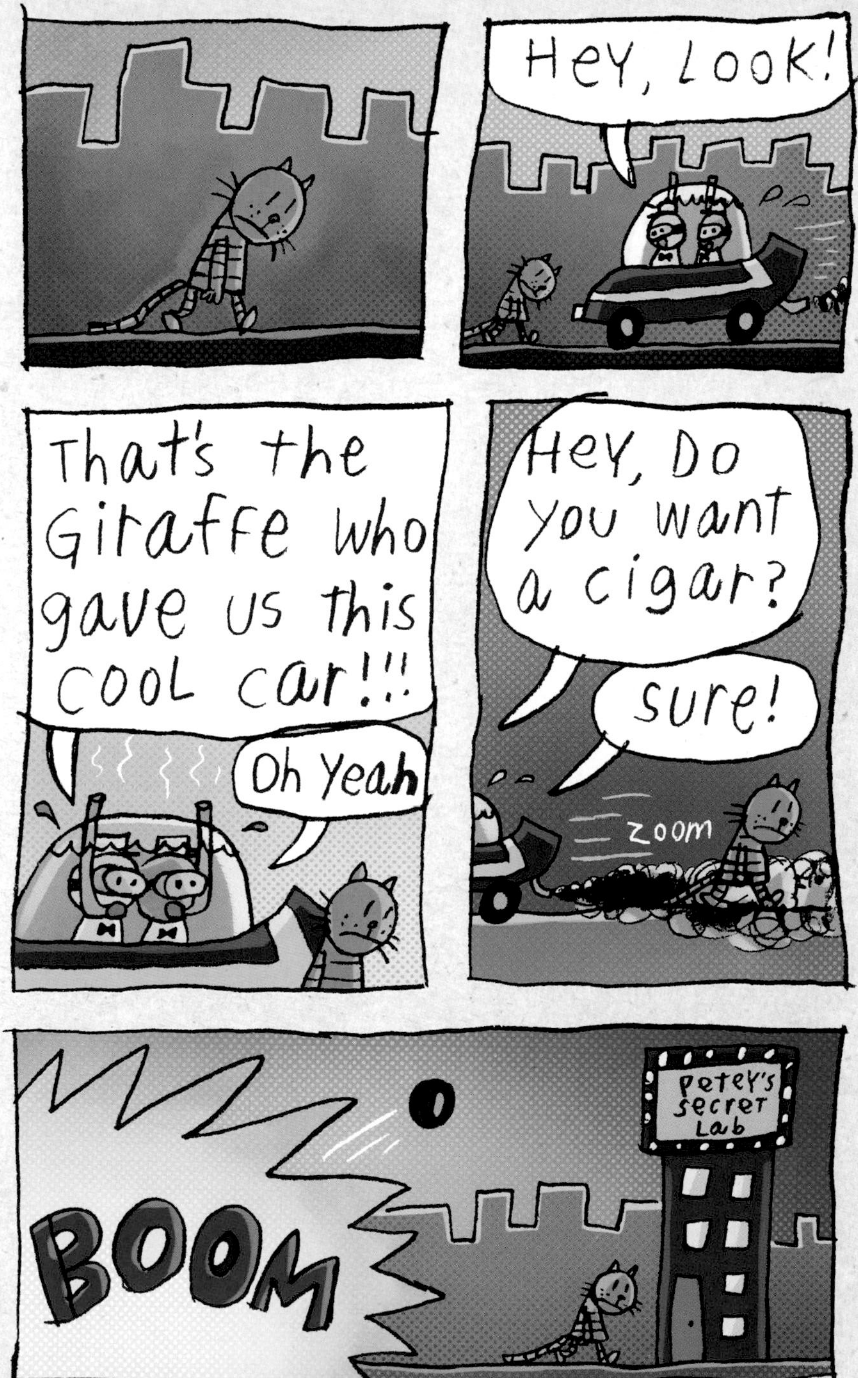
HEY, LOOK!
That's the Giraffe who gave us this cool car!!!
Oh Yeah
Hey, Do you want a cigar?
sure!
zoom
BOOM
petey's secret Lab

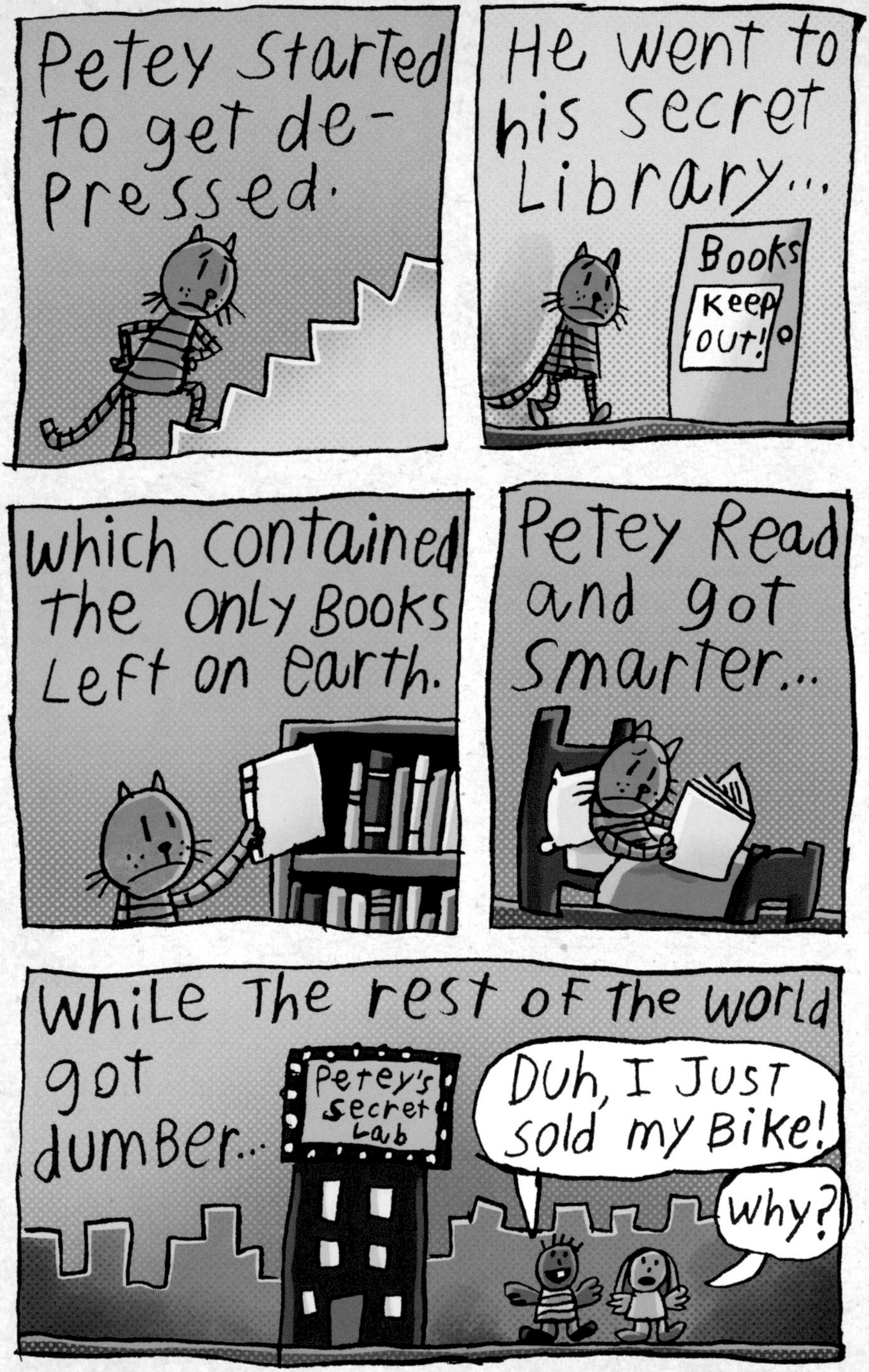
Petey Started to get de-pressed.
He went to his secret Library...
Books
Keep out!
which contained the only Books Left on earth.
Petey Read and got Smarter...
while The rest of the world got dumBer...
Petey's Secret Lab
Duh, I JUST sold my Bike!
why?

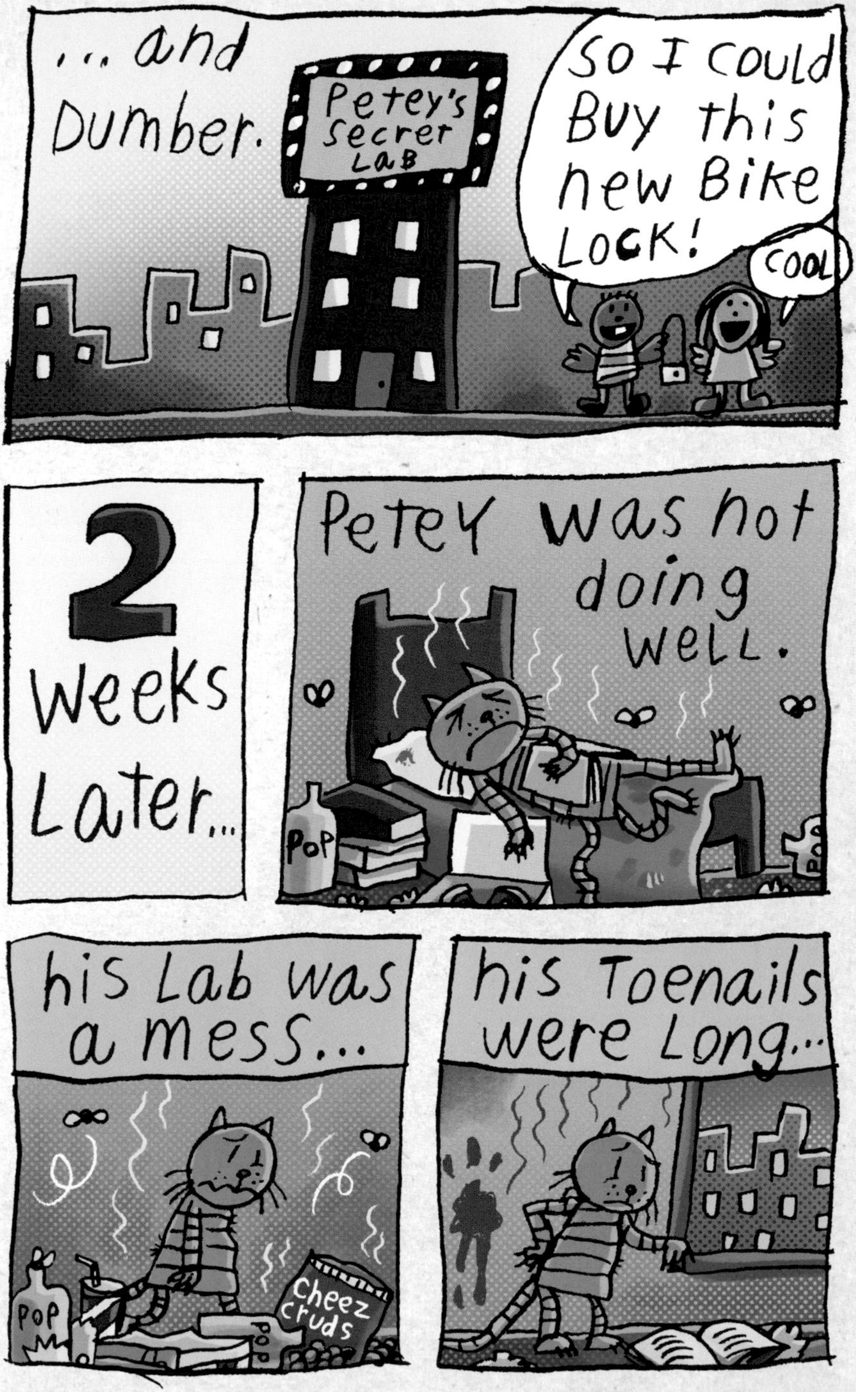

... and Dumber.
Petey's Secret Lab
So I could Buy this new Bike Lock!
COOL
2 Weeks Later...
Petey was not doing well.
POP
his Lab was a mess...
POP
Cheez Cruds
POP
his Toenails were Long...

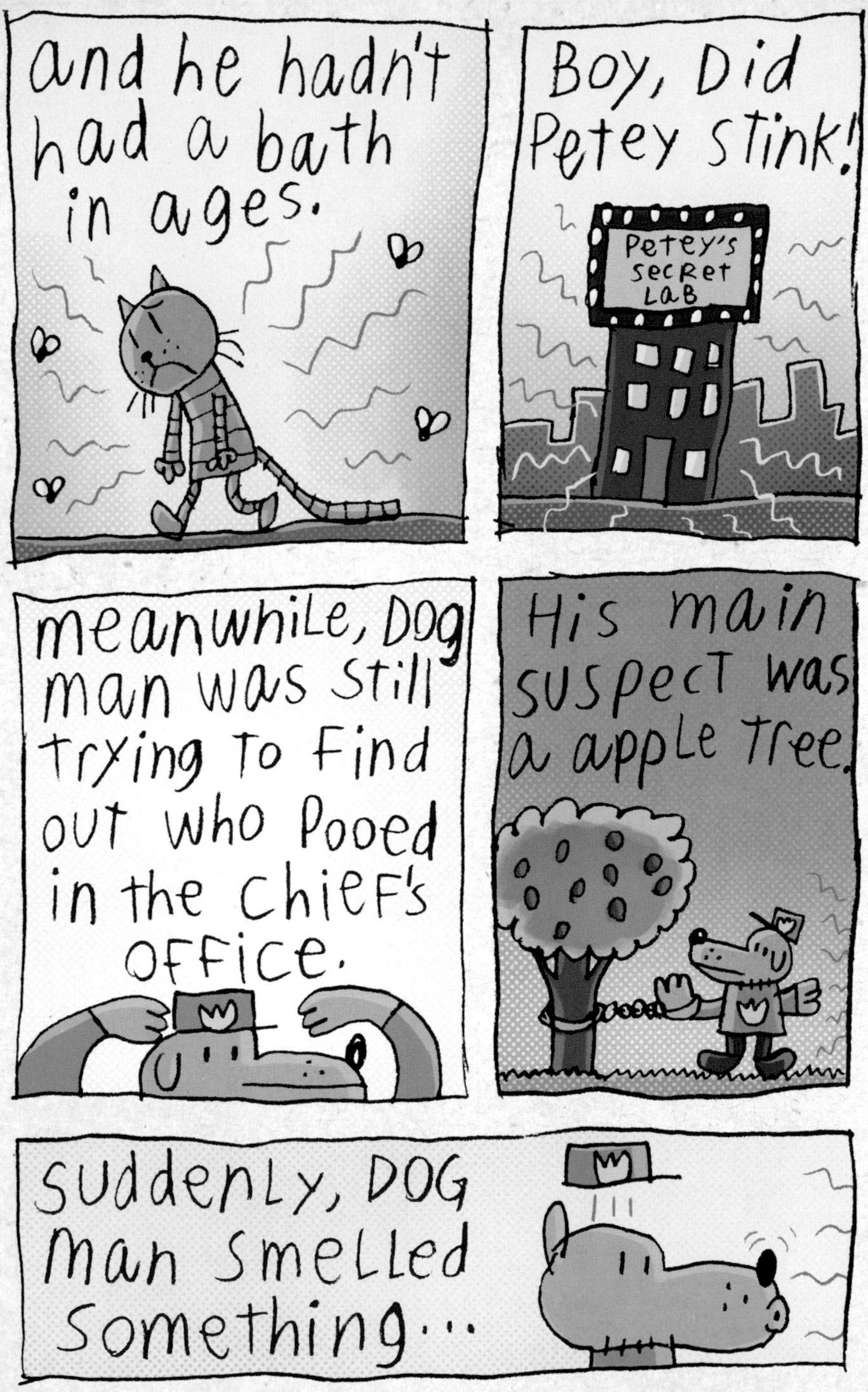
and he hadn't had a bath in ages.
Boy, Did Petey Stink!
Petey's Secret Lab
meanwhile, Dog man was still trying to Find out who Pooed in the Chief's office.
His main suspect was a apple Tree.
suddenly, Dog man smelled something...

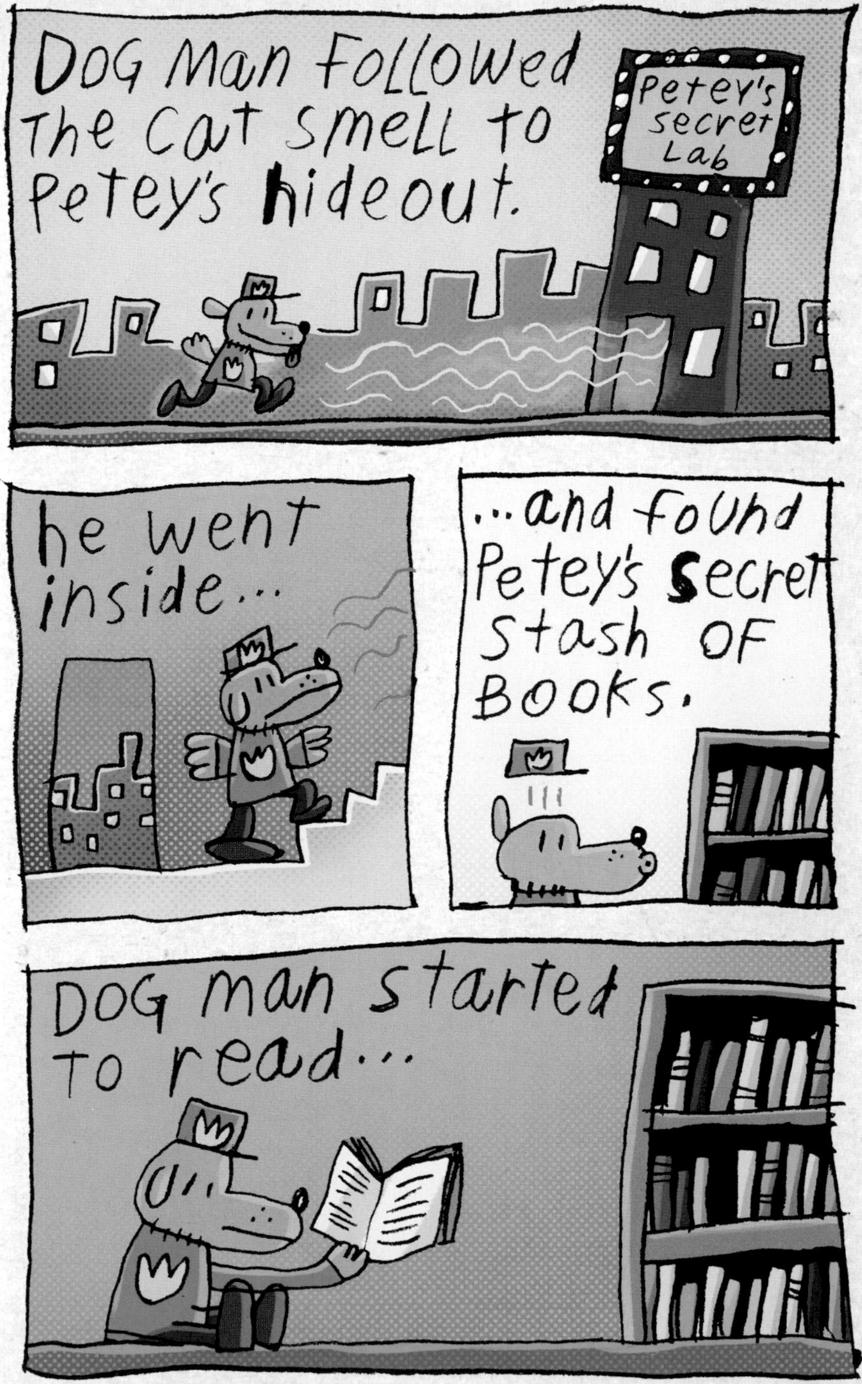

DOG MAN FOLLOWED THE CAT SMELL TO PETEY'S HIDEOUT.
Petey's secret Lab
he went inside...
...and found Petey's Secret Stash OF BOOKS.
DOG man started TO read...

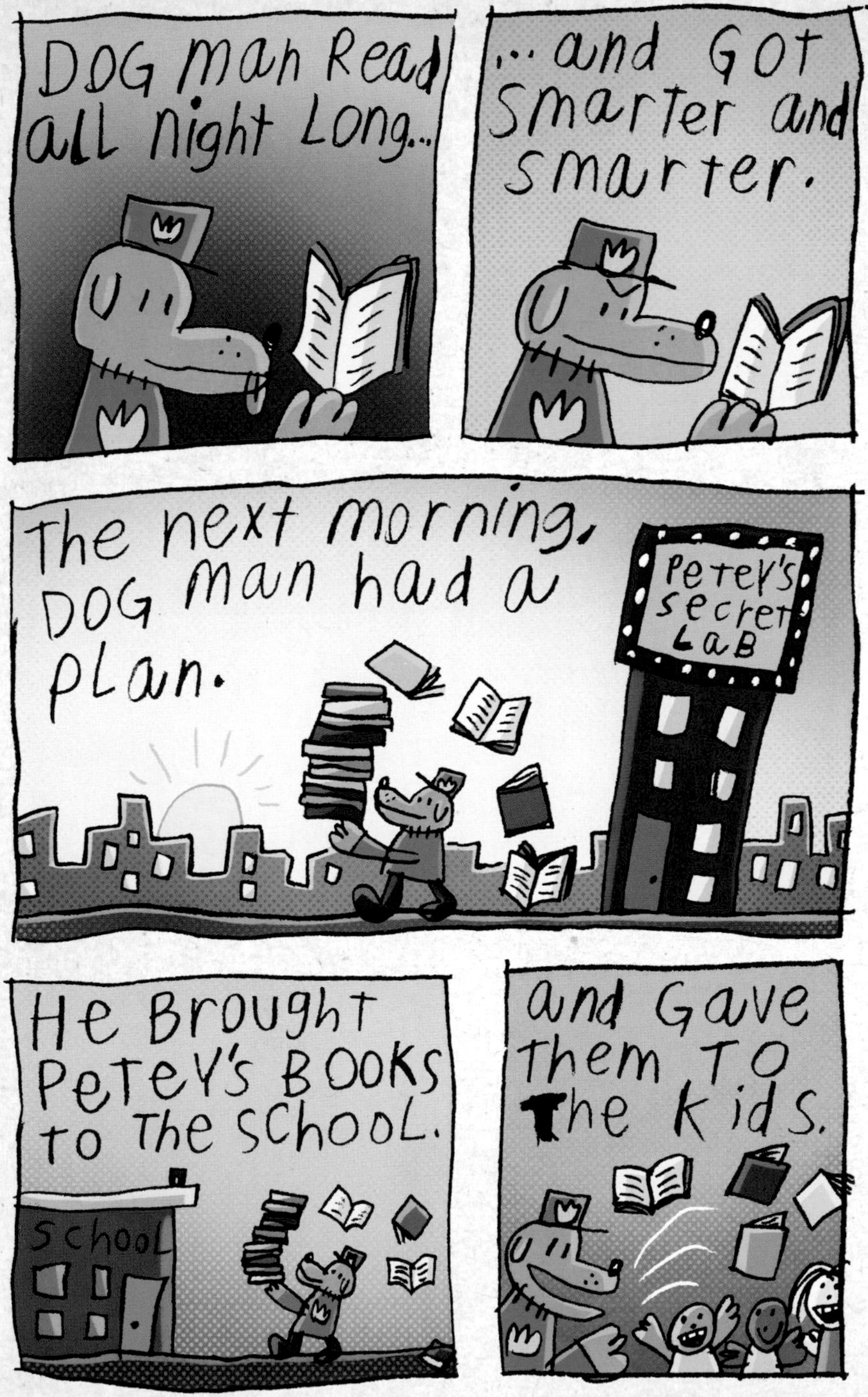
DOG man Read all night Long...
...and GOT Smarter and smarter.
The next morning, DOG man had a plan.
Petey's secret LaB
He Brought Petey's BOOKS to The SchooL.
SchooL
and Gave them TO The Kids.

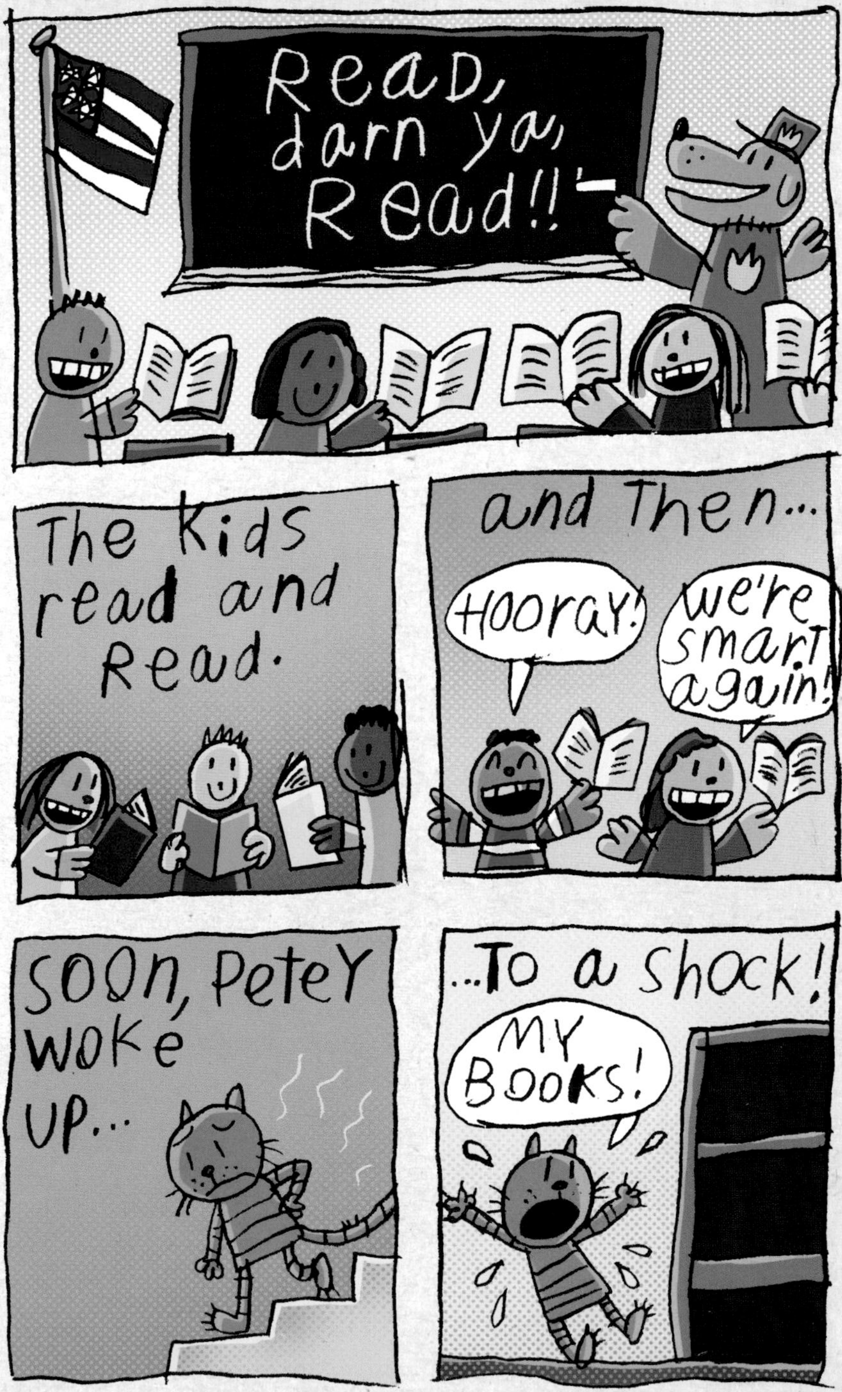
Read, darn ya, Read!!
The kids read and read.
and Then...
HOORAY!
We're smart again!
Soon, Petey woke up...
...To a shock!
MY BOOKS!

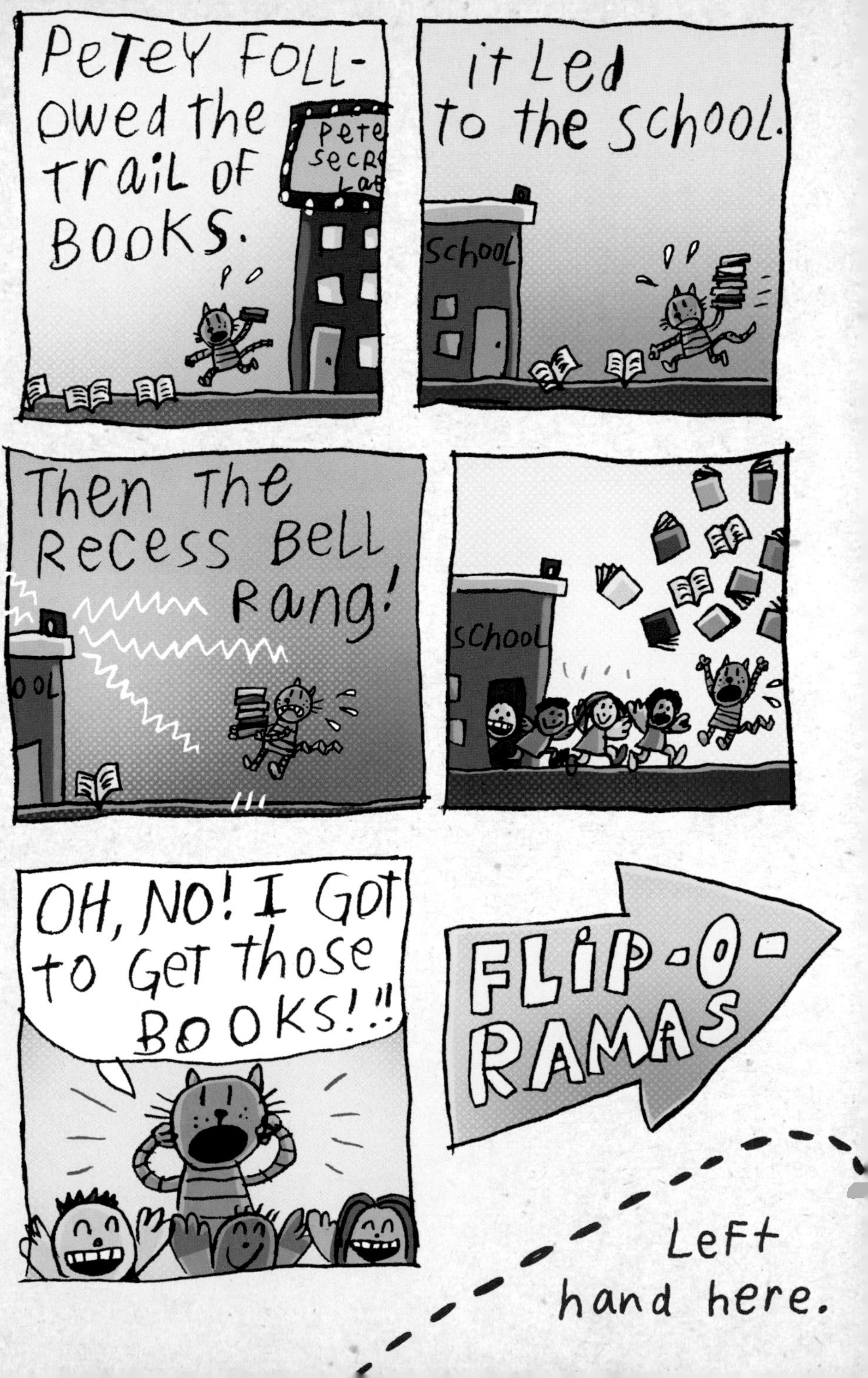
PETEY FOLL-owed the trail of BOOKS.
it Led to the school.
SCHOOL
Then The Recess Bell Rang!
SCHOOL
OH, NO! I GOT to Get those BOOKS!!!
FLIP-O-RAMAS
Left hand here.

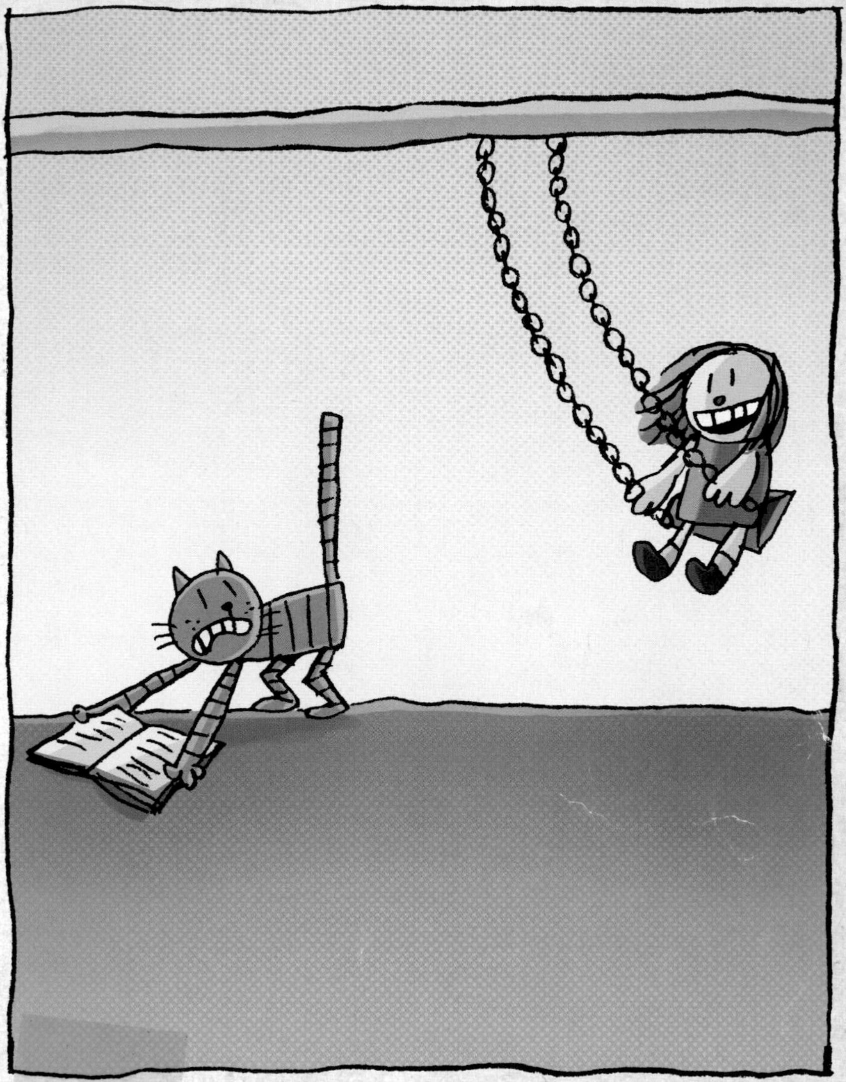

The Swing Set Smacker

Right Thumb here

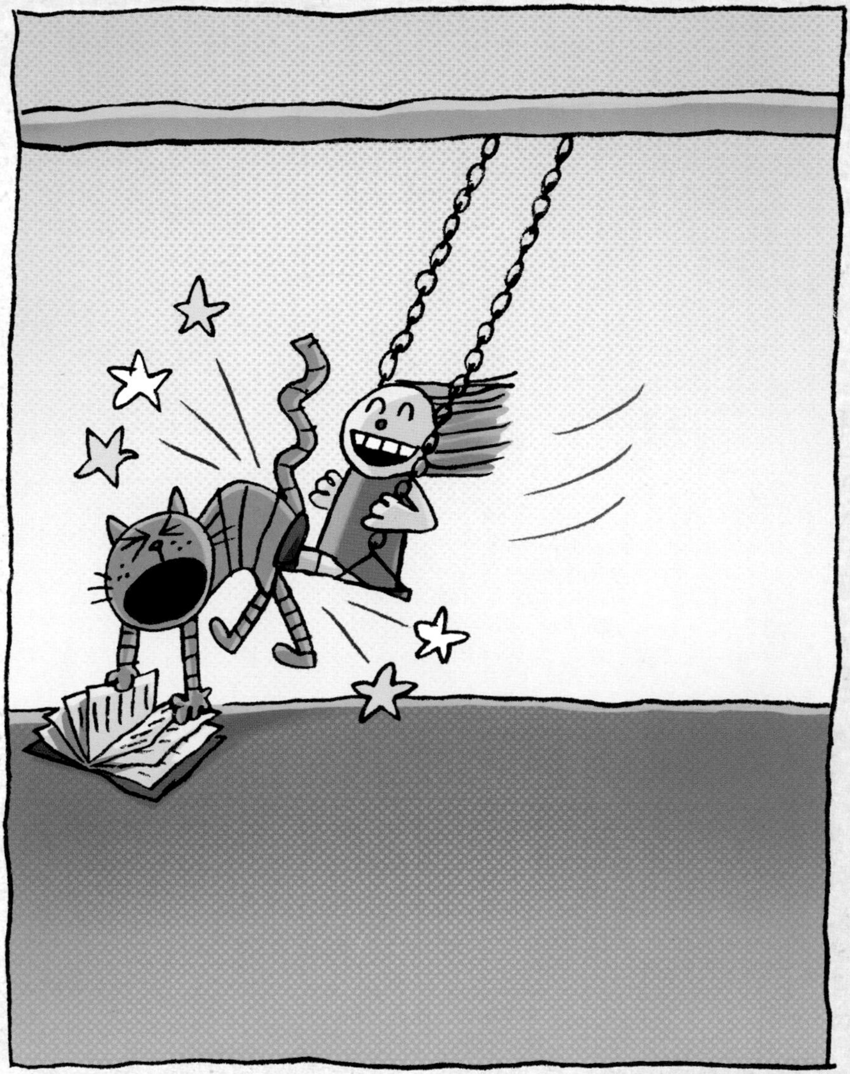

The Swing Set Smacker

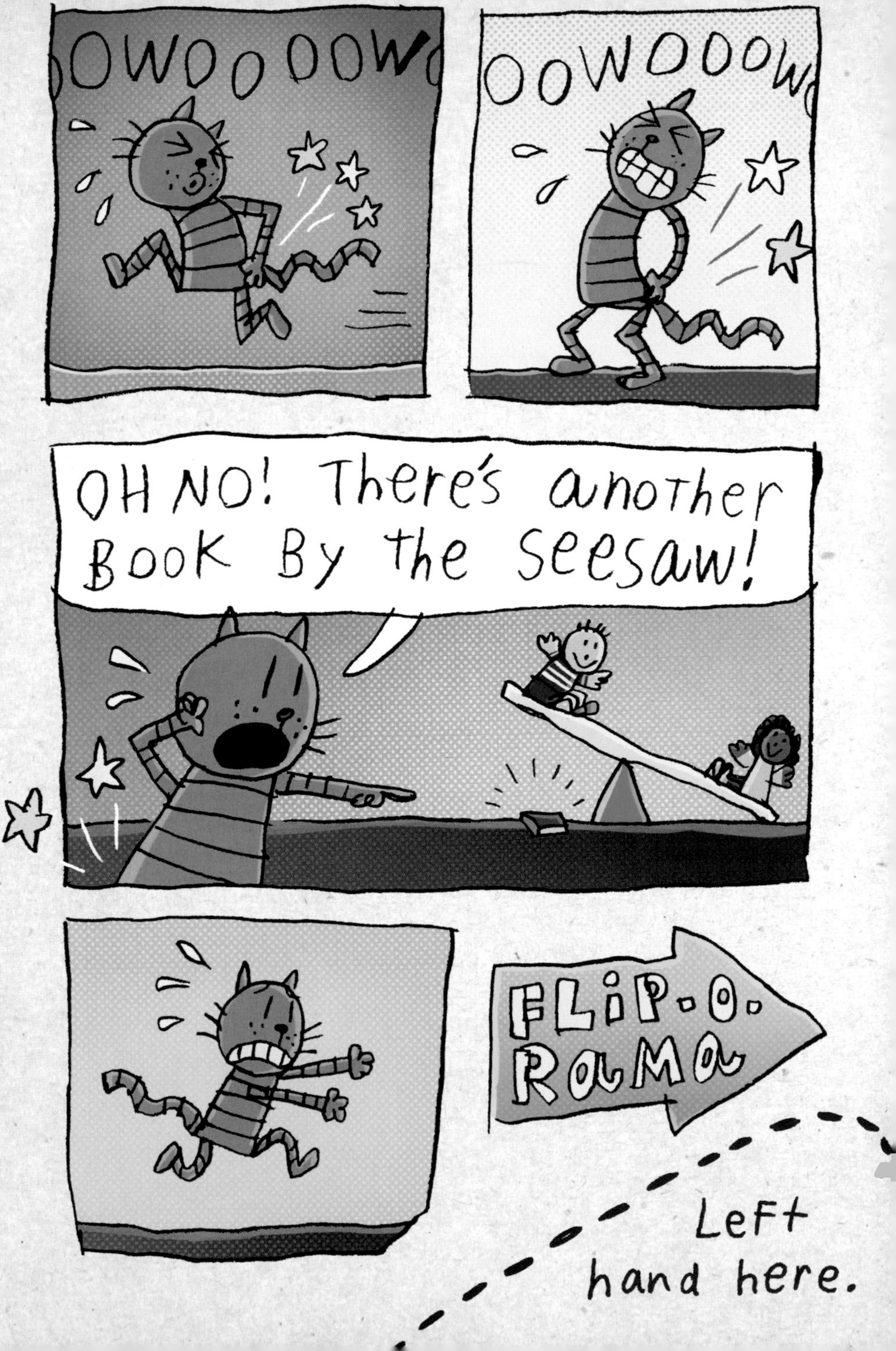

OOWOOOOOW
OOWOOOOOW
OH NO! There's another Book By the seesaw!
FLIP-O-RAMA
Left hand here.

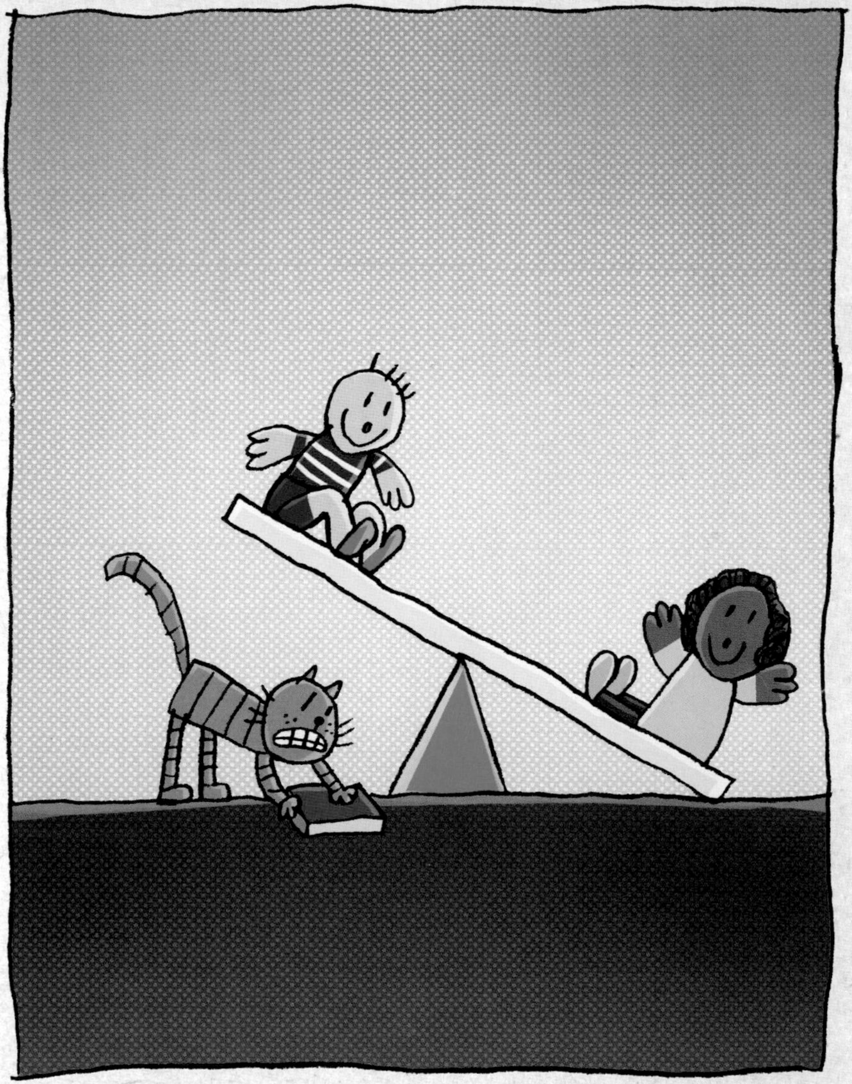

The Seesaw Smoosher

Right Thumb here.

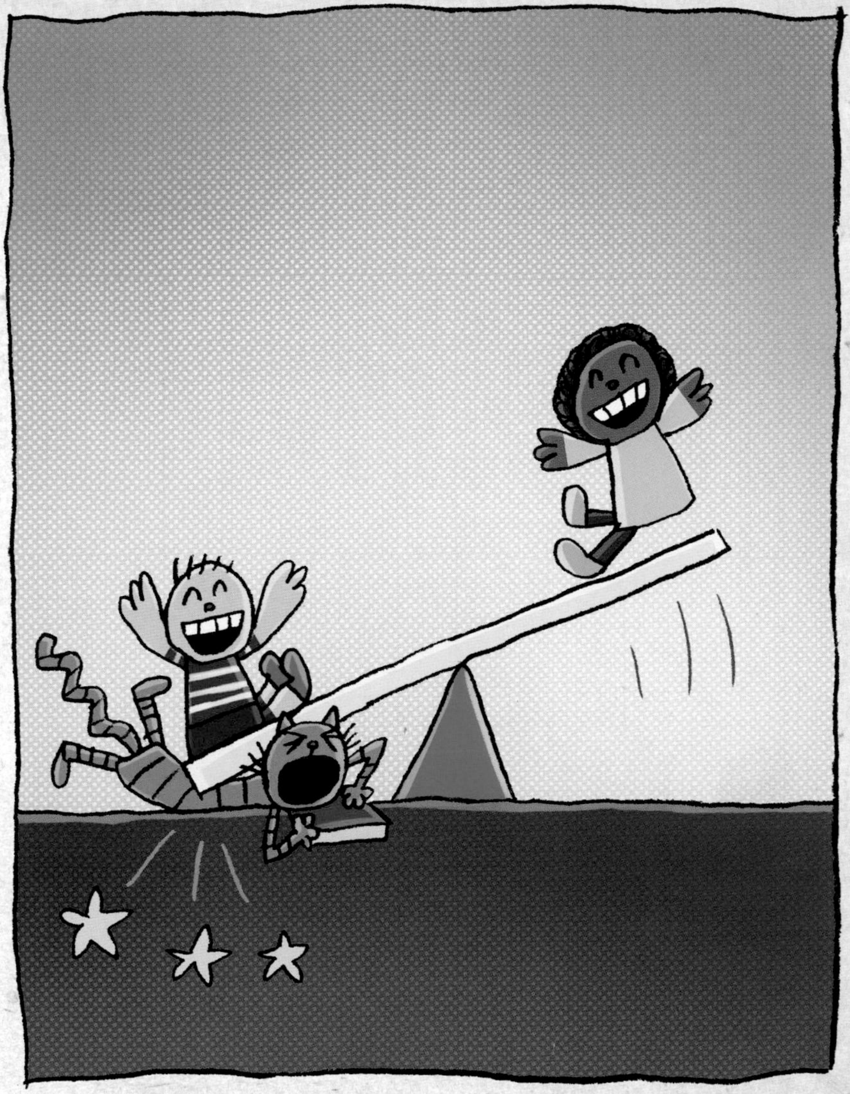

The Seesaw Smoosher

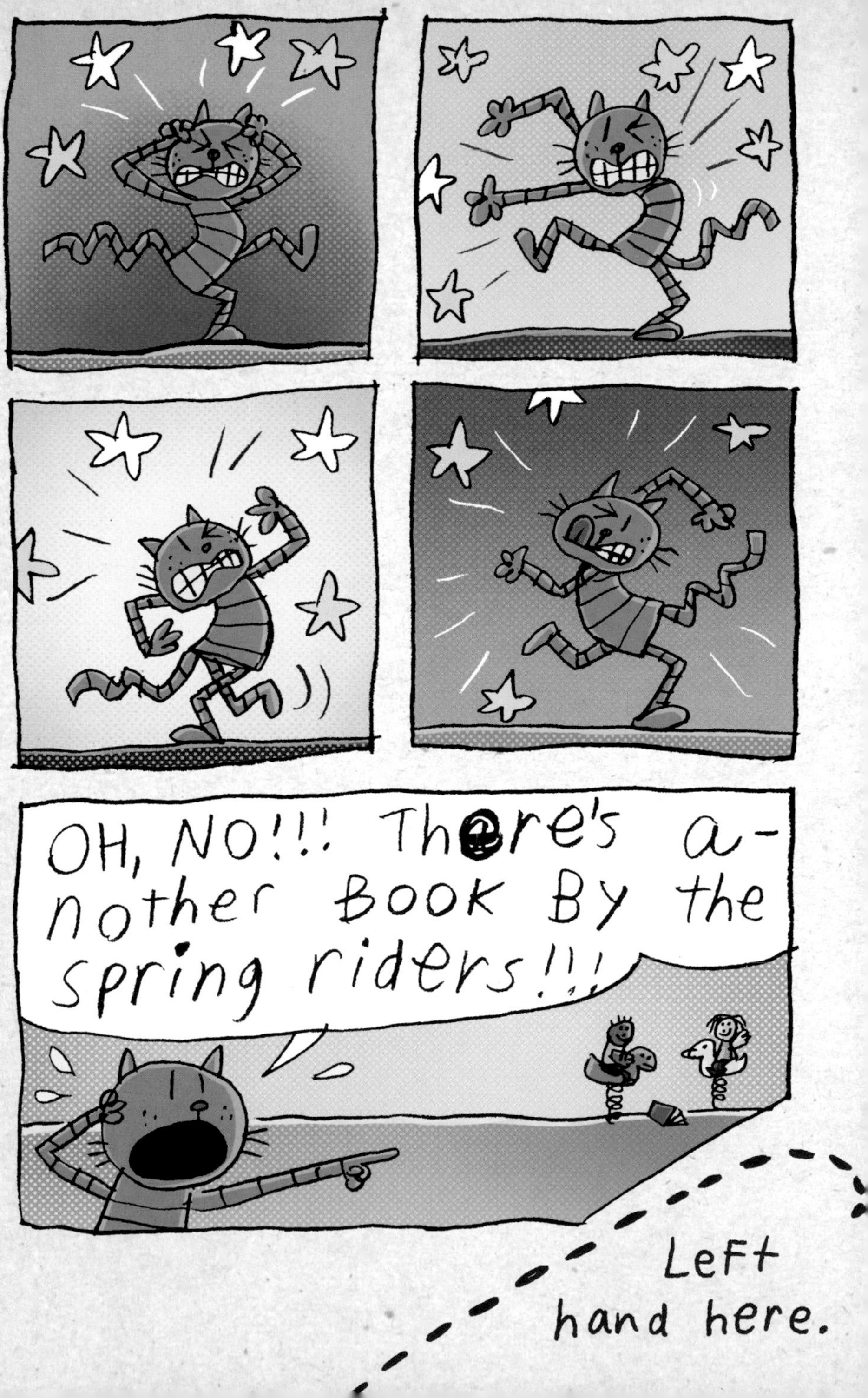
OH, NO!!! There's a-nother Book By the spring riders!!!
Left hand here.

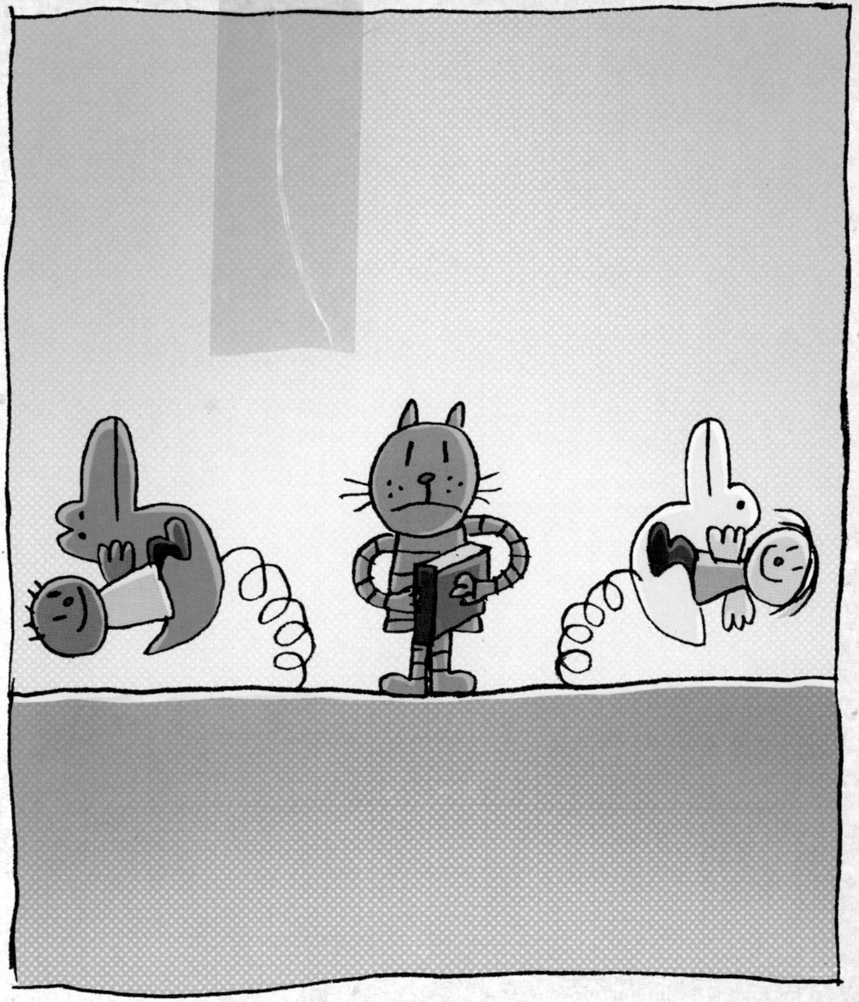

Spring Break

Right Thumb here.

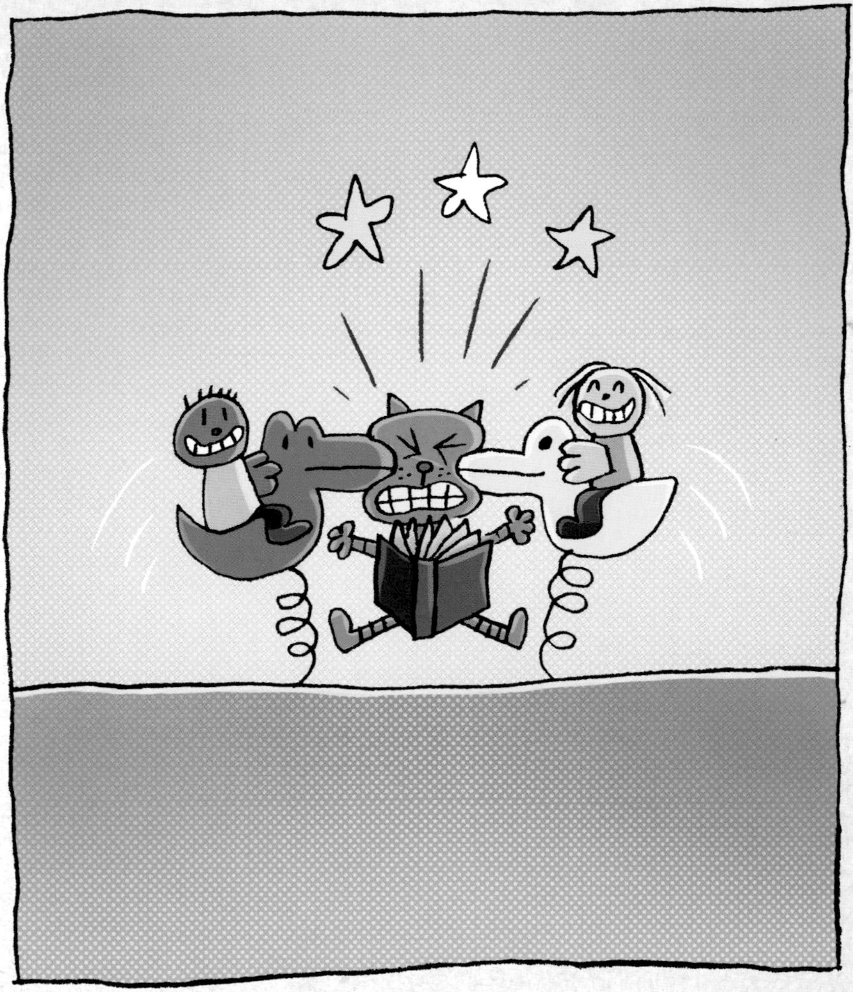

Spring Break

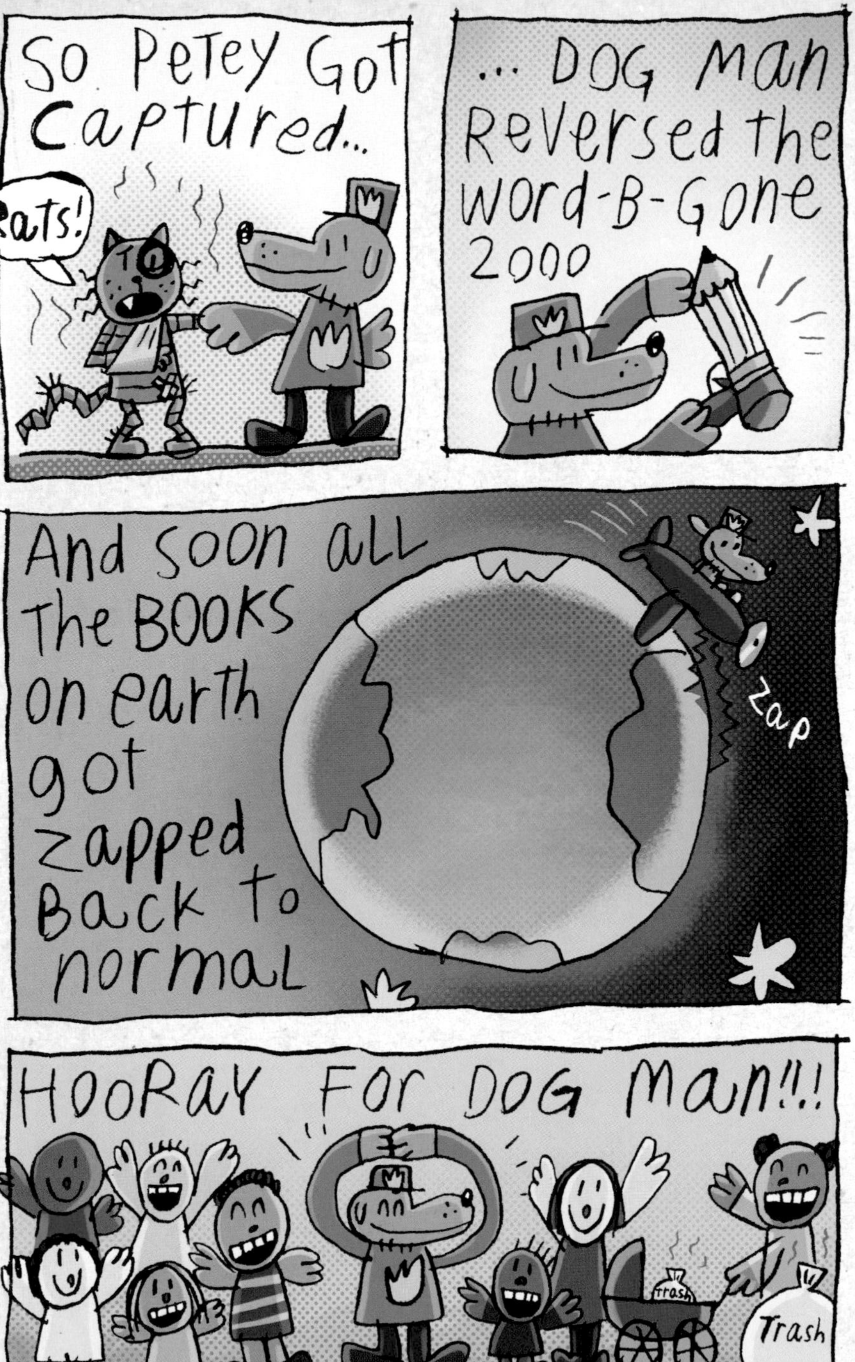
So Petey Got Captured...
Rats!
... Dog Man Reversed the Word-B-Gone 2000
And soon all the Books on earth got zapped Back to normal
Zap
Hooray for Dog Man!!!
Trash
Trash

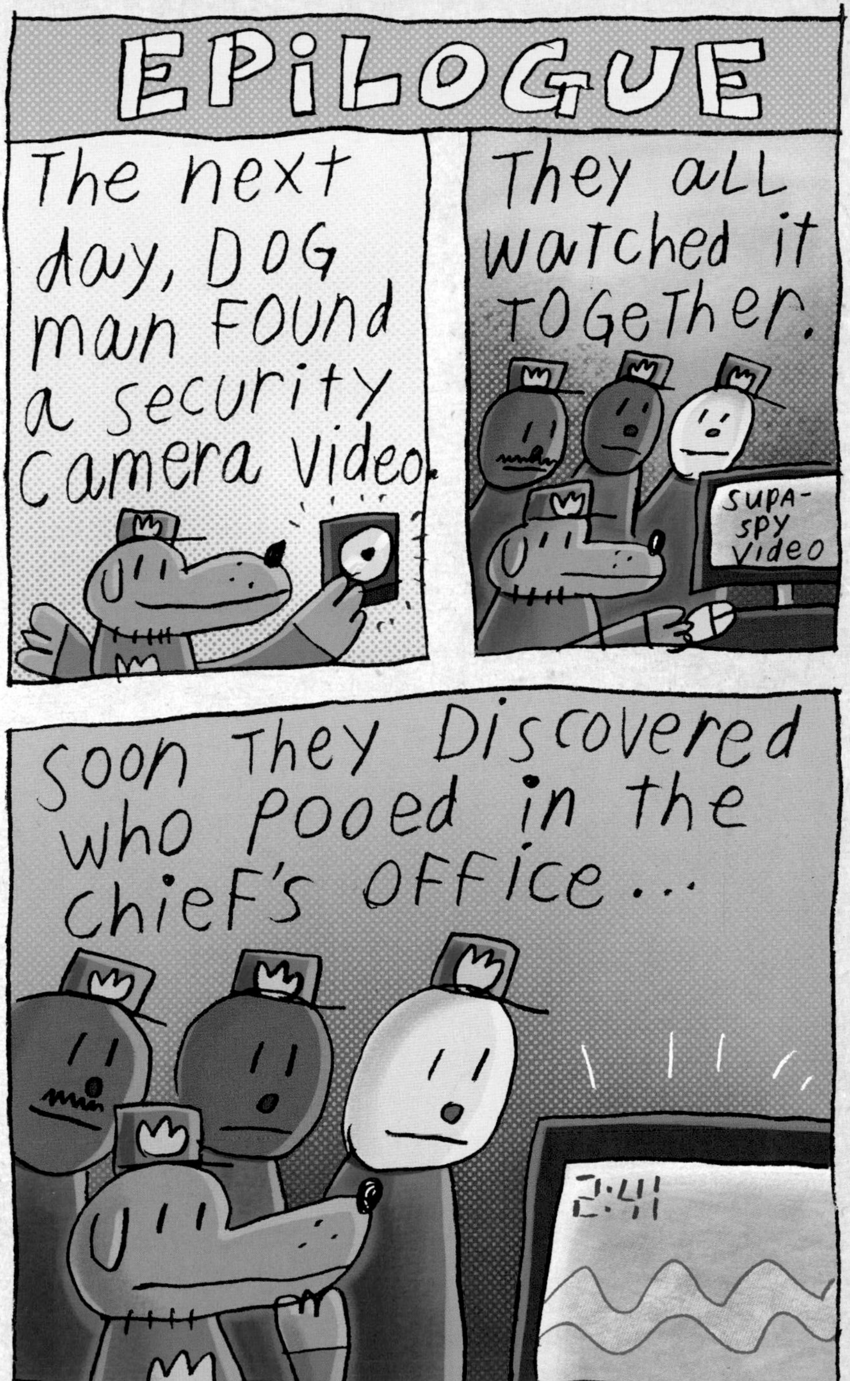
EPILOGUE
The next day, DOG man FOUND a security camera video.
They all watched it TOGether.
SUPA-SPY Video
Soon They Discovered who Pooed in the chief's office...
2:41

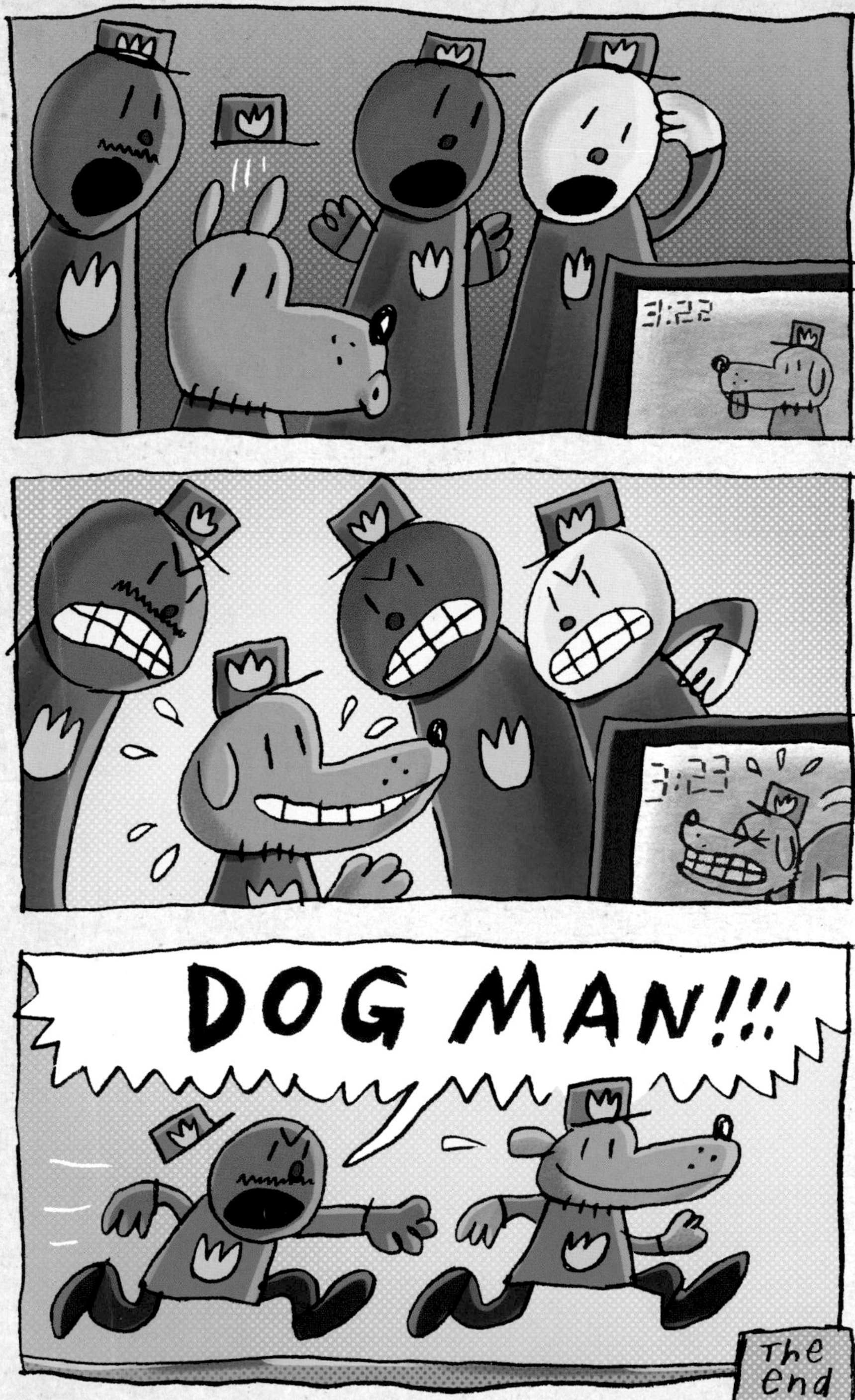
3:22
3:23
DOG MAN!!!
The end

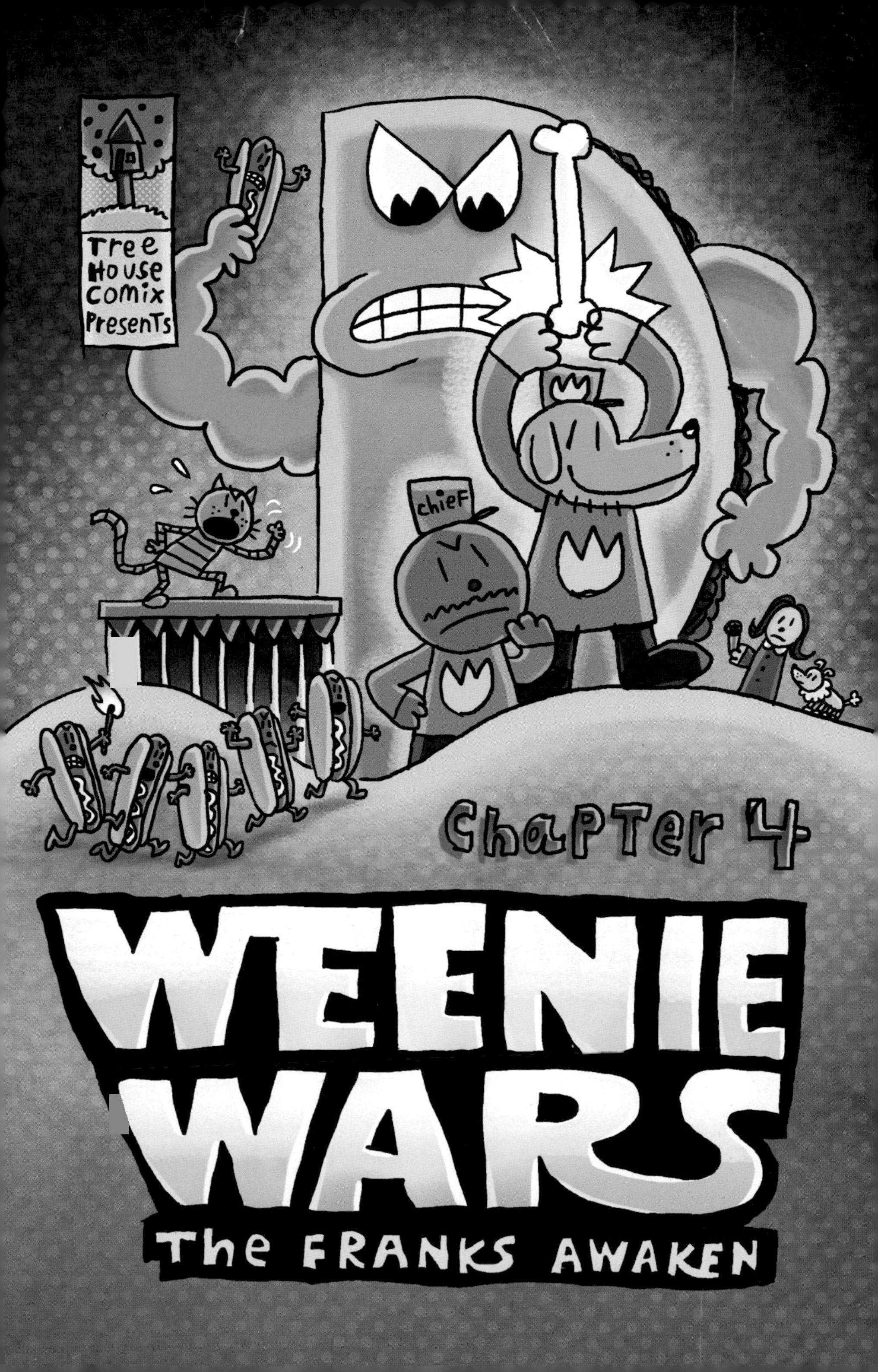
Tree House Comix Presents
chief
Chapter 4
WEENIE WARS
The FRANKS AWAKEN

DOG MAN in WEENIE WARS:
THE FRANKS awaken

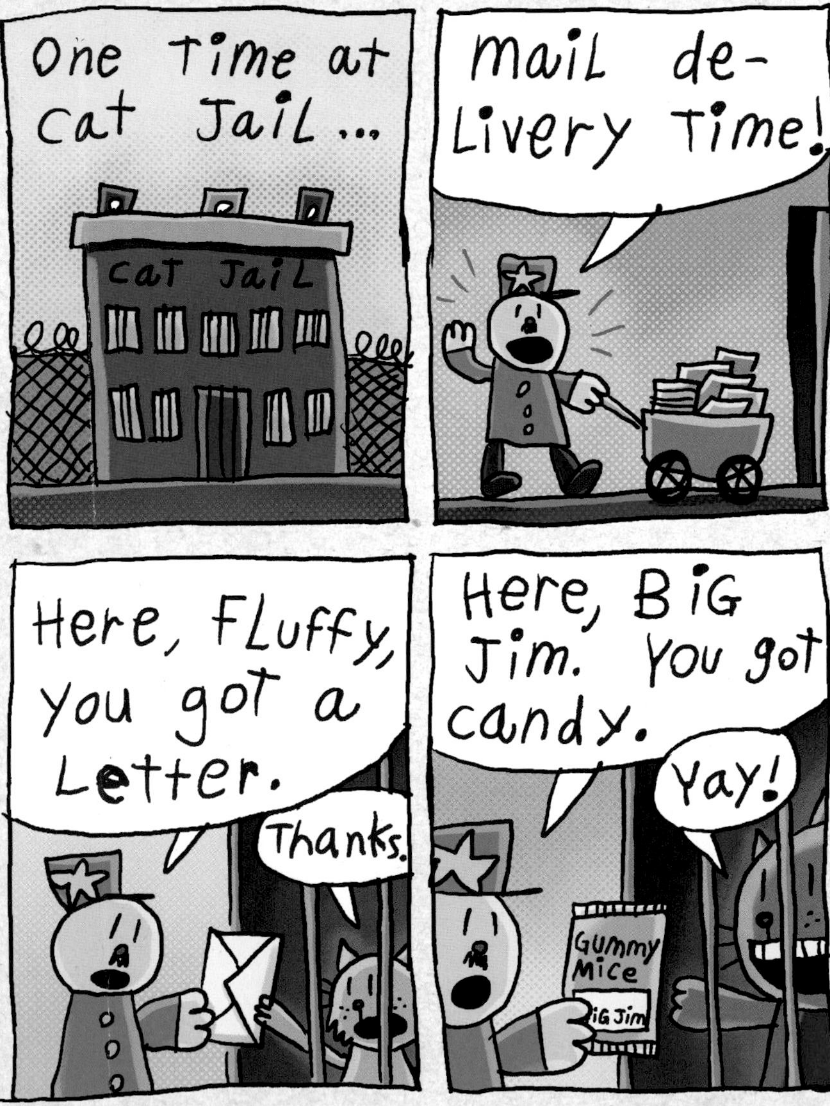
One time at cat jail...
CAT JAIL
Mail de-livery time!
Here, Fluffy, you got a letter.
Thanks.
Here, Big Jim. You got candy.
Yay!
GUMMY MICE
BIG JIM

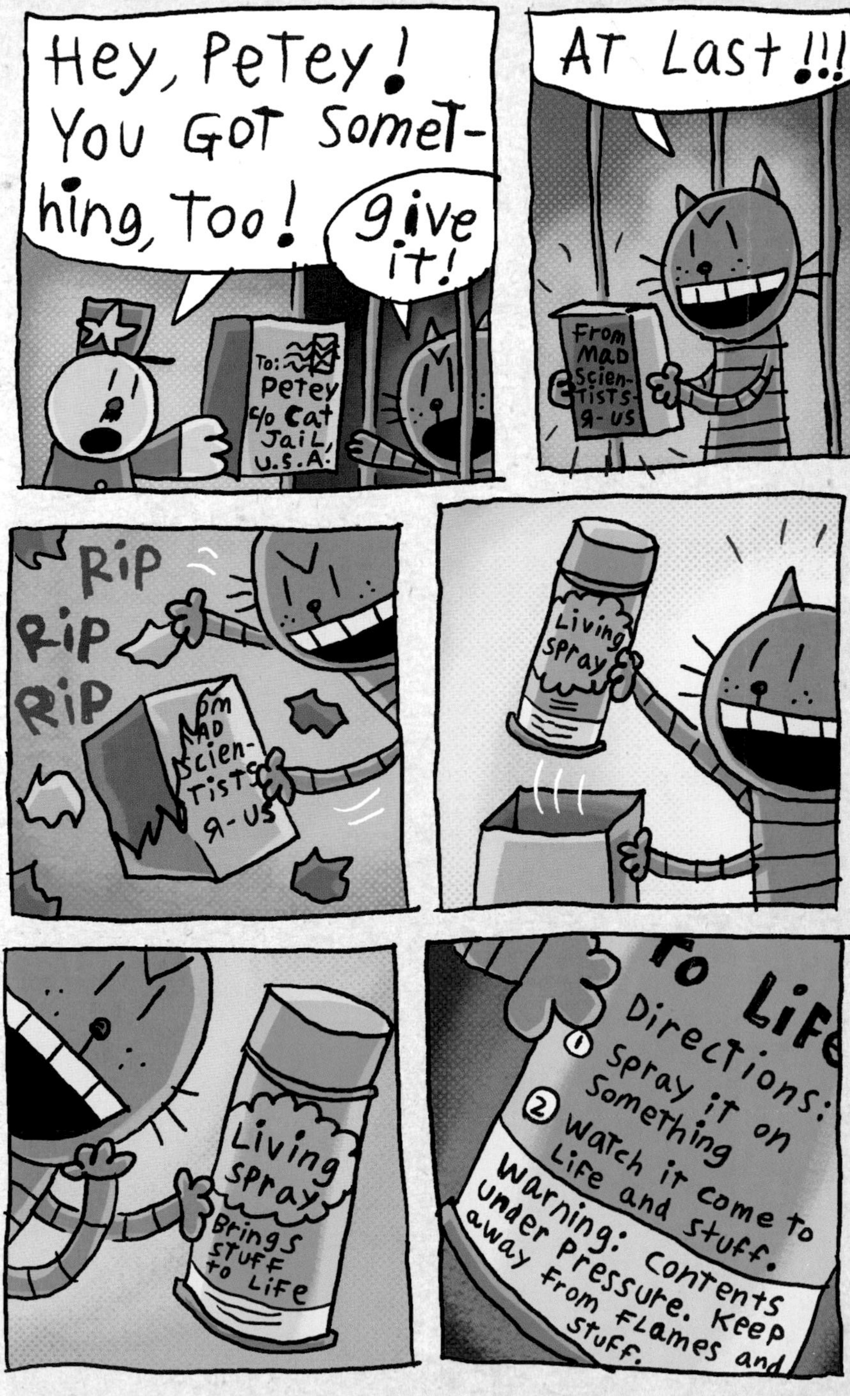
Hey, Petey! You Got Somet-hing, Too!
give it!
To: Petey c/o Cat Jail, U.S.A.
AT Last!!!
From MAD Scien-TISTS-R-US
RiP
RiP
RiP
Living Spray
Living Spray
Brings STUFF to LiFe
To LiFe
Directions:
① Spray it on Something
② WaTch it come to Life and stuff.
Warning: contents under Pressure. Keep away from FLames and stuff.

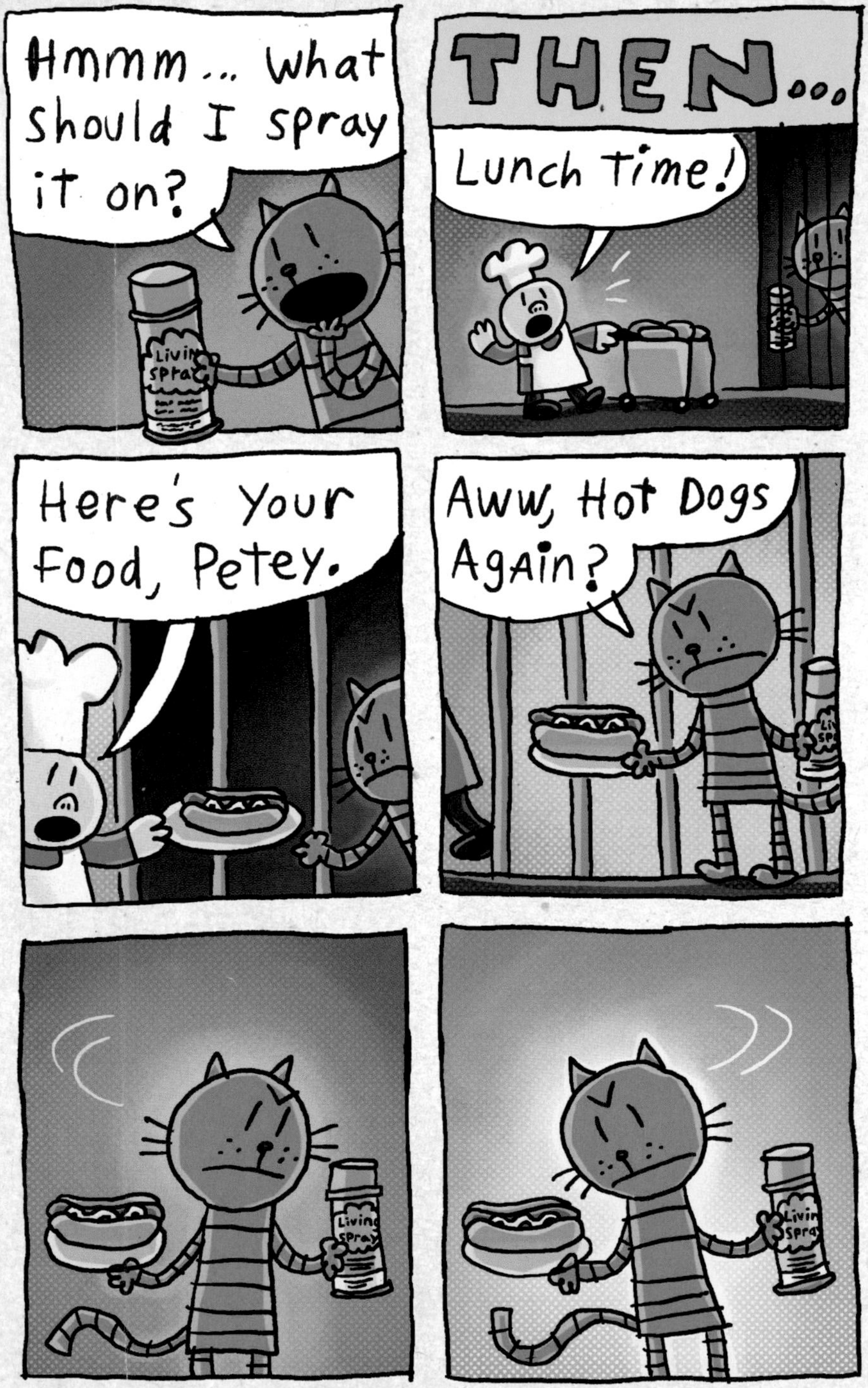
Hmmm... What should I spray it on?
Living Spray
THEN...
Lunch Time!
Here's Your Food, Petey.
Aww, Hot Dogs Again?
Living Spray
Living Spray

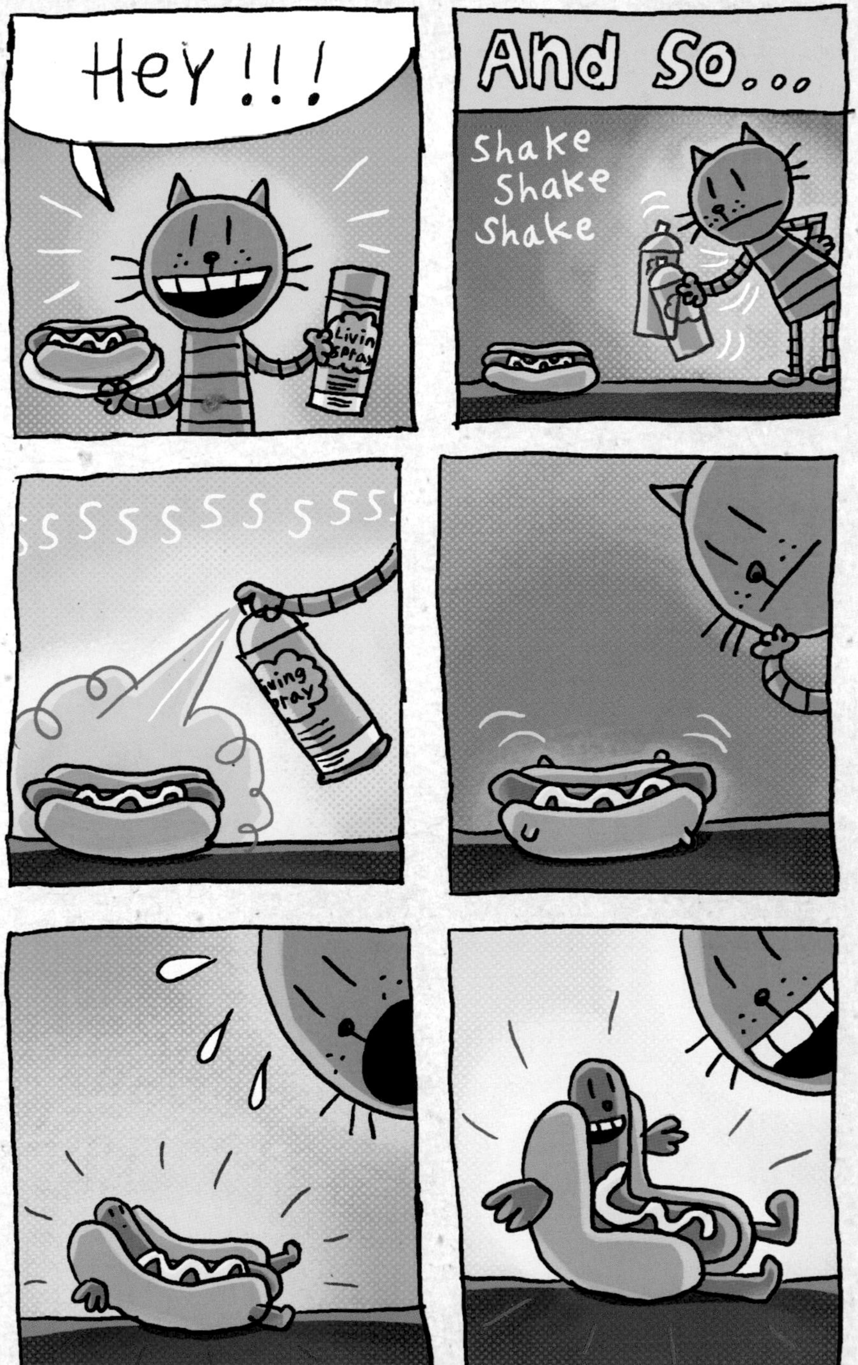
Hey!!!
And So....
Shake
Shake
Shake
SSSSSSSSSSSS

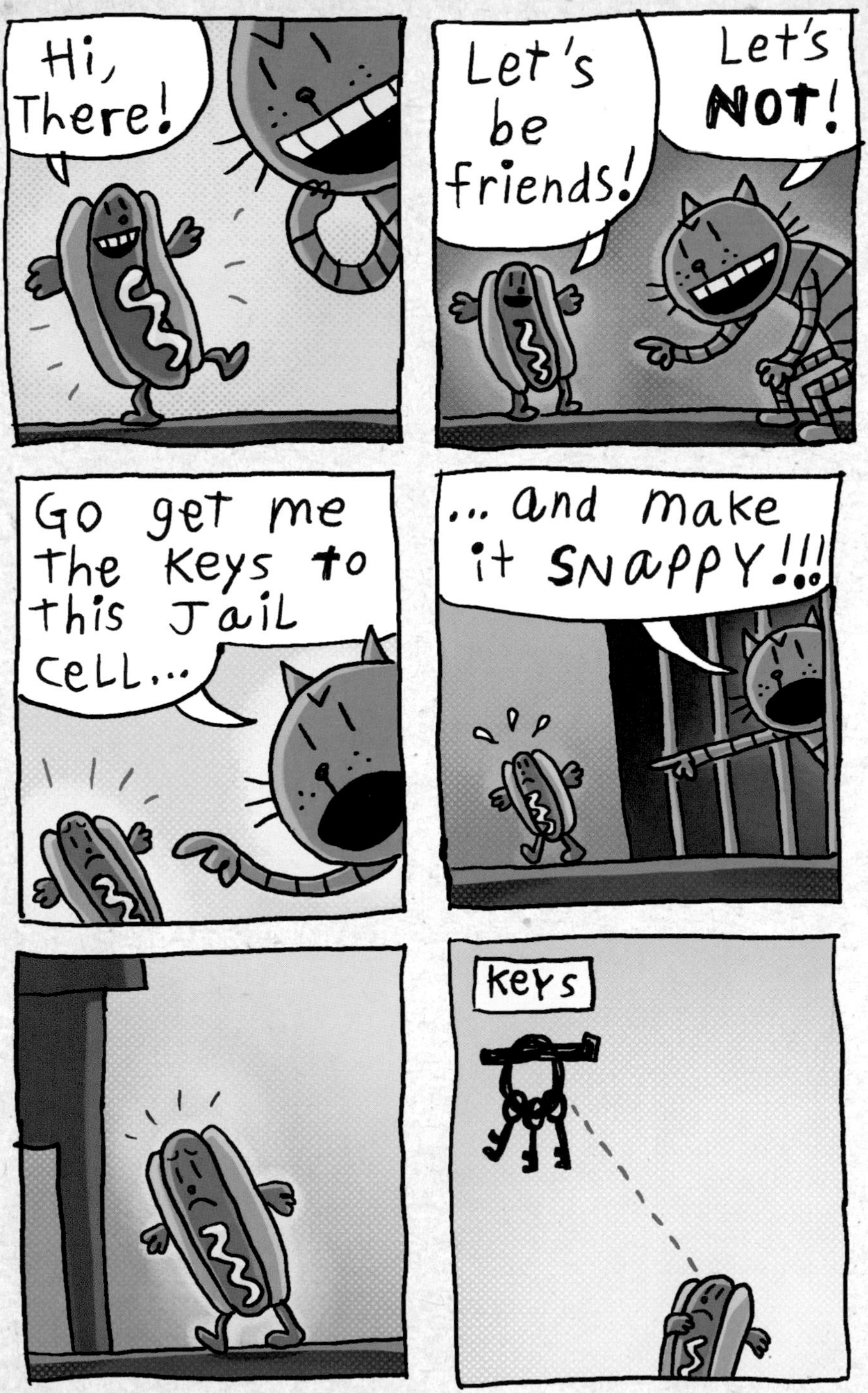
Hi, There!
Let's be friends!
Let's NOT!
Go get me the keys to this jail cell...
... and make it SNAPPY!!!
KEYS

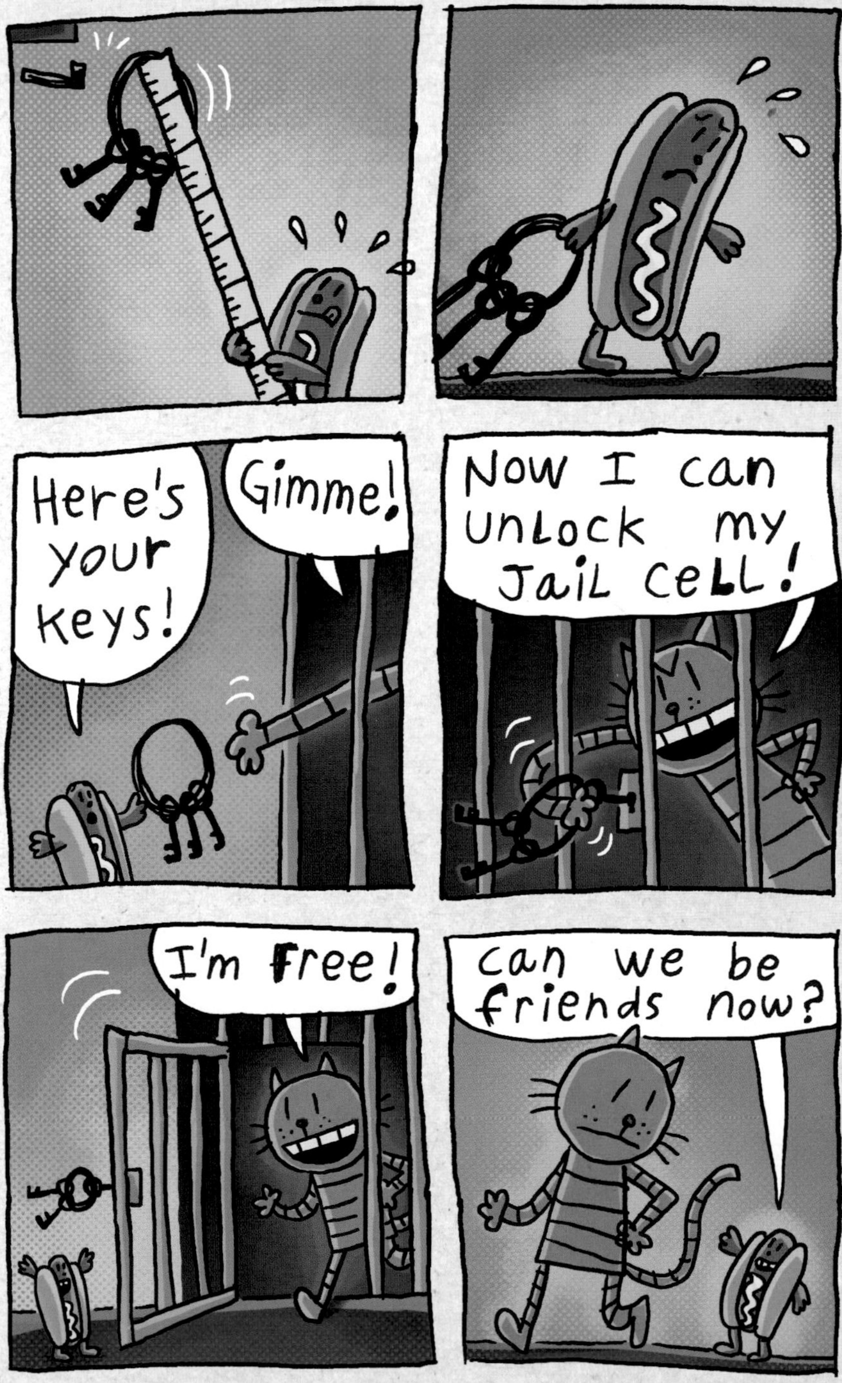
Here's your keys!
Gimme!
Now I can unlock my jail cell!
I'm free!
Can we be friends now?

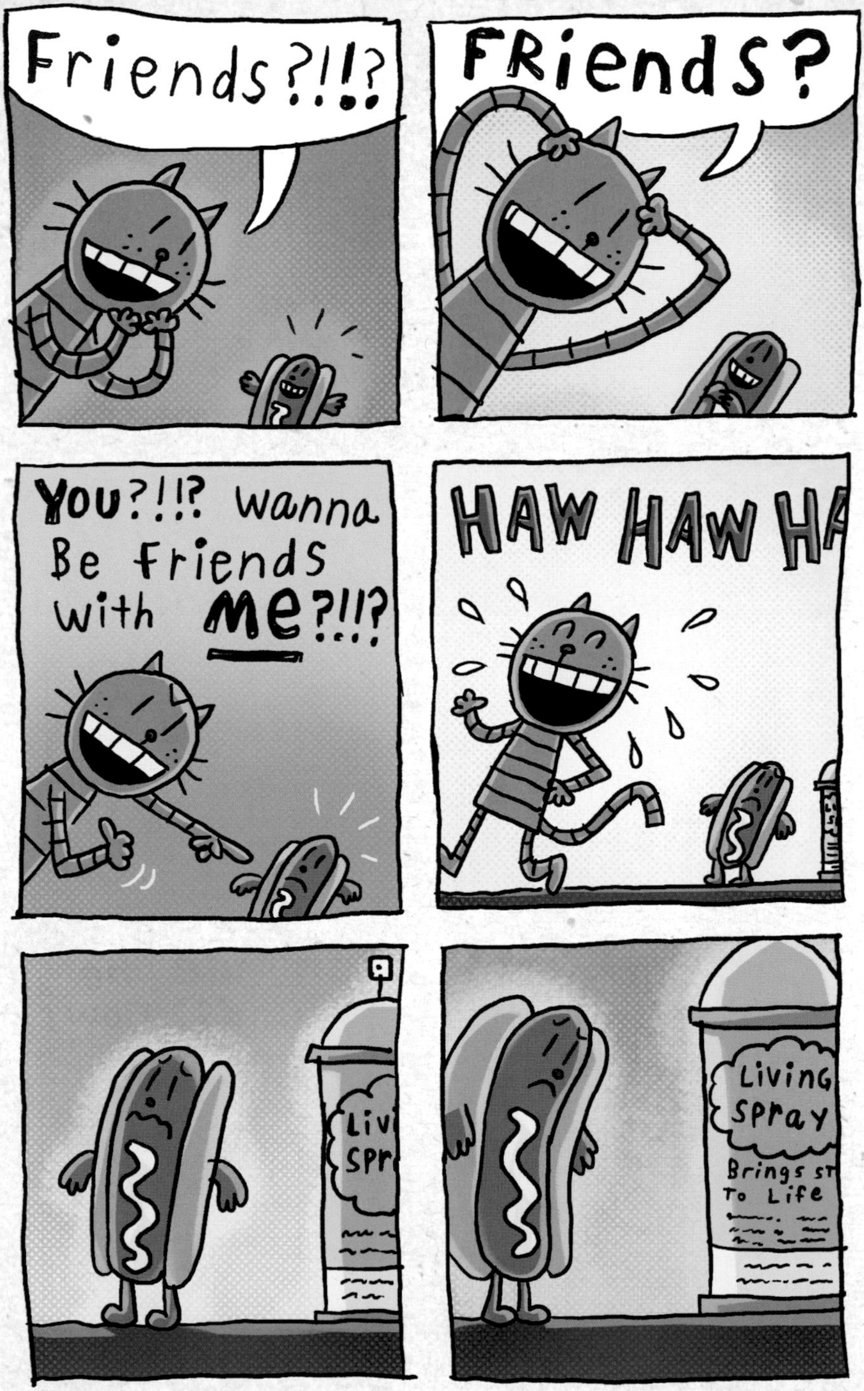
Friends?!!?
FRiends?
YOU?!!? wanna Be Friends with ME?!!?
HAW HAW HA
LIVI
SPR
LIVING SPRAY
Brings ST
To Life

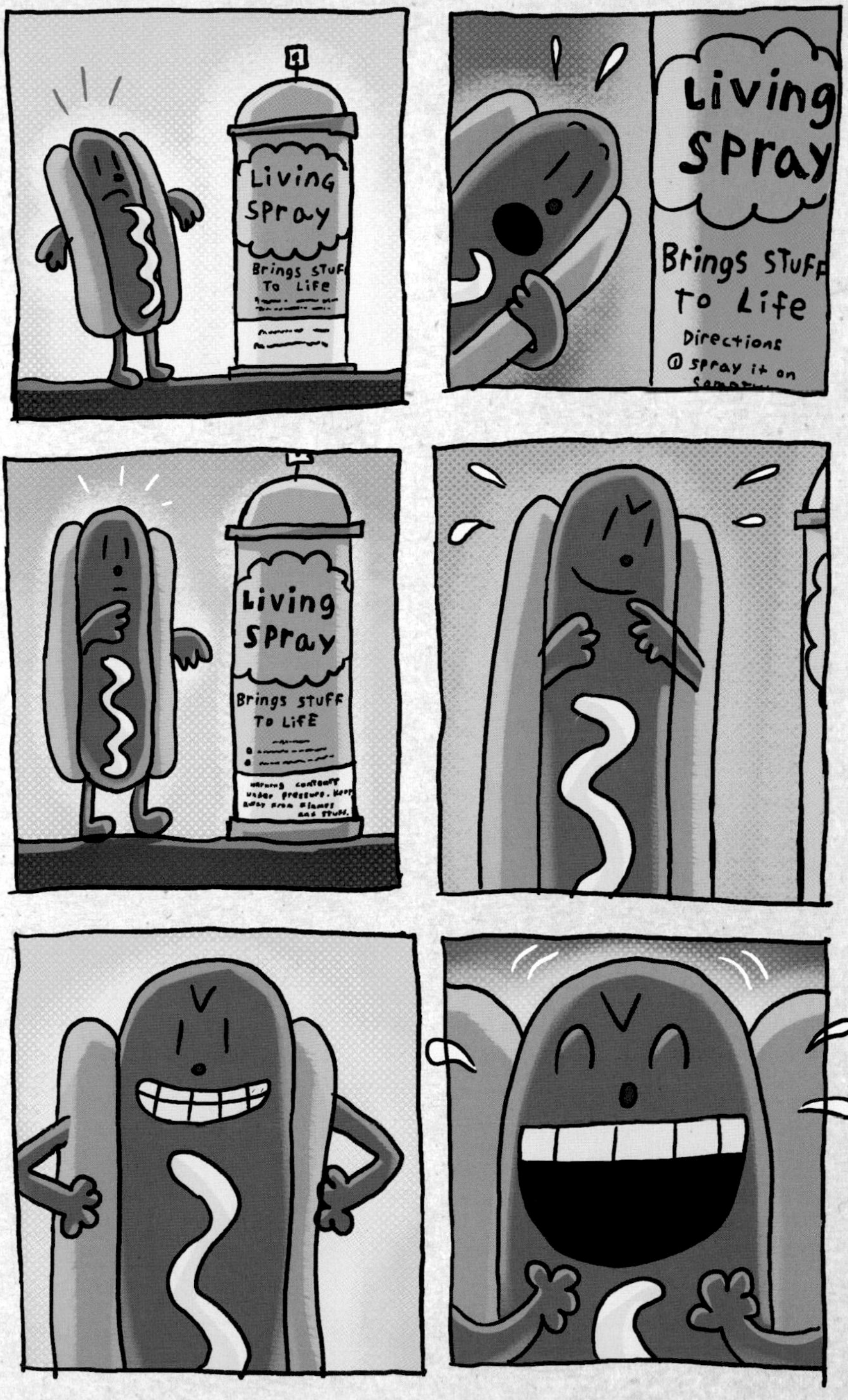
Living Spray
Brings Stuff To Life
Living Spray
Brings Stuff to Life
Directions
① spray it on
Living Spray
Brings stuff To Life
warning contents under pressure. Keep away from flames and stuff.

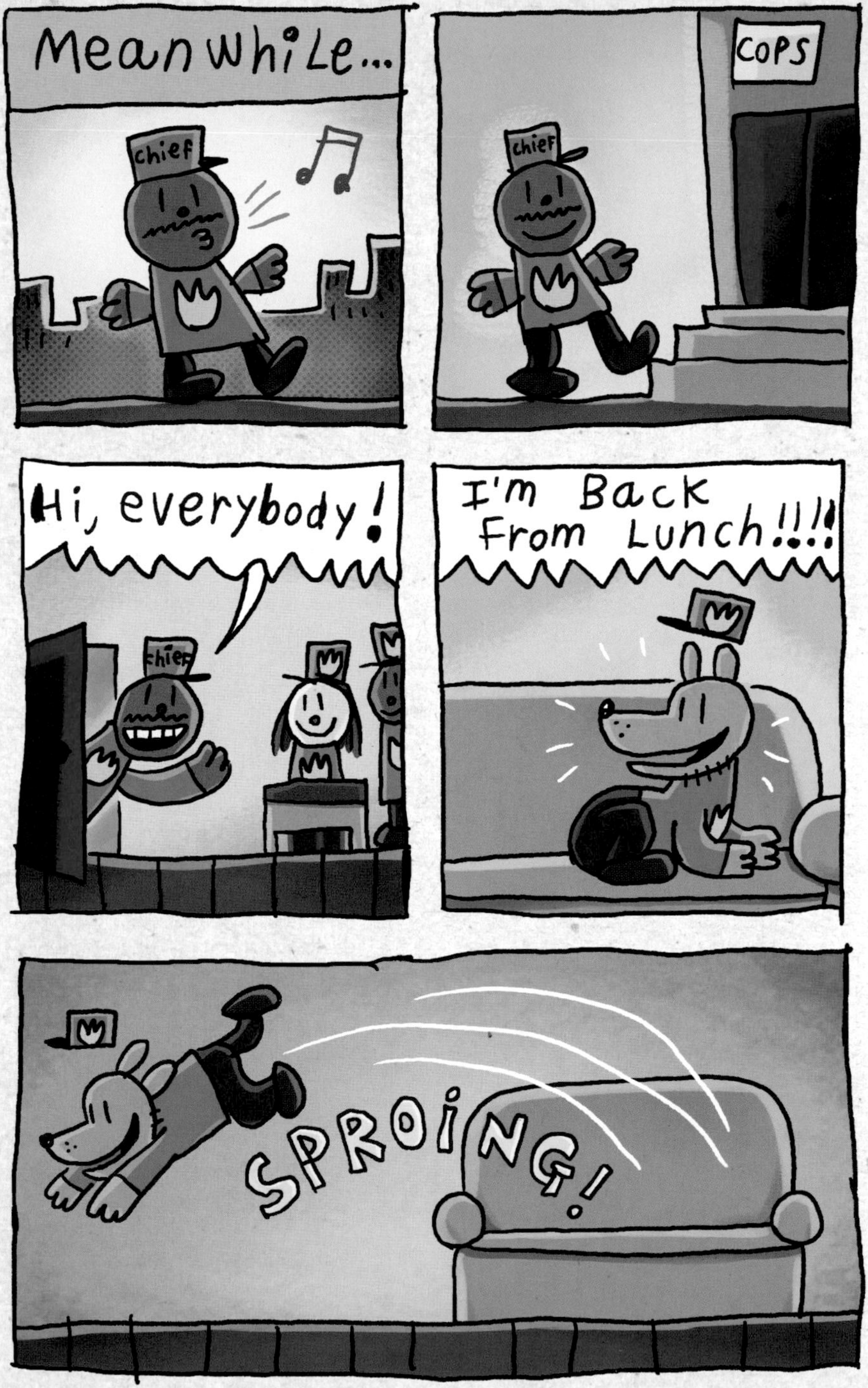
Meanwhile...
chief
COPS
chief
Hi, everybody!
chief
I'm Back From Lunch!!!!
SPROING!

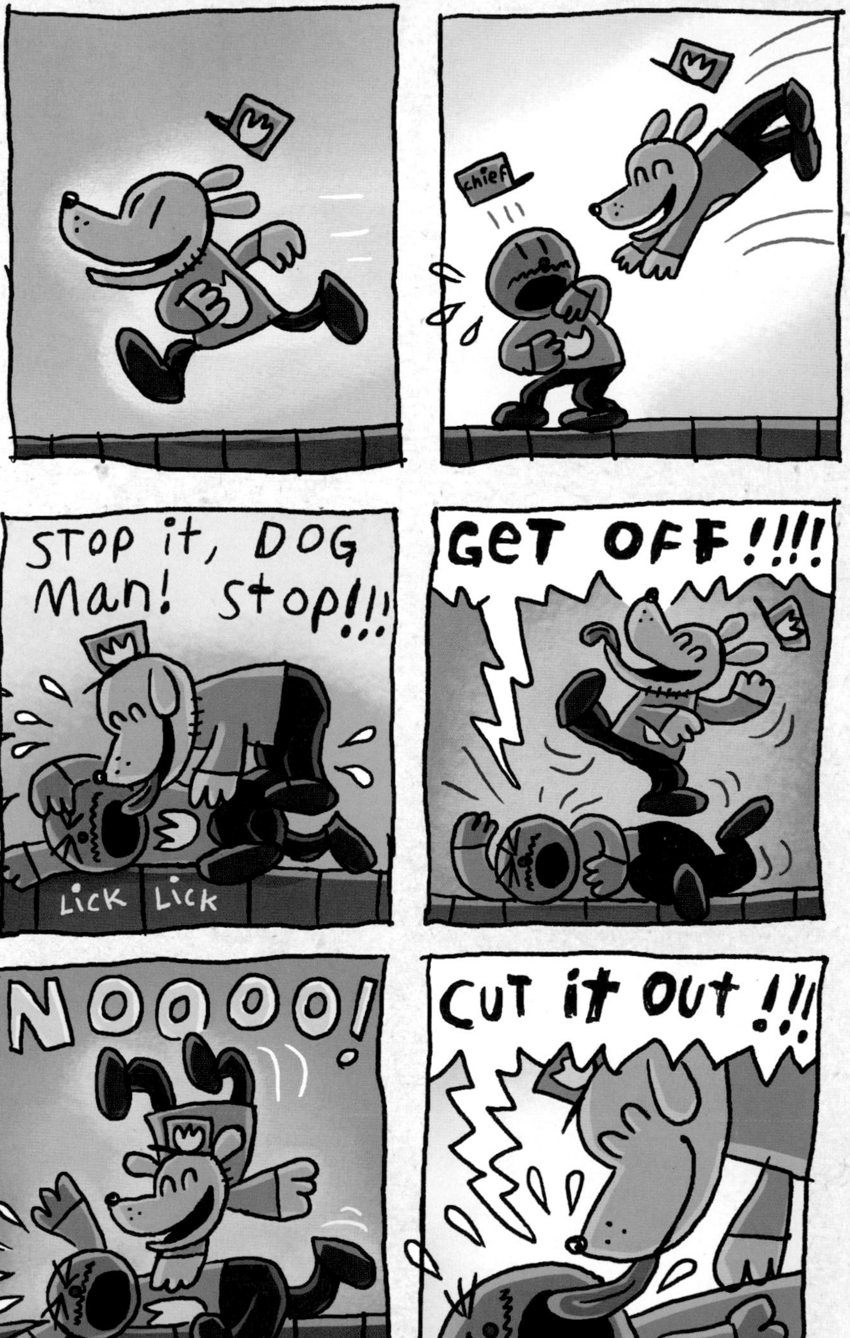
chief
STOP it, DOG Man! stop!!!
LiCK LiCK
GeT OFF!!!!
NOOOO!
CUT it OUT!!!

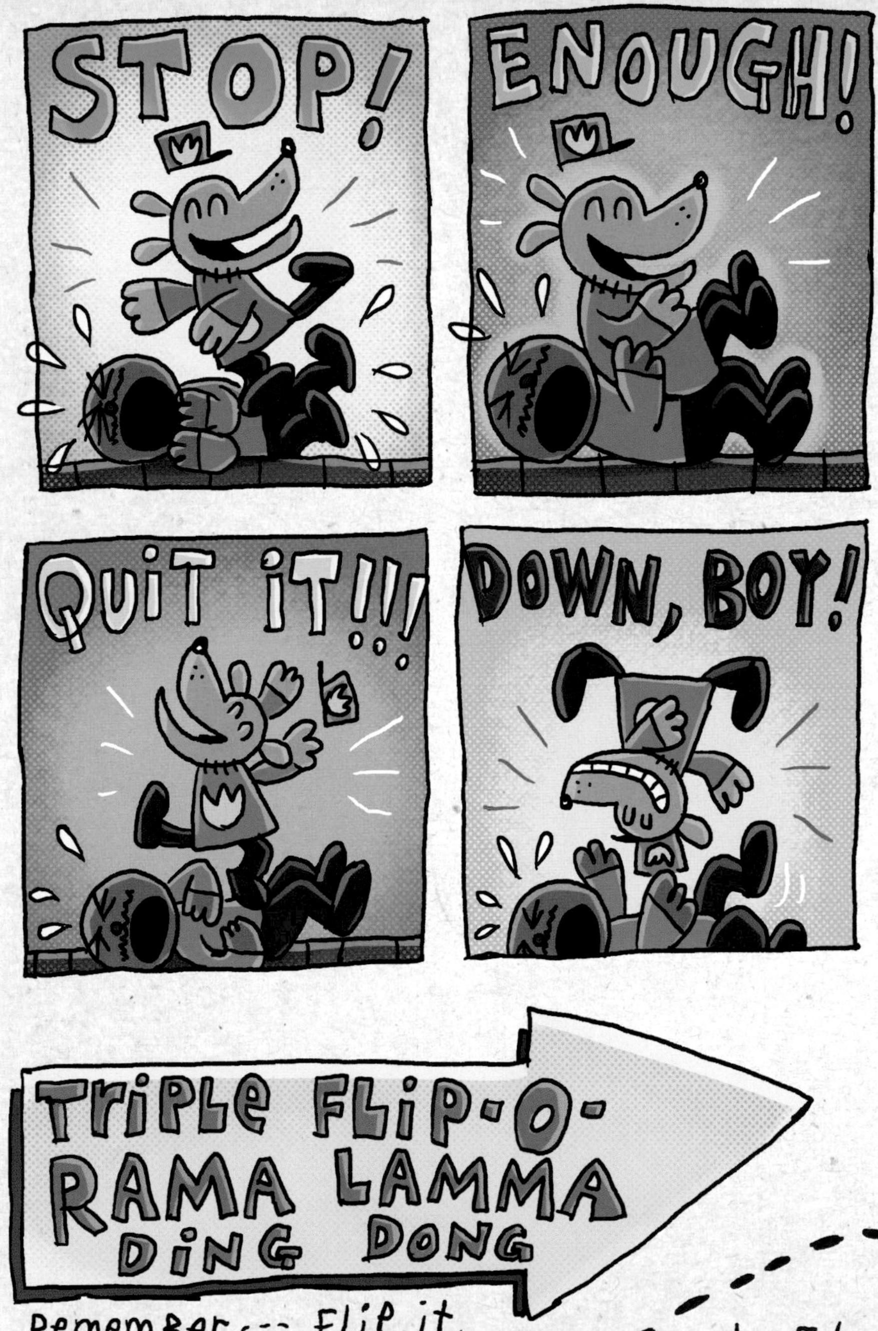
STOP!
ENOUGH!
QUIT IT!!!
DOWN, BOY!

TRIPLE FLIP-O-RAMA LAMMA DING DONG

Remember--- Flip it, Don't Rip it!!!!!!

Left hand here.

Welcome

Back,

Chief!

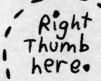

Right
Thumb
here.

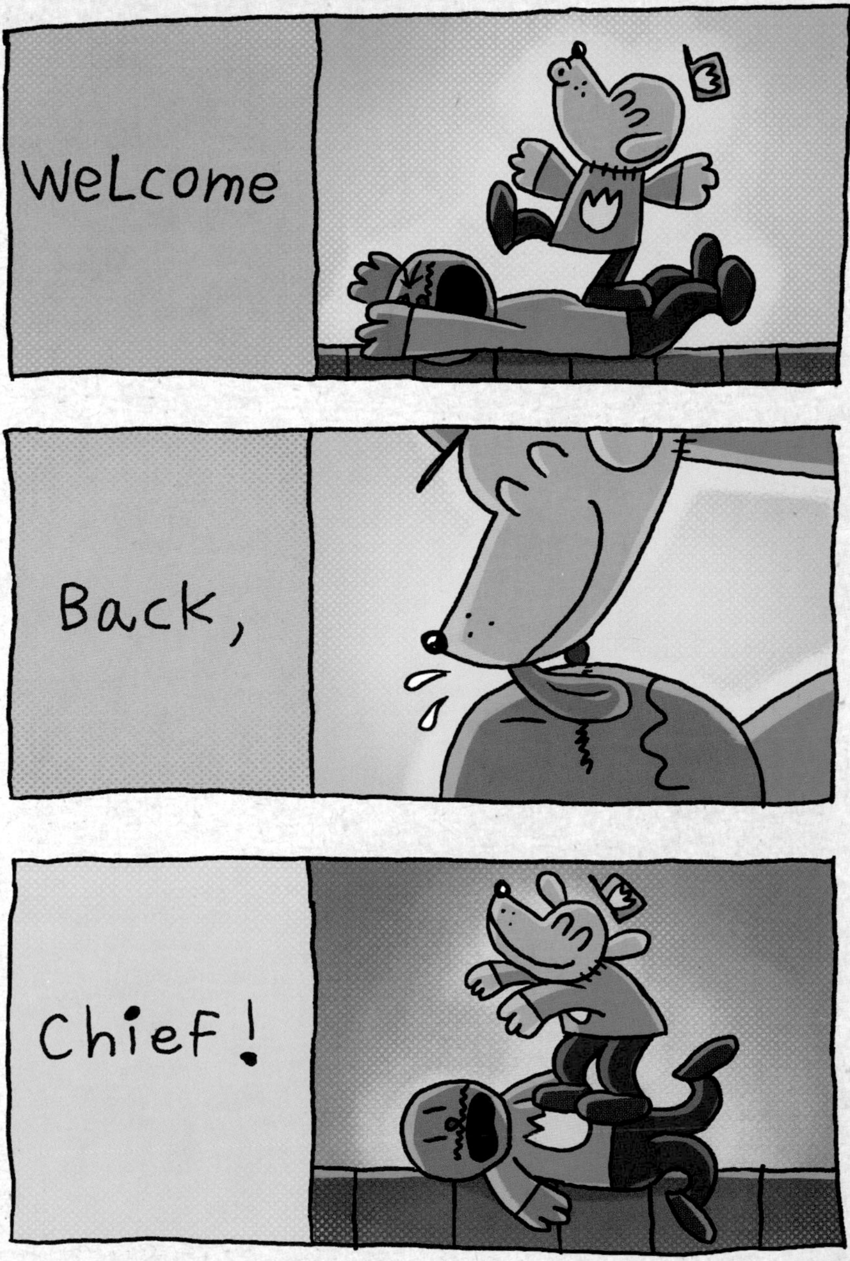
Welcome
Back,
Chief!

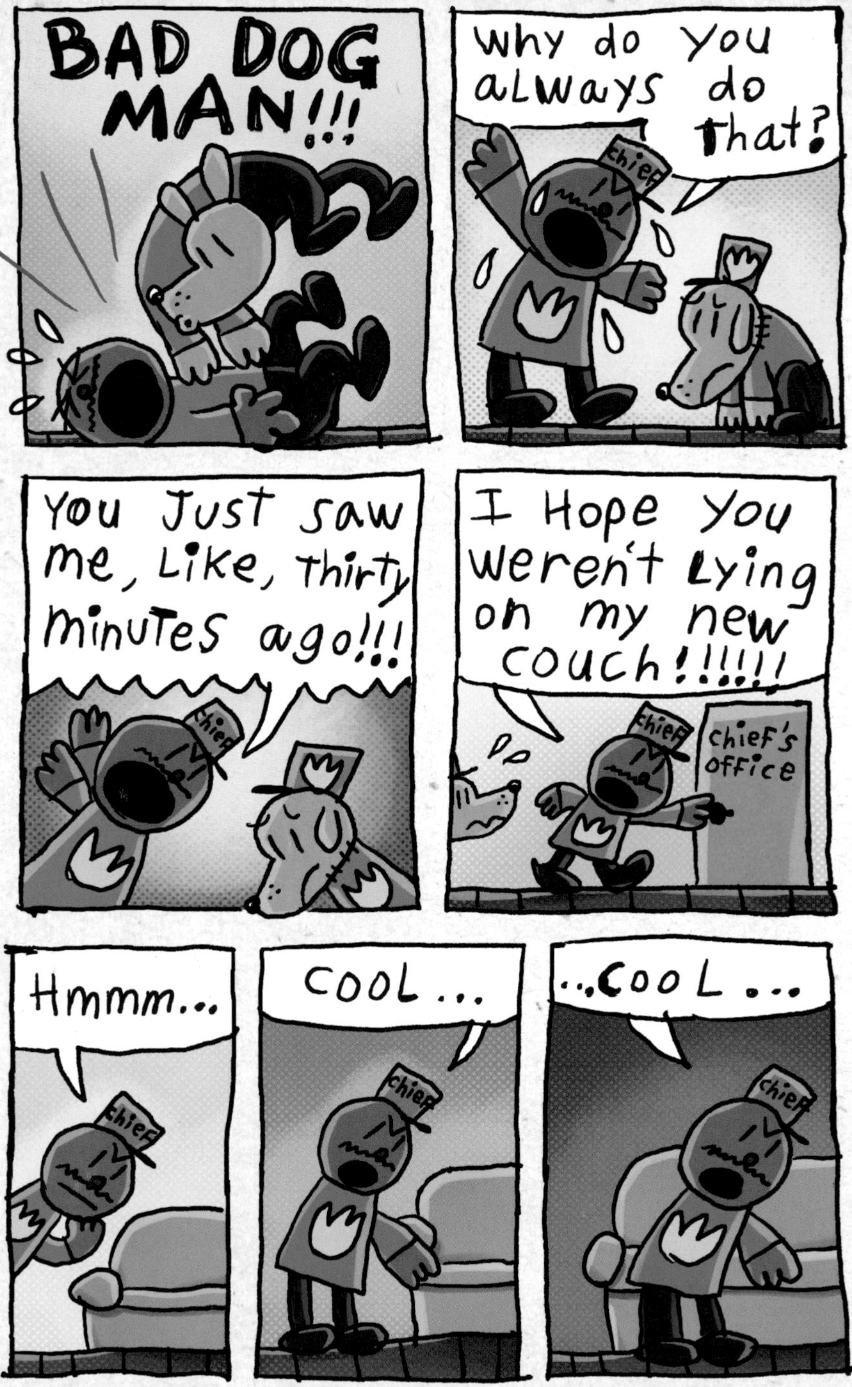
BAD DOG MAN!!!
Why do you always do that?
chief
You just saw me, like, thirty minutes ago!!!
chief
I Hope you weren't Lying on my new couch!!!!!!
chief
chief's office
Hmmm...
chief
COOL...
chief
...COOL...
chief

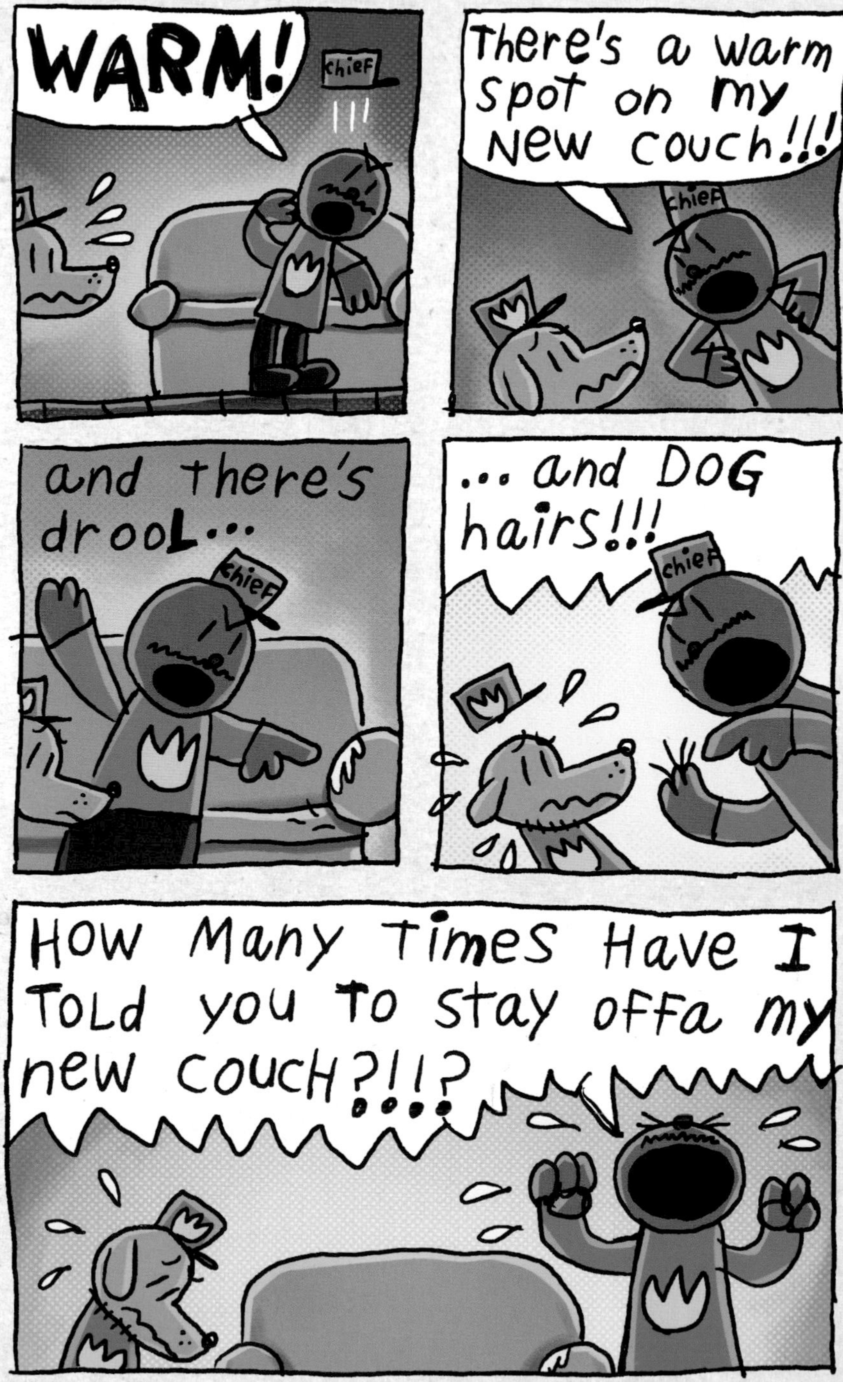
WARM!
chief
There's a warm spot on my new couch!!!
chief
and there's drool...
chief
...and DOG hairs!!!
chief
How Many Times Have I Told you To stay offa my new couch?!!?

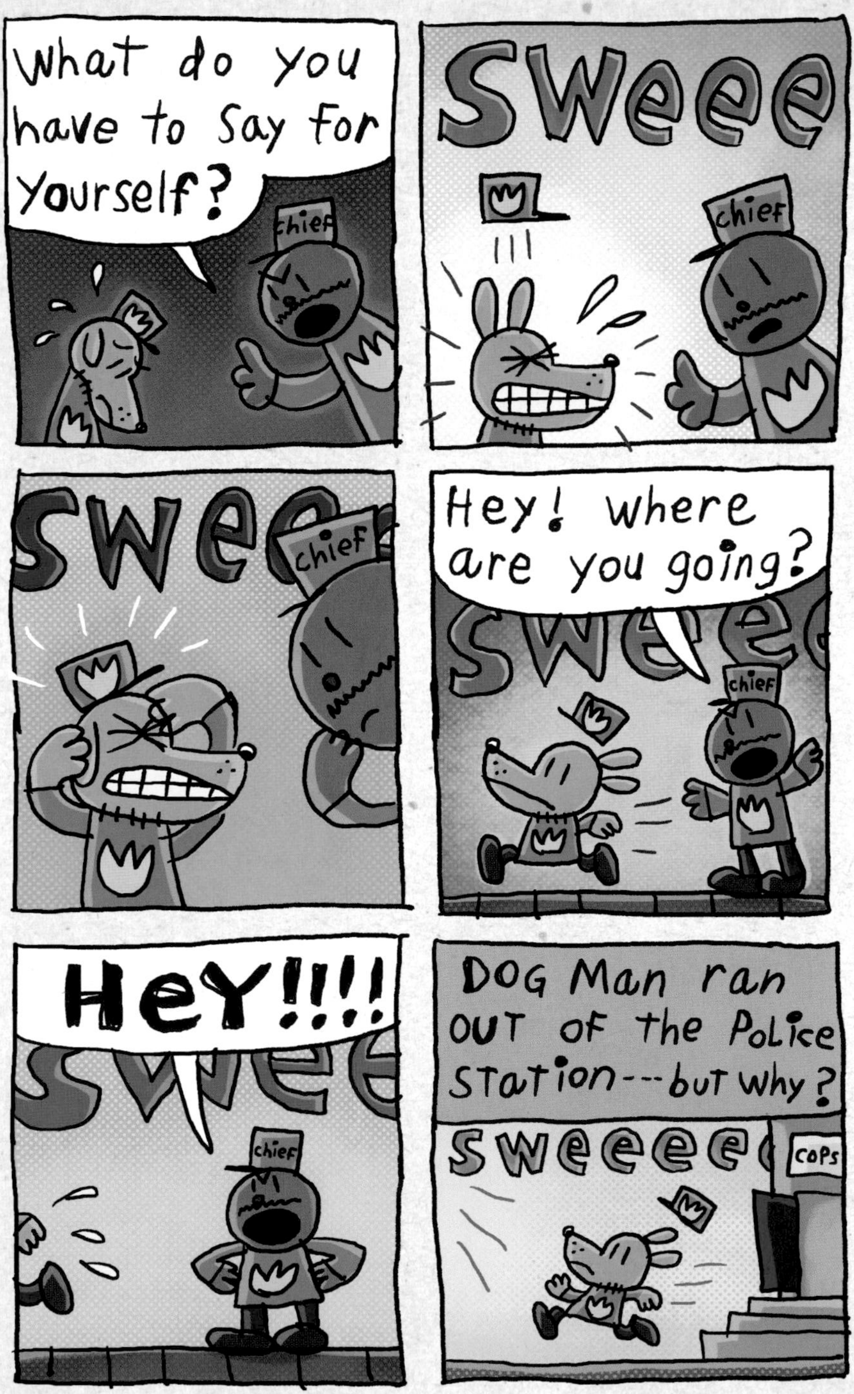
What do you have to say for yourself?
chief
SWEEE
chief
SWEE
chief
Hey! Where are you going?
SWEEE
chief
HEY!!!!
SWEE
chief
DOG MAN ran OUT OF the Police station---but why?
SWEEEE
COPS

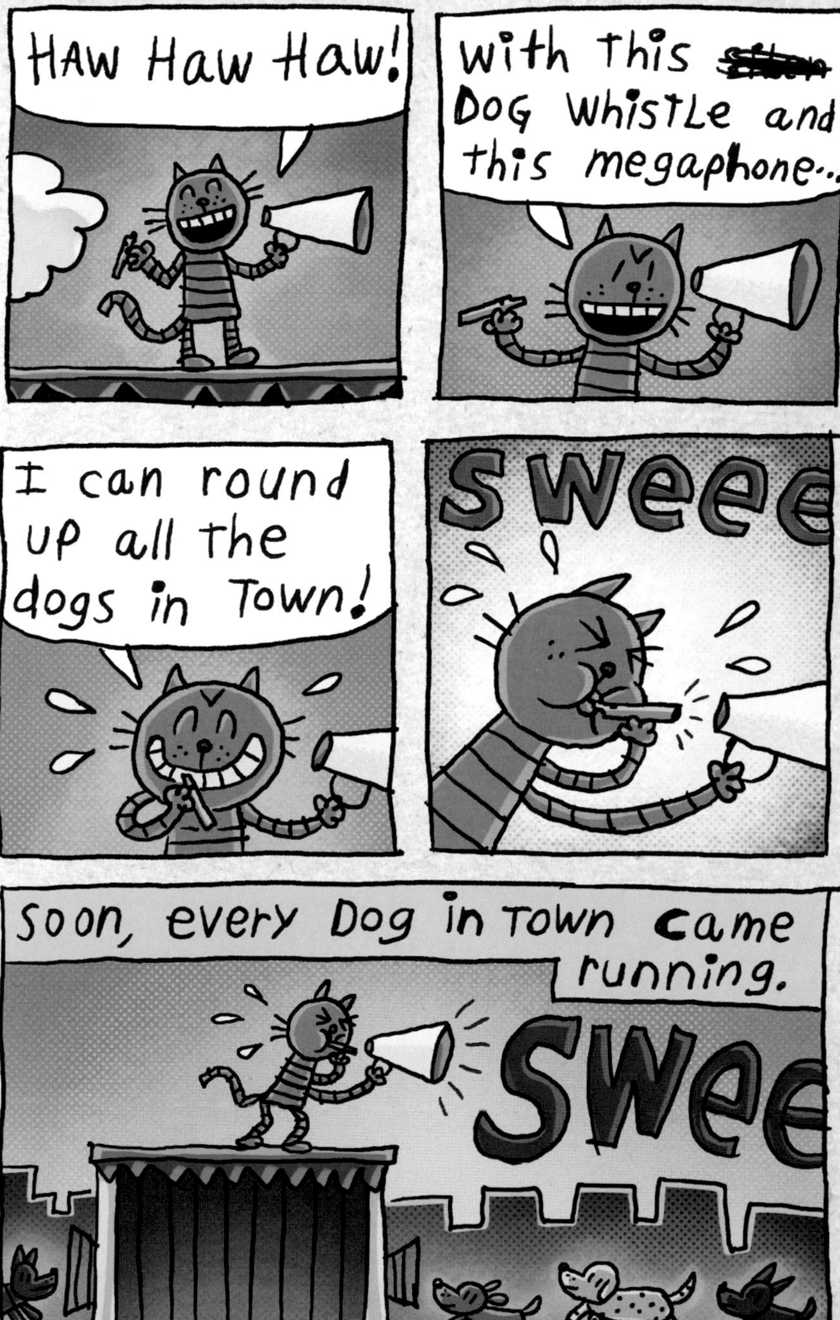
HAW Haw Haw!
With this Dog WhisTLe and this megaphone..
I can round up all the dogs in Town!
SWEEE
Soon, every Dog in Town came running.
SWEE

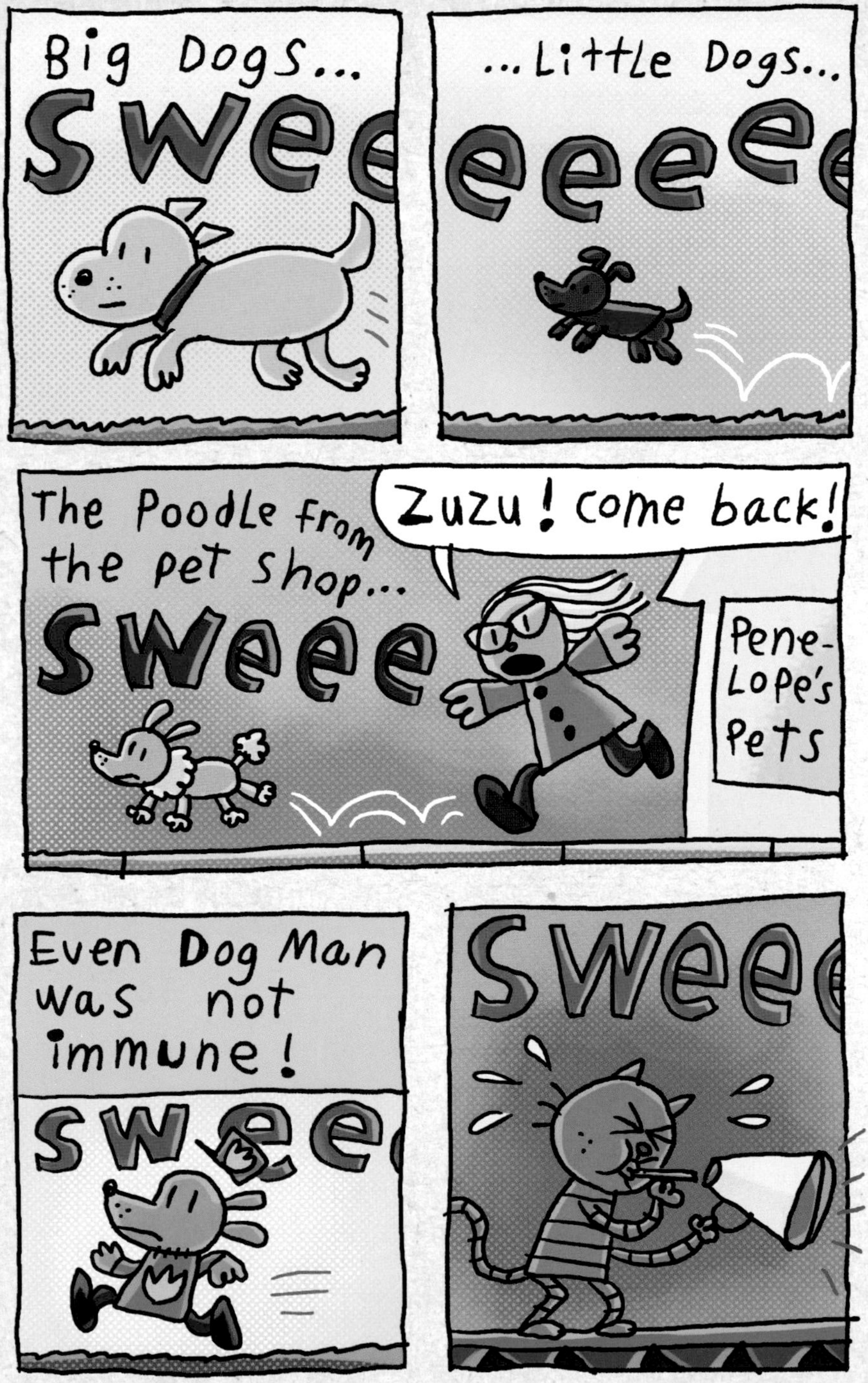
Big Dogs...
SWEE
...Little Dogs...
EEEEE
The Poodle from the pet shop...
Zuzu! come back!
SWEEE
Pene-Lope's Pets
Even Dog Man was not immune!
SWEE
SWEE

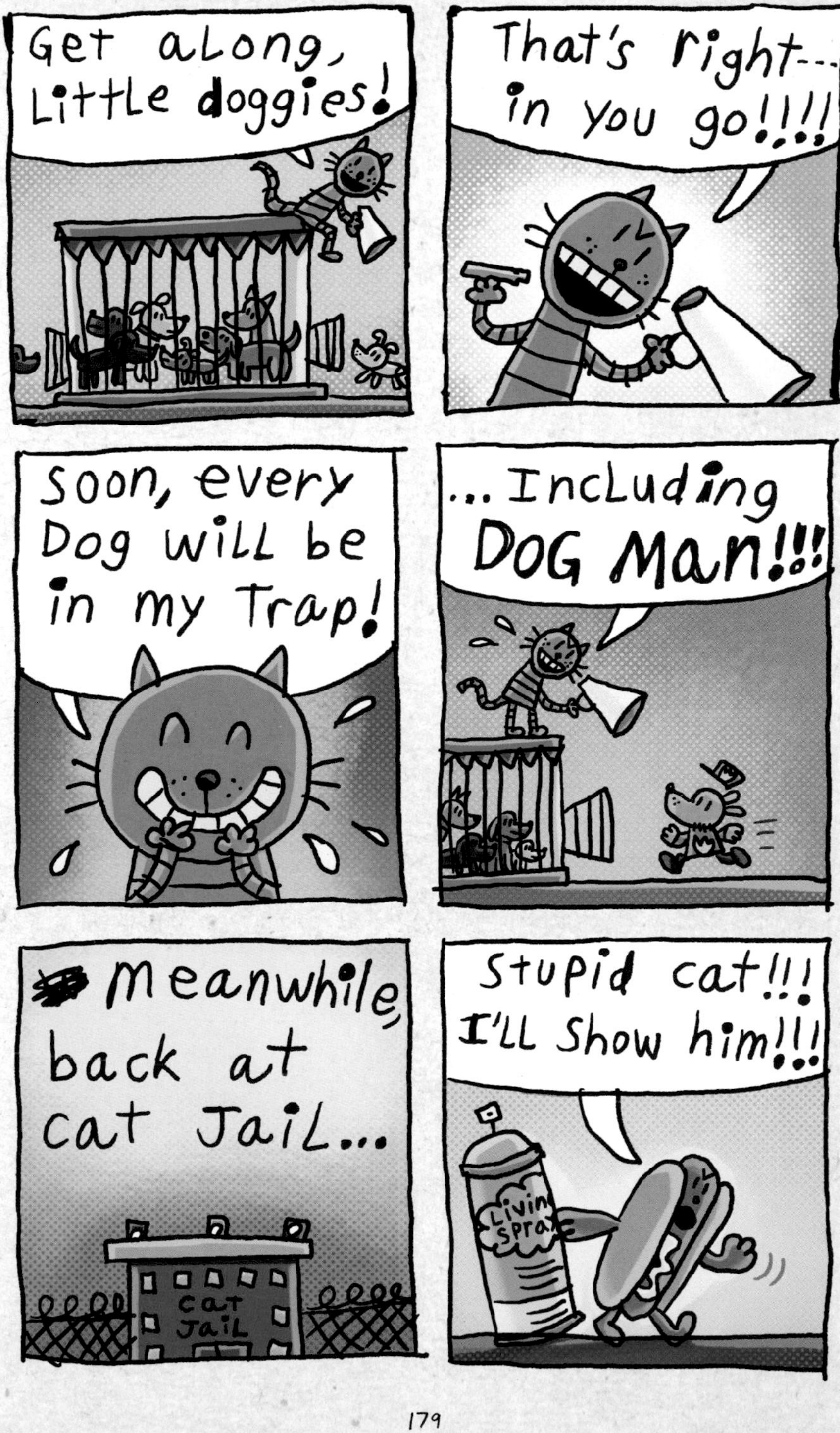
Get aLong, Little doggies!
That's right... in you go!!!!
Soon, every Dog will be in my Trap!
...IncLuding DOG Man!!!
Meanwhile, back at cat JaiL...
CAT JAIL
Stupid cat!!! I'LL Show him!!!

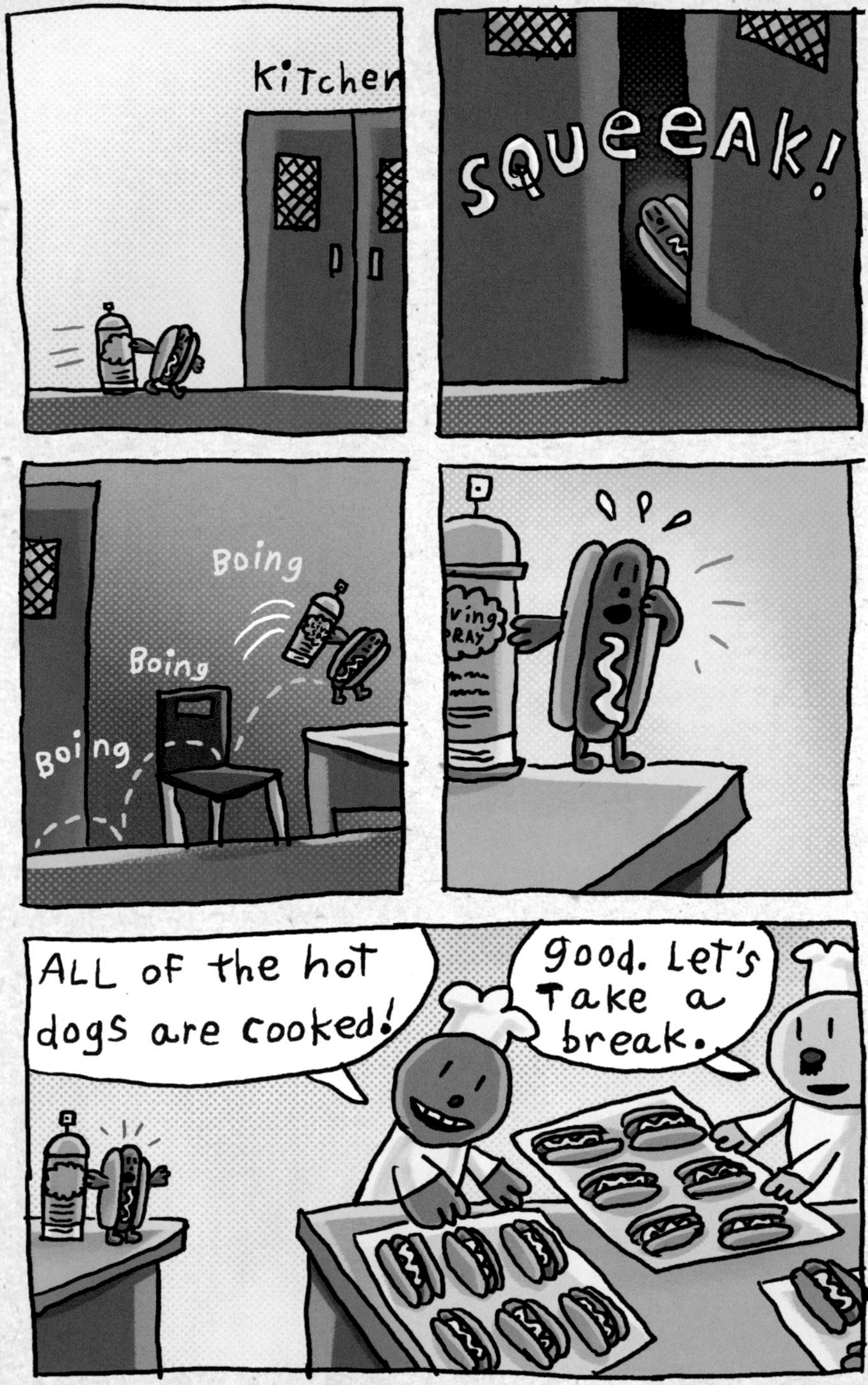

KiTchen
SQUEEAK!
Boing
Boing
Boing
ALL of the hot dogs are cooked!
good. Let's Take a break.

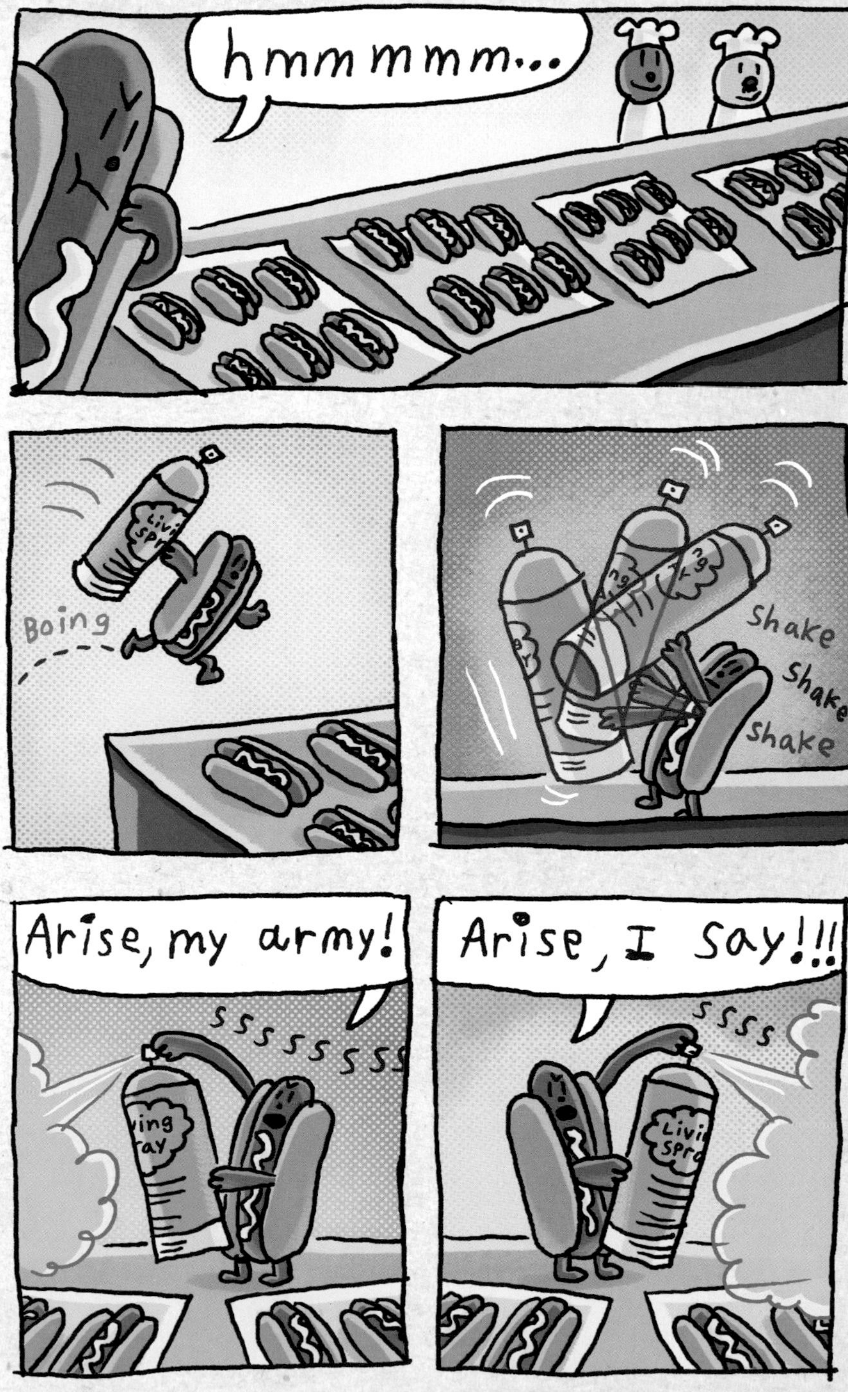
hmmmmm...
Boing
Shake
Shake
Shake
Arise, my army!
SSSSSSSSS
Arise, I say!!!
SSSS

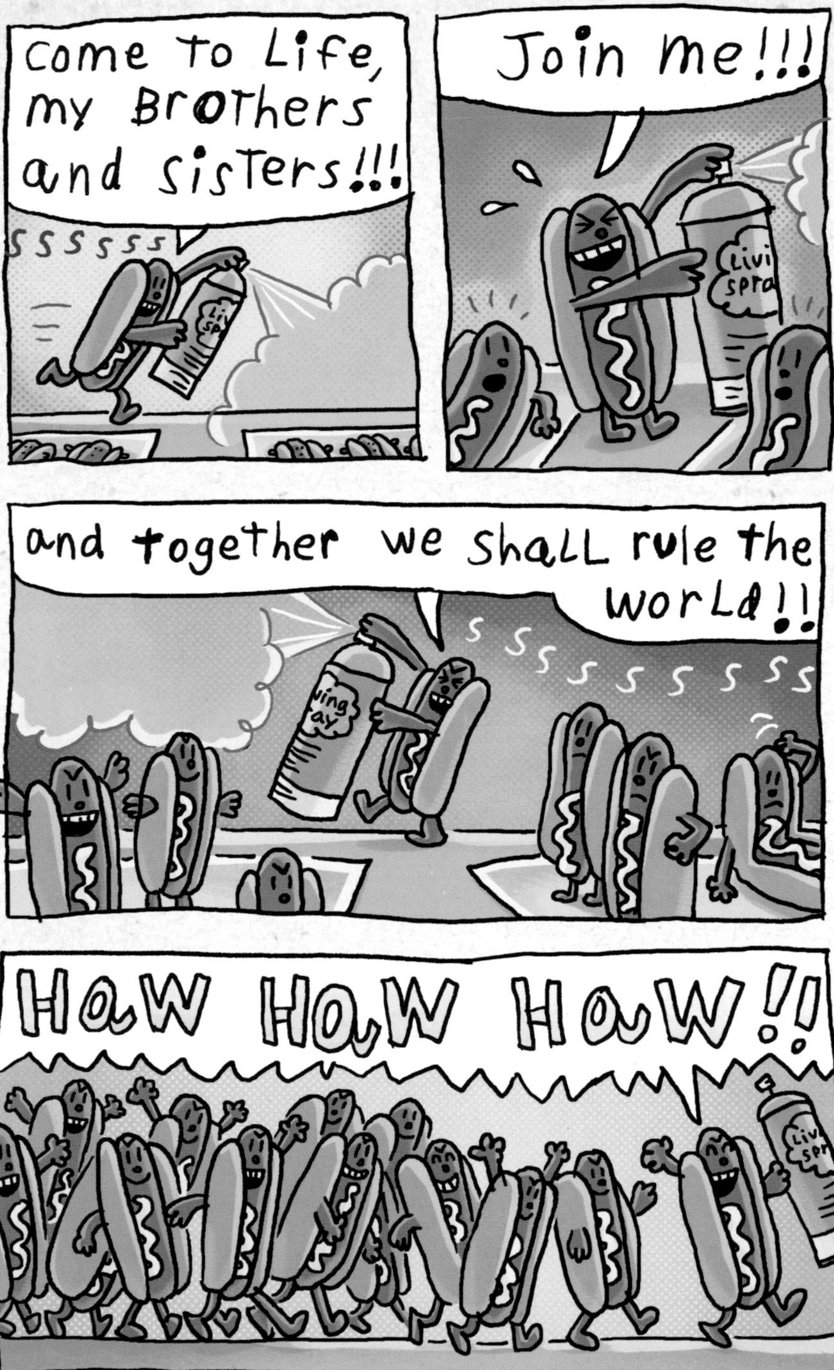
Come to Life, my Brothers and Sisters!!!
SSSSSS
Join me!!!
and together we shall rule the world!!
HAW HAW HAW!!

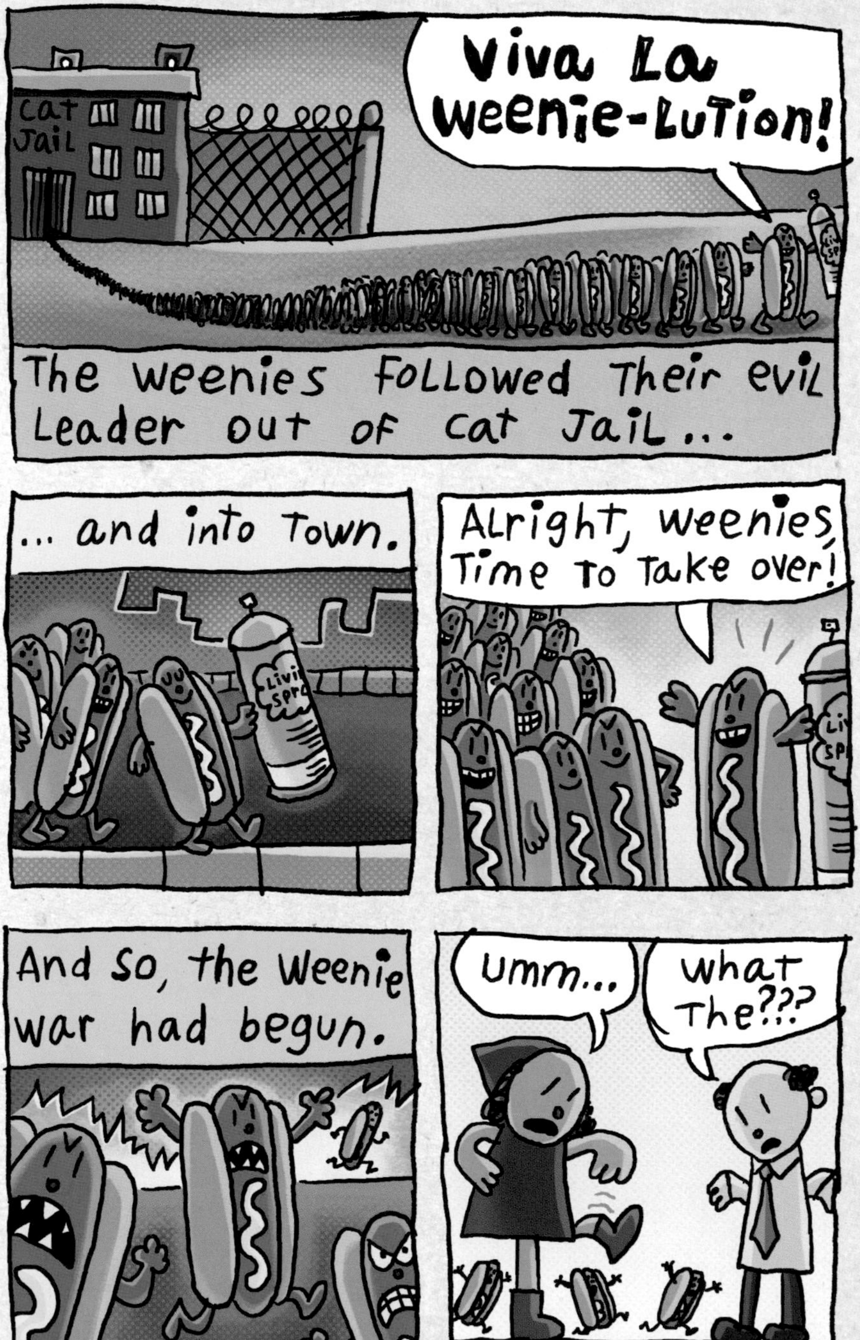
Viva La Weenie-Lution!
CAT JAIL
The weenies followed their evil leader out of cat jail...
... and into town.
Alright, weenies, time to take over!
And so, the weenie war had begun.
Umm...
What the???

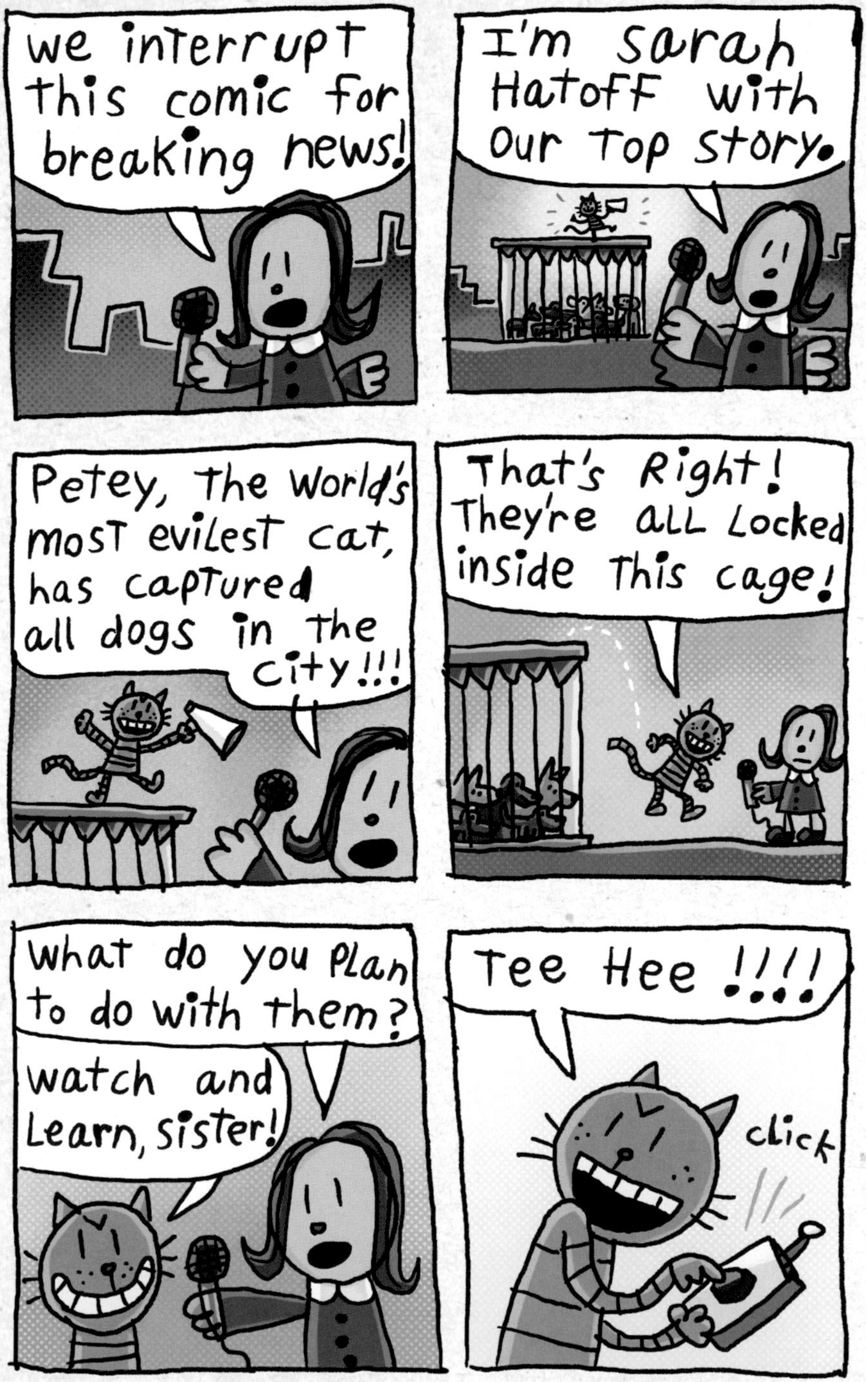
we interrupt this comic for breaking news!
I'm Sarah Hatoff with our top story.
Petey, the world's most evilest cat, has captured all dogs in the city!!!
That's right! They're all locked inside this cage!
What do you plan to do with them?
Watch and learn, sister!
Tee Hee!!!!
click

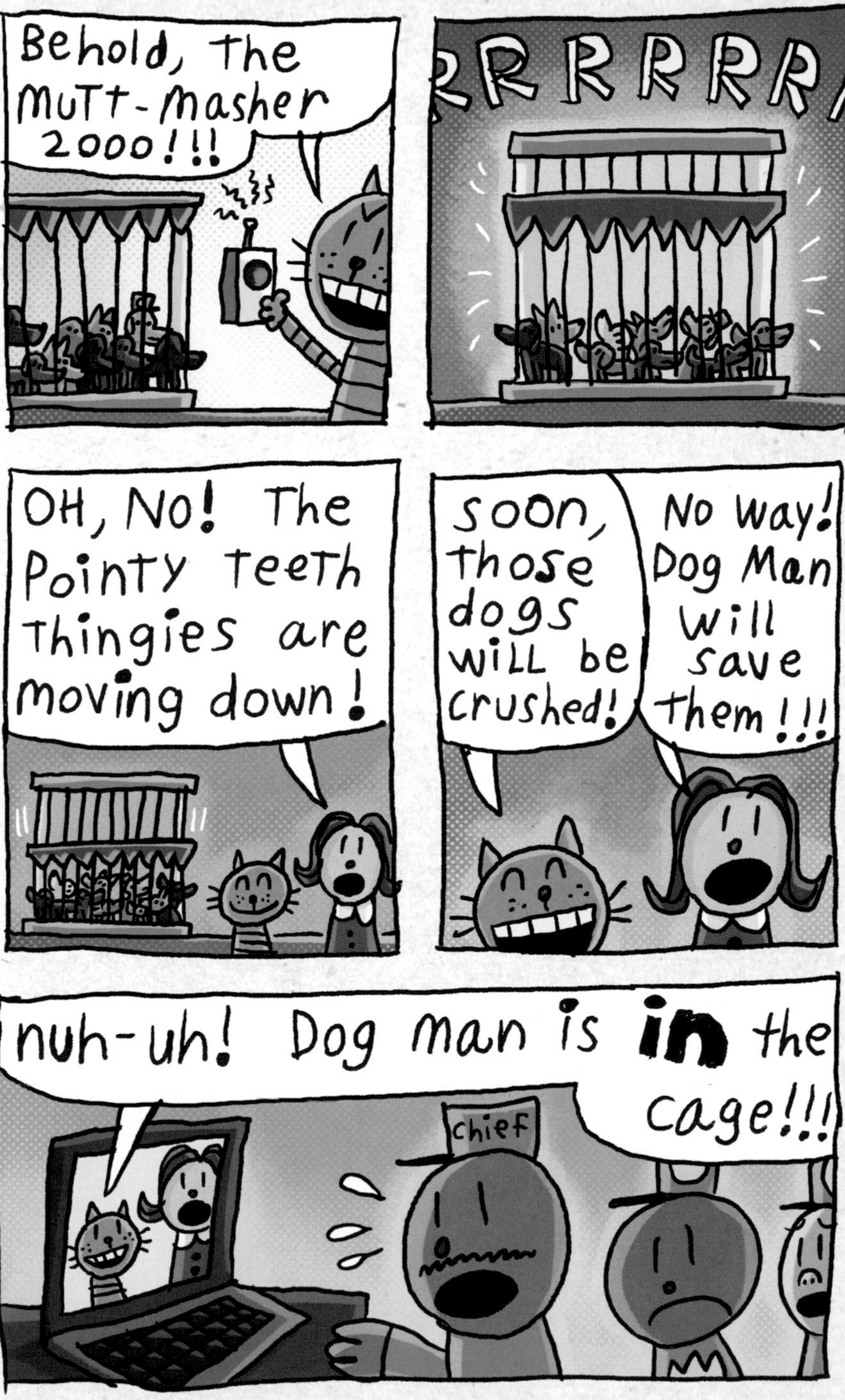
Behold, the Mutt-Masher 2000!!!
RRRRRRA
OH, NO! The Pointy teeth thingies are moving down!
Soon, those dogs will be crushed!
No way! Dog Man will save them!!!
nuh-uh! Dog man is **in** the cage!!!
chief

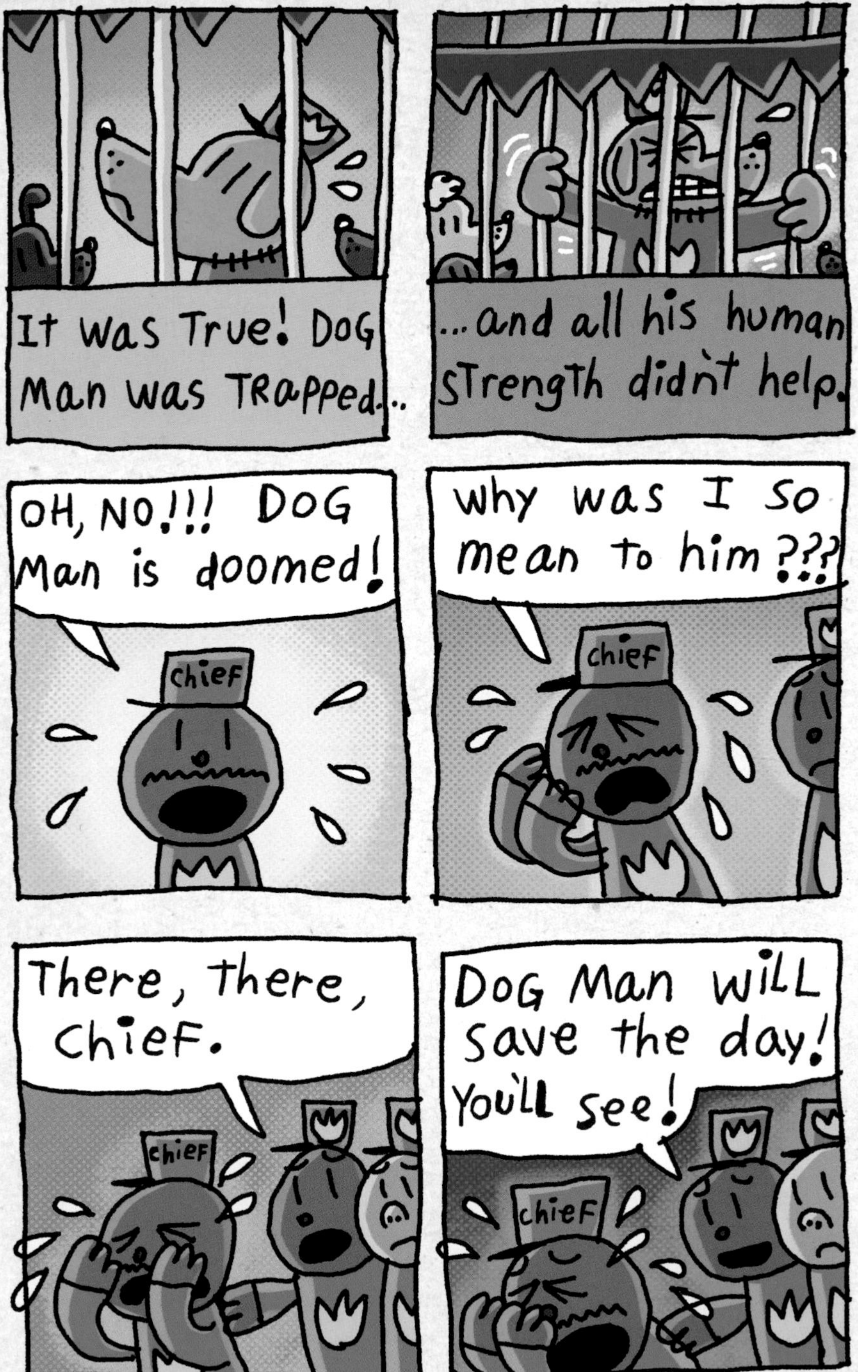
It was True! DOG Man was TRapped...
...and all his human STrength didn't help.
OH, NO!!! DOG Man is doomed!
Why was I so mean to him???
There, there, Chief.
DOG Man will save the day! You'll see!

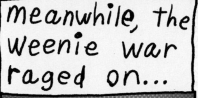

meanwhile, the weenie war raged on...

...It looked like the end was near...

...but it wasn't.

awww... Look!

how cute!

say "cheese"!

click

Hey! That one made a little campfire!

Oh, how precious!

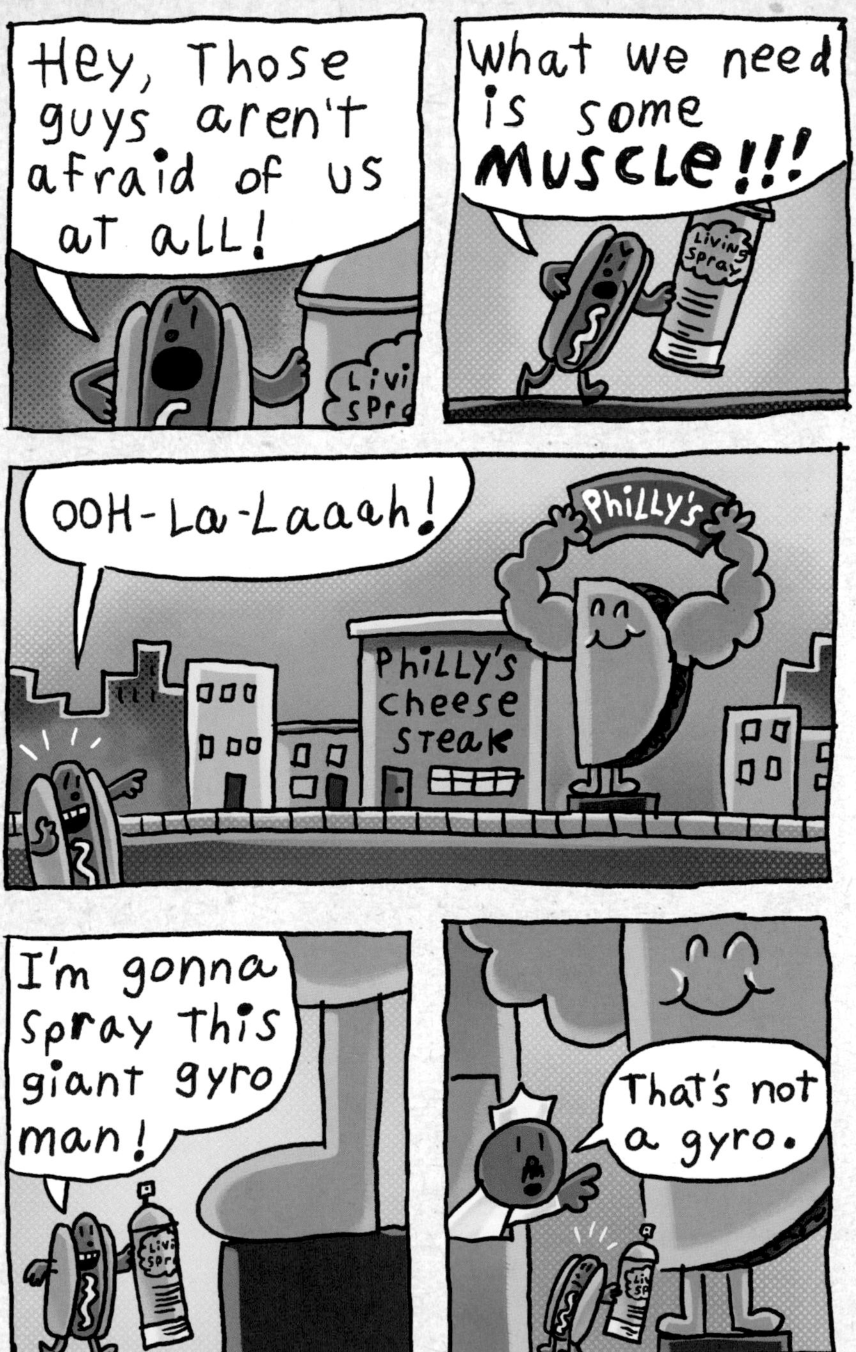
Hey, Those guys aren't afraid of us at all!
Livi
SPr
What we need is some MUSCLE!!!
Living Spray
OOH-La-Laaah!
PhiLLy's
PhiLLy's cheese STeak
I'm gonna spray this giant gyro man!
That's not a gyro.

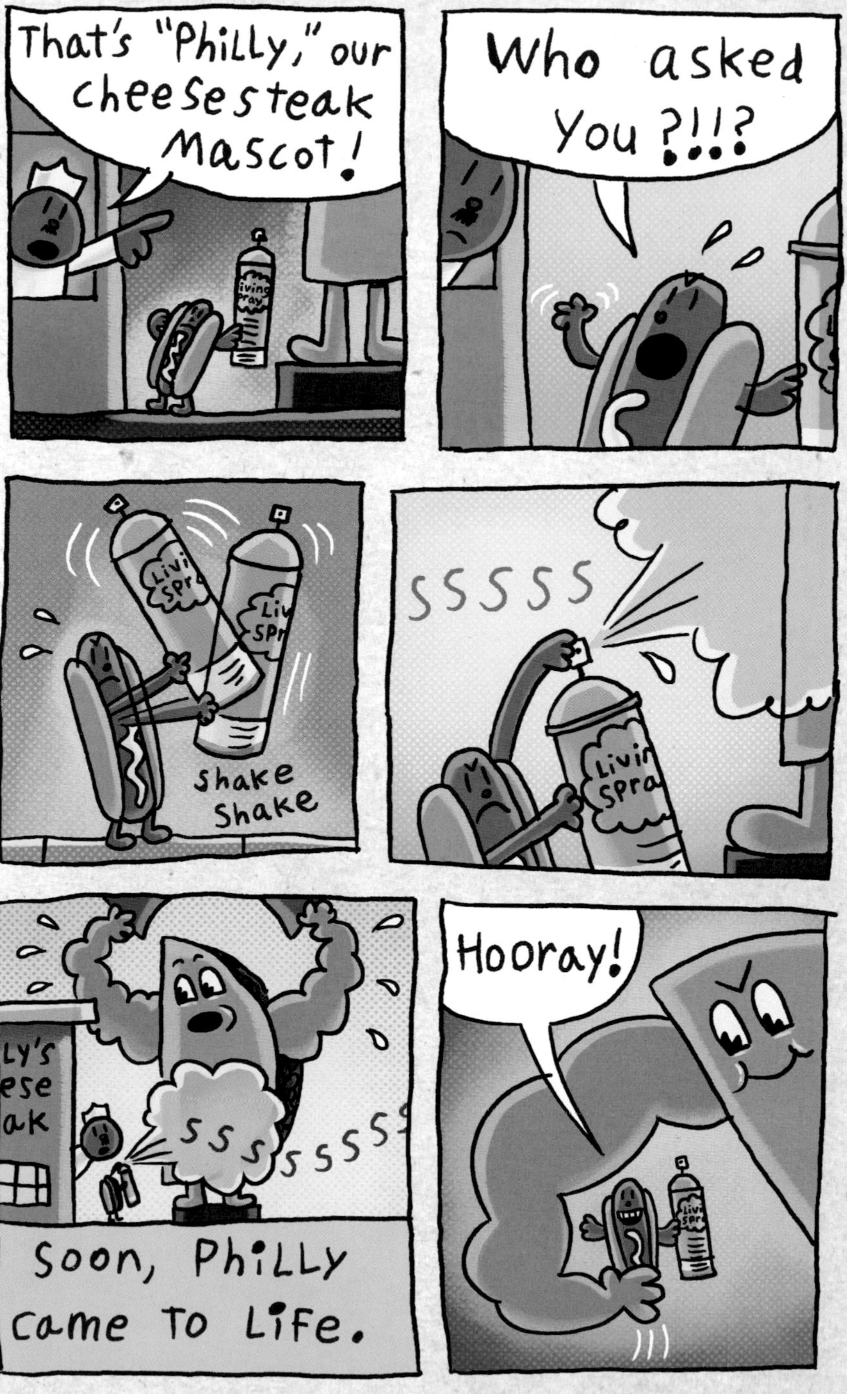
That's "Philly," our cheesesteak mascot!
Who asked you?!!?
Shake Shake
SSSSS
LY's
ese
ak
SSSSSSSS
Soon, Philly came to life.
Hooray!

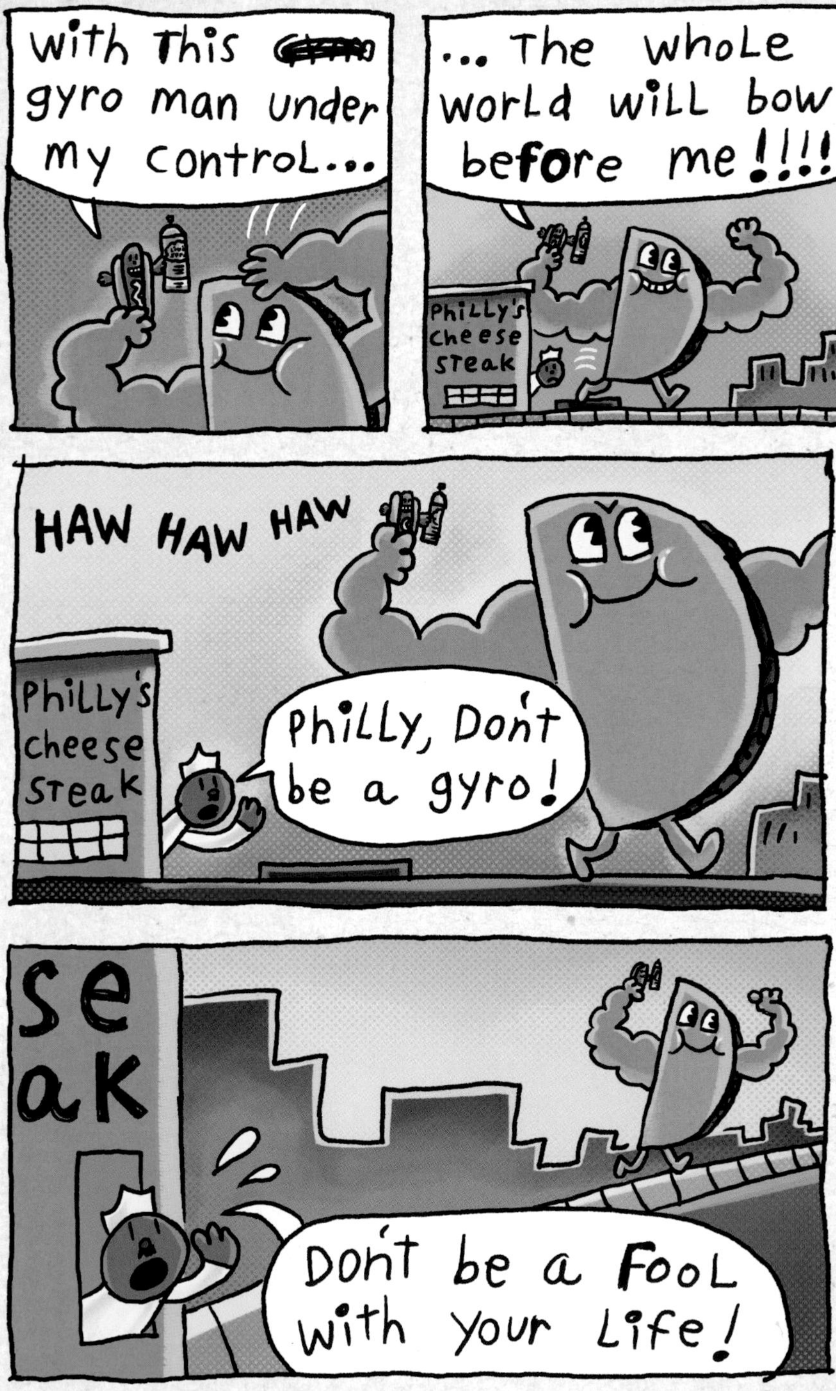
With This
gyro man under my control...
... The whole world will bow before me!!!!
Philly's Cheese Steak
HAW HAW HAW
Philly's cheese Steak
Philly, Don't be a gyro!
se ak
Don't be a Fool with your Life!

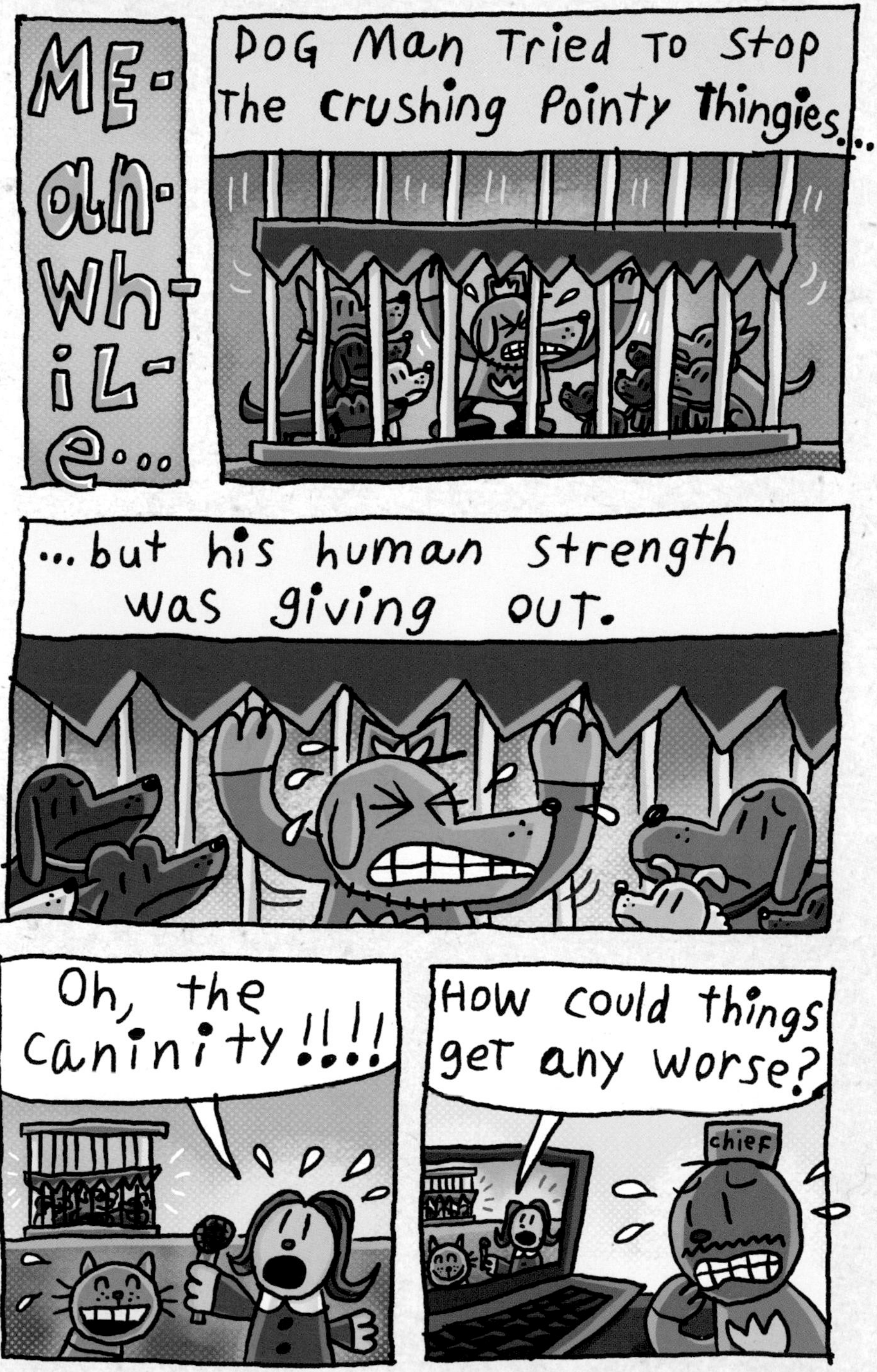
ME-an-wh-iL-e...
DOG Man Tried To Stop The crushing Pointy thingies...
...but his human strength was giving out.
Oh, the caninity!!!!
HOW could things get any worse?
chief

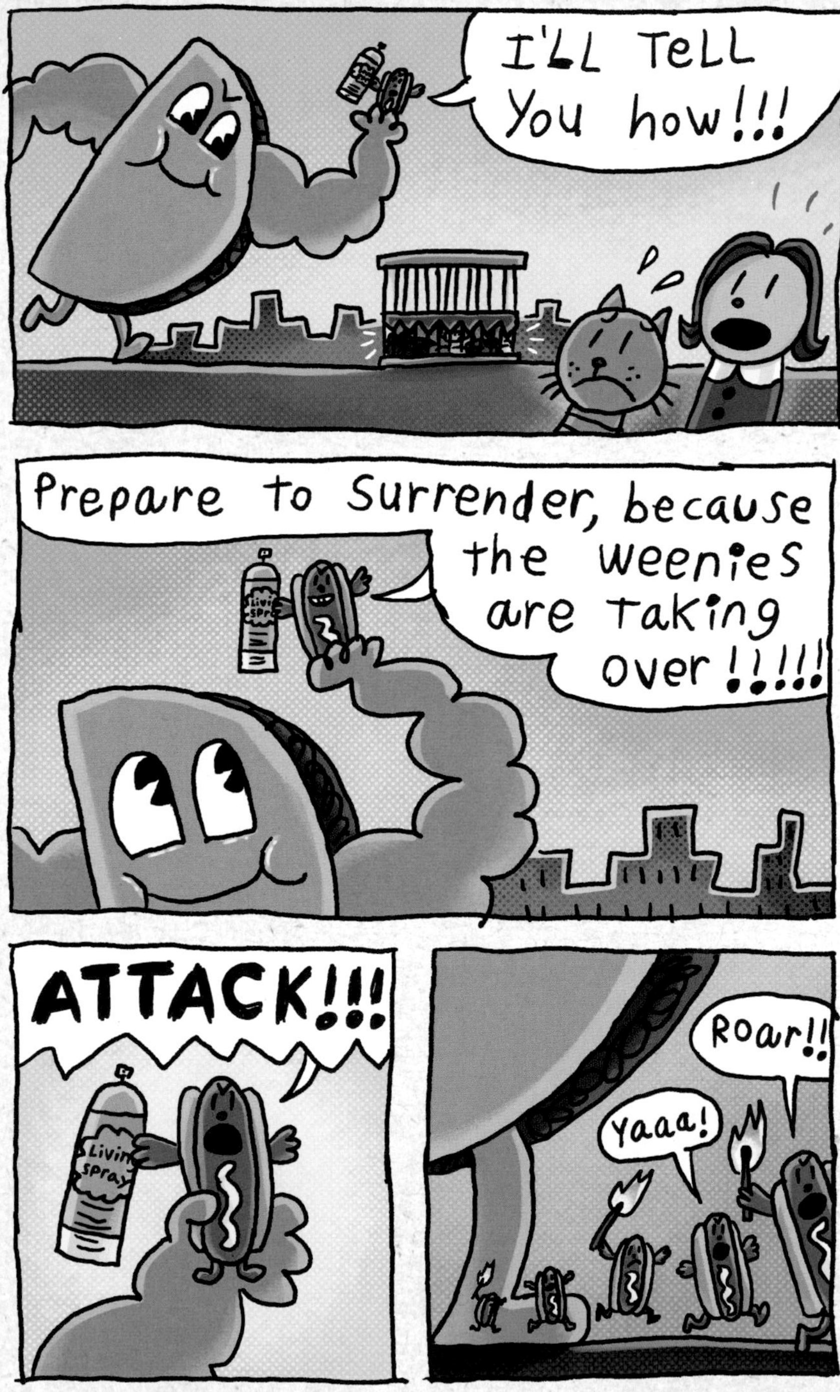
I'LL TeLL You how!!!
Prepare to Surrender, because the weenies are Taking over!!!!!
ATTACK!!!
Roar!!
Yaaa!

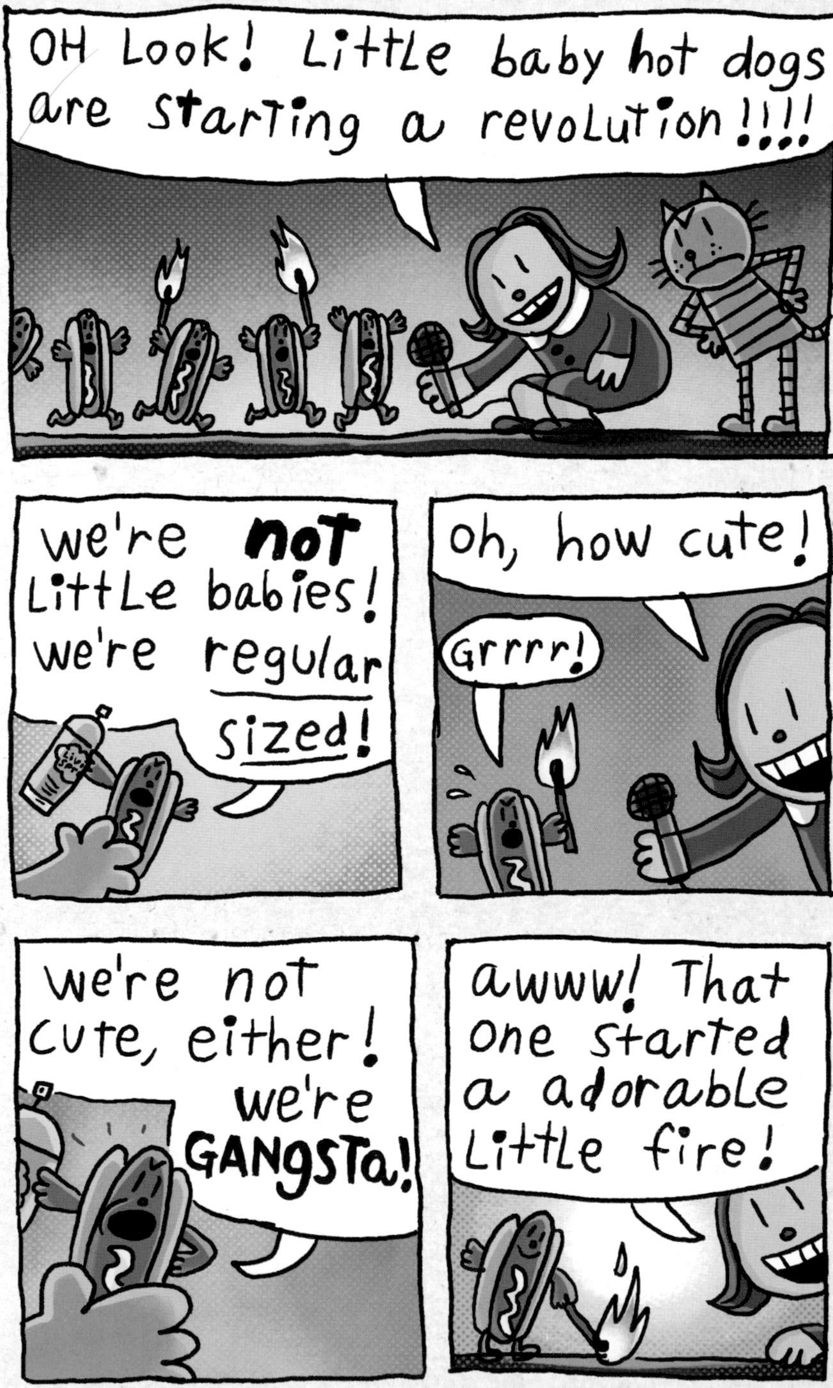
OH Look! Little baby hot dogs are starting a revolution!!!!
We're NOT Little babies! We're regular sized!
Oh, how cute!
Grrrr!
We're not cute, either! We're GANGSTA!
awww! That one started a adorable Little fire!

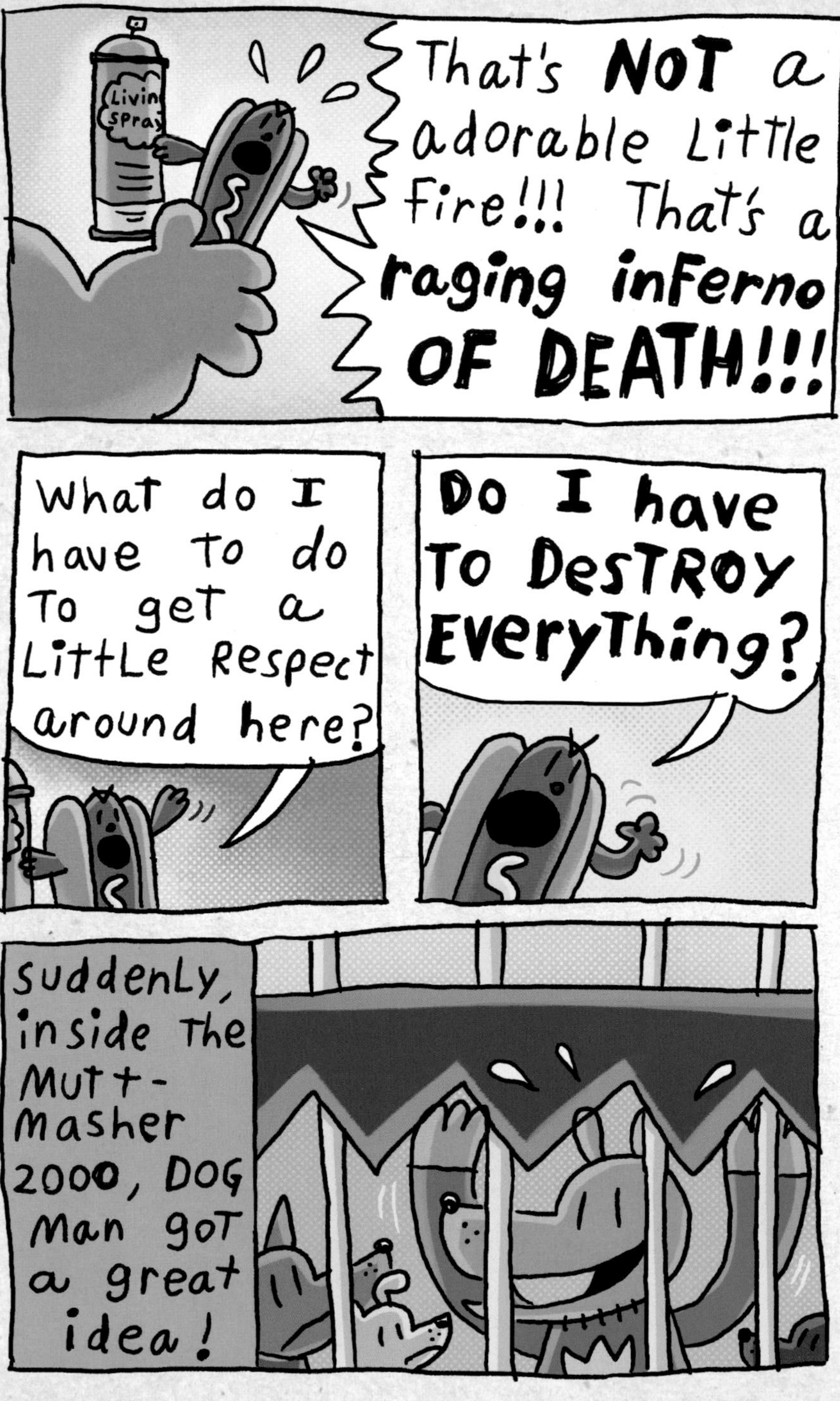
Living spray
That's NOT a adorable Little Fire!!! That's a raging inFerno OF DEATH!!!
What do I have to do to get a Little Respect around here?
Do I have to Destroy Everything?
suddenly, inside the Mutt-Masher 2000, Dog Man got a great idea!

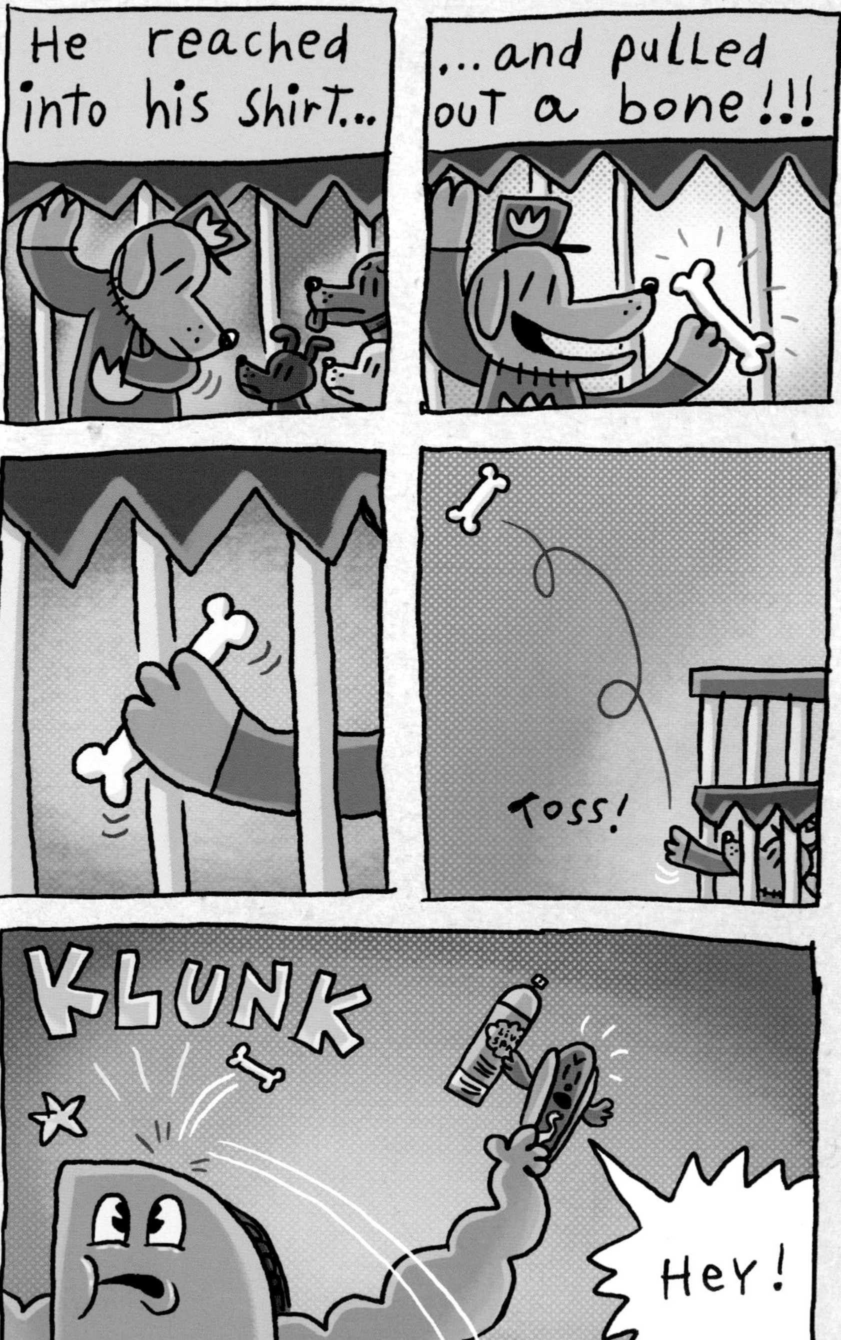
He reached into his shirt...
...and pulled out a bone!!!
TOSS!
KLUNK
HEY!

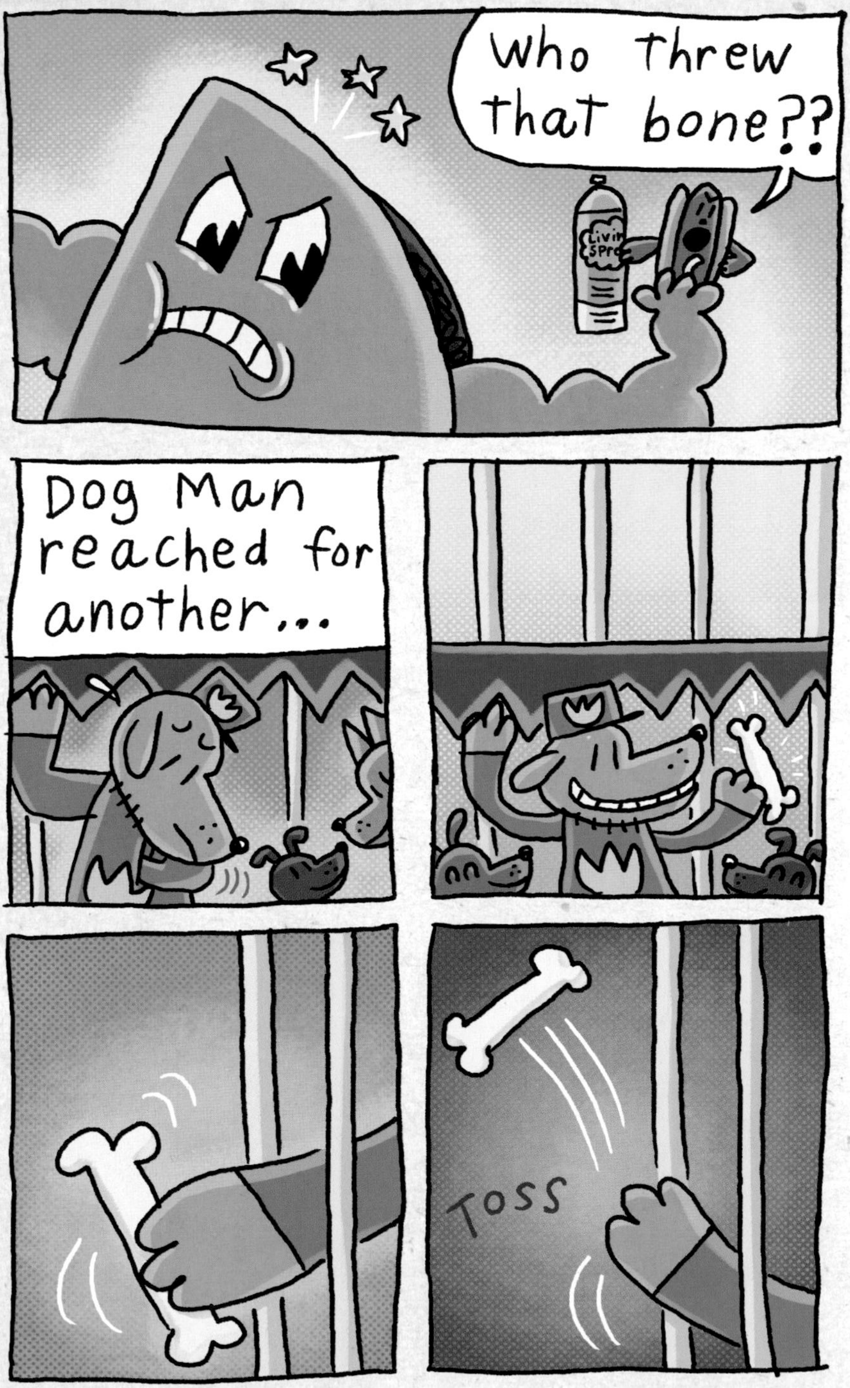
Who threw that bone??
Dog Man reached for another...
TOSS

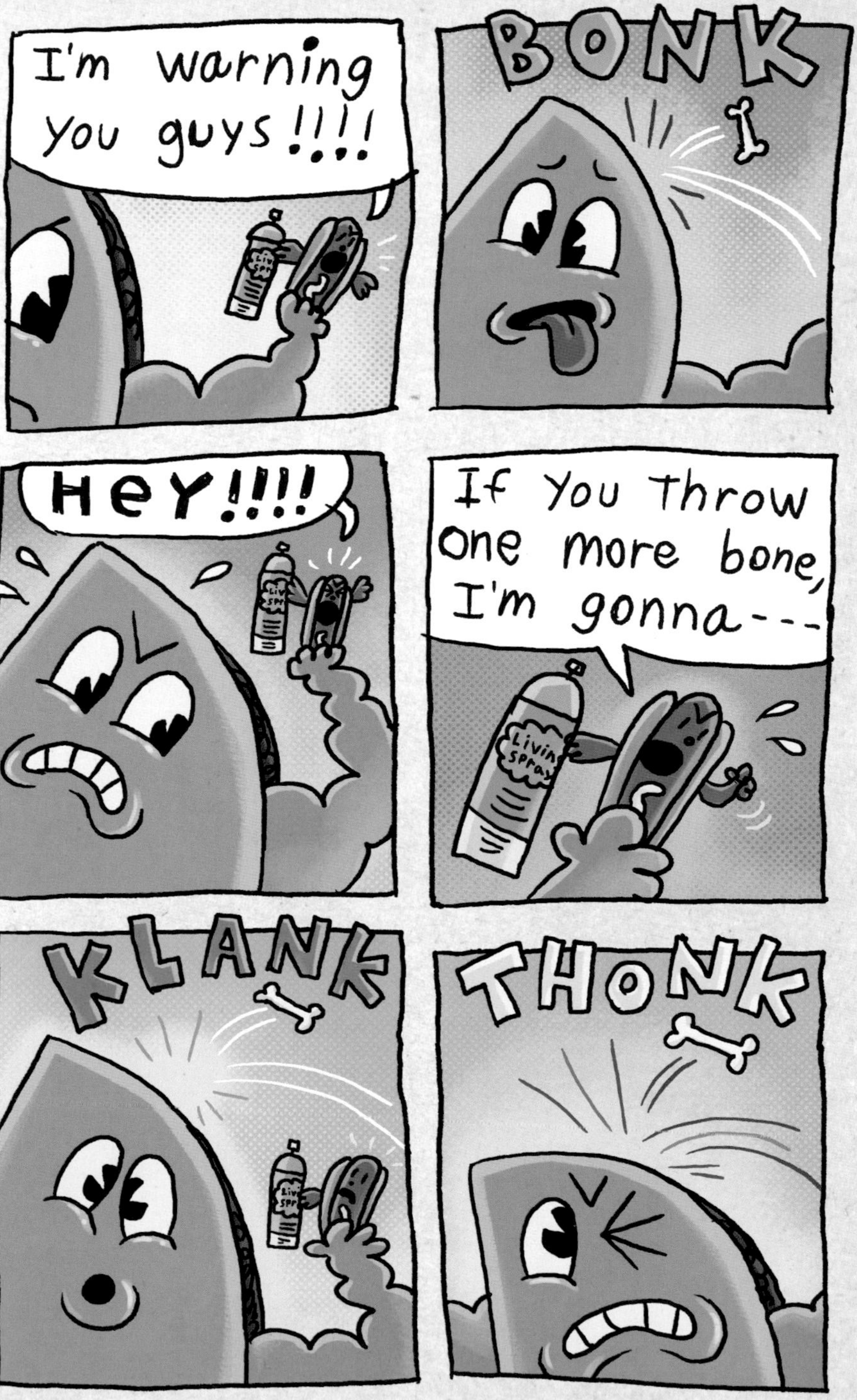
I'm warning you guys!!!!
BONK
HEY!!!!
If You Throw one more bone, I'm gonna---
KLANK
THONK

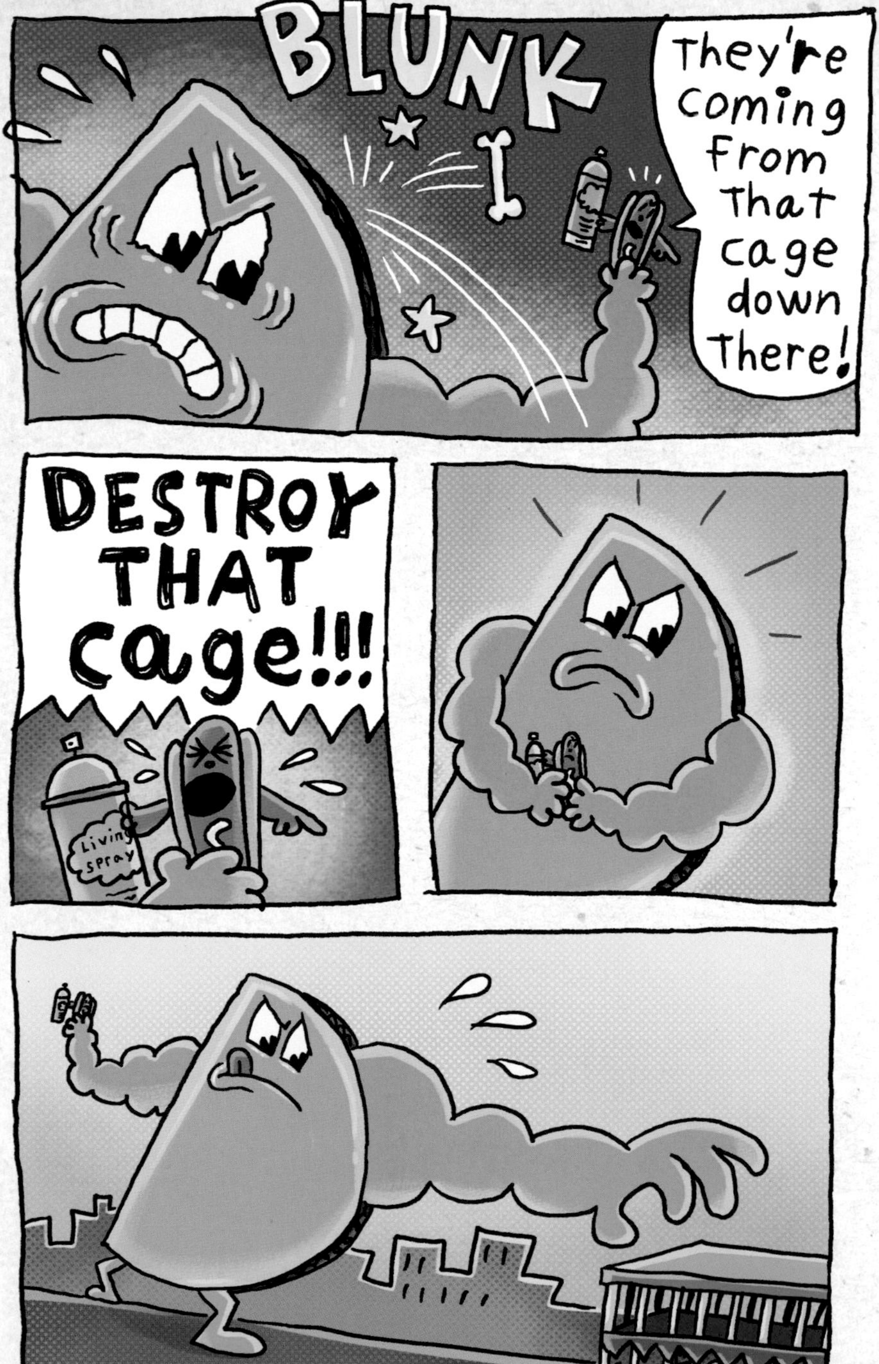
BLUNK
They're coming from That cage down There!
DESTROY THAT Cage!!!
Living spray

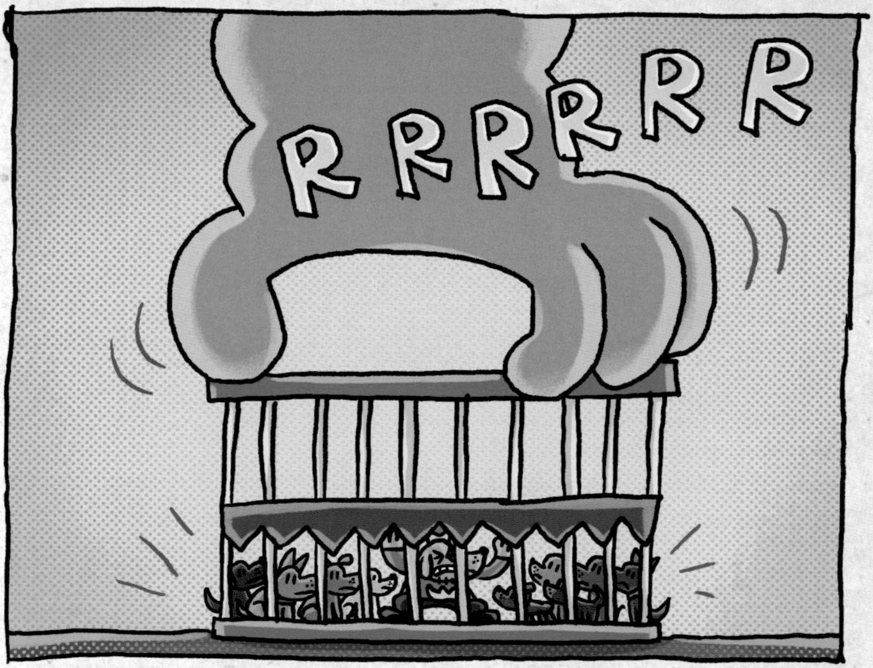
RRRRRRR

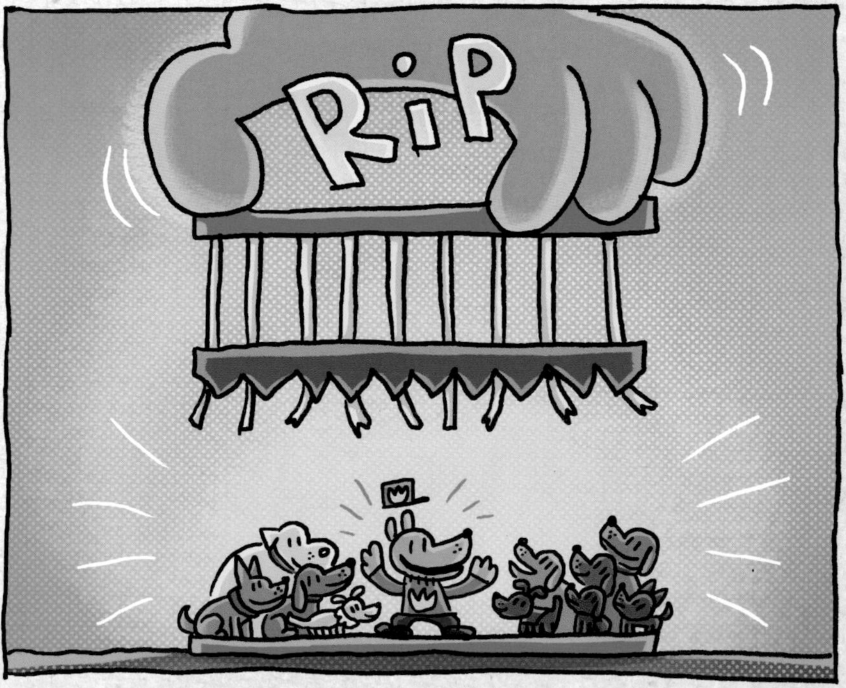
RiP

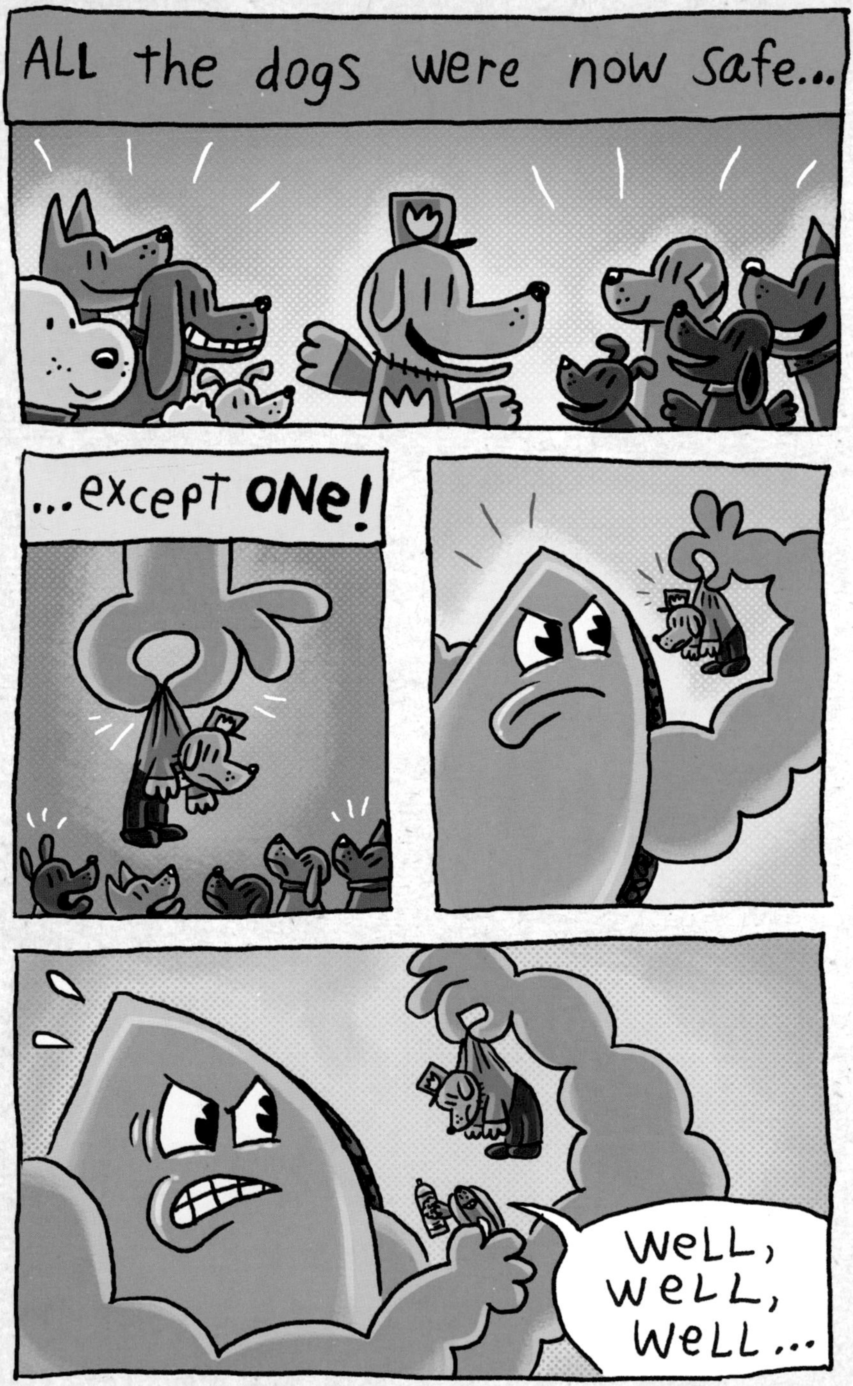
ALL the dogs were now safe...
...except ONE!
WELL, WELL, WELL...

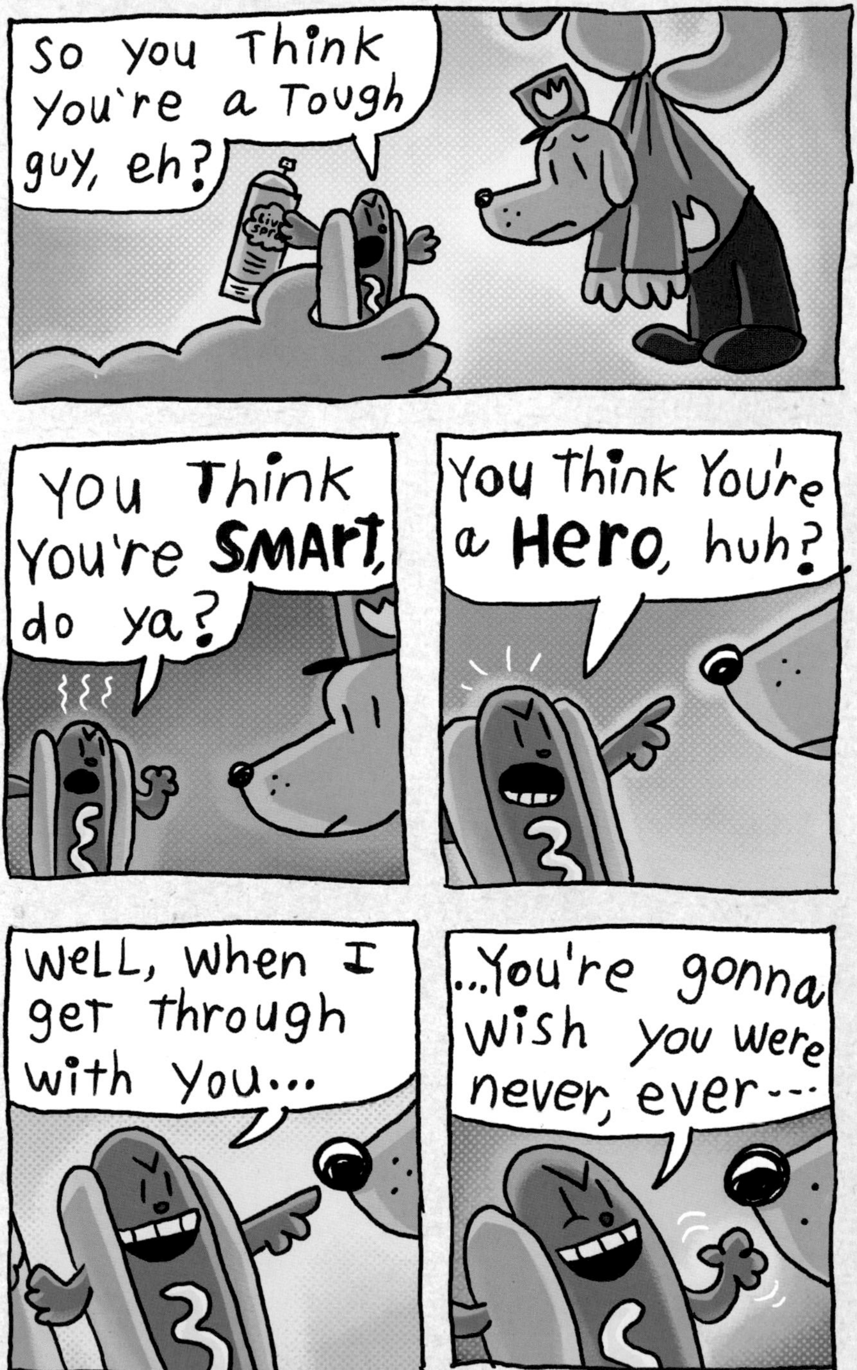
So you Think You're a Tough guy, eh?
You Think You're SMART, do ya?
You Think You're a Hero, huh?
WELL, when I get through with you...
...You're gonna wish you were never, ever---

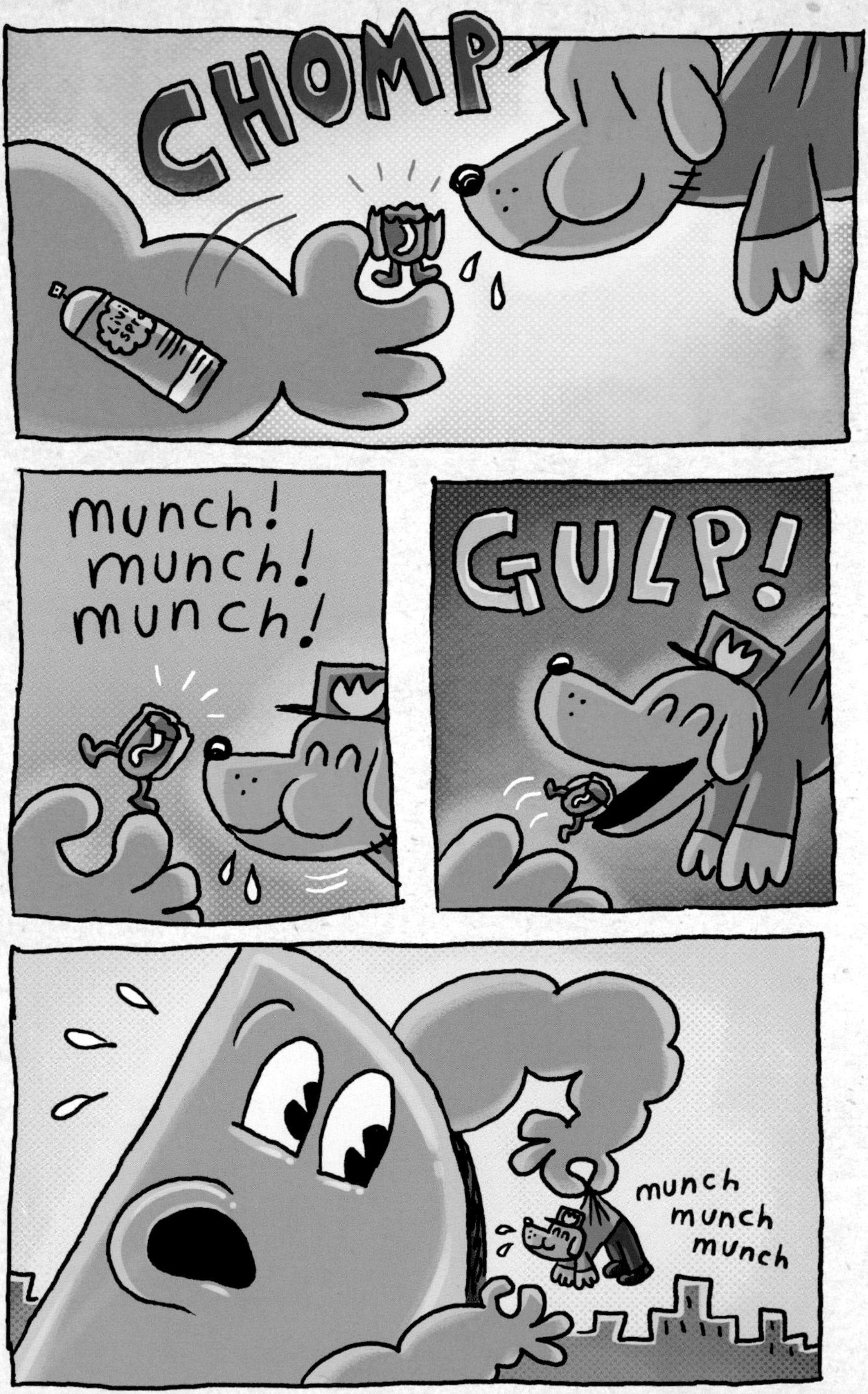
CHOMP
munch!
munch!
munch!
GULP!
munch
munch
munch

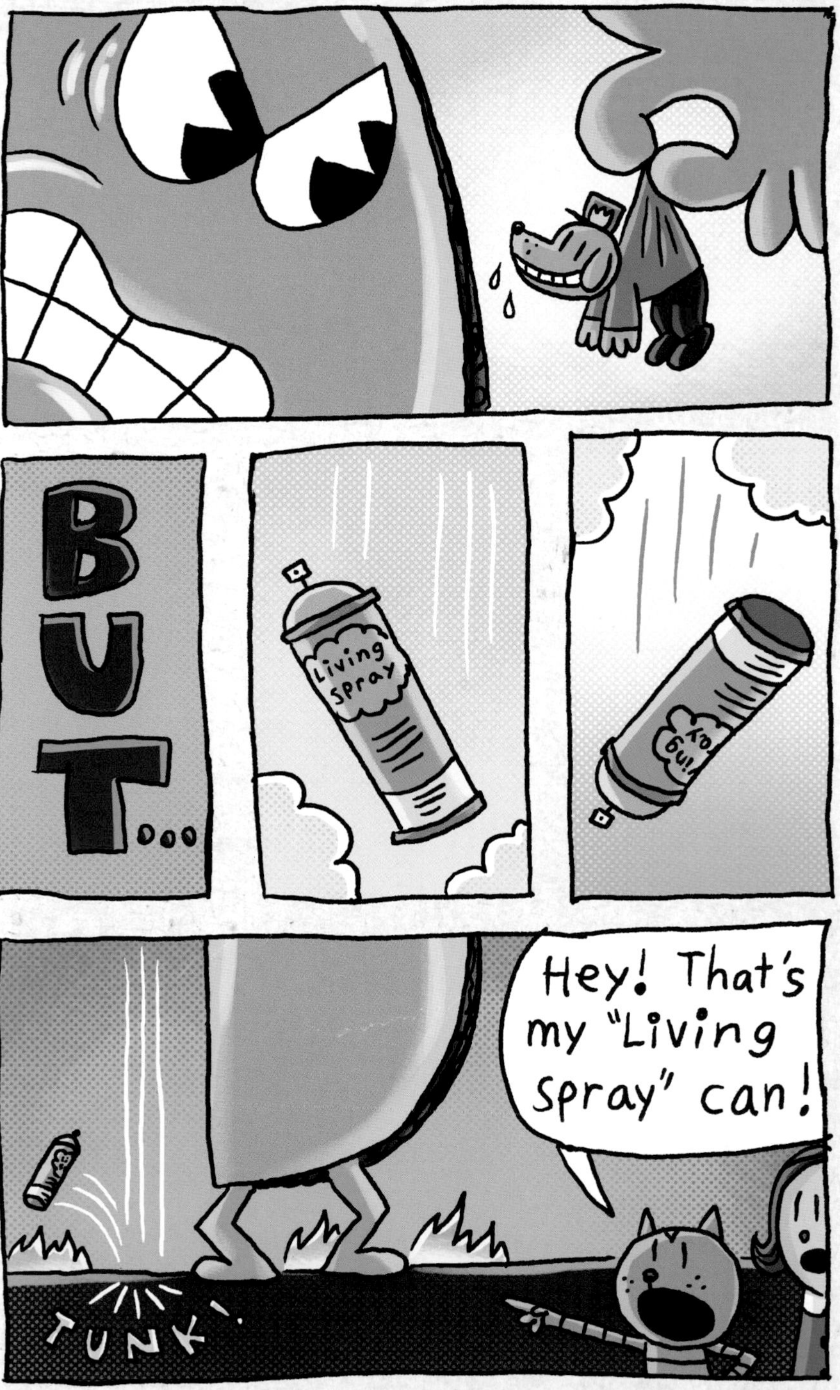

BUT...
Living spray
Hey! That's my "Living spray" can!
TUNK!

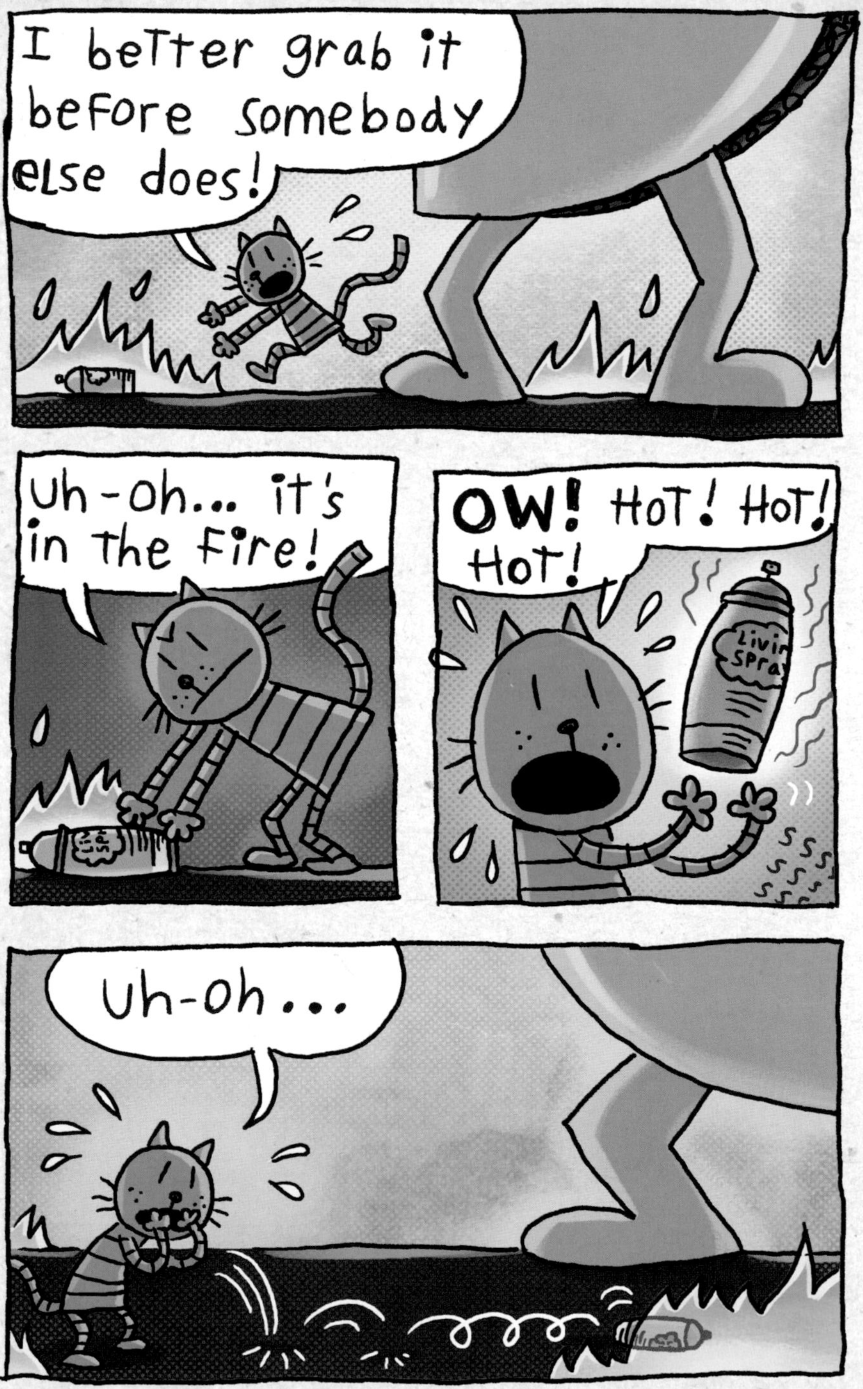
I better grab it before somebody else does!
Uh-oh... it's in the fire!
OW! HOT! HOT! HOT!
Livin Spray
Uh-oh...

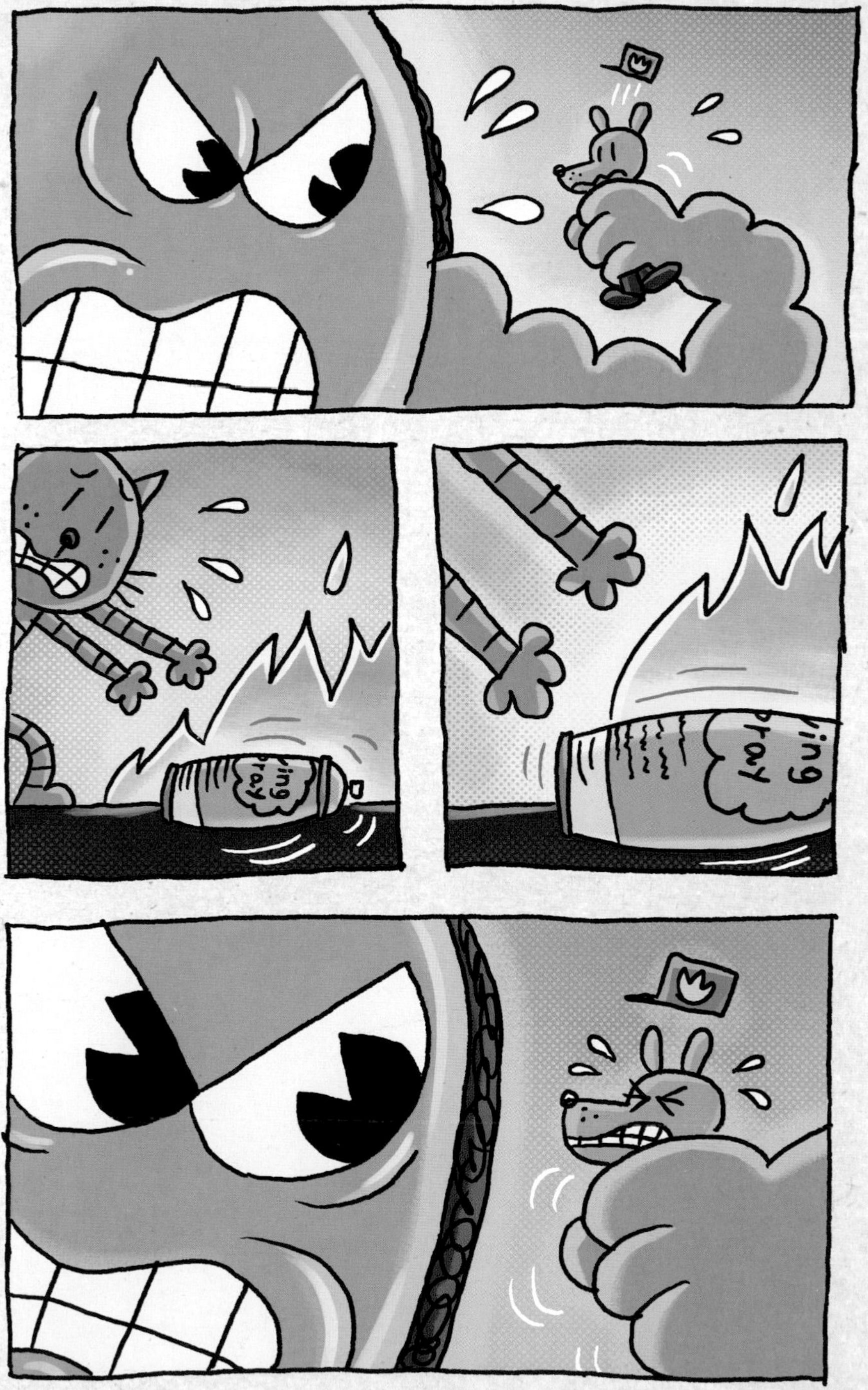

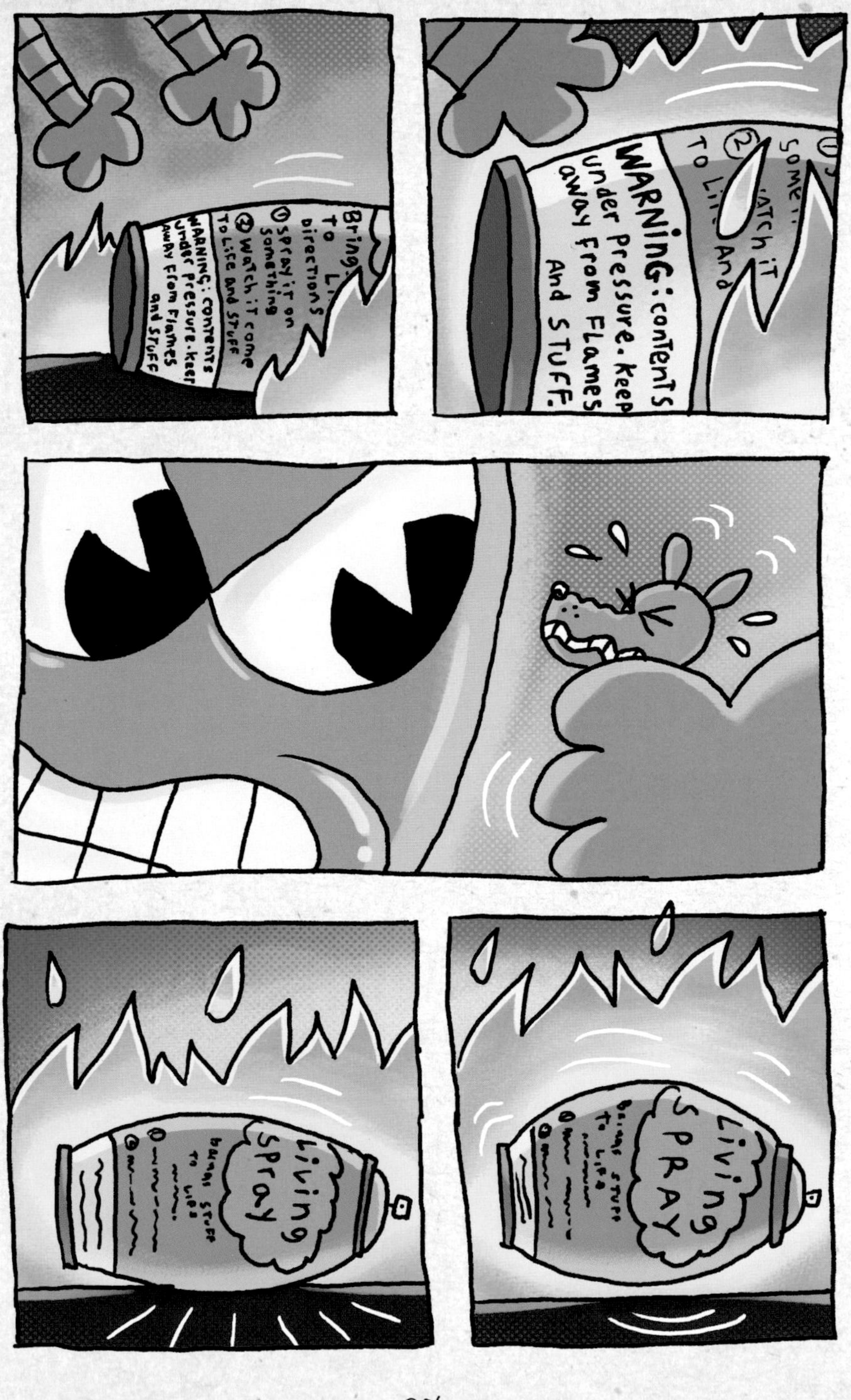

Bring
To
directions
① spray it on something
② Watch it come To Life and stuff
WARNING: contents under pressure. keep away from flames and stuff
WARNING: contents under pressure. Keep away from flames And STUFF.
Living Spray
Living SPRAY

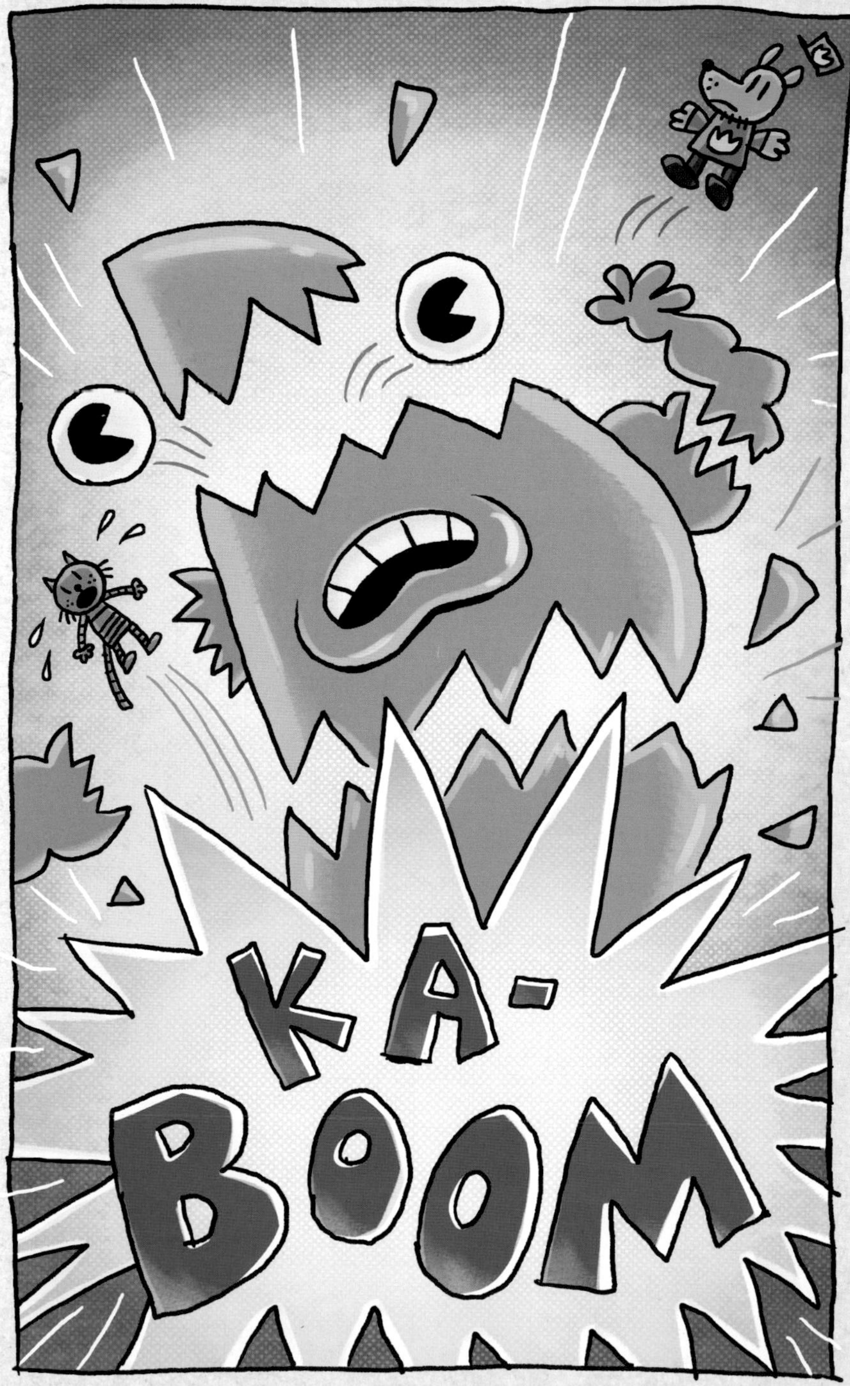
KA-
BOOM

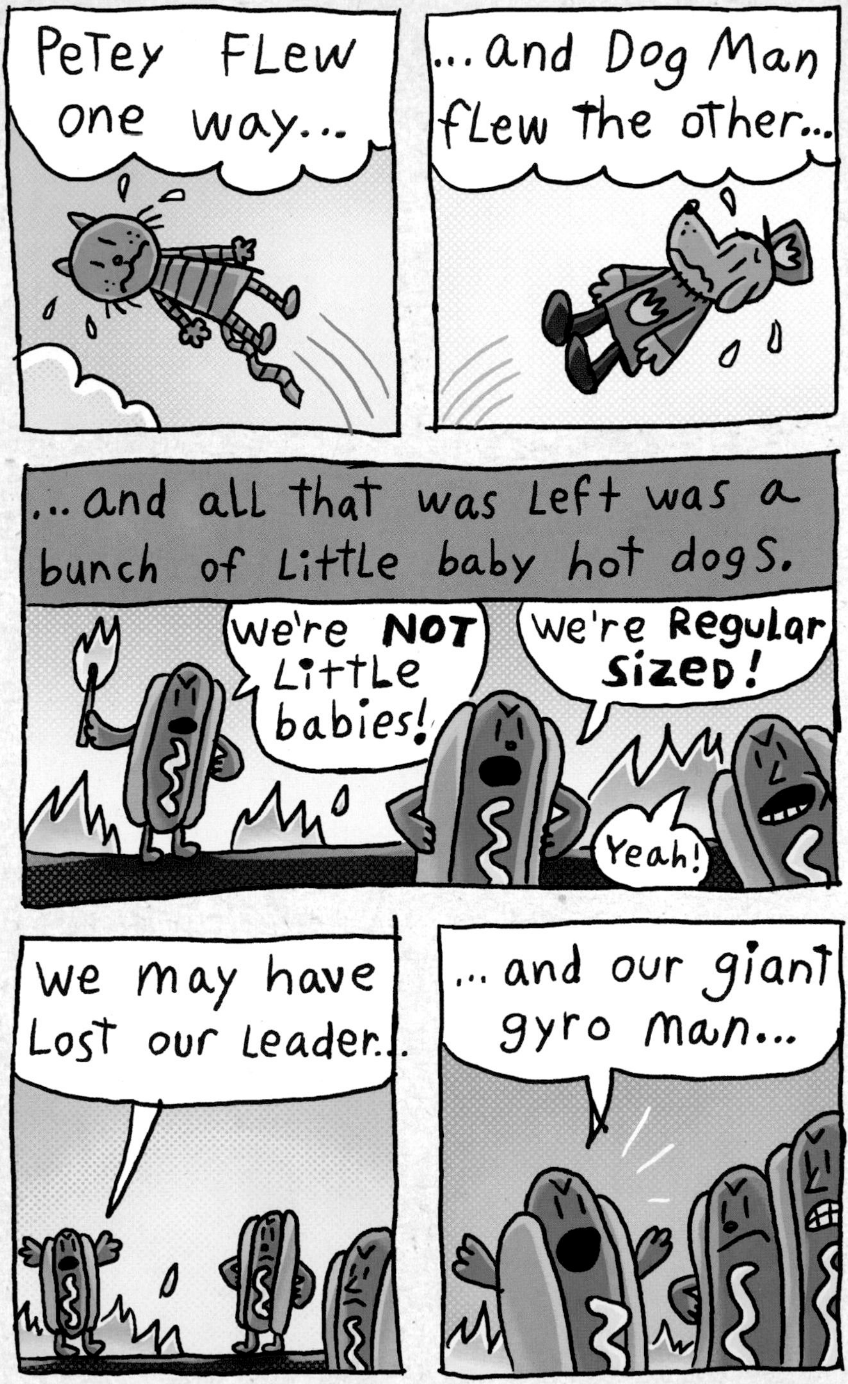
PeTey FLew one way...
...and Dog Man fLew The other...
...and all That was Left was a bunch of Little baby hot dogs.
we're NOT LitTLe babies!
we're Regular SIZED!
Yeah!
we may have Lost our Leader...
...and our giant gyro man...

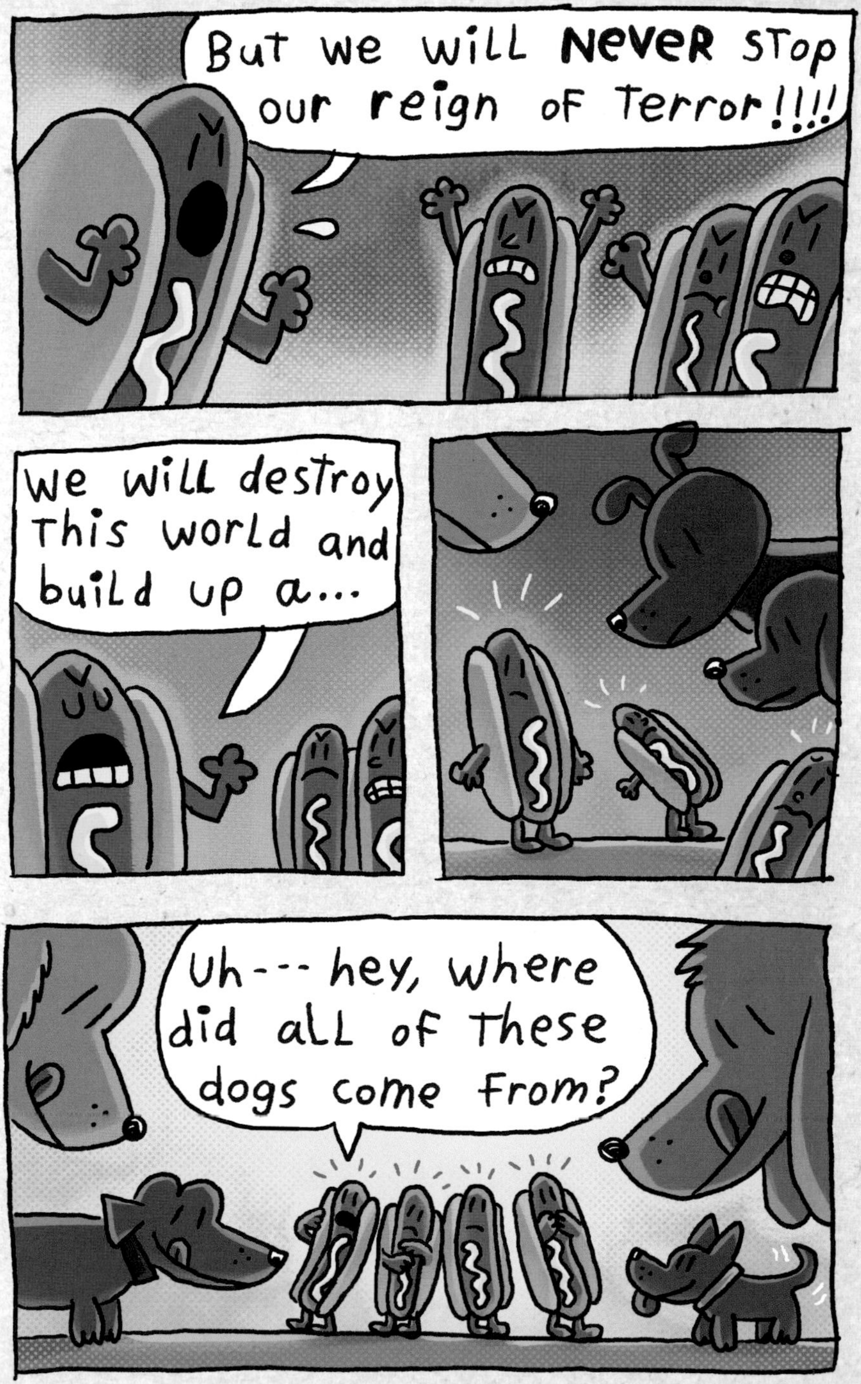
But we will NEVER stop our reign of Terror!!!!
We will destroy This world and build up a...
Uh--- hey, where did all of These dogs come from?

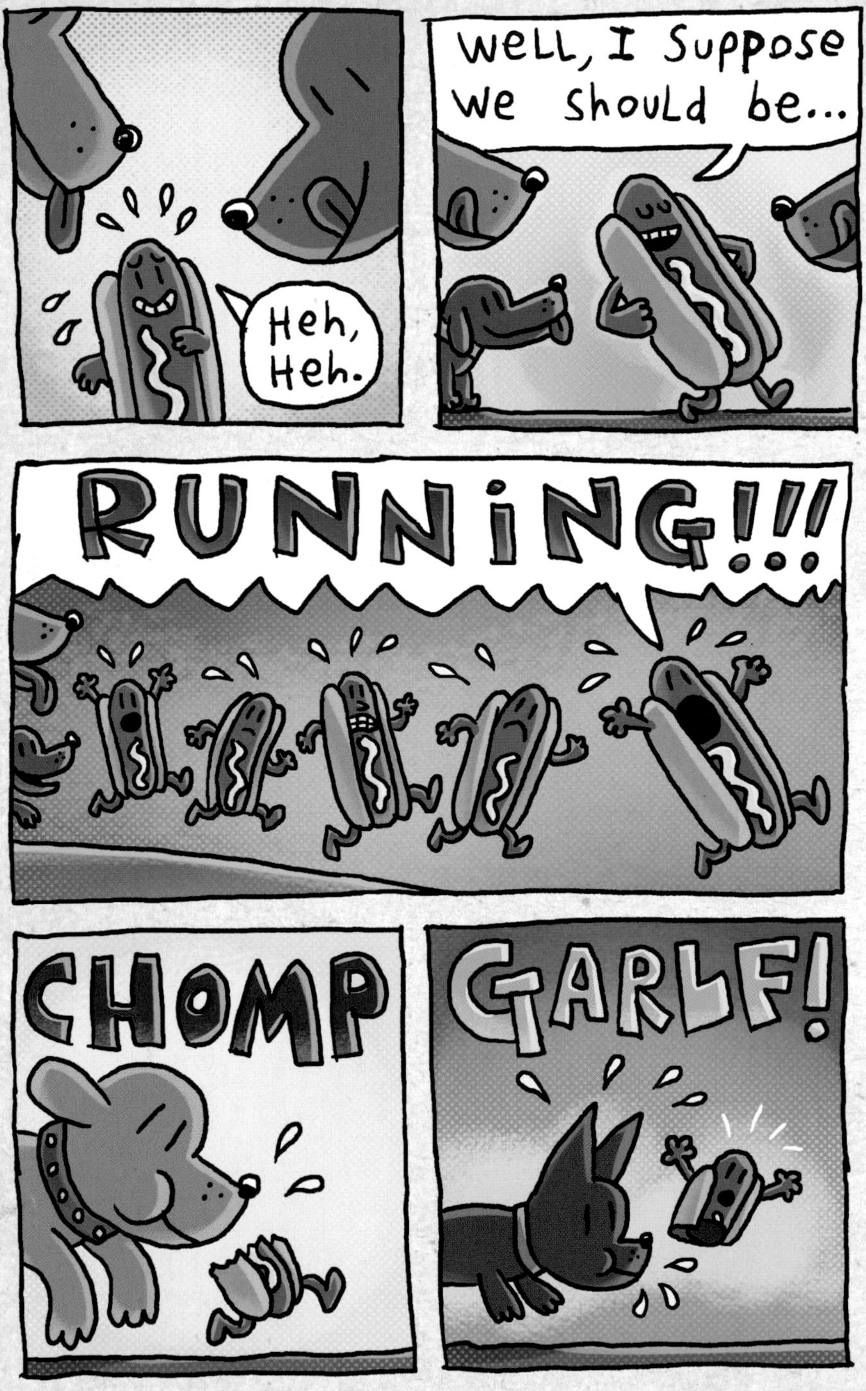
Heh, Heh.
WELL, I Suppose we should be...
RUNNiNG!!!
CHOMP
GARLF!

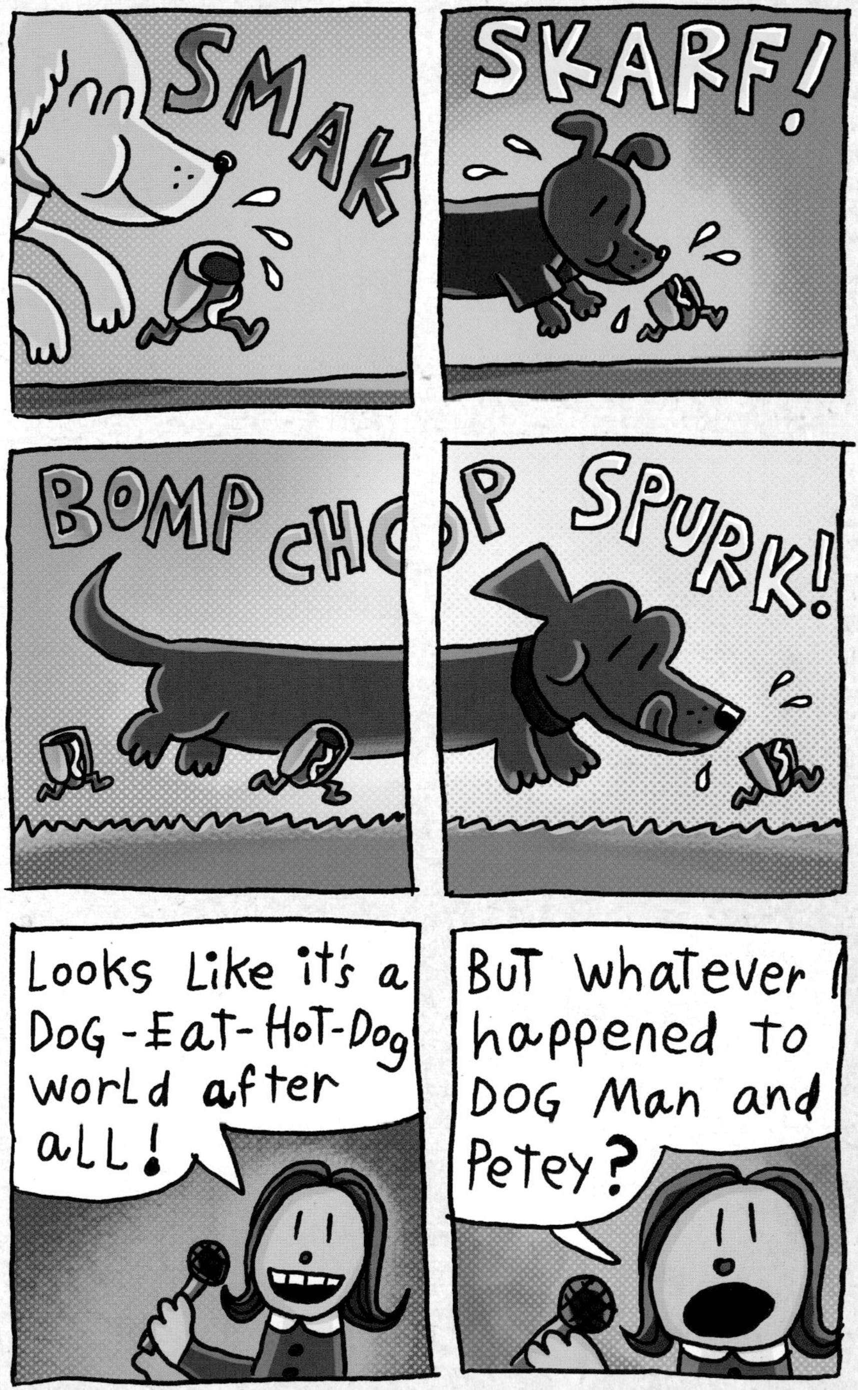
SMAK
SKARF!
BOMP
CHOP
SPURK!
Looks Like it's a DoG-Eat-HoT-Dog worLd after aLL!
BuT whatever happened to DOG Man and Petey?

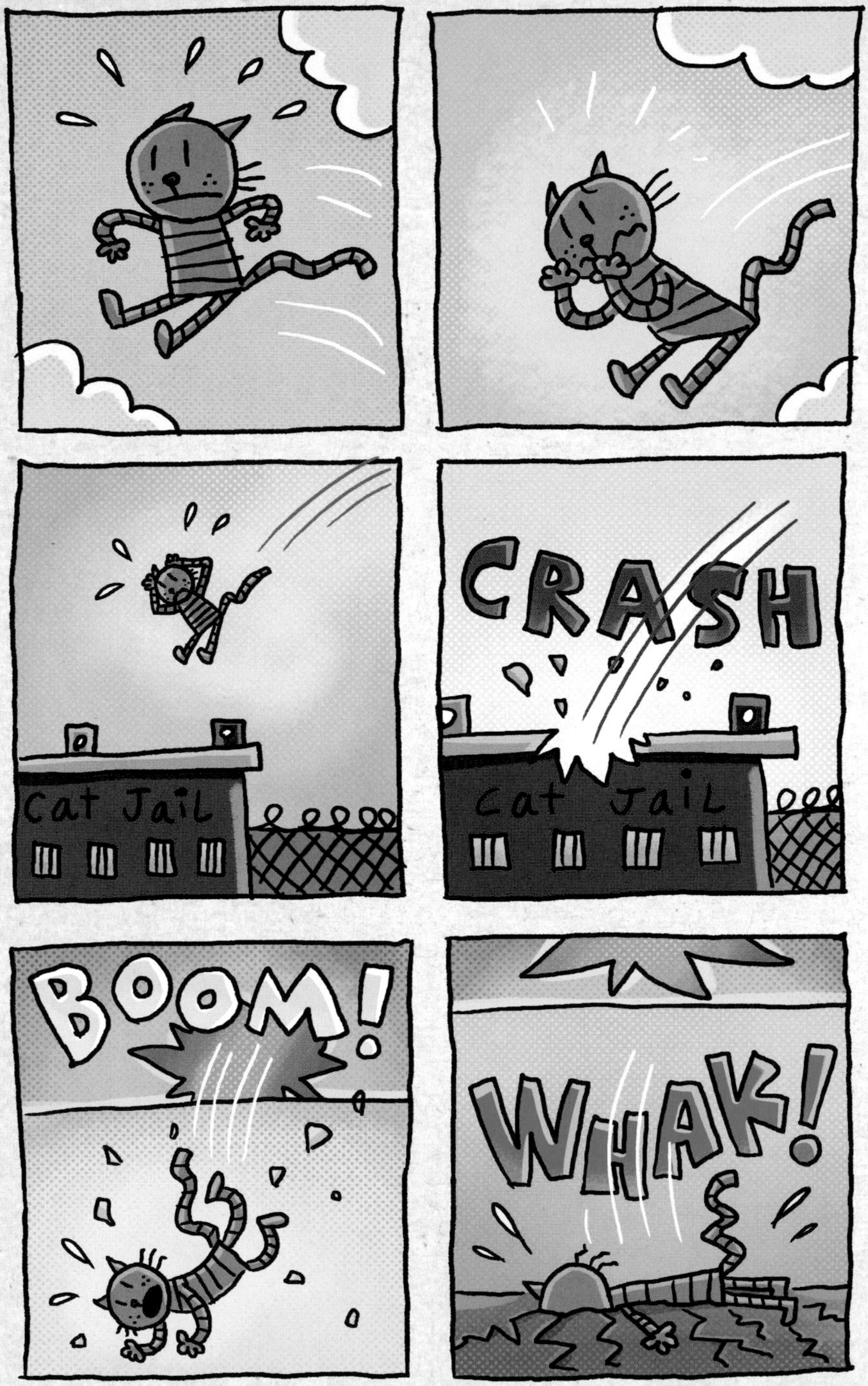
Cat Jail
CRASH
Cat Jail
BOOM!
WHAK!

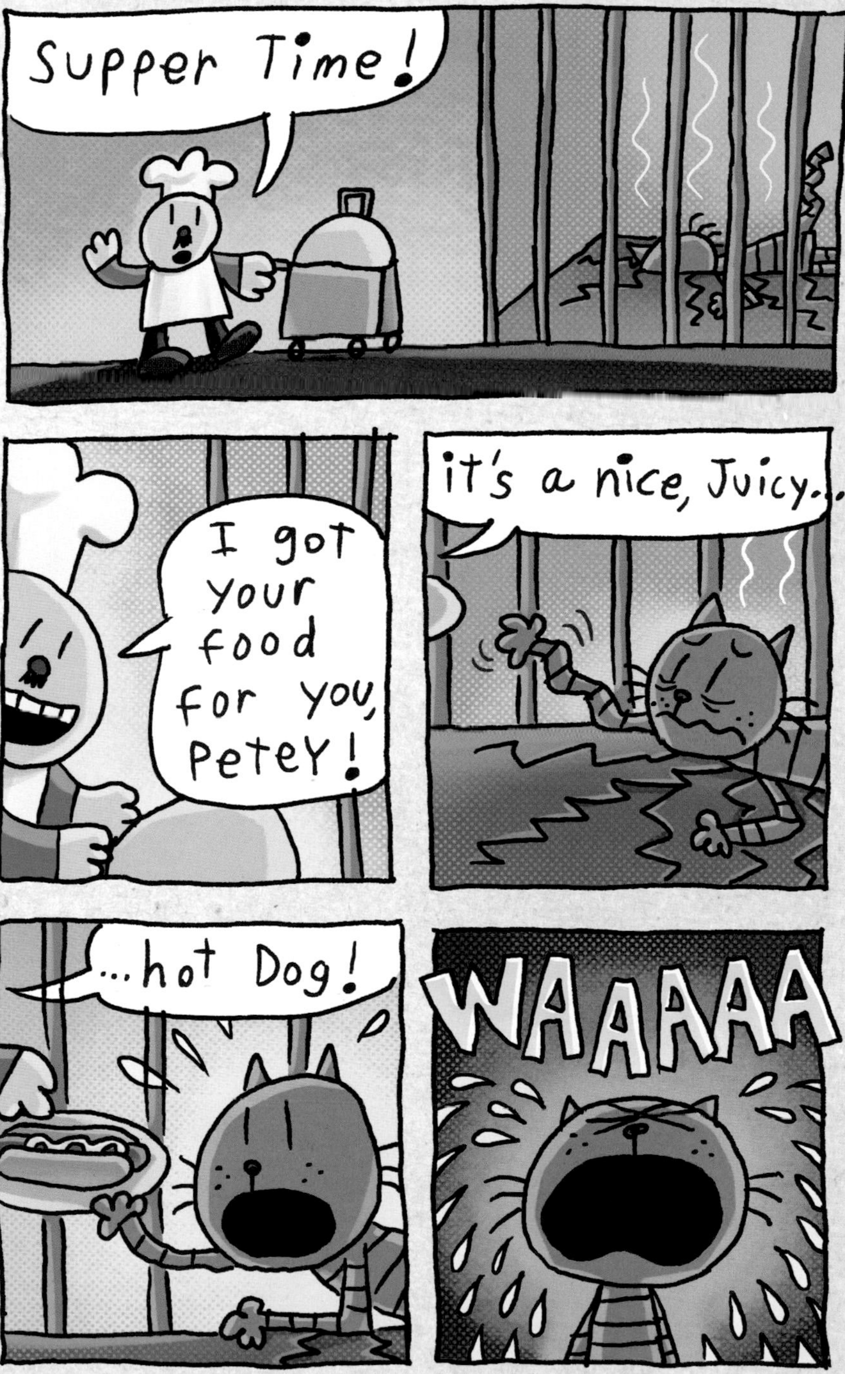
Supper Time!
I got your food for you, Petey!
it's a nice, Juicy...
...hot Dog!
WAAAAA

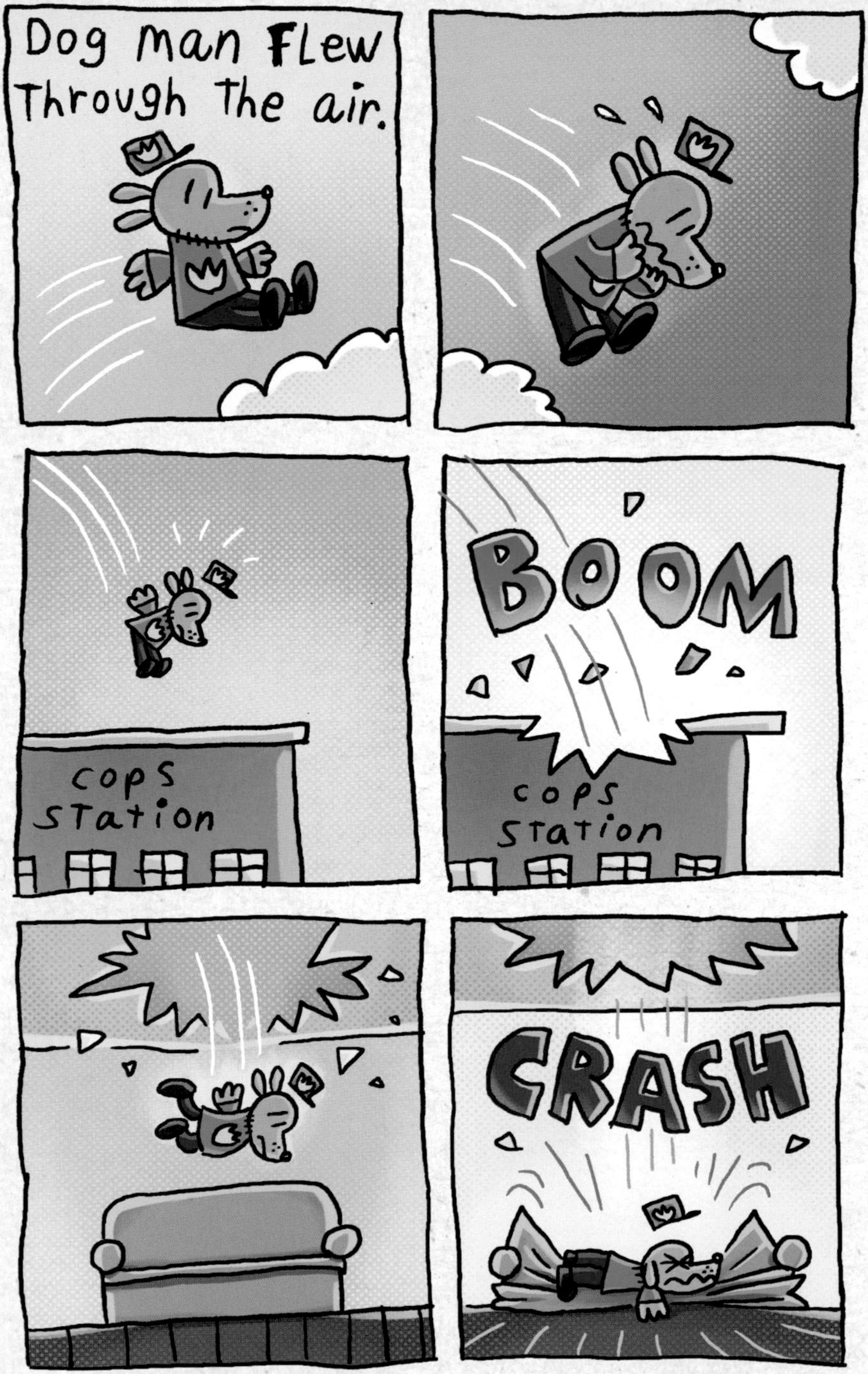
Dog man Flew Through the air.
BOOM
cops station
CRASH

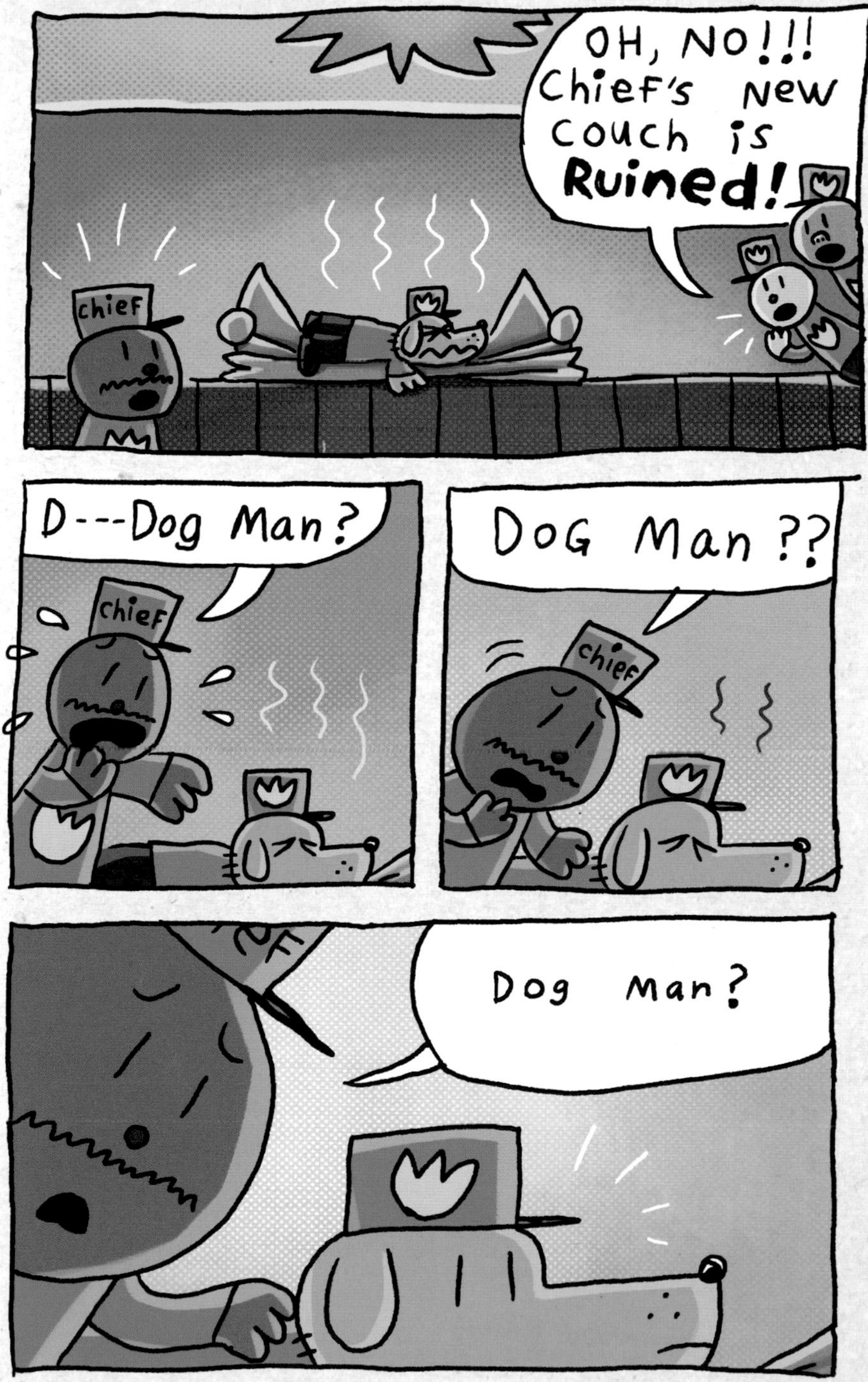
OH, NO!!! Chief's new couch is Ruined!
chief
D---Dog Man?
chief
Dog Man??
chief
Dog Man?

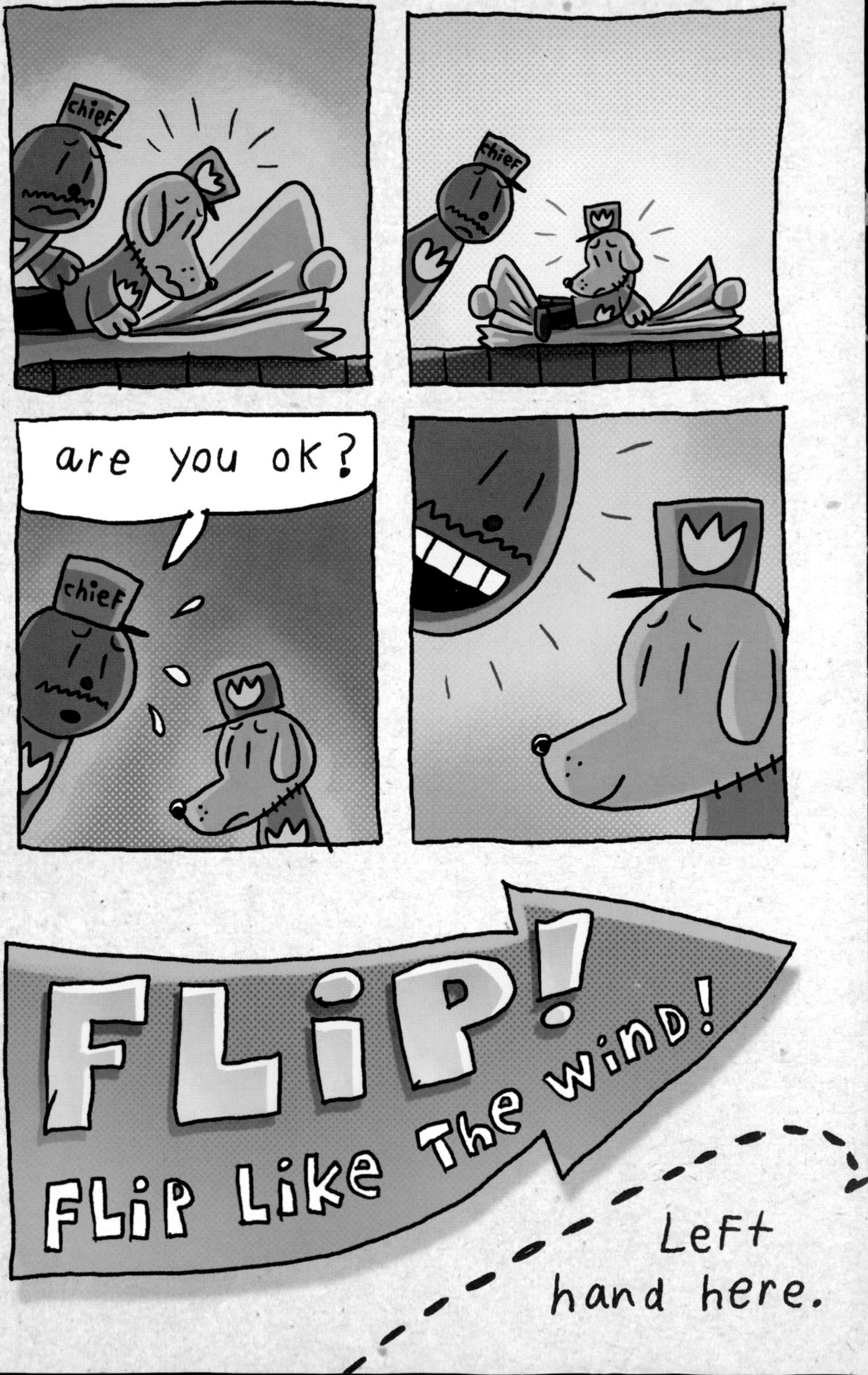
chief
chief
are you ok?
chief
FLIP!
FLIP Like The wind!
Left hand here.

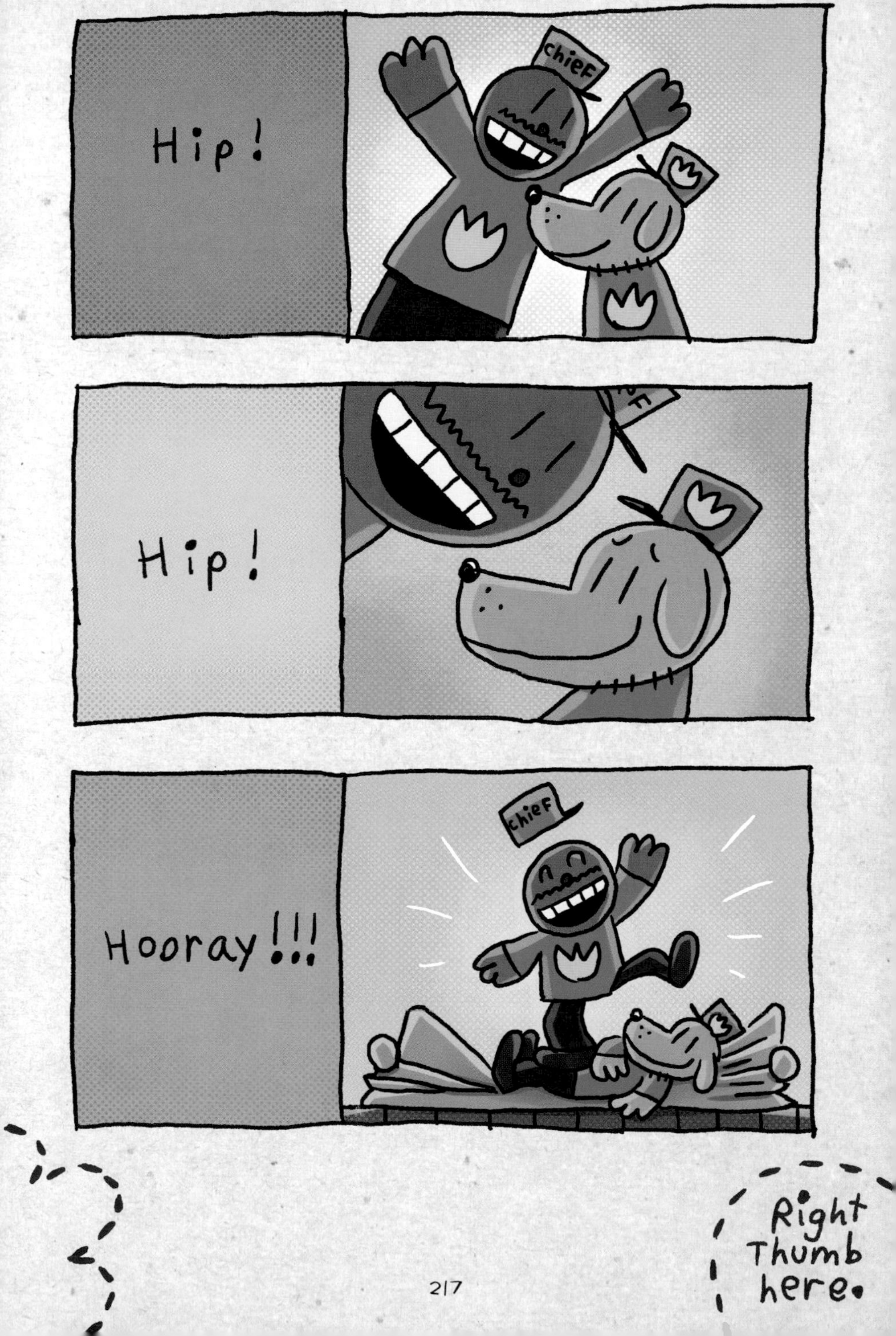
Hip!
chief
Hip!
Hooray!!!
chief
Right Thumb here.

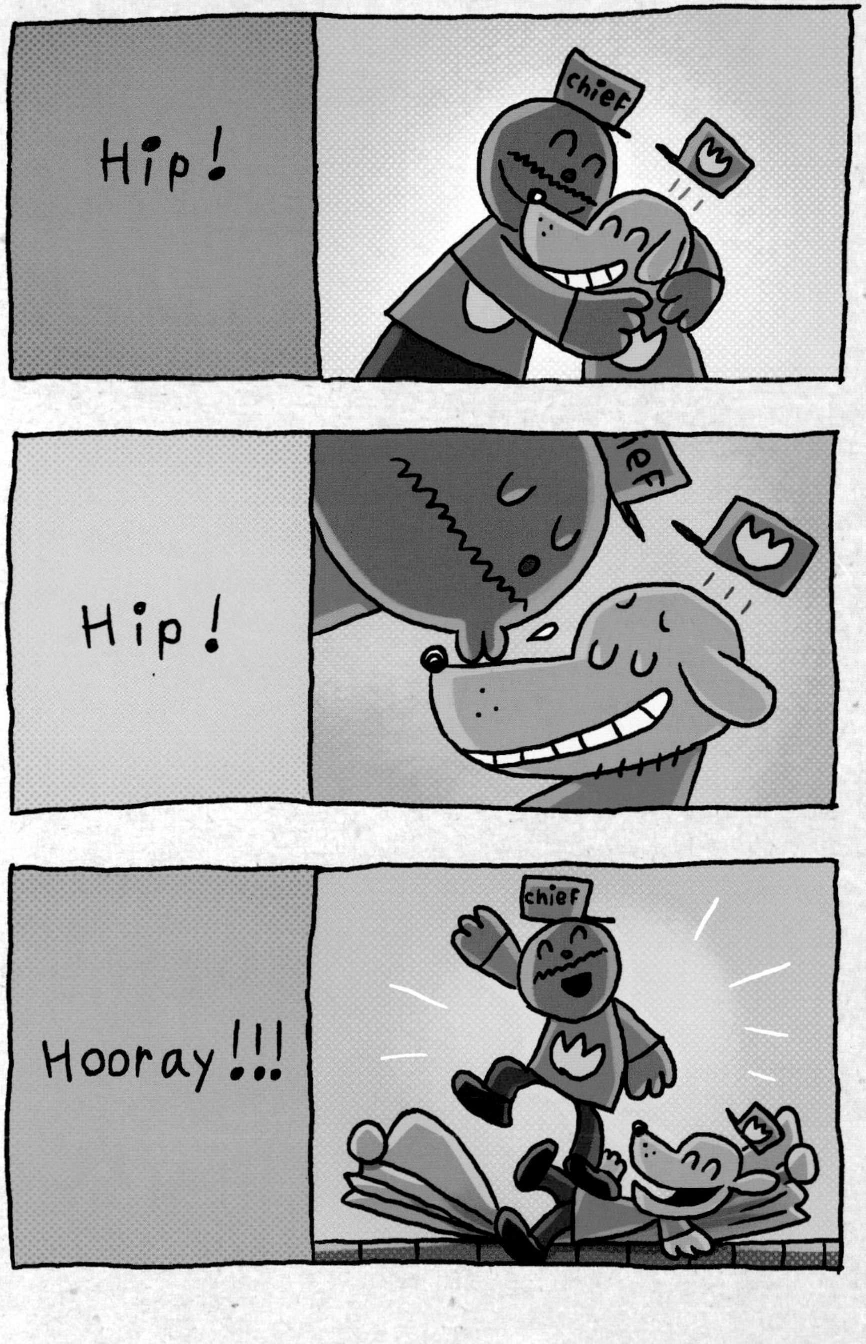

Hip!
chief
Hip!
Hooray!!!
chief

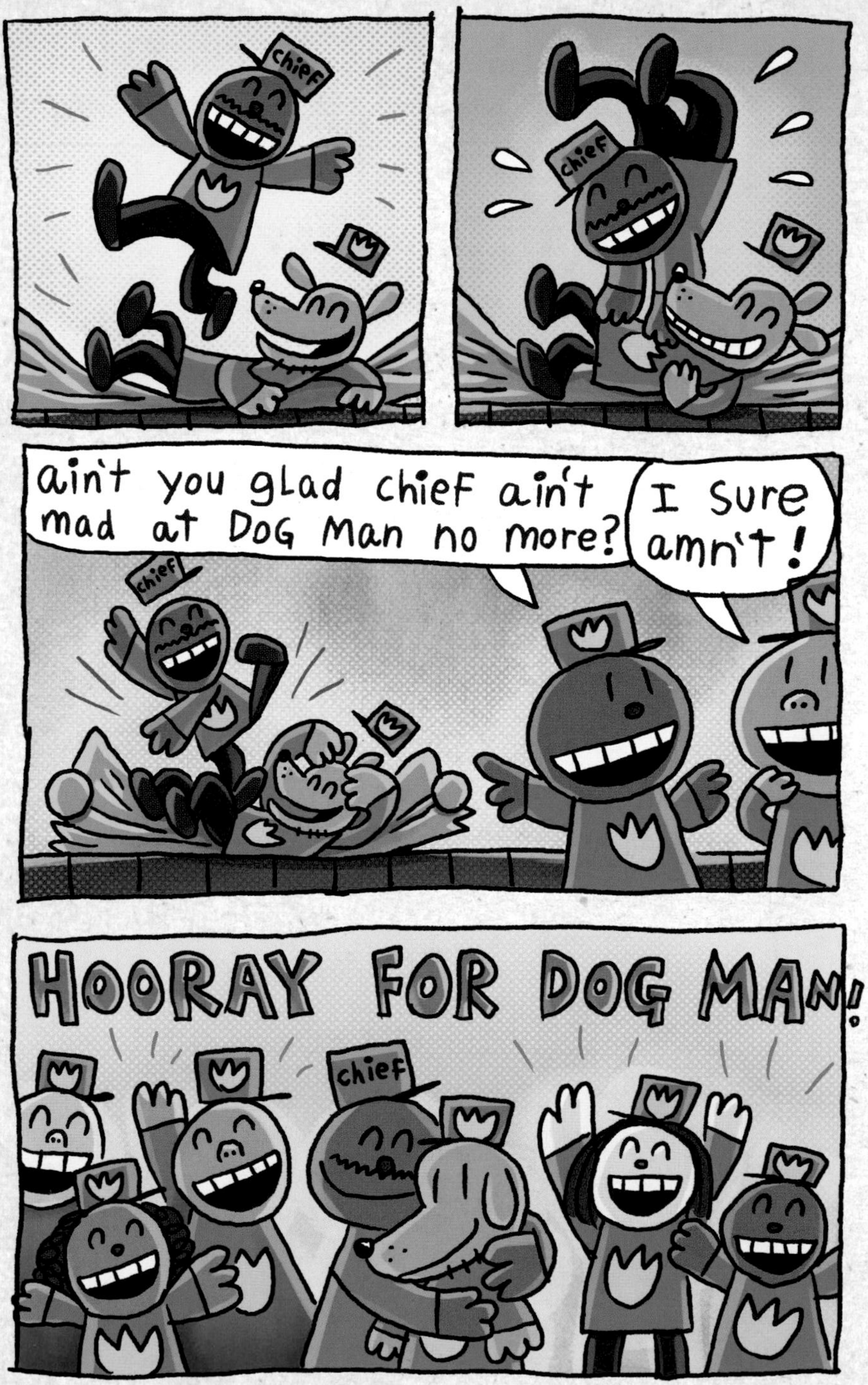
chief
ain't you glad chief ain't mad at DOG Man no more?
I sure amn't!
HOORAY FOR DOG MAN!

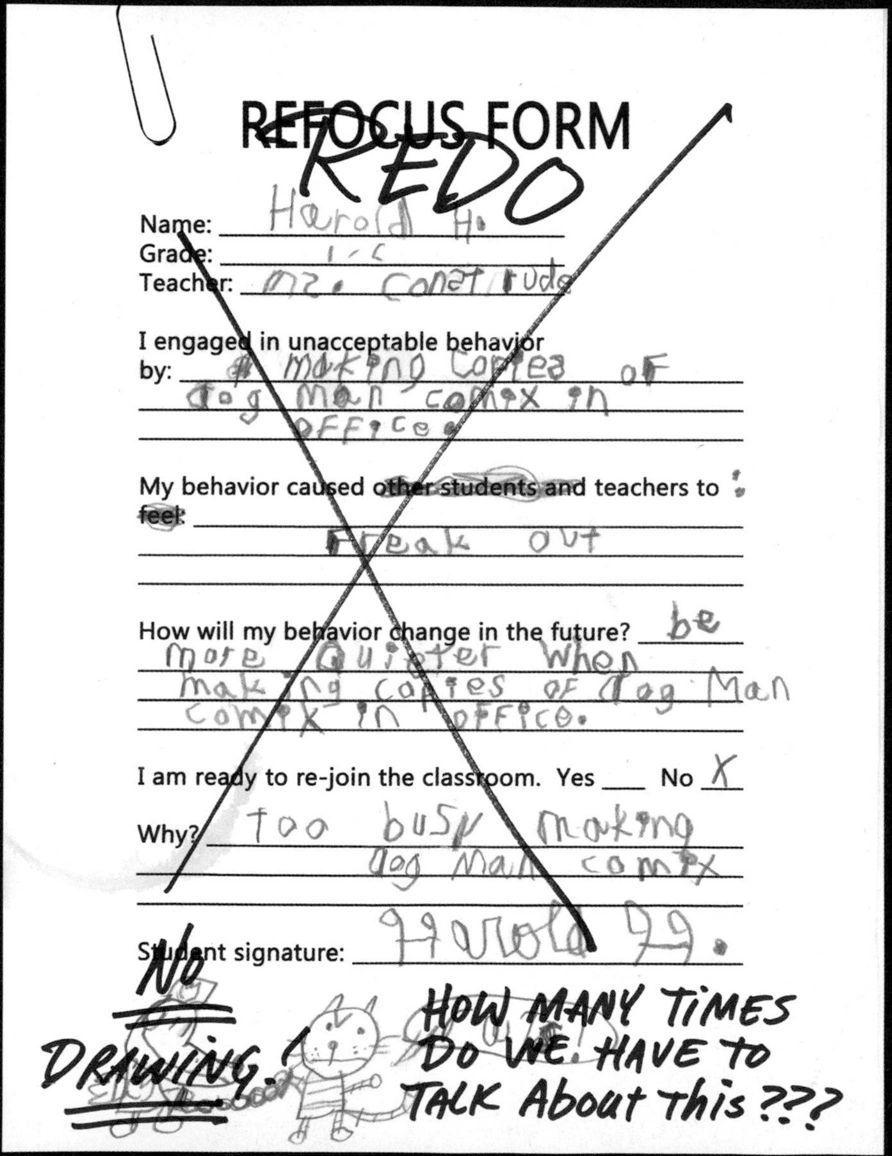

REFOCUS FORM

REDO

Name: Harold H.

Grade: 1-C

Teacher: Mz. Construde

I engaged in unacceptable behavior by: making copies of dog man comix in office.

My behavior caused other students and teachers to feel: Freak out

How will my behavior change in the future? be more Quieter when making copies of dog Man comix in office.

I am ready to re-join the classroom. Yes ___ No X

Why? too busy making dog Man comix

Student signature: Harold H.

NO DRAWING!

HOW MANY TIMES DO WE HAVE TO TALK About this???

HOW 2 DRAW DOG MAN

IN 28 RIDICULOUSLY EASY STEPS!

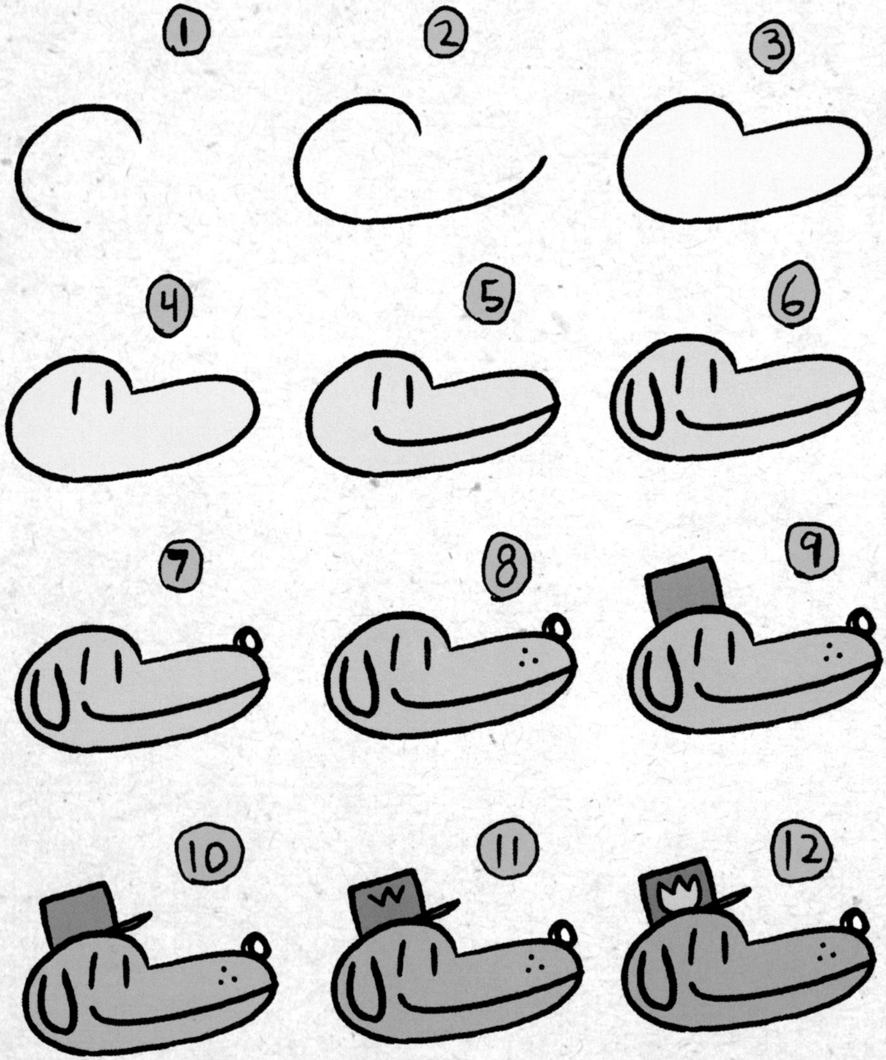
1
2
3
4
5
6
7
8
9
10
11
12
W

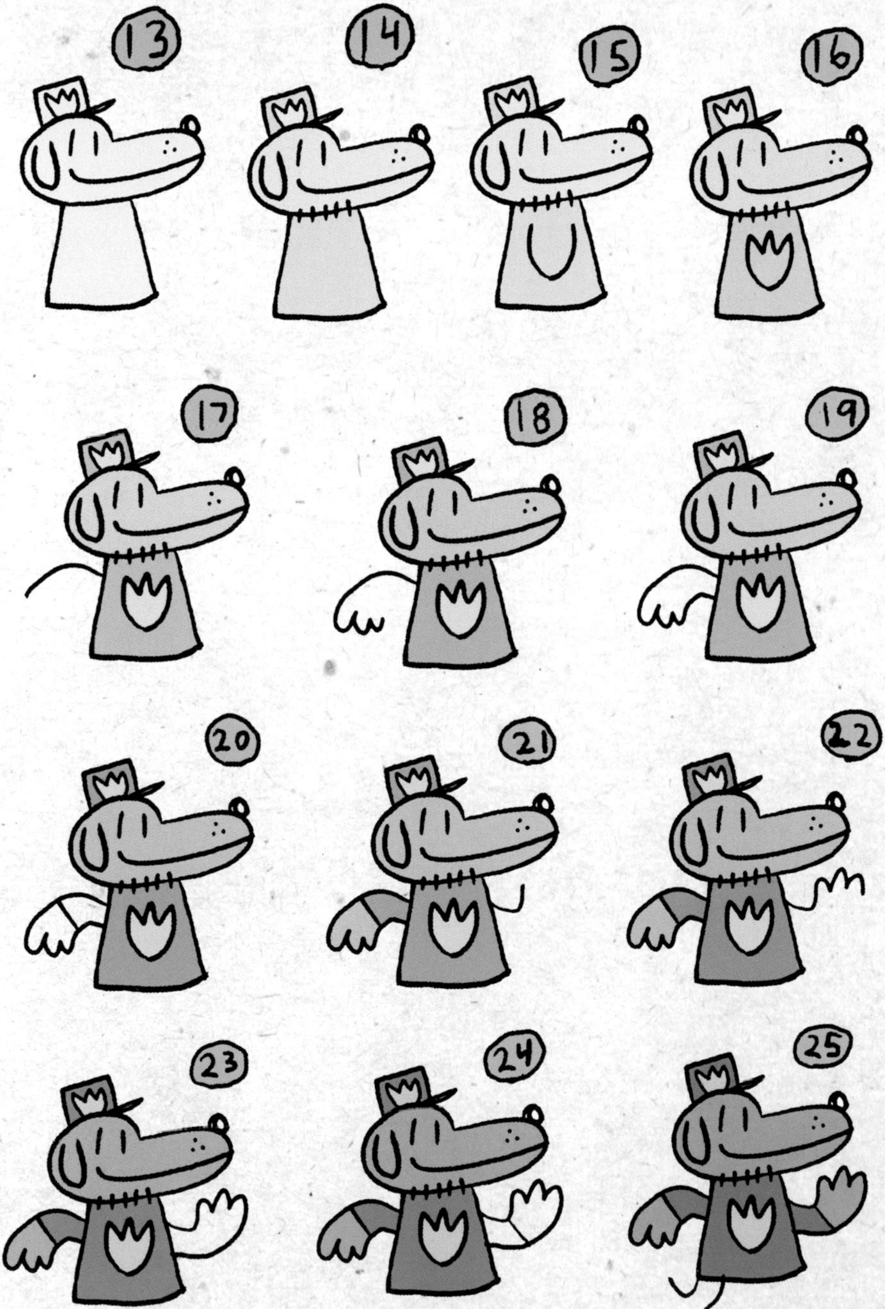
13
14
15
16
17
18
19
20
21
22
23
24
25

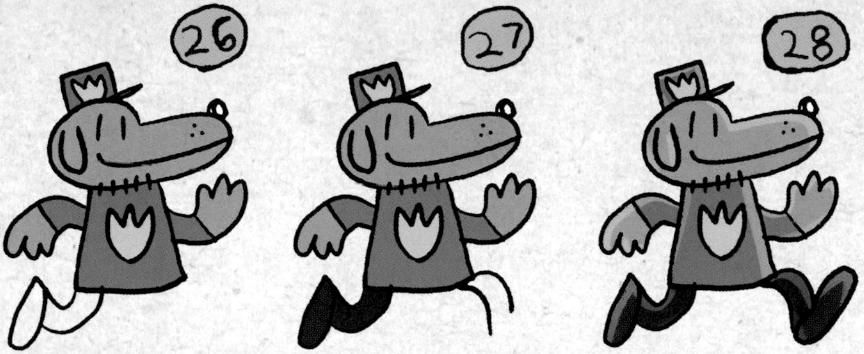
26
27
28

BE EXPRESSive!!!

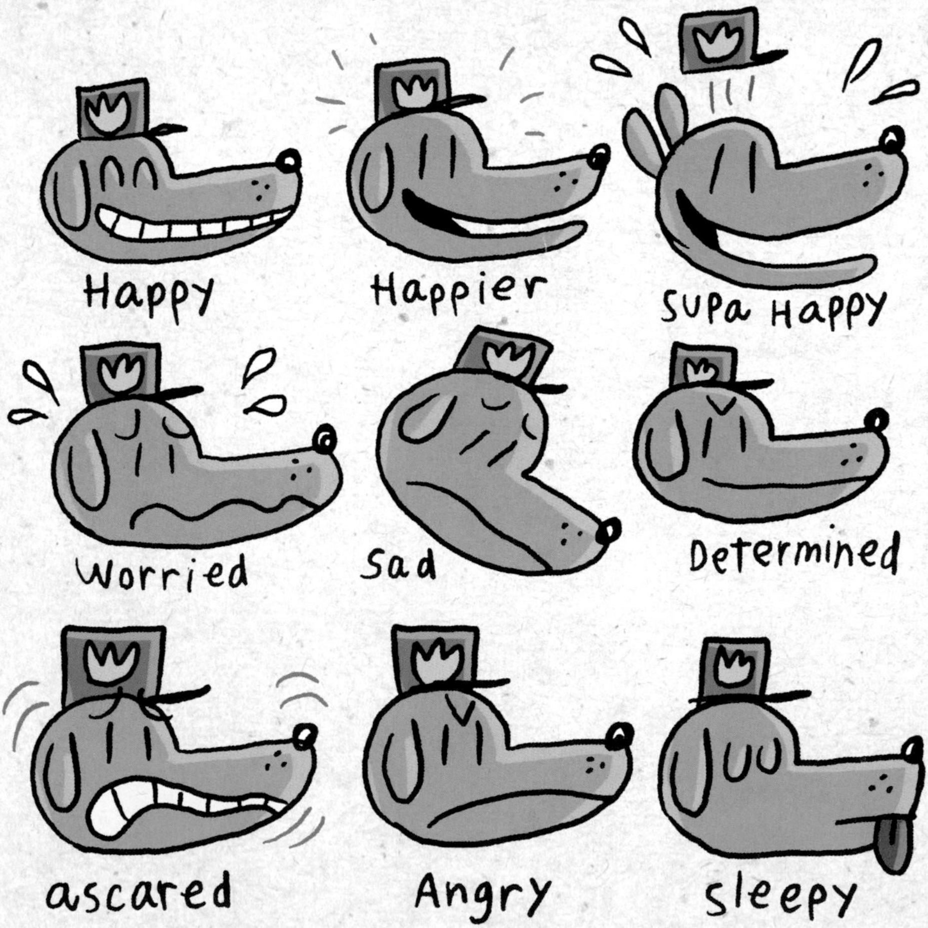
Happy
Happier
Supa Happy
Worried
Sad
Determined
ascared
Angry
sleepy

HOW 2 DRAW

PETEY

in 24 Ridiculously easy steps.

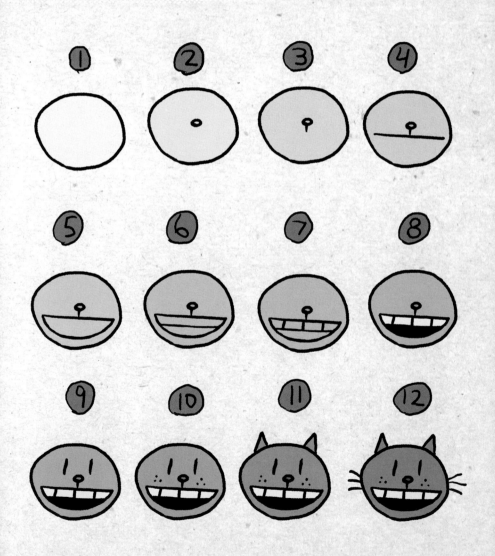

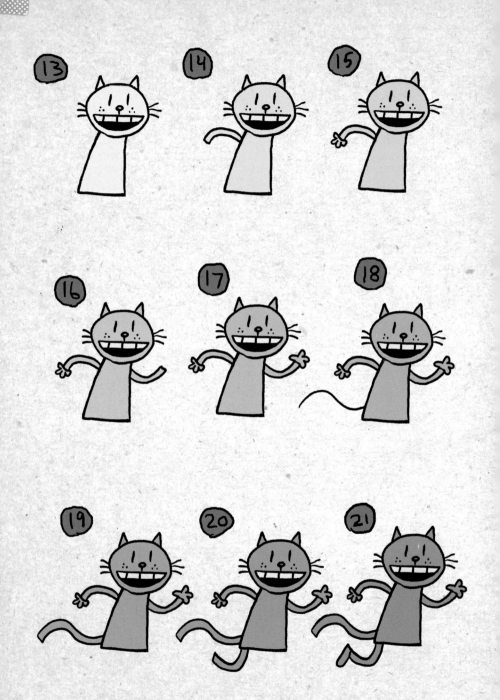

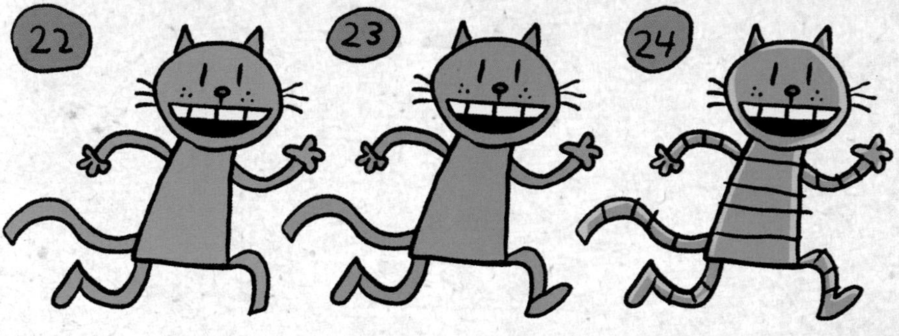
22
23
24

BE EXPRESSIVE

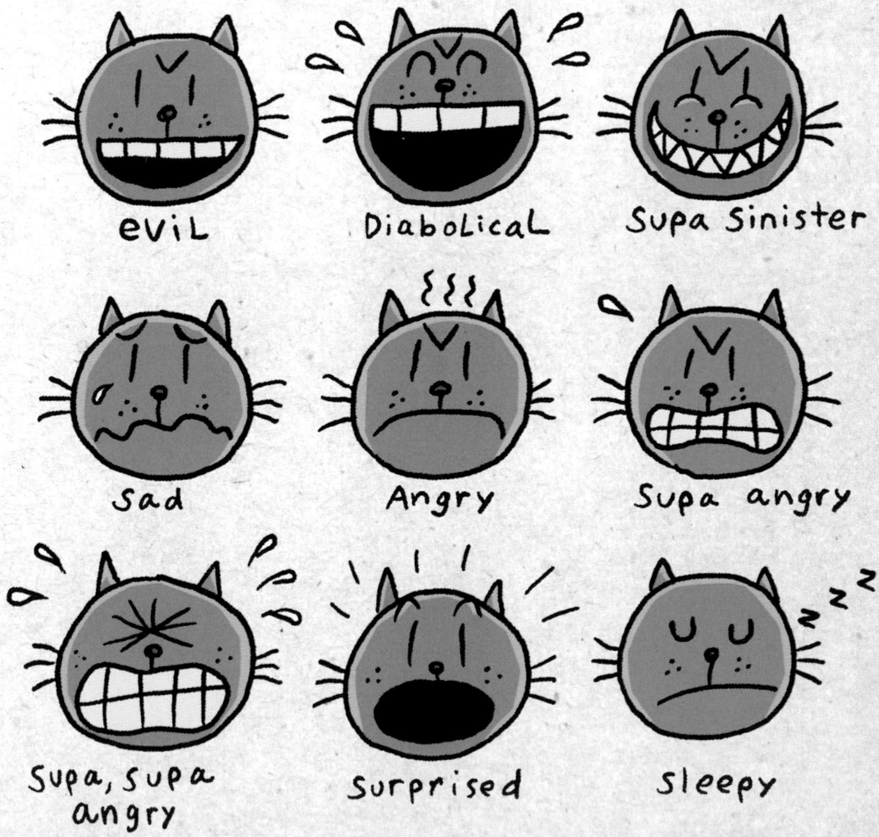
eViL
DiaboLicaL
Supa Sinister
Sad
Angry
Supa angry
Supa, Supa angry
Surprised
Sleepy

HOW 2 DRAW PhiLLY

in 24 Ridiculously easy Steps!

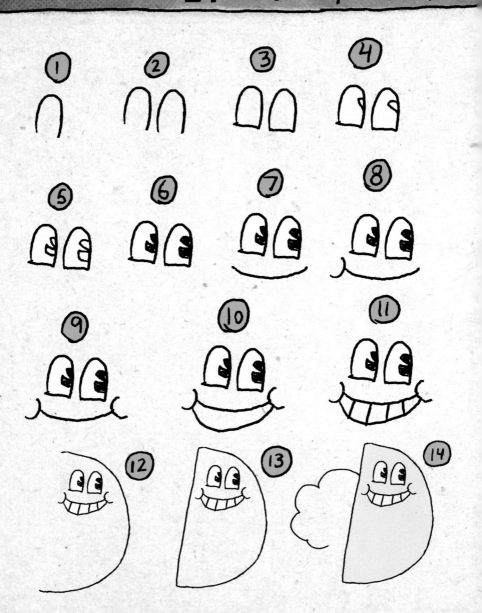

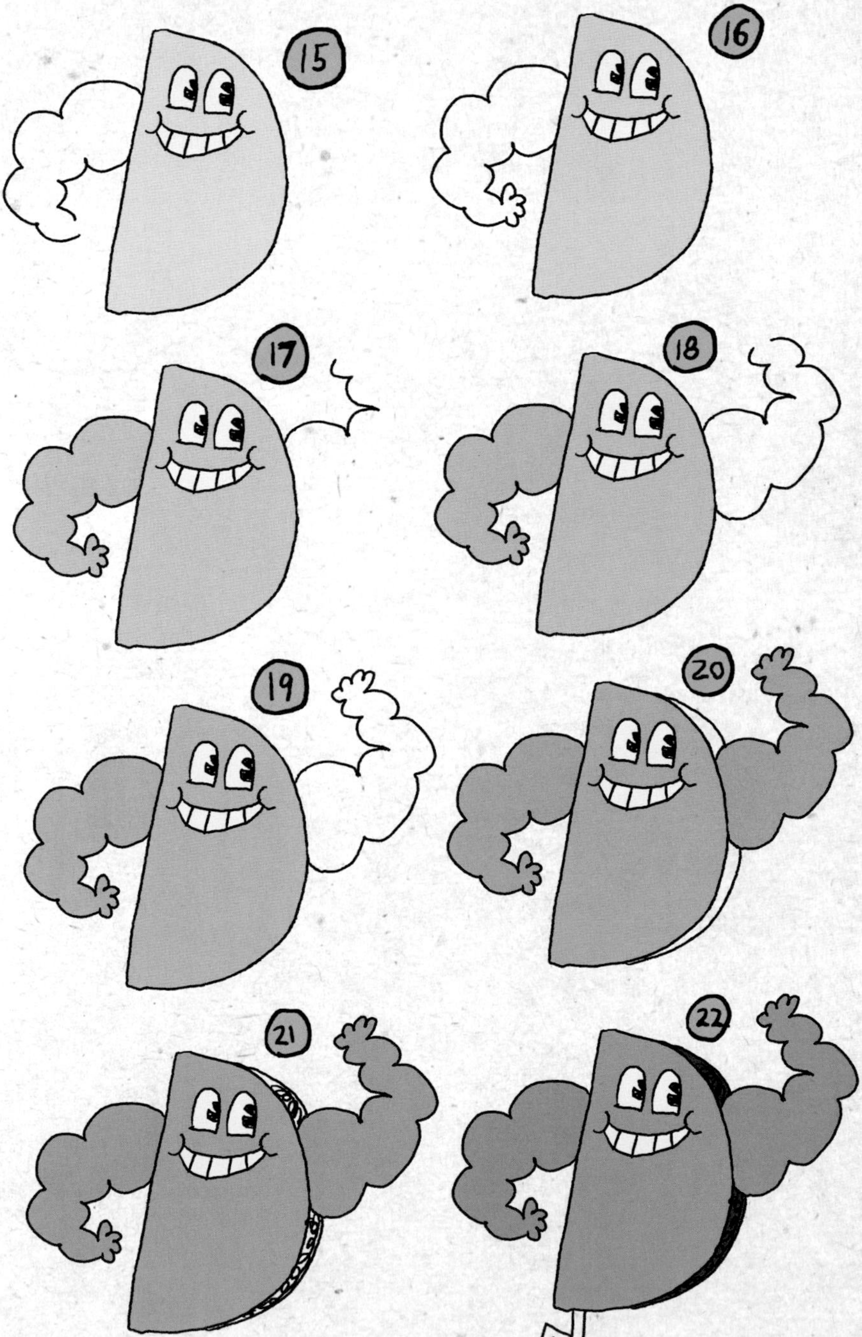
15
16
17
18
19
20
21
22

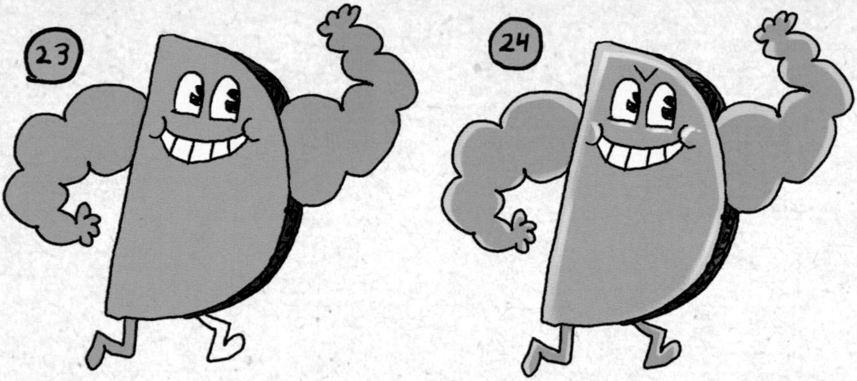
23
24

BE EXPRESSIVE!!!

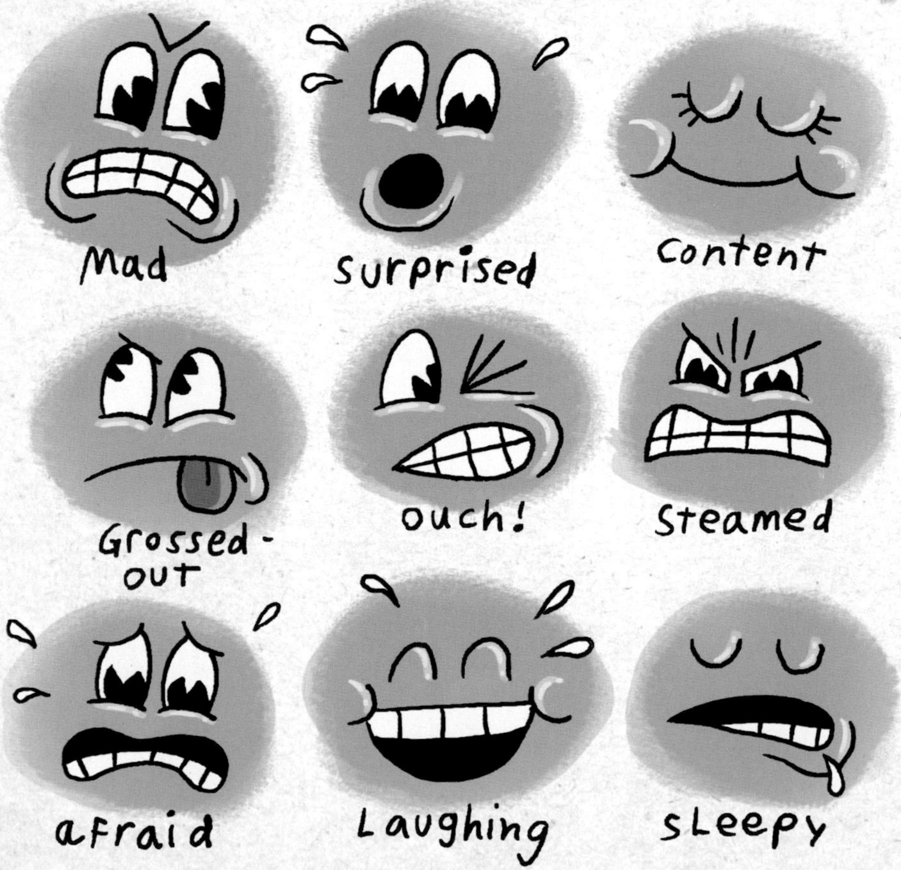
Mad
surprised
content
Grossed-out
ouch!
Steamed
afraid
Laughing
sleepy

HOW 2 DRAW INVISIBLE PETEY

in **8** easy steps.

 ① ② ③ ④

 ⑤ ⑥ ⑦ ⑧

BE EXPRESSIVE!!!

Happy   angry   sad   obsequious

ABOUT THE AUTHOR-ILLUSTRATOR

When Dav Pilkey was a kid, he was diagnosed with ADHD and dyslexia. Dav was so disruptive in class that his teachers made him sit out in the hall every day. Luckily, Dav loved to draw and make up stories. He spent his time in the hallway creating his own original comic books.

In the second grade, Dav Pilkey made a comic book about a superhero named Captain Underpants. Since then, he has been creating books that explore universally positive themes celebrating the triumph of the good-hearted.

ABOUT THE COLORIST

Jose Garibaldi grew up on the South Side of Chicago. As a kid, he was a daydreamer and a doodler, and now it's his full-time job to do both. Jose is a professional illustrator, painter, and cartoonist who has created work for many organizations, including Nickelodeon, MAD Magazine, Cartoon Network, Disney, and THE EPIC ADVENTURES OF CAPTAIN UNDERPANTS for DreamWorks Animation. He lives in Los Angeles, California, with his wonder dogs, Herman and Spanky.

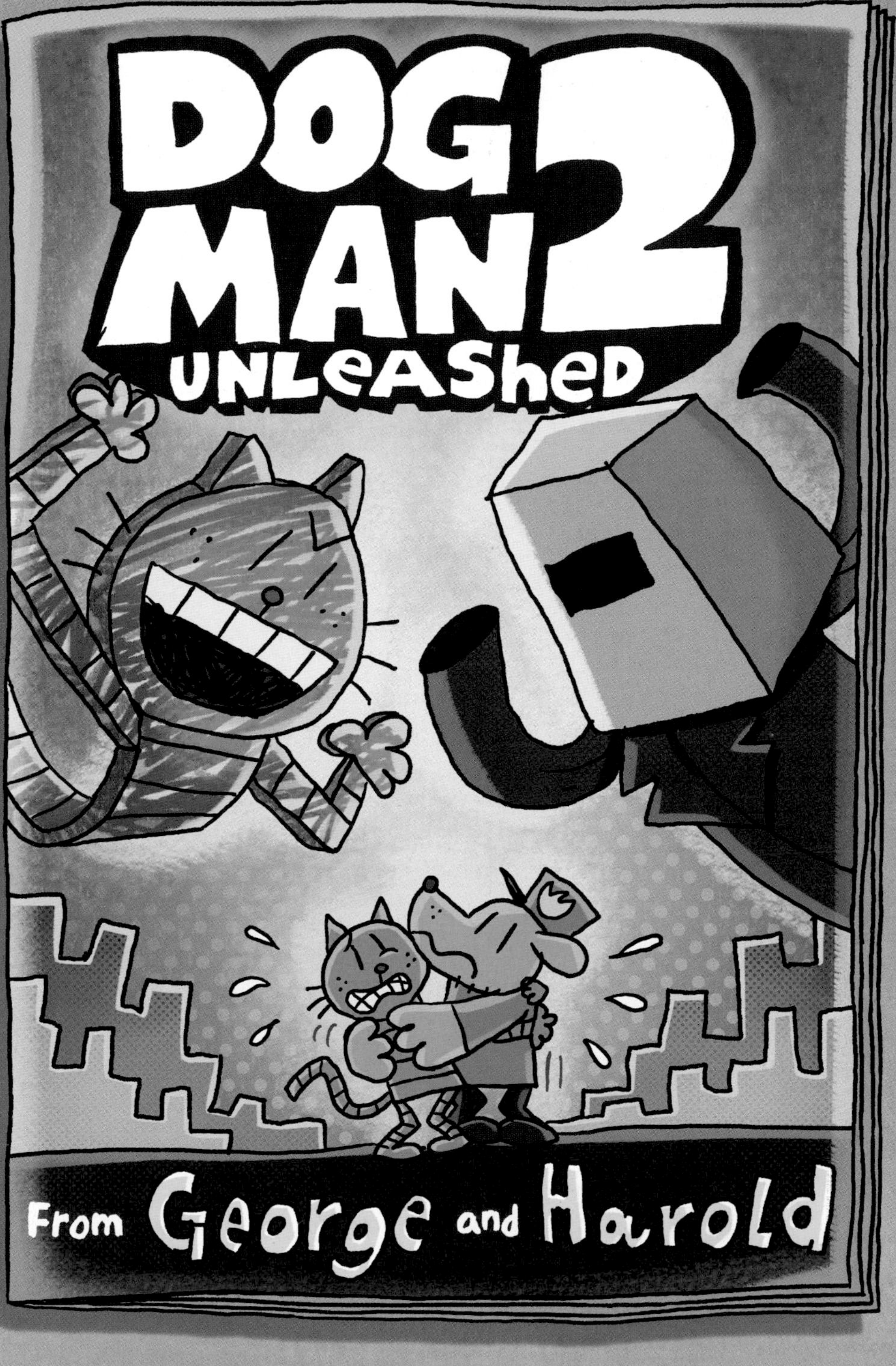
DOG MAN 2
UNLEASHED
From George and Harold

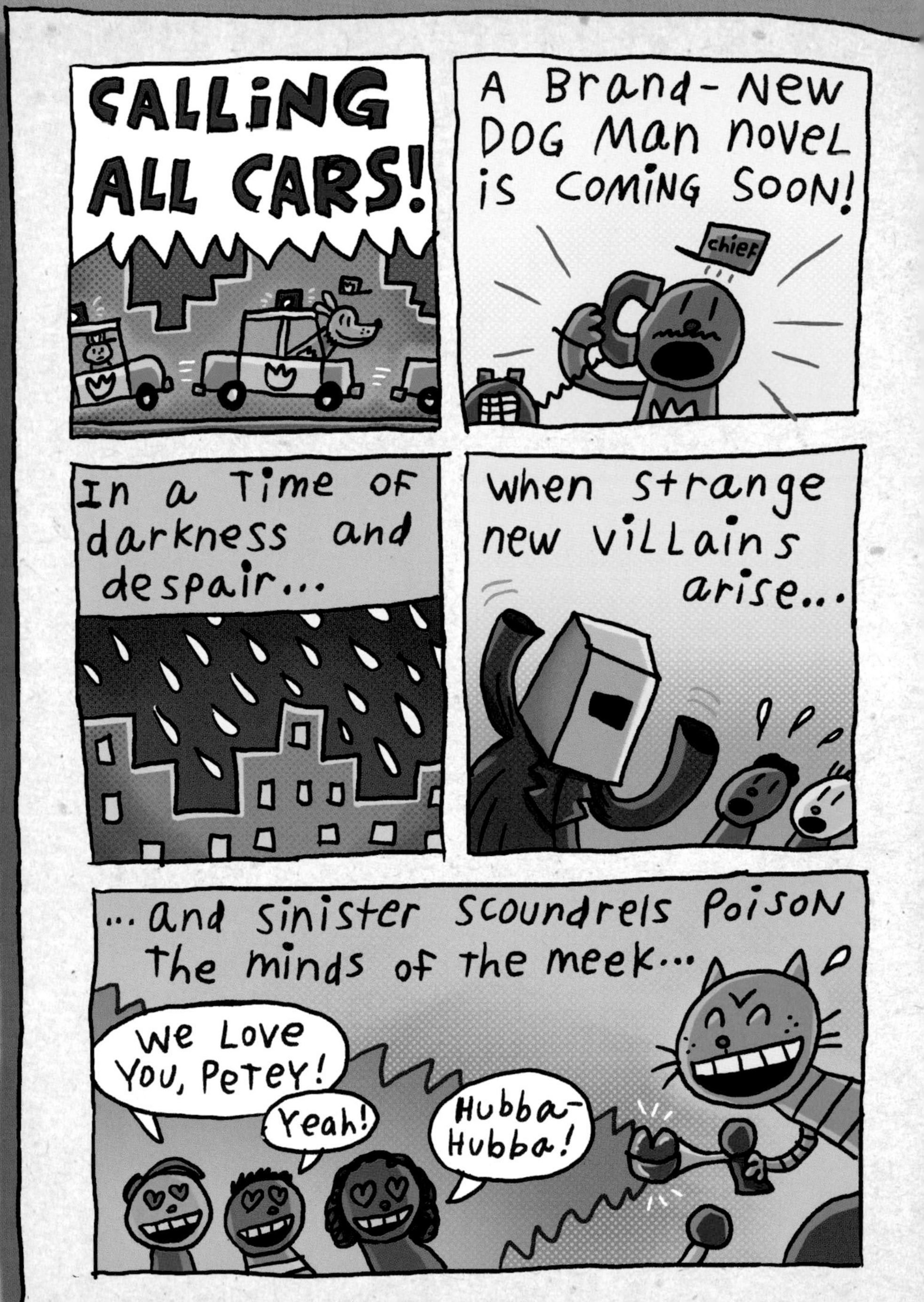
CALLING ALL CARS!
A Brand-New DOG Man novel is COMING SOON!
chief
In a Time of darkness and despair...
when strange new villains arise...
...and sinister scoundrels Poison the minds of the meek...
We Love You, Petey!
Yeah!
Hubba-Hubba!

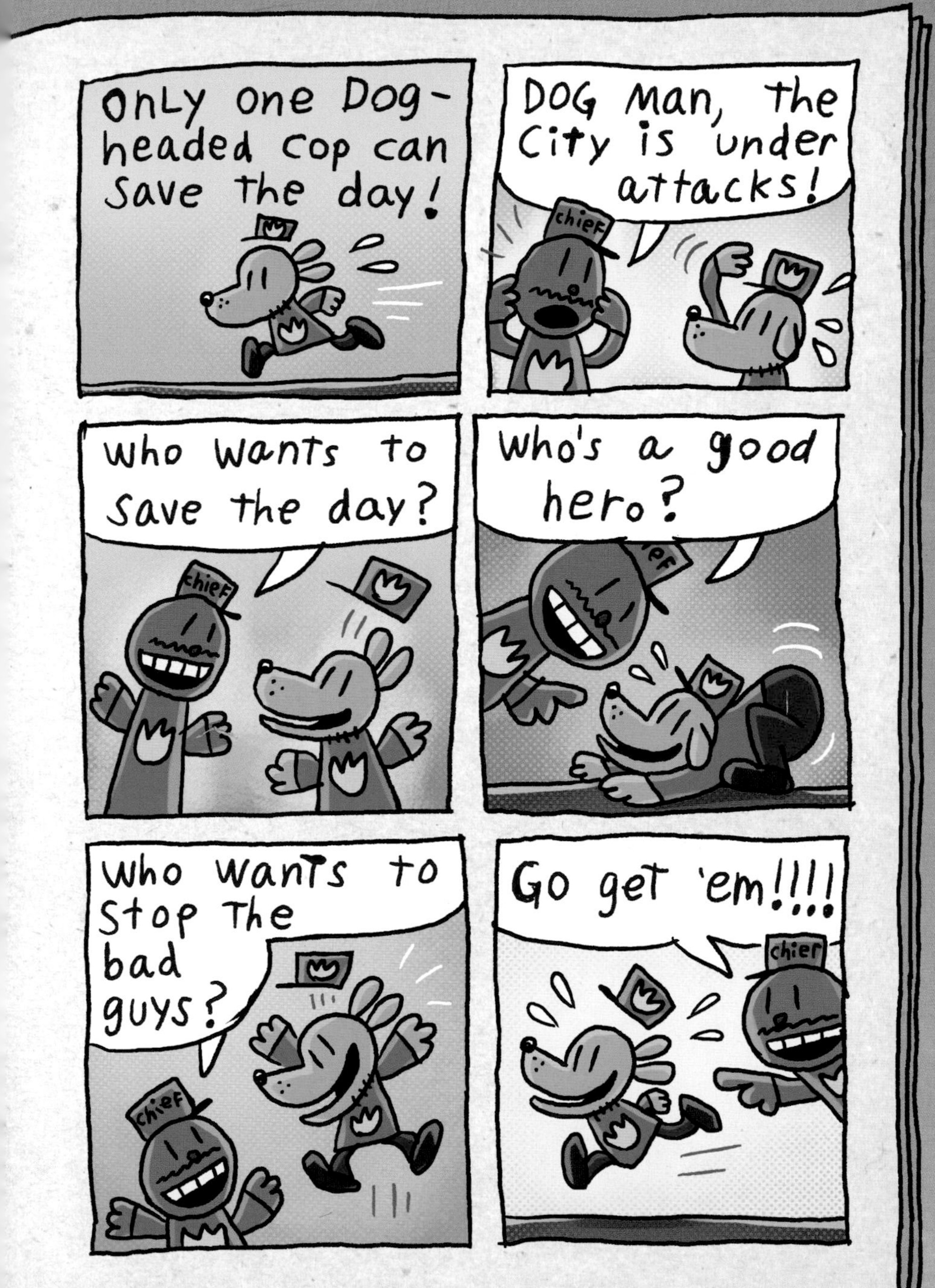

OnLy one Dog-headed cop can Save the day!
DOG Man, the City is under attacks!
chief
Who wants to Save the day?
chief
Who's a good hero?
Who wants to Stop the bad guys?
chief
Go get 'em!!!!
chief

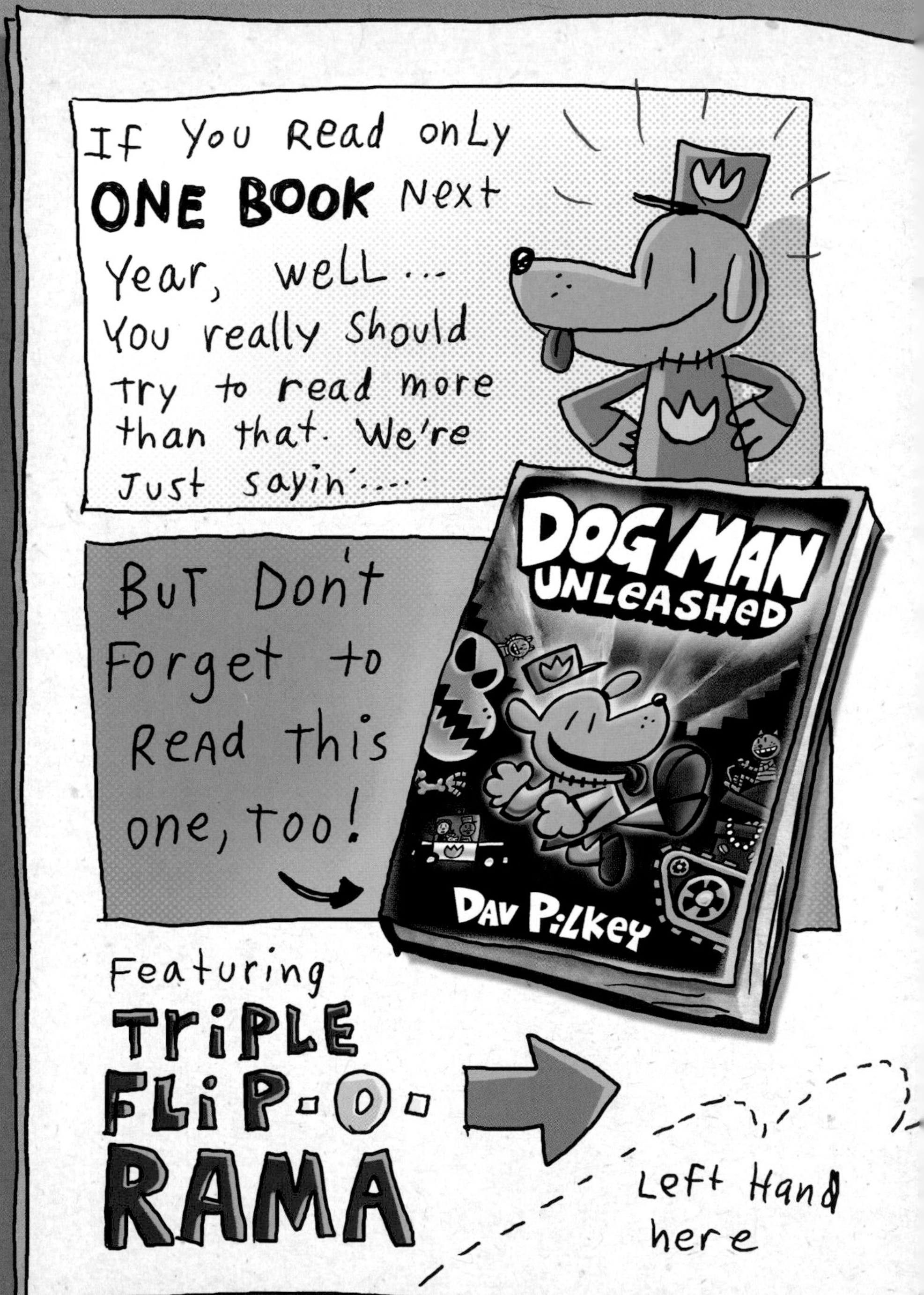
If You Read onLy ONE BOOK Next Year, weLL... You really Should try to read more than that. We're Just sayin'....
BuT Don't Forget to Read this one, too!
DOG MAN
UNLEASHED
DAV PiLKEY
Featuring
TriPLE FLiP-O-RAMA
Left Hand here

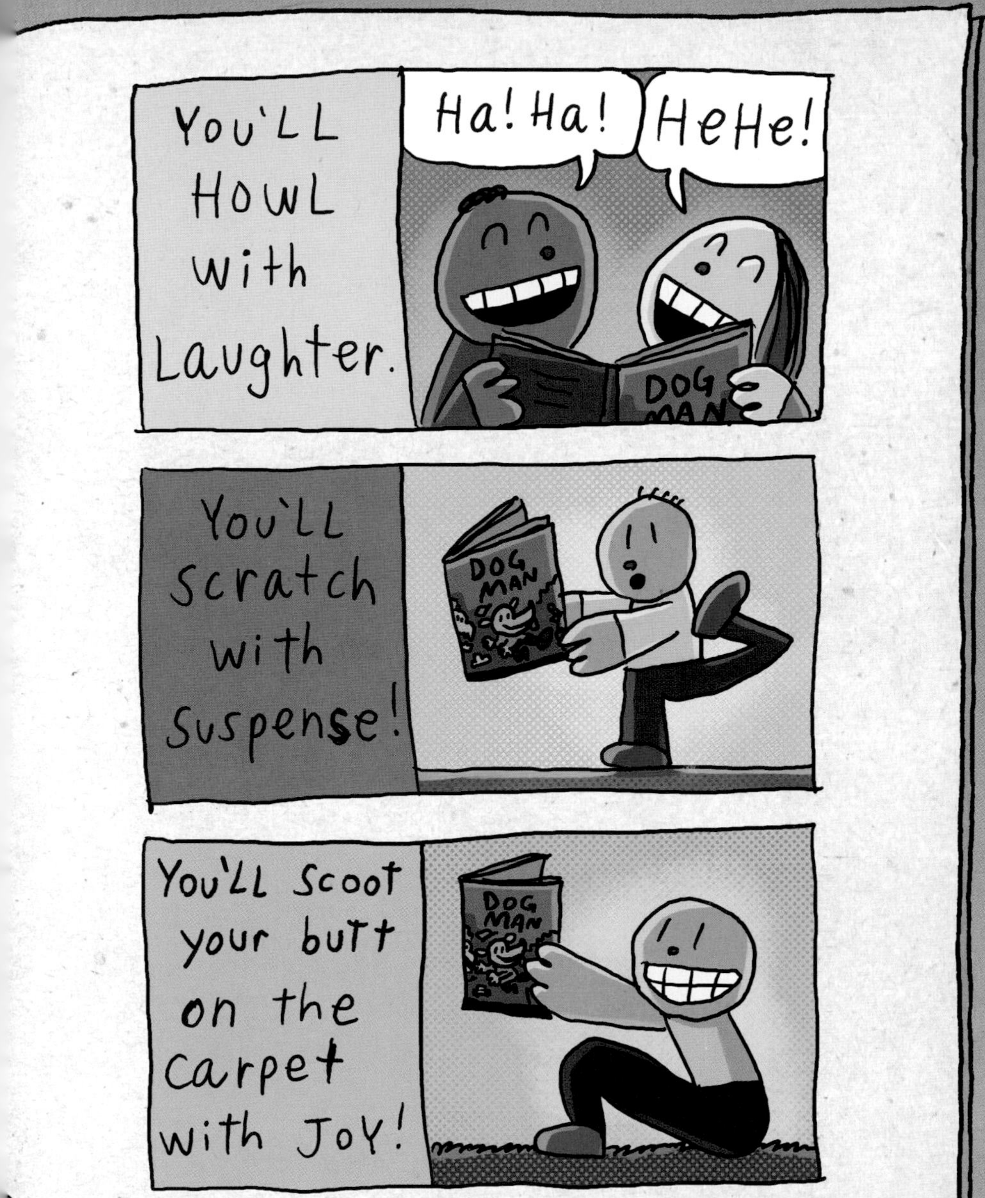
You'll HOWL with Laughter.
Ha! Ha!
HeHe!
DOG MAN
You'll scratch with suspense!
DOG MAN
You'll scoot your butt on the carpet with JOY!
DOG MAN
Right THUMB here

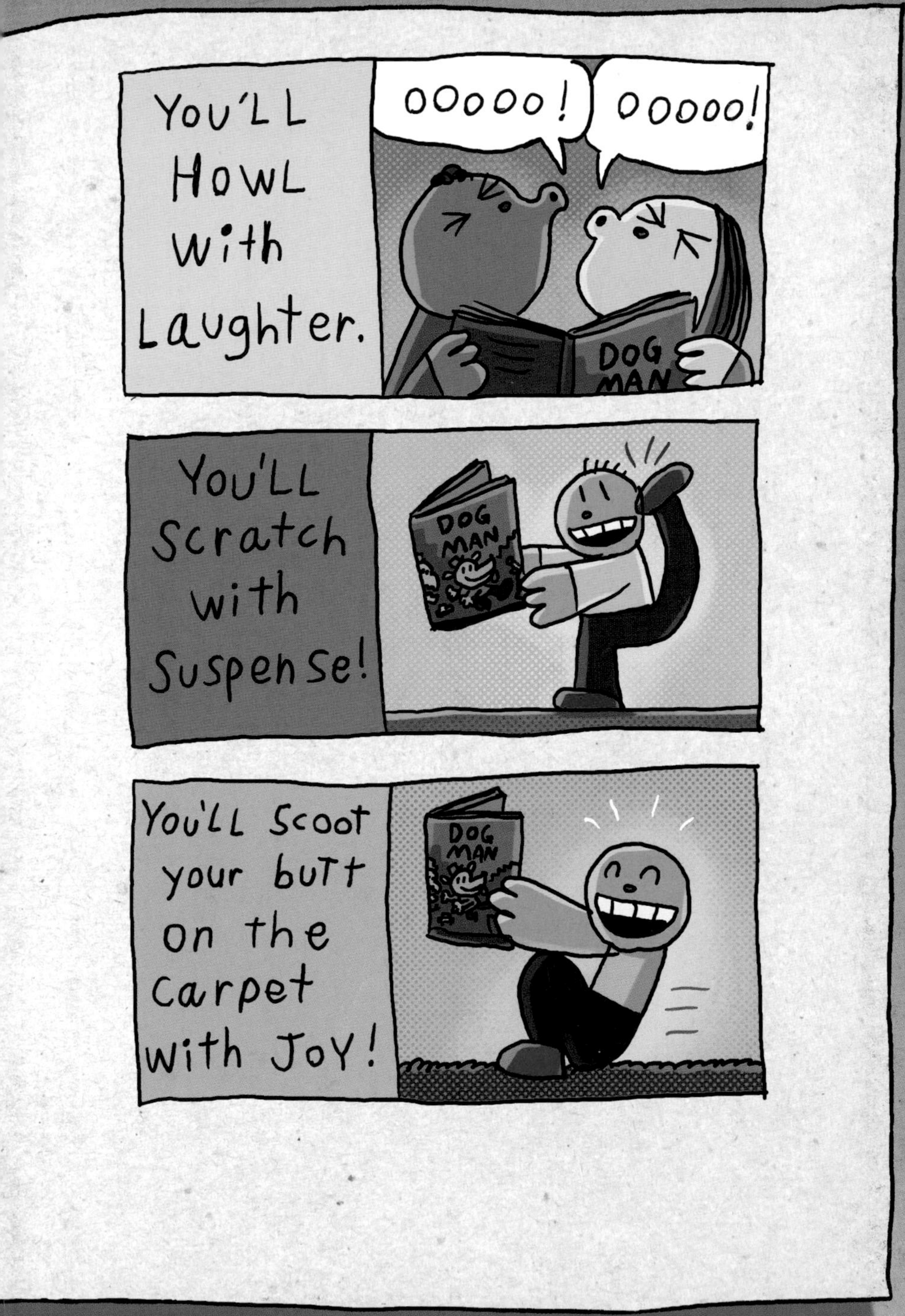
You'll howl with laughter.
Ooooo!
Ooooo!
DOG MAN
You'll scratch with suspense!
DOG MAN
You'll scoot your butt on the carpet with joy!
DOG MAN

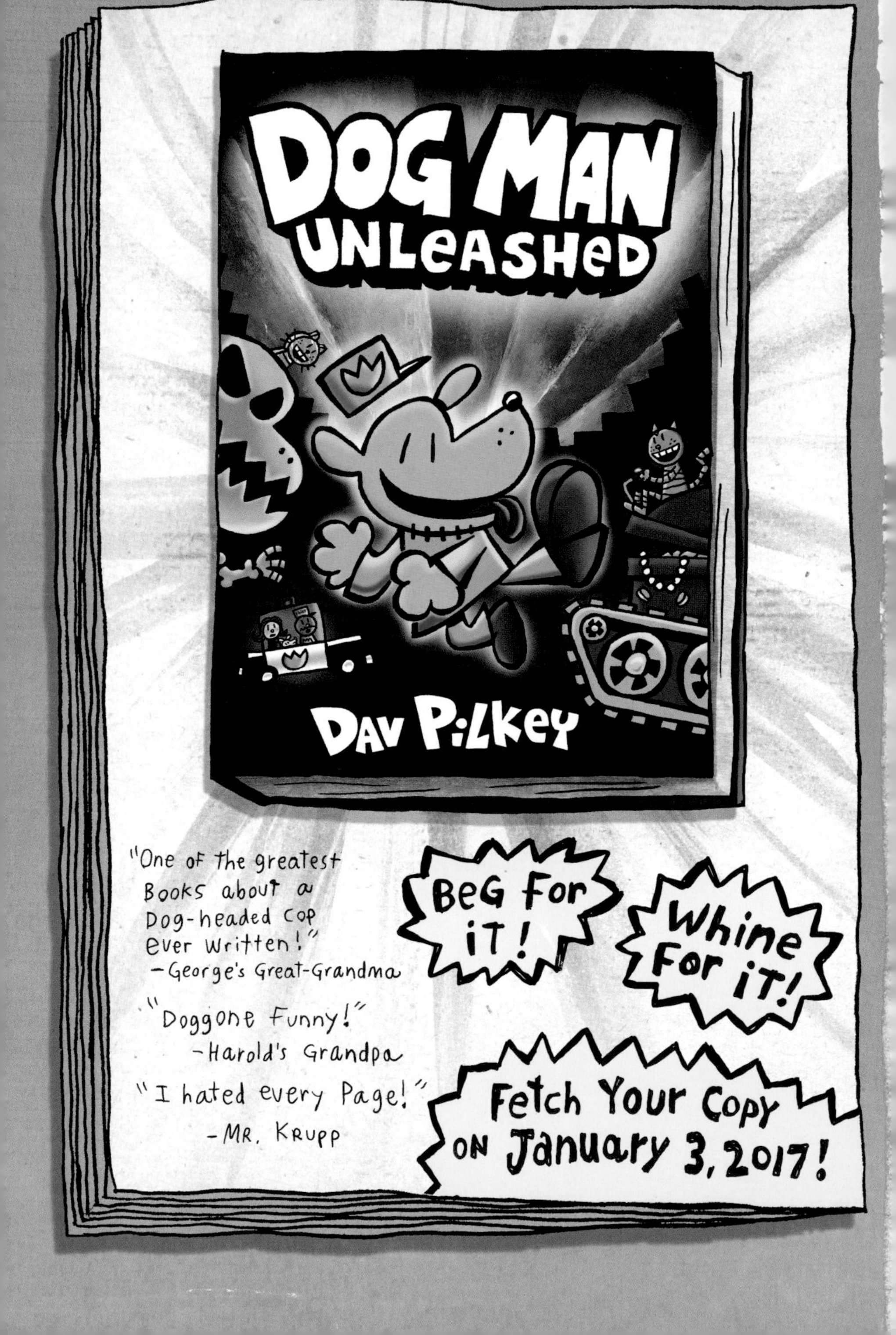
DOG MAN
UNLEASHED
DAV PILKEY
"One of the greatest Books about a Dog-headed Cop ever Written!"
—George's Great-Grandma
"Doggone Funny!"
—Harold's Grandpa
"I hated every Page!"
—MR. KRUPP
BeG For iT!
Whine For iT!
Fetch Your Copy on January 3, 2017!